THE MAY-WEEK MURDERS

THE
MAY-WEEK MURDERS

BY
DOUGLAS G. BROWNE

Author of
"PLAN XVI," "THE DEAD DON'T BITE"
"THE COTFOLD CONUNDRUMS,"
"THE 'LOOKING-GLASS' MURDERS," ETC.

Ostara Publishing

First Published by Longmans Green & Co 1937

Every reasonable effort has been made by the Publisher to establish whether any person or institution holds the copyright for this work. The Publisher invites any persons or institutions that believe themselves to be in possession of any such copyright to contact them at the address below.

ISBN 978-190628802-0

A CIP reference is available from the British Library

Printed and bound in United Kingdom

Published by   Ostara Publishing
                      13 King Coel Road
                      Lexden
                      Colchester
                      CO3 9AG

CONTENTS

OPUS ONE

OPUS TWO

IMPROMPTU—AND OPUS THREE

FINALE: UNREHEARSED

TO

MY FRIENDS

JOHN FARQUHARSON

AND

INNES ROSE

OPUS ONE

CHAPTER I

1

I HAD been staying with the Nugents at Clayhythe since the beginning of May Week. Maurice, who always dodges festivities, or as much of them as he can, was coming down on the Tuesday evening, 15th June. He and Chester Nugent had soldiered together in the dim past; and now they had another link, for Chester—Colonel Nugent to the multitude, but Puffin to his friends—had just been made Chief Constable of South Cambridgeshire. Since Maurice took up criminology we have rather gone in for collecting chief constables, but Puffin was the first exhibit we had acquired extra-professionally, so to speak. And he didn't keep his amateur status long.

The races were finished on Saturday, the 12th, and on Monday, the 14th, we all went to the Trinity Ball—"all" comprising Puffin and Vera Nugent, their daughter Averil, and myself. Maurice says I'm not to write about balls and frocks and frivolities of that sort, so I'll only mention that among those present were the Rowsell-Hoggs and the Tullises. James Tullis was a sort of connexion of mine, but only by marriage, and that a long time ago, and I had never met him before; but recently I had run across his son Ian, who was at Clare, and who insisted on calling me his cousin. That night he introduced me to his father, who danced like a poker and talked continually (except for intervals of glooming morosely over something or the other), about the tedious ramifications of our families. Afterwards Ian made amends by dragging up some more youthful and entertaining partners, among them being Hereward Rowsell-Hogg, who was at Trinity himself, and who pointed out *his* parents to me. I didn't pay much attention to them at the time: they looked very like other parents to me, and in the crush I never noticed when they left, which they did about midnight on Lady Rowsell-Hogg's account. I had been kept pretty well on the hop dodging James Tullis, who was always appearing in the offing, obviously dying to reminisce about his Great-aunt Julia, who lived at Harrogate and married my grandmother's brother-in-law; but somewhere about this time he vanished too. At any rate I didn't see him again till much later, and then he seemed to have lost interest in me.

It must have been nearly two o'clock when Vera Nugent caught my arm as I was passing and said that Puffin had been called away to the police station, and that we were not to wait for him.

"What's up?" I asked.

But Vera didn't know. "I hope he isn't going to make a habit of it, anyway," she said. "It will be as bad as being married to a doctor."

Vera, of course, was still in the age of innocence, and saw nothing very odd in a chief constable being called away from a ball, like Wellington—or was it Blucher?—at two in the morning; and I didn't want to spoil her fun by suggesting horrors. Besides, I had an idea it might be nothing more than some undergraduates' rag. But Puffin was still absent when we left, soon after three, and I had begun by then to wonder what *was* up.

It was Averil who brought me the news, with a cup of tea, about twelve o'clock that morning.

"I say, do you know what happened last night?"

I was barely awake, and had forgotten all about it. I just blinked at her.

"Murder and robbery at the 'Eagle,' " said Averil, with relish.

"Nonsense!" I said.

"It's true. Daddy's there again now."

"Who was murdered?"

"Sir Vyvyan Rowsell-Hogg."

"I danced with his son," I said stupidly, gulping down some tea. Averil looked envious. It's odd what prestige you get if you are connected in any way with a murderer or his victim.

"I don't know any of them," she said.

"What about the robbery?" I asked.

"Lady Hogg's jewels were taken."

This was about all Averil knew, for she'd been having breakfast somewhere up the river when her father got back, and didn't get home herself, to tumble into bed for a couple of hours, till after he'd had his own breakfast and gone off again. But he was expected home to lunch, and putting politeness before her natural impulse—she's only eighteen—to get out the other car and rush off to Cambridge to be in the thick of things, she sat and talked to me while I dressed. She seemed to think it a bit of luck for all concerned that Maurice was coming that night.

"Except for the murderer, of course," she added. "Major Hemyock is so clever, isn't he?"

"Perhaps your police won't want him butting in," I said.

"Daddy told Mummy he'd be very glad of his help. Mummy says he's very worried. It's his first big case, you know."

Puffin, of course, is a born worrier, and he'd only had this job about three months. And I knew Maurice *would* butt in if he was given half a chance.

When I was dressed, Averil and I went down to look up Sir Vyvyan in *Who's Who*. Vera Nugent, very sensibly, was only just getting up.

According to *Who's Who*, Sir Vyvyan was born in 1891. He was educated at Eton and Trinity, entered his father's business (stockbroking), m. Eugenie, d. of Wilbraham Foster, Esq., and succeeded his father, the 1st baronet, in 1917. One s., Hereward Vyvyan, b. 1916. Clubs: Carlton, Bath, Royal Thames Yacht. Recreations: yachting, golf. Evidently one of our plutocrats.

Vera Nugent floated down, very placid about it all, while we were digesting this information; and just as the gong went for lunch Puffin arrived from the scene of the crime. (Clayhythe, by the way, is six miles from Cambridge, and Hythe House stands a mile farther down the Cam). Averil leapt at her father with squeals of excitement, but Vera, in her sensible way, insisted on his having a drink and beginning his lunch before he uttered a word.

He looked very gloomy. A murder was bad enough, and a murder in Cambridge, of all places, and in May Week, too, was worse; but what really put the tin hat on it was the baronetcy and the Bath and Carlton. As Puffin said—it was his first remark—it was going to raise the deuce of a stink.

"Devilish glad old Maurice is coming along," he mumbled, giving me a hopeful but doubting look—the sort of look Holmes's clients gave Watson when the head of the firm was out.

"Well, what *did* happen?" I asked, assuming the ban to be raised, and beating Averil by a short head.

"Fellow was run through the back," Puffin said.

"*Run* through. . .? What with?"

" Something like a French bayonet, the doctor says. Long, three-edged blade. Went slap through and came out in front——"

"And this was in the 'Eagle'?" I said incredulously.

"Good God, no!" Puffin's tone implied that that would have been the last straw.

"But Mummy said——" Averil began.

"Fellow was *staying* at the 'Eagle,' " Puffin explained to me. "He was killed in King's Lane. Know it?"

I nodded.

"There's a bend in it, with some garages and bicycle racks, between King's and the back of the 'Eagle' "—I nodded again—"Hogg must have been stabbed there. There's a spot or two of blood on the pavement. Then he was dragged round the corner and shoved in a doorway."

"What time was this?" I asked, trying to remember when I had last seen the Rowsell-Hoggs at the ball.

Puffin was mixing himself another stiff whisky and soda.

"Round about one," he said. He took a drink and helped himself to more kidneys. "Restoring the tissues," he added, "and, by gad, they need it! It's the devil of a business . . ."

"But what about the jewels?" Averil cried.

"I'd forgotten them," I said. "*Was* there a robbery, too?"

Puffin nodded, his mouth being full of kidney.

"Very much so," he said, when he could speak again. "And there's another rum go. Fellow walked in, cool as you please——"

"Walked in where?" Averil asked. "And what fellow? Daddy, you're telling this awfully badly. Begin properly, at the very beginning."

Vera told her to let her father tell it in his own way. But as Puffin's narrative style is in fact the reverse of lucid, so that it took us half an hour, and from the dining-room to the garden, to reduce his story to an intelligible form, I'll give a précis of it myself.

2

As I mentioned before, Sir Vyvyan and his wife left Trinity at midnight. It was barely dark then, and a lovely night, and they walked to the 'Eagle' along Trinity Street and King's Parade. A man named Mercer was with them. He'd been at Trinity with Sir Vyvyan in the old days, and was now an assistant tutor at Queens'. Having left Lady Rowsell-Hogg at the hotel, the two men went on to Queens', by King's Lane, to have a talk together in Mercer's rooms. This programme—and as it turned out, the point was an important one—had been fixed up earlier in the day. Lady Hogg was in poor health, and intended to leave the ball early, and as her husband was going back to London next morning, he'd arranged to have this chat with Mercer after she had gone to bed.

The two men, by Mercer's account, were together for about an hour. Just after one in the morning Mercer let Sir Vyvyan out by Doket's Gate, in Queens' Lane. So far as was known when Puffin came home to lunch, this was the last seen of Rowsell-Hogg alive—by anyone, that is, except his murderer.

In the meantime, his wife had not gone to bed. She slept badly, and having undressed just sat about, reading and waiting for her husband. Outside the room, in the corridor, a chambermaid was also waiting up, to minister to more belated revellers from the ball. As it happened, no one else came to the rooms on that landing for more than an hour.

It was ten past one, or thereabouts, when a man appeared in the corridor. He wore evening dress, with a light black overcoat and a black felt hat (which he kept on). He had a dark moustache and tinted glasses, and carried a thick stick. The maid noticed this because gentlemen, in her experience, didn't carry sticks with evening dress. The man, who was a stranger to her, came along quickly, and spoke rather breathlessly, as if he had run up the stairs. He also spoke with a slight stammer.

He asked the maid if Lady Rowsell-Hogg slept on that floor. The maid said yes. Then the man told her to call Lady Hogg, as Sir Vyvyan had met with an accident, and was lying in the lounge. He wanted his wife to go to him. The man added that the maid was to go too, as another woman was wanted.

Rather flustered, and having no reason to doubt all this, the maid ran to Lady Hogg's door. She had an impression that the strange man had turned to run down the stairs again. Anyway, when she came out of the bedroom with Lady Hogg, which was almost at once, he was nowhere to be seen in the corridor. The two women rushed downstairs, to find perfect calm reigning everywhere, the lounge empty, and only the night porter at his desk.

The porter knew nothing about any accident. A gentleman had just come in, nodded to him, and gone up. The porter didn't know him, hadn't bothered about him, and wouldn't know him again. During May Week, or at any rate while the balls were on, people were coming and going at all hours. One or two parties had come in in the last fifteen minutes. He supposed the unknown gentleman, as he hadn't asked for his key, had gone to join someone already upstairs.

What they ought to have done now, of course, was to rush up at once, though probably it was already too late. Instead, they all dithered about for some minutes in the lobby. Poor Lady Rowsell-Hogg was still rather worried about her husband, wondering if something *had* happened to him—as indeed it had, for his body was then lying in a doorway round the corner. The porter, who had lived all his life in Cambridge, talked of practical jokes. It was the chambermaid who remembered her duties upstairs, and then began to think of thieves and wonder where the stranger with the stick and the stammer had got to: and now at last they all three trooped up. Everything seemed in order until Lady Rowsell-Hogg, with this talk of thieves in her mind, looked in her jewel-case, which she had left on her dressing-table, the key in the lock, just as it was when she took off her jewellery on her return from the ball. She cried out at once, for a valuable pendant of nine fine diamonds was missing.

Oddly enough, nothing else had been taken; and while the porter went off to find the manager of the hotel, the two women searched the room, on the chance that Lady Hogg, who was careless with her things, had put the pendant down somewhere else. They were still looking for it when a police whistle blew outside.

A constable on his beat, walking up King's Lane, had found the body of Sir Vyvyan in the doorway.

Within a few seconds the decorous calm of the 'Eagle' was shattered with a vengeance. A party just returning heard the whistle, ran whooping down the Lane, and got the shock of their lives. They identified the body, which was carried in. The news was broken to Lady Hogg, who fainted. What with these people, the police, the staff, and other guests roused by the hubbub, the lobby was soon crowded; and in the babel and excitement it was not for several valuable minutes that anyone thought of the man with the stammer, and the missing pendant. There was not much hope of finding either then.

For those who don't know Cambridge, I'll add a description of the locality. Four streets make a rectangle: Trumpington Street and Queens' Lane, parallel and running north and south, are linked up by Silver Street and King's Lane, also parallel and running east and west. The junction of King's Lane and Trumpington Street forms the north-east corner of the rectangle, and the ' Eagle,' in Trumpington Street itself, is on the opposite side to the Lane. Queens' College faces on the parallel Queens' Lane, on which it has two gates. Doket's Gate, where Mercer let Sir Vyvyan out, is the nearest to King's Lane, and therefore to the 'Eagle.' From the gate to the hotel is not two minutes' walk.

King's Lane is no thoroughfare, being blocked at the Trumpington Street end by wooden posts. Halfway to its junction with Queens' Lane it makes a double bend, and it was here they found the spots of blood. The body of Sir Vyvyan had been dragged out of the bend to a doorway a few yards nearer Trumpington Street, in a part of the Lane which at one o'clock in the morning, even in May Week, is little used, and is not overlooked at all. If the body had been left in the bend, where there was a lamp, it might have been seen at any moment by someone leaving or entering King's College Buildings, at the head of Queens' Lane, or using one of the garages in the bend itself. The murderer didn't know that a constable would be taking King's Lane on his beat so soon after the crime. That, at least, was the police theory, according to Puffin. Anyway, the body must have been lying in the doorway for ten minutes before it was found—ample time for the rest of the business. That is, of course, if the murder and the theft were committed by the same man.

3

At the end of his story, I asked Puffin about this.

"Devilish odd coincidence if they weren't," he said.

"He must have had plenty of nerve," said I

Puffin nodded. Averil was listening with eyes like saucers, but Vera Nugent took it all with her usual massive calm.

"But if the man was after the jewels," I went on, "why did he kill Sir Vyvyan at all? Did he steal anything from him?"

"Not so far as we know," Puffin said. "Bloke had the usual things on him—gold dress watch, cigarette-case, a quid or two. Nothing touched, apparently."

"Do you think they met in the Lane? I mean, did the man overtake him, and kill him to stop him coming in? It seems rather drastic. And it would mean he knew who Sir Vyvyan was."

"Oh, he knew all right——" Puffin stopped and chewed on his pipe.

"What do you mean?"

"Tell you later, Myra—perhaps."

"Besides," I added, "I thought burglars stuck to burgling, and never killed."

"They don't often use side-arms, anyway."

"You're sure it was a bayonet?"

"Something very like. French type, you know."

"Perhaps he's a Frenchman?" Averil suggested brightly.

We all smiled, even Puffin. But I was thinking of an expression he had just used.

"Side-arms," I repeated. "How long, O Lord?"

"Eh?" said Puffin.

"Sorry. I mean how long would it be?"

"How long would what be?"

"A French bayonet."

"Oh, a couple of feet, or nearly, I should say. They're nasty things."

Averil, who has her moments, looked at her father, winked at me, and murmured, "Un-British."

"Then how would the man carry it?" I went on. "Did that maid at the 'Eagle' say if he seemed to be holding something under his coat, or if he walked stiffly?"

13

"Why stiffly?" Averil asked.

"Trouser leg," I explained.

I got this idea out of a book, but Puffin, as well as his daughter, looked at me with respect.

"No," he said. "According to the gal, he walked all right and had both his hands free. But you've forgotten something."

I racked my memory. Watson's stock must be kept up.

"Something the girl said?" I asked.

Puffin nodded.

"I've got it!" I cried. "The stick. He had a thick stick——"

"Good for you, Myra," Puffin said.

"Then it *was* a sword-stick?"

"Well, it's a possibility. Probability, I should say—if the bloke who had it was the murderer. And I'll bet he was. As a matter of fact, our doctor suggested a sword-stick. It would fit the wound. The blade, I mean . . . They're usually three-edged, like skewers. And why a stick, anyway? A fellow in evening kit doesn't carry 'em nowadays."

I could have told Puffin that some fellows did. But they weren't the sort of fellows he and the ' Eagle's' chambermaid meant.

"Let's get the whole thing straight," I said. I was warming up now, and getting interested, and in Maurice's absence I felt I must do the firm, credit. "Do you think the thief met Sir Vyvyan by chance, and killed him on the spur of the moment?"

"No."

"Then everything that happened must have been premeditated?"

"Looks like it."

"But premeditated from *when?*"

"Eh. . .? Don't get you there."

"I mean," I said, "either he was someone who knew beforehand that Rowsell-Hogg and his wife were leaving the ball early, and that Sir Vyvyan was going on with this man Mercer to Queens', or he had just been following him about, waiting for a chance to get him in a quiet spot like King's Lane. But in that case he couldn't have guessed it *would* be King's Lane, and so handy for the 'Eagle,' so that he was able to nip in, tell his tale, grab the jewels, and be off again, all in five minutes. All *that* part must have been improvised on the spot. And would a man who'd just committed a murder *think* of it, or dare to do it. . .?" I stopped to sort out my ideas a bit further. "I'm not making myself very clear, am I?" I added.

"You're doing jolly well," said Puffin. " Carry on."

"You see what I mean?"

"Oh, lord, yes. Iliff—he's my Superintendent here—puts it in the same way, but not half so well."

"What does he think? And you?"

"Well, we don't *know,* of course, but it looks as if the fellow had been following the Hoggs."

"From the ball."

"Yes. He'd have plenty of time to think everything out, while Hogg was at Queens'."

"That's a pity," I said.

"Why?"

"If it had been the other way, you ought to be able to spot him pretty quickly."

"As how?"

"There can't be so many people who knew all about the Hoggs' movements last night."

Puffin grunted, and fiddled with his pipe. He'd as good as admitted that he'd got something up his sleeve, and he was trying to keep it there. But he wasn't very subtle, and I thought I might get it out of him with a little patience.

"Well, we've got as far as this," I said. "The murder was premeditated. The man was waiting for Sir Vyvyan to leave Queens'. But why? What was the motive?"

"Ask me another," Puffin mumbled. "Dash it, Myra, we've only had twelve hours."

He wasn't a bit convincing, but I let it pass.

"All right," I said. "We'll go on to the theft. Also premeditated, I suppose?"

"Seems to follow, doesn't it?" Puffin said, looking relieved, as if he thought we were on safer ground.

"The man didn't go downstairs after he'd spoken to the maid, but nipped into a bathroom or something, and as soon as the women had gone walked into Lady Hogg's room and took the pendant?"

"That's it, I should say."

"Then how did he get out of the 'Eagle'?"

"Window at the back, probably," Puffin said. "It was the first floor, you know. Half the bedrooms were still empty, and the fellow could slip away easily enough over the roofs below—coal-houses and things—and across the yard into one of the streets behind. Though if he did, he didn't leave any tracks, and I wouldn't put it past him to lie doggo till the shindy began in the lobby, and then just walk down and out of the door."

15

"Having removed his moustache and glasses."

Puffin nodded at me with approval. "Don't forget much, do you? Must come from living with old Maurice."

"I've got brains of my own, thank you," I said. "But you know, Puffin, if the man did walk out like that, he *must* have a nerve!"

"Well, he has. Doesn't it stick out a mile? And he knew there'd be a rumpus pretty soon, when they found the body. And there was. Place was full of people barging about, and Lady Hogg was fainting upstairs, and they were all yelling blue murder and wanting sal volatile and doctors, and for five minutes or so there was only the one constable there—chap who found Hogg—and he couldn't keep an eye on every one——" Puffin stopped for breath, and made noises of disgust. "My men had their hands full looking after traffic," he said. "Damn it, this isn't a normal town at any time, and in May Week it's bedlam. People don't go to bed at all, and they pop in and out of hotels at all hours of the night."

"Poor daddy," said Averil. "Don't you wish it was Wigan?"

"I want to know more about the robbery," I said. "Why did he only take the pendant? What else was there? I should have thought a woman like Lady Hogg would go about with masses of jewels. Though," I added, on second thoughts, "she wasn't wearing many last night. I remember the pendant, and diamond ear-rings. . . ."

"She didn't bring anything more with her," Puffin said, "bar a few rings and oddments. And she only wanted the pendant for a special do." "The ball?"

"No. Rowsell-Hogg gave a dinner at the 'Eagle' last night, to do with a club he belonged to when he was at Trinity. Reunion of old members, and all that—though there were only two of 'em—plus the younger generation up here now. Sons and daughters, you know."

"Daughters?"

"Well, there was a girl from Girton, though I believe she's down now."

"And what had the pendant to do with it?"

"It was a wedding present to Lady Hogg from the original members."

"And now it's gone—and everything else was left," I said. "And those ear-rings looked valuable. Isn't that suggestive? Or isn't it?"

From the way Puffin began to fiddle with his pipe again, I suspected it *was* suggestive.

Vera Nugent, who hadn't said a word for half an hour, now asked a question. Like most of Vera's questions, it proved to have its point.

"What was this club, Chester? What was it called?"

"Oh, one of those dinner clubs. Fellows dined once a month at the 'Eagle' in sky-blue coats, or some damn-fool toggery like that. Called 'emselves the Nine Bright Shiners." Puffin looked at me. "Suggest anything *to you?*" he said. "You read, and all that . . ."

Books, to Puffin, are divided severely into two classes: those about sport, and the others, which are all closed to him.

"I've heard the name," I said. "It's out of some old rhyme—"

Here Averil chipped in with a contribution:

"Why, it's one of the college songs. King's, I think. The refrain's 'Green grow the rashes, O!' and it begins:

> 'Twelve are the Twelve Apostles;
> Eleven are the eleven who went to Heaven,
> And ten are the Ten Commandments:
> Nine are the Nine Bright Shiners. . . .'"

Puffin stared at his offspring with naïve surprise.

"Out of the mouths of babes . . ." he said. "Go up one, Averil. It *is* King's."

"Uses of Girl Guides," Averil explained. "It's in one of our song-books, and I asked about it."

"What are the Nine Bright Shiners?" I inquired.

But Averil didn't know that. Her father threw a chest and looked superior.

"According to one school of thought," he said, "they're nine heroes. Old mediæval idea. Three Christians, three Jews, and three what-d'you-call-'ems."

Averil and I asked together what he meant by that.

"Oh, *you* know. . . . What aren't Jews or Christians?"

"Buddhists?" Averil suggested.

"Infidels?" I said.

"That's it." He pulled a bit of paper from his pocket and studied it. "Here you are. . . . Joshua, David, Judas Mac—Maccabæus—whoever *he* was. Sounds Scotch, but those are the Jews. Arthur, Charlemagne, Godfrey de Bouillon. Don't know anything about *him*, either—unless he invented soup. And the infidels are Cæsar, Alexander, and Hector."

"It reads like a selection from the Positivists' calendar," I said. "But what do you mean by one school of thought? Is there another explanation?"

"So I gathered. But this is good enough for me. It's the one this club used. They all took the names. Rowsell-Hogg was Hector. He chose the right one, from all I hear."

"You seem to have heard quite a lot," I remarked.

Puffin put his paper away. "Well, I got most of it from your cousin," he said.

I stared. "My *cousin?*"

"Mr. James Tullis."

"He's not a cousin. His great-aunt married my great-grandmother, or the other way about. But how does *he* come in?"

"He was a member of this tomfool club. He was Judas Thingumbob."

I chuckled. I couldn't imagine anyone less like my notion of Judas Maccabæus than James Tullis. But no doubt he got the name from an association of ideas—if you can call it that—supplied just now by Puffin himself, whose mind runs rather on undergraduate lines.

"Well, he *is* a Scot," I pointed out. "Of course I remember now Ian telling me his father had been at Clare. But I'd never met James before last night, and then he insisted on delving into much more ancient history. . . . So he knew Sir Vyvyan, did he?" I added.

"Oh, rather."

"When was all this, by the way?"

"The club? It was formed in 1910. The whole lot came down together in 1912."

Vera stirred herself again. "What happened to it then?" she asked.

"Died a natural death, I should hope," Puffin said. "But for the last year or two Rowsell-Hogg has been giving a dinner in May Week to the survivors and their kids who are up here—which seems to mean all of 'em, except the Girton girl, who went down last year."

"Are there any more girls among them?" Vera asked.

"One. But she wasn't at the dinner——"

He pulled himself up and coughed.

"Why not?" said I.

"Oh, I dunno. . . ."

But it was obvious that he did know, and that Vera, in her uncanny, casual way, had hit on something.

"Who is she?" I asked.

Puffin coughed again. "Er—girl named Lanham."

"At Girton too?"

"No. Newnham."

Here he stopped coughing and wriggling, tried to be official, looked at his watch, and mumbled something about having to go. But I wasn't going to let him off, just when it was plain that at last we were getting warm.

"Come on, Puffin!" I said. "This hush-hush stuff won't work. I'll get it all out of Ian Tullis—to say nothing of Cousin James. Ian's coming to fetch Averil and me in an hour or so. He told me last night he'd come on from some reunion, which seemed to have bored him. I thought he meant an old boys' gathering, but of course it was this dinner. And James was there too, I suppose. . .? So out with it, Puffin. What's the mystery of Miss Lanham?"

Puffin grinned. He's a simple soul, even for a chief constable, and still very much of a boy. He'd spent half the night and most of the morning with his policemen, and came home tired and worried and full of official inhibitions. But food and drink and the domestic atmosphere had worked wonders, and I think for some time he'd been itching to let a cat or two out of the bag. And now, after a little more humming and hawing, he began to find excuses for letting the whole lot out together.

"Oh, well, if it's like that . . . And then there's old Maurice. It's all in the family, eh. . .? And it'll be all over Cambridge in two two's, with that mob at the dinner, and the girl at the 'Eagle'. . . ."

"Oh, go *on,* Daddy!" Averil cried.

He eyed her severely. "But there's to be no gossip from *this* house, mind."

"Cross my heart!"

"There may be nothing in it. We may be on the wrong track altogether. I hope we are——"

"Oh, go *on!*"

He ignored Averil, and looked at me.

"Well, it's this way," he said. "It's all mixed up with these Nine Shiners and their silly club. There were only three of 'em left—Rowsell-Hogg, your pal Tullis, and the father of this Lanham girl——"

"Out *of nine?*" I put in. "If they came down in 1912, they'd only be in the forties now. Isn't that a pretty heavy casualty list?"

"And you a soldier's wife? Though you've got the right word. Ever hear of the war?"

"Oh, of course. . . ."

"It killed off three or four of 'em, and one got drowned at sea, and one or two just died. . . . Anyway, there've only been these three left for some years."

Vera put in another of her quiet questions.

"How many children are there?"

Puffin scratched his head. "Wait a minute. . . . I've got it. Six. There were seven, but a boy called Henderson was done in in a motor smash last Christmas. His twin's still up here at Queens'."

Vera went on: "Didn't you say they're all up here—or were?"

"Rather. Parents' *alma mater,* and all that. Mustn't have any truck with Oxford."

19

"And there are no more coming up? Or not coming up?"

"Lord knows. Haven't heard of any. Why?"

"Oh, I don't know," Vera said. "I suppose I'm more interested in the children than in their parents. I keep thinking of that poor Rowsell-Hogg boy. It ought to be the happiest time of his life—and it was, till this morning. How did you tell him, Chester?"

"I went round myself and fetched him away from the ball later on. Nasty business. . . ."

He looked as if it had been.

"Poor fellow!" I said.

I'd been so interested in the crime that I'm afraid I hadn't thought much about the victim and his wife and son till Vera's remark brought that side of it home to me. The fact that I had actually danced with Hereward Rowsell-Hogg now seemed to make it all the more shocking. He had been so much on top of the world only twelve hours ago.

In the meantime, while Vera, though we little knew it then, was calmly putting her finger on the root of the whole matter, I'd been doing some more arithmetic.

"Then with six children left—if there *are* no more—and the three original members, there were another nine of the two generations."

"I'll take your word for it," Puffin said. "And now there are only eight. . . . Does it matter?"

"I wanted to be tidy."

"Like old Maurice, eh. . .? Well, where was I? You've put me off between you."

We told him where he was.

"Oh, yes. . . . Well, there were these three left out of the original nine. Now there are two. And if it wasn't for something else"—Puffin chuckled and cocked an eye at me—"I might be keeping an eye on both of 'em."

"What has James done?"

"Nothing, that I know of. . . ." He looked at his watch again. "By gad, I *shall* have to be off——"

"What's this something else?" I said firmly, for he seemed in a hurry again to cut his revelations short. "The real Simon Pure?"

"That isn't his name."

"No," I said, wondering if he was serious or pulling my leg. Puffin isn't so simple as he sometimes pretends to be. "No, obviously it's Lanham."

He nodded. "Yes, we'd like to see Mr. Lanham."

"Was he at the dinner?"

"He's never been to any of 'em."

"Oh . . . Nor his daughter?"

"No."

"And he's one of the original members. . . ."

"He founded the bally thing."

"Curiouser and curiouser," I said. "All the same, why do you want to see him?"

"You seem to have hit on it yourself. I told you the murder's mixed up with the club."

"But you haven't explained in what way."

Puffin got up. "I want a drink," he said. "Well, for one thing, there was a drawing on the body."

"A *drawing?*"

"Yes, stuffed in Hogg's shirt-front. A dozen people saw it, so it isn't much of a secret, as I said. The point is, it's a drawing of Hector."

CHAPTER II

1

PUFFIN refused to tell us any more. He had his drink and left us in a tearing hurry to take up chief constabulary duties again. He was a good deal more cheerful than when he came home to lunch. As I guessed at the time, his superintendent and inspectors were inclined to be a bit superior, in a perfectly disciplined and respectful way (which is more infuriating than any other), towards a chief who was so new to his job; and Puffin, who has no illusions about himself, was suffering from a slight inferiority complex. He was too decent to get his own back, as he might have done, by coming the heavy army officer over his subordinates. I believe he's very popular now, but at this time he was still being tried out, and he knew it. As he said afterwards to Maurice, in some ways it was like being a raw subaltern again. His men didn't know him, and he didn't know his men, and they were much the more experienced and critical of the two.

The murder in King's Lane was a pretty severe test for all concerned—and they little knew what was to follow!—so that although being able to relax before a sympathetic audience had soothed Puffin's nerves, he was still anxious for Maurice's arrival and moral support. Maurice, in the circumstances, looked like being a godsend. Superintendent Iliff, as we were to learn, already regarded the case as solved; and this was what worried Chester Nugent most of all. He was praying that it wasn't. A case of murder in which every person involved had been to a public school and belonged to the best clubs, and which had as a background Cambridge and its colleges and dons and all the imported rank and fashion of May Week, was very shocking to the conventional mind. The Superintendent had no social prejudices; in fact, he rather relished figuring in a sensation in high life; but it was gall and wormwood to poor Puffin, who was still hoping against hope that the criminal would prove to belong to the criminal classes after all. And Maurice, who talked the same language and would understand, might find a flaw or two in Mr. Iliff's theories, or—who knew?—even produce on the spot an old lag out of a hat. Such faith, as I told my husband, would move mountains.

The garden at Hythe House slopes down to the Cam; and Vera Nugent, Averil, and I were still discussing the inevitable topic there half an hour later when Ian Tullis came charging down the river in a minute motor-boat to take Averil and me to tea at the university motor-boat club just below Waterbeach. Of course he was full of the murder too, but it was only a few minutes' run up to the club and he'd only time to tell us (with the air of a host who is doing his guests proud) that we should meet there several more of the junior protagonists in the case—if that's the right word. At the now famous dinner at the 'Eagle' the night before, the younger Bright Shiners present had arranged to meet at the boat club this afternoon, Ian himself and a boy called Ince being members. One of the five was unavoidably absent, but the others thought a murder no reason for changing their plans. Rather the reverse—there was so much to talk about, and they were in the news themselves now. As Ian said, "We mustn't disappoint our public."

The lawns of the club were crowded, but we were barely ashore when he hailed a girl who was strolling by with a tall, saturnine young man in impossibly perfect flannels.

"Hi, Claudia!"

The pair waited for us, and Ian introduced Miss Claudia Farleigh. I didn't catch the name of her escort—I learnt later it was Armfeldt—and that of Miss Farleigh herself conveyed nothing to me till Ian explained:

"She's one of us, you know. But she's gone down."

So this was the young lady from Girton.

She hadn't got over it yet. She was beautifully dressed, in a rather arty style, extremely slim, distinctly pretty, and terrifyingly superior.

Ian mentioned that I was staying with the Chief Constable, and that Averil was his daughter. After all, this gave us a sort of *cachet* just then. But Miss Farleigh smiled pityingly.

"Oh, yes?" she said to me, completely ignoring Averil. "I hope you suffer the police gladly, Mrs. Hemyock. I've been a little bored by them this morning."

"So they've been after you too?" Ian said.

"A man with waxed moustaches—an Inspector or something— had the bad taste to call at Girton. I'm staying there, you know. It made a bad impression, and of course I wasn't up——"

"What did he want? Your views on Lanham?"

"Did they ask you about him too?" said Miss Farleigh, with a flicker of interest. "Of course I told him he'd better go to Newnham, and that I didn't know a thing about the man—or his daughter either."

Her tone dismissed Newnham and Miss Lanham to outer darkness.

Her tall, saturnine companion, who'd been staring at me—I thought with interest—put in a word.

"An extraordinary affair, Mrs. Hemyock."

I agreed that it was. Mr. Armfeldt did not look English, and spoke with a slightly foreign accent. He was handsome, in his dark way, with very liquid brown eyes and a silky little black moustache. His clothes were too perfect, and, like Claudia Farleigh's, had a touch of extravagance that might be foreign too, or merely meant to suggest the æsthetic. Even flannels can do this, given a certain cut. He was, I could see now, considerably older than the boys about us.

"Let's collar a table," Ian said, with a return of his showman's manner, "and I'll round up the others and we'll compare notes on the third degree."

He moved on with Claudia Farleigh, while Armfeldt walked between Averil and me.

"I find it extremely interesting," he observed.

"You mean the murder?" I said.

"Yes." He waved a beautifully manicured hand. "Claudia thinks it too highly coloured—she works in very subdued tones herself—but I feel that an artist ought to be able to see nuances even in the dramatic."

"You're an artist?" I said, failing, on the spur of the moment, to think of an intelligent reply.

"I decorate," said Mr. Armfeldt.

"And Miss Farleigh decorates too?"

"Oh, no. She writes. Exquisite work—very modern. All subfusc tones, you know. Patterns in grey."

"Dear me!" said I, stealing a glance at Averil, who was grinning broadly. "You're not a Cambridge man yourself, Mr.——?"

"Armfeldt. Oh, no, no!" He seemed slightly horrified at the idea. "If one must go to a university, I should choose Oxford. Between two impossibles, one should always choose the most extreme."

I rallied after a moment. "But Miss Farleigh," I said, "modern though she is, chose Cambridge."

Mr. Armfeldt shrugged—a definitely foreign shrug, bringing into play arms and hands as well as shoulders.

"Her parents did," he explained. "The sins of the fathers, you know . . . And then Claudia got her wages."

Of course I didn't understand then what he meant, and mercifully we were spared any more of this, for Ian had found a table, and at the same moment was loudly hailing another boy, with a long, solemn face and horn-rimmed glasses, who edged his way out of the crowd to join us. He was introduced as Roy Henderson, and I remembered that his twin brother had been killed in a motor smash.

"Where's Patrick?" Ian asked him.

"Somewhere about." Young Henderson looked vaguely round him. He was a nice lad, with a look of reserve and melancholy, which was not surprising. His dark eyes, behind their round lenses, seemed to see through you to other and less palpable worlds. Poor fellow! I have often wondered since what he saw.

Have I mentioned that it was a gorgeous day? This may be taken as read of that afternoon, and of the days that followed. May Week, cursed in other ways, was blessed with its traditional weather. The sun blazed down. The green lawns of the boat club, vivid with boys in prismatic blazers and their young womenfolk in pretty frocks, made a charming picture—though I refrained from commenting on this to Mr. Armfeldt, who, I suspected, would scarcely find enough nuances in this kind of thing. Motor-boats, paint and varnish flashing in the sunshine, scudded up and down the river, or drew in to disembark more laughing passengers. An occasional canoe or punt, like some shy ghost of a quieter age, slid by under the willows on the farther shore. Presently from the university yacht club, whose lawn marched with ours, a little flock of triangular white sails was loosed and went drifting away down stream, leaning to the breeze. There was no hint of tragedy here, still less of more to come. Not even at *our* table. . . .

But I never think of that tea-party now without a shiver.

While we found our chairs—the suave Mr. Armfeldt found mine for me— and Ian conferred earnestly with a waiter, I heard Claudia Farleigh's cool, over-modulated voice uttering one of those sweeping assertions young women of her kind affect. She was speaking to the Henderson boy.

"It would be hypocritical to pretend one's really sorry. I never liked him, and, of course, he was merely a social parasite."

I wondered who this unfortunate might be.

"You are a Socialist, Miss Farleigh?" young Henderson asked—I thought with a touch of sarcasm. If so, the literary Claudia, like most of her type, was impervious to it.

"Of course," she said. "Socialism is the only creed for intelligent people."

Mr. Armfeldt, who had taken a chair beside mine, turned his rather silky smile on me.

"Two questions, Mrs. Hemyock. A. Are you intelligent? And B. Is it possible that Lanham is really a Socialist, carrying our creed to its logical conclusion ?"

"'Our' creed?"

"Oh, I have none, of any sort. But I am engaged to Claudia, and hers— while they last—are mine."

25

So that explained Mr. Armfeldt. I'd been wondering what he was doing in this galley.

"Whom was Miss Farleigh speaking of?" I asked, though I'd guessed by now.

"The murderee."

"You talked of conclusions," I said. "Aren't you rather jumping to them?"

"About Lanham?"

"Yes. Unless you've more information than I have——"

"And yours comes from the horse's mouth?"

"I was going to add, 'Surely it's a little early to accuse anyone?'"

"Ah, I fancy your horse was discreet." He called across to Ian, who had just sent his waiter flying and was pulling up a chair for himself. "Tullis, tell Mrs. Hemyock your story about Devine and Lanham."

"Oh, don't you know that, Myra?" Ian said. (I'm not old enough to be his mother, but this fact, and a very distant relationship, are no excuse for his calling me Myra, as he did the second time we met. But the youth of to-day hurl Christian names about with less excuse than that.) "The police have had us all on the mat about it," he went on. "I should have thought old Nugent—oh, sorry, Miss Nugent—"

"Don't mind my feelings," said Averil. "Go on."

"Well, there's a chap called Devine," Ian said, "who has a cottage up the river here, at Horningsea. Or rather his mother has. He's a journalist, and pops up and down. . . . The Devines are friends of the Lanhams, and Lanham was coming down last night to stay with them, to see the girl. She's at Newnham, you know, and Lanham wouldn't want to put up in Cambridge just now, because he might run across Rowsell-Hogg or my father at any moment——"

"Without implying anything," Armfeldt murmured, with another of his cynical smiles at me, "he needn't worry about Hogg any longer."

"But why should he want to avoid either?" I asked.

"He hates 'em both," Ian said. "It's part of the story. . . . But to go back to Devine, I met him near the station last night, just before the dinner. You know my rooms are down that way. . . . Well, Devine had been to meet Lanham, as per arrangement, and Lanham hadn't turned up. And he hasn't turned up yet. Or he hadn't this morning, because as Devine didn't hear from him he rolled along to Newnham to find out if the Lanham girl knew anything about it, and *she* thought her father was at Horningsea, and was expecting to see him. I got this out of old Breeze—he's one of the cops here, a sergeant, and a pal of mine—he ran me in once— when he came round to ask *me* about it.

26

We're all mixed up in it, you know." Ian waved a hand round the table. "Well, Breeze wanted to know if I'd seen Lanham, or would know him if I did. As the last time I saw him was when I was about five, I don't suppose I should. . . . Anyway, it seems that the Superintendent here, Iliff, went round to see Miss Lanham too, and found Devine there. And then the fat was in the fire. . . ."

2

If none too lucid, when sorted out this filled in some of the gaps in Puffin's story. I wondered if Ian and his friends knew yet about the drawing of Hector. But without this, the police inquiries after the missing Lanham accounted in themselves for every one's readiness to suspect him of the crime. And obviously there was still more behind—some knowledge of the past shared by all these descendants of the original Nine Bright Shiners. And, *ex officio,* by Mr. Armfeldt too.

Speculations about the drawing were answered at once.

"Never having been run in," Claudia Farleigh drawled, "the police don't confide in me, so I haven't yet grasped what put them on to Lanham in the beginning."

"My dear girl," Ian said, "you've heard of the drawing?"

"What drawing?"

"The 'Eagle's' buzzing with it."

"Possibly. I'm not staying there."

"But what the 'Eagle' knows at one a.m., all Cambridge knows. . . . However, this is the story, or one version of it. A large cartoon of Hector was gummed on Hogg's shirt-front."

Even Miss Farleigh was surprised out of her careful poise.

"Hector . . .?" she exclaimed, in quite a natural voice. "Nonsense!"

"On the contrary," Ian said. "There *was* a drawing, with 'Hector' scrawled over it. Father told me, at lunch. He'd seen it."

I felt Mr. Armfeldt's liquid glance on me again.

"Rather bizarre, eh . . .?" he murmured. "Did your horse tell you this, Mrs. Hemyock?"

I nodded. "So the police showed it to your father? " I said to Ian.

"Oh, rather. Poor old Hereward told them what it meant, so they put father through the hoop. Very natural too. No one ever thought of Rowsell-Hogg *père* as Hector except the members of the old club. And there are only Father and Lanham left. It was fifty-fifty."

The idea of his father being put through the hoop seemed to amuse Ian. I wondered what James Tullis thought about it.

"*We* all knew," young Henderson said. He'd been sitting silent, his large spectacles turning from one to the other of us, but always with that curious distant gaze that seemed really fixed on something beyond.

"Oh, we're *in statu pupillari,*" Ian said. "And minors can't commit murder. Or can they. . .?"

"I'm not a minor," Claudia remarked.

"Don't give yourself away," said her fiancé, smiling at me. "Mrs. Hemyock's in with the police."

"Go on about your father," she said to Ian.

Ian grinned. "Well, the rum thing was, the old boy had been round to the 'Eagle' to see Hogg about a dog—loud laughter—and when d'you think? Between the witching hours of twelve and one last night. . . . But Hogg was pow-wowing with some don at Queens', so father trotted back to Trinity to shake a sober leg again."

"That accounts for it," I said, remembering Puffin's little joke about keeping an eye on James. "Your father was lost to sight, to memory dear, for some time. But he was there again afterwards, till quite late."

"He might have had a job to prove *when* he got back, as I told him," Ian said, with a chuckle. "No one notices the time in the middle of a dance. But what happened was, luckily for him, that after they'd roasted him a bit, Iliff went to Newnham to put Mary Lanham through it about *her* father, and there was Harry Devine on the same job. But I told you that. Anyway, Iliff got the story out of him, rang up Lanham's flat in town on the spot, and found he *had* left yesterday—for Cambridge. Breeze told me this, and I passed it on to father, to ease his mind. . . . By the by, Miss Nugent, don't give Breeze away to the Colonel. He only told me official secrets because I wouldn't say a word about Lanham till he did. What we classical pundits call *quid pro quo*—and I got the quids, because I hadn't really anything to tell him. . . ."

Averil nodded. "By the way," she said, "I know the Devines. I've got some girl guides at Horning-sea——"

"Then where *is* Lanham?" Claudia interrupted.

"Lord knows," Ian said.

"He may merely have changed his mind," I remarked, "and gone to Brighton or Wootton-under-Edge, or anywhere. All this doesn't amount to much. Besides, there's the robbery."

"Oh, there's a lot more," Ian said. "Even the pendant comes into it. And between father and the rest of us, our zealous police have got it all. . . . As *you* ought to know, Myra. What's the good of staying with the Chief Constable if you don't? And I've been boasting in every bar in Cambridge about my lovely cousin who's hand in glove with the Force, and her husband the Major, England's premier amateur sleuth. . . ."

Miss Farleigh, evidently, did not frequent bars, for at this she stared at me; and Mr. Armfeldt turned to me again.

"Really?" he said. "Your husband is the Major Hemyock one read of in the papers a year or so back? What they called the Looking-Glass murders, wasn't it?"

"He is," I said. "Go on, Ian. You may assume I don't know much yet."

But before he could go on we were interrupted by the return of the waiter, staggering under a tray. And behind him came another young man, whom Ian hailed as the missing Patrick. Loud and hearty, and wearing an Old Malvernian blazer, he was introduced to Averil and me as Mr. Ince, of Jesus.

"Well, fellow suspects!" he said, squeezing his large form in between Claudia Farleigh and Roy Henderson. "How goes it? All wobbly at the knees? I had some girls in tow—wonderful how popular I am just now—but I shook 'em off. I thought this would be a council of war. But I didn't know it would be semi-officially blessed."

He grinned amiably at Averil and me. Unlike Miss Farleigh, he had heard, in bars or elsewhere, about Ian's lovely cousin. I liked Mr. Ince, who reminded me of an Airedale puppy. Fair and muscular, bursting with energy, he regarded life as one enormous joke—except in the matter of games, about which he was immensely serious. He was the very antithesis of the dreamy and wistful Roy Henderson beside him. The only bond between them was the queer fellowship of inheritance which brought them together once a year at Sir Vyvyan's dinners at the 'Eagle.' That, and its consequences. Of one of the most important of these I was still ignorant, and another none of us suspected then.

Mr. Ince's boisterous arrival drew general attention to a gathering already of considerable interest to those in the know. I saw people stop to stare and point us out to others less well informed. Our party was now complete. Somewhere Hereward Rowsell-Hogg, with whom I had danced little more than twelve hours before, was adjusting a dazed mind to the crash of his happy world; and Mary Lanham, who was only a name to me, was fretting herself ill at Newnham with fears for her father. But all the available descendants of the Nine Bright Shiners were present.

3

As Ian made me deal with the tea, I was kept busy for some time, for we were all hot and thirsty. Every one else now seemed to be chattering at once, but this was an illusion produced by Ian himself and the exuberant member from Jesus, whose tongue was never still. On general principles, I fancy—she is a pretty child—Mr. Ince drew in Averil whenever he could. Mr. Armfeldt, if slightly over-mannered about it, conveyed by his attentiveness in handing cups that he preferred more mature charms. Claudia Farleigh looked supercilious and said little, though once or twice I caught her rather cold blue eyes resting a little bleakly on her fiancé and me. Roy Henderson sat smiling mechanically at jokes he scarcely heard. Names of the dramatis personæ in the sensation of the hour were bandied about with the cheerful callousness of youth, and listening as well as I could amid my duties and the clatter of tea-things, I managed to pick up a few facts and impressions. Nobody, I noticed, pretended to grieve for Sir Vyvyan, and there were only somewhat perfunctory expressions of sympathy with his widow. "H.R.H." or "Poor old Hoggins" (this was Here-ward) was referred to with more genuine feeling. The guilt of the missing Lanham was, of course, taken for granted, but only Ian seemed ever to have met him, and that, as he said, about fifteen years earlier, when Lanham was still a young man himself and friendly with James Tullis. Miss Lanham, who had been at Newnham for two years, was known only to her fellow student from Girton, and that was rather ancient history too.

It was Armfeldt, suddenly remembering that a fiancé has duties as well as privileges—perhaps he caught one of those bleak looks—who drew Claudia out on this subject when the other girl's name came up.

"Mary Lanham?" Claudia said in her bored way. "I haven't seen her since her first term. I was in my second year then. I looked her up, out of politeness —she's no grudge against *my* father: he died when she was about eight— but she made it quite plain she didn't want to know me. Which was just as well. . . ."

"What's she like?" Patrick Ince inquired.

"An insignificant little thing. I don't suppose I should know her if I met her again."

"What is she taking?" Ian asked.

"History, I believe."

"Clever?"

"Good heavens!" said Miss Farleigh, who had taken high honours in history herself. "How should I know?"

The Lanhams' friends at Horningsea, the Devines, were mentioned. Oddly enough—at least by contrast with the general lack of knowledge of the Lanhams themselves—all three boys knew Harry Devine and his mother, though he wasn't even up at Cambridge, and never had been.

The Devines' cottage, it appeared, like Hythe House, stood on the river bank, and was used as a port of call.

"Good fellow, Devine," Patrick Ince said.

"I think Mrs. Devine has an awfully interesting face," Averil remarked, adding, as though the fact explained this: "Of course she's not English."

"You know 'em, do you, Miss Nugent?" Mr. Ince inquired.

"Very slightly. I've only met Mr. Devine once."

The jovial Patrick guffawed. "I gave him a ducking. That's how *we* met."

"A ducking?" said Averil. "What for?"

"Oh, I didn't do it to annoy, like the fellow in Shakespeare." (Miss Farleigh's expressive eyebrows went up.) "I was dawdling along in the *Slug*—my motor-launch, you know—you must come out in her some day, Miss Nugent—and Devine's canoe got too much of her wash. He swims like a fish, so there was no harm done, except that the canoe went down. He wouldn't let me help with the damage—said it was his fault, and so it was. He ought to have got out of the way, but as he said, he isn't used to toy rivers like the Cam. He's been in the States, you know. Learnt his canoeing on the St. Lawrence or Mississippi or somewhere. Interesting bloke, when you can get him to talk. Gang warfare in Chicago, and all that. He was doing newspaper work there."

"I wonder he came back here," I remarked.

"You wouldn't," Mr. Armfeldt's soft voice murmured, "if you knew Chicago."

"Which you do?"

"For my sins. A dreadful place. All American towns are dreadful. Life is so crude there. Art should sometimes be crude, but life never——"

"I meant," I interrupted ruthlessly, "that to get to America seems to be the ambition of most writers. They're always talking about it, and about their sales there."

"Not our highbrows, eh, Claudia?" Ian put in, with a grin, adding, as Miss Farleigh shrugged, "Oh, you'll grow out of it when you do sell a book there. She's quite human really," he explained, with another grin to the company at large.

This goaded Miss Farleigh into proving that she was, considerably to my amusement. She retorted tritely and rather crossly:

"Money isn't everything, you know."

"Not to you, just now," Ian said. "But wait till you've blown it all, my girl."

There was obviously something behind this sparring, but it was cut short by an exclamation from Averil.

"Why, surely that *is* Mr. Devine!"

A man in flannels was just landing on the club lawn from a canoe. He stood looking about him till a stentorian shout from Patrick Ince made him (and about fifty other people) turn in our direction. He waved a hand and came towards us.

"Hullo, hullo, hullo!" Mr. Ince cried. "The very man we want. Bag a chair."

"May I butt in?" Harry Devine asked. "I took a chance and stepped on your sacred turf, Ince, hoping you might be here."

"Meet my cousin Myra," Ian said, "and Miss Nugent. Myra's the dark one. Oh, and you don't know our Claudia. Miss Farleigh, Mr. Devine. And the dark gent's called Armfeldt."

Mr. Devine distributed bows. Then he pulled up a chair, and we made room for him somehow. He was a tall young man, rather older, like Armfeldt, than the others, and, like that exquisite too, with something vaguely foreign about him. It was not his voice, though that had transatlantic inflexions and rang a little harshly among the standardised accents of three public schools and the soft modulations, less easily placed, of Mr. Armfeldt himself. But Harry Devine was so very blond, and had a long, narrow head in which were set deeply a pair of curious pale blue eyes. Nordic was the word that came to my mind, though I've only the haziest idea of what it means.

"Well, what d'you think of May Week now?" Ince asked him. "And where's your friend Lanham? Any news yet?"

"It's a queer business," Devine said cautiously, looking from me to Averil.

"Oh, they're all right," Ian explained. "They're in it too. Miss Nugent's father is no less a person than our Chief Constable, and Myra, as well as being my cousin, is staying with them. Give the gent a cup of tea, or a bag of nuts, or something, Myra."

"I was waiting to ask him," I said.

Harry Devine was looking at me again. "Is that so?" he said. Then he smiled, showing strong white teeth. "I was not referring to the tea, though I'd like a cup. I was digesting Tullis's information."

"It interests you?" I asked.

"Naturally."

"Well, what about Lanham?" Patrick Ince asked impatiently.

"I don't know anything about him," Devine said.

"No sign of him?"

"None."

"Well, what d'you *think*?"

"That probably there's some rational explanation."

"But, my dear chap——"

"He's a friend of ours, you know," Devine said quietly. He added to me, as I handed him a cup, "Thank you, Mrs.—I'm afraid I didn't catch your name."

"Hemyock," I said. "Ian omitted to mention it."

I reflected that he had sharper eyes than most men, who never notice things like wedding rings. Ian explained with gusto once more that Maurice was the well-known archæologist and amateur detective.

"I'm afraid I haven't heard of your husband," Harry Devine said to me. "But I've been out of England. Is he here now?"

"He soon will be," said I, looking at my watch. "Ian, the train's 5.10. If you're going to run me into Cambridge, isn't it time we started?"

Ian said his motor-boat would get us to Ditton in a quarter of an hour, and that I could take a taxi from there.

Devine had turned to Patrick Ince again.

"I was hoping you people would have some news," he said. "I know practically nothing. I only heard of the murder when I went to see Mary Lanham this morning, and found a policeman there. And he wasn't giving much away."

"We know all about that," Ince said. "Nothing is hid from us."

Devine glanced at me. I shook my head.

"Not guilty. I know less than anyone," I said, keeping an eye on my watch, for it was now half-past four, and I was full of wifely anxiety to meet Maurice. I hadn't seen him for a week, and there was this murder to talk about.

"And now there's a plain-clothes dick snooping about the cottage," Harry Devine went on.

"What's a dick?" Averil asked.

"American for bobby, Miss Nugent."

"In case Lanham turns up, eh?" Ince said.

"Presumably."

"A bit shattering for Mrs. Devine, all this."

"Yes, she's not too happy about it."

I collected my bag and parasol.

"Come on, Ian," I said firmly. "I'm sorry to drag you away, but you'll have to throttle down that boat of yours. I'm not dressed for speed, and I've no intention of turning up in Cambridge looking as if I'd been blown there. You can tell me some more of the story on the way. Are you coming, Averil?"

"I'll look after Miss Nugent," Patrick Ince said promptly. "Run her home, and all that. She'll be perfectly safe with me, Mrs. Hemyock. I'm the mothers' joy. They simply fight to have me take their daughters home."

As Averil seemed very happy where she was, I left her in charge of the mothers' joy, and saying good-bye to the party, propelled a rather reluctant Ian to his launch.

CHAPTER III

1

I'D forgotten that you can't exchange much light chat with the man at the wheel of a motor-boat, and what with holding my hat on and arguing with Ian in shouts about what constituted a reasonable speed, I'd heard no more of the story after all by the time we reached Ditton. As I'd suspected, Ian had been a bit optimistic when he talked airily of finding a taxi there, but he raised a sort of car at a garage, and I bumped into the yard at Cambridge station, rather hot and bothered and wispy, just as the 5.10 drew in.

Maurice, who looked offensively cool and tidy—although he's so pink and well-covered he never feels the heat, even in a train—had an evening paper under his arm, one of those things labelled 6.30 edition which you get at places like Stow-on-the-Wold hours before that.

The first thing he said was: "What have you let me in for now?"

But I knew he was really rather thrilled about it.

We got a real taxi, with springs, and drove out to Hythe House, where we found Puffin home again, recuperating on the lawn with a gin and lime. Vera was out, and Averil hadn't come back from the boat club.

Puffin danced round Maurice, saying, "My dear old chap! It's topping to see you. Have a drink," and so on, rather incoherently. It reminded me of the meeting between Wellington and Blücher on the playing fields of Eton, or wherever it was. Of course they hadn't seen one another for a year, but obviously Puffin's first murder case was still worrying him, and he'd been praying for the Prussians to come, like the Duke. (It's odd to think, by the way, that we've never prayed for them since.) But as I needed a wash, I dragged Maurice in to have one too, because I wasn't going to let the pair get going without me.

When we joined Puffin again, he'd collected all the drinks in the house, and we got down to it.

I asked him at once if he'd found the missing Lanham, or had any news of him.

He shook his head gloomily. He'd been hoping the man would turn up with some perfectly good alibi from the other end of England, so that Superintendent Iliff would have to drop that line and start again among the lower classes. And all the more because what had transpired, as they say, since the morning tended, with Lanham still missing, to make things blacker than ever against him.

Before he came to this, Puffin ran over the points I'd already heard, for Maurice's benefit—the murder itself, the bayonet or sword-stick theory, the man with the stammer, the theft of the pendant, and the story of the Nine Bright Shiners. The first novelty on the agenda, and in fact most of the new items, proved to come from James Tullis, who'd been through the hoop again. After all, as the only surviving Shiner except Lanham himself, James was a star witness, and having got really going he'd been pulling cards out of his sleeve like a conjurer. Instead of being grateful, Puffin was rather annoyed about it.

"Can't think why the fellow didn't tell us everything before," he grumbled. "Of course we didn't ask him. How were we to know there was anything of the sort behind it?"

"You haven't explained what you're talking about yet," I pointed out.

"The club, of course," Puffin said. "We thought it was the ordinary dining club. There were any number of 'em here before the war, when people had more money."

"And wasn't it?"

"That's what it started as. But I'll have to begin at the beginning again. . . . Well, it was founded by this chap Lanham, as I told you, Myra. It was his idea, anyway—and a damn silly one, if you ask me. He was at King's, and he got the name from that college song, or whatever it is. They called themselves after these heroes, and he bagged Charlemagne. . . . Ever heard of 'em, by the way, Maurice?"

Of course Maurice had. Though he pretends his antiquarian studies haven't got any further than the Norman period, he has acquired an extraordinary amount of miscellaneous and useless information from all ages, and he offered at once several alternative ideas about the meaning of the Nine Bright Shiners. The Nine Kings of Lunnery, the Nine Tent Makers, the Nine Muses——

"That's enough," I said. "Go on, Puffin."

"Well, in 1912," Puffin said, after gaping at Maurice in admiration, "that's to say, when the club had been going for two years, these fellows were about due to come down. And one night, when they must have been doing 'emselves pretty well, Lanham—Lanham again, mark you—had another of his ideas. Did I say they were all filthily well off? Well, they were, or their people were——"

"James Tullis doesn't talk as if he was filthily well off now," I said.

"I dare say not. You're forgetting the war again. And it's part of the story. . . . Anyway, they'd all got more money than they knew what to do with *then*, so what does this ass Lanham do but propose that they start a fund, for the benefit of their children. He had one gleam of sense, because he pointed out, according to Tullis, that in twenty years' time things might be jolly different. As they are. . . . He said that by then, after they'd sent their kids to public schools and then on to Cambridge, there mightn't be much left over to start 'em on careers afterwards, and he talked of fellows they knew who'd have to begin as office boys, or underpaid schoolmasters, as soon as they went down. . . ."

"Very sound," Maurice said. "The descent from the sublime to the ridiculous, and sometimes to a struggle for bread-and-butter, is a well-known catch in our university system."

"Oh, yes, I suppose the idea was all right," Puffin agreed dubiously. "But it seems to have led to the deuce of a lot of trouble. It wanted thinking out a bit more, but they just rushed at it."

"They were only boys themselves," I said.

"And they'd had a good many drinks," he added. "They seem to have got the scheme practically cut and dried that evening. Your cousin James shakes his Caledonian head now when he thinks of it."

"Yes, he must have had a few," I said. "How much did they put up?"

"You'll never guess." Puffin paused to have a drink himself and make his effect. "A thousand apiece."

"Gracious!" said I.

"I told you they were beastly rich. And you know what it was in those days before the war. Chaps like these had no sense of money. . . . Of course they couldn't put their hands on all that then, but they could in a few months' time, when they all came of age—or they could raise it. And they did."

"Nine thousand pounds?" Maurice said.

"Yes."

"And what was to become of it?"

"Oh, they were quite business-like about that. It was made a fund, with trustees, and put away in a bank at compound interest till the children of these idiots came to Cambridge. That's to say, for at least twenty years."

"I could have worked that out," I said. "What does it come to by now?"

"Actually it's been accumulating from 1912 till last year. That's twenty-three years. According to Tullis, it doubled itself in fifteen, and a year ago it was nearly £25,000. Then *the* Girton girl drew her share, about £4000, when she went down."

"That explains it," I said, half to myself, thinking of the sparring between Claudia and Ian. Miss Farleigh could afford to be highbrow while her share lasted.

"Let's get it tidy," Maurice said. He has a mania for getting things tidy. "What precisely were the conditions of the trust? And who were the trustees?"

"Your glass is empty," Puffin said, pushing some drinks across the table. "The trustees," he went on, "were two of these blessed Shiners and the manager of the Cambridge branch of the National Southern Bank, where the money is. If a trustee died, or went batty, or something, another member of the club was to be elected by the rest, who weren't trustees, except in the case of the bank manager, who's succeeded by his successor."

Maurice had fished out one of his little notebooks, and Puffin winked at me.

"Getting the great mind interested, eh?"

"And the conditions?" Maurice said.

"One," said Puffin, stimulated by this display of order and method, "the what-d'you-call-'ems—beneficiaries—the kids, you know—must graduate from Cambridge. Two, the cash is to be divided equally among 'em when they go down. That's all. Any who don't get a degree, or go to Oxford or any other university, are disqualified. Quite simple, what?"

"A lawyer told me once," I said, "that any trust is the devil."

"I wouldn't contradict him."

Maurice had turned a page of his notebook.

"Before we go any further," he said, "let's have the names of the original members, and what happened to them, and their children, and who were the trustees, and who are now."

Puffin groaned. "Must we?" he asked, fumbling half-heartedly in his pocket. "What d'you want all that for?"

"It's tidy. And I like to know the background. You may have it all in your mind, but it isn't in mine yet."

It evidently wasn't all in Puffin's mind, and for some time it seemed doubtful if it was in his pockets. But at last he produced, with his tobacco-pouch, a crumpled sheet of typescript, which he looked at distastefully.

"Iliff wished this on me," he said. "He's like you, Maurice—too damned conscientious."

It was a neat list of names and dates. Here it is:

THE NINE BRIGHT SHINERS

Cambridge, 1909–1912

Name	College	Died	Children
W. A. Lanham (Charlemagne)	King's	—	1; Mary (Newnham)
V. H. Rowsell-Hogg (Hector)	Trinity	—	1; Hereward (Trinity)
J. O. Farleigh (Alexander)	Pembroke	1925	I;Claudia (Girton)
J. S. Tullis (J. Maccabaeus)	Clare	—	I; Ian (Clare)
H. R. Ince (Jesus) (Caesar)	Jesus	1917	1; Patrick
R. D. Henderson (David)	Queens'	1918	2; Rex, Roy (Queens'); (Rex k. 1935)
G. A. Frome (Arthur)	Trinity	1915	None
K.H.Hope (Joshua)	Jesus	1915	None
O. E. Jevons (Godfrey de Bouillon)	St. John's	1914	None

Members living in June 1936 . 3
Issue „ „ „ ,, . 6

2

Maurice studied this for a while. Then he said:

"Mortality chiefly due to the war, obviously."

"Four were killed," Puffin said. "The last man, Jevons, was drowned at sea on his way home to join up. Farleigh, the father of the Girton girl, died of pneumonia or something."

"And now about these trustees?"

Puffin leaned over to study the list for himself.

"I can remember *them,*" he said. "The first three were Rowsell-Hogg, Frome, and the bank manager *pro tem.* I forget his name. When Frome was killed, Farleigh was elected. He'd been out, but had a dud heart, and was sent home. When *he* died, in '25, Myra's cousin James stepped in. There've been two or three bank managers. The present trustee's a man named Blewitt. He'd have been at this dinner, but he's away. Comes home to-day, I believe."

"Then Lanham," Maurice said, "who founded the club, and proposed the fund, was never a trustee?"

"No. He refused to be one at the beginning, Tullis says, and afterwards, when he'd changed his mind and wanted to be elected—that was after Farleigh's death—the others wouldn't have him."

Maurice screwed in his eyeglass and stared at the list.

"But after Farleigh's death, in '25," he said, "there was only one other candidate—Tullis. Making two with Lanham himself. If only the non-trustees had the right of election, which was what I gathered from you, Puffin, those two would cancel each other out if they didn't agree. How *did* they decide who was to succeed Farleigh?"

Puffin scratched his head. "Eh. . .? Oh, I see what you mean. But my dear fellow, they weren't sticking to the rules then. There weren't enough of 'em— the ordinary members, I mean. Two didn't form a thingumbob."

"A quorum?" I suggested.

"That's it. So every one had a say—Rowsell-Hogg and the other trustee, the bank manager. He was the chap before the present one, Blewitt. In fact, I fancy they did all the deciding. Used their discretion, was the way Tullis put it, and elected him instead of Lanham."

"Yes, they were in a bit of a difficulty," Maurice said. "They couldn't have foreseen that six out of nine young men would die in twelve or thirteen years. Example of what Myra pointed out—the trickiness of trusts. And when it came to this election in '25, if Tullis had sided with Lanham there'd have been an *impasse* again—two against two- So what did he do? Nothing? Or vote for himself?"

Puffin looked at me. "Is he always like this now?" he asked. "Regular cross-examination, what. . .?" Then he went on, "Of course we've only got Tullis's account. *He* says he stood out. Didn't want to be a trustee, anyway. But the other two wouldn't have Lanham, and there had to be three, so he took it on."

"Very irregular," Maurice remarked. "If Lanham had cared to take it fur-ther, I should say he'd have had a case."

"He threatened to."

"Oh, did he? They seem to have fallen out pretty thoroughly. What was the beginning of the trouble? Why this animus against Lanham?"

Puffin had another drink and settled himself in his chair.

"Dry work," he said. "And now we'll have to go back again. . . . It's all part of the story."

Maurice turned another page of his note-book.

"Shall I dictate slowly?" Puffin asked, grinning.

"He learnt shorthand in his spare time in the service," I explained.

"Good lord! What spare time? I never had any."

"Go on," Maurice said, "or go back, or whatever it is you want to do."

Puffin said he didn't want to do anything more now, except leave the witness-box and have a nap: but he went on.

"Can you do 1912 in shorthand?" he asked. "Because we're back there again. All these nine chaps came down then, and the club stopped functioning. But they kept in touch—dined in town, and so on. And early in 1914 there was a thumping big do when Rowsell-Hogg got married. They were still chucking money about in the good old pre-war way—Myra's James groaned when he talked about it—and Lanham had another of his theatrical ideas, and sent the hat round, and the other eight of 'em gave the bride a pendant as a what-d'you-call-it of their precious club. Nine stones, you see. It's worth a thousand or two now, though diamonds have slumped since then."

"And Lady Hogg wears it at these dinners for old lang syne," I added for Maurice's benefit as Puffin paused for breath.

"Or she did," Puffin said. "Well, then the war came along. It killed off four of 'em, and some of those who weren't killed were pretty hard hit, and one or two of the casualties left young widows with devilish little to live on. New poor, and all that. You know what it was. . . ." He stopped to squint at the typewritten list again, and dabbed a finger at two of the names. "These two," he said, "Frome and Henderson. And Henderson left two kids as well—twins. Well, now, the point is, Mrs. Frome and Mrs. Henderson knew about the fund, of course. So they applied to the trustees for help, and got it— a few hundred each, in advance."

Maurice put in his eyeglass to have another look at the list himself.

"The trustees now being Hogg, Farleigh, and the bank manager of the period?" he said.

"Yes. The bank manager was the original one, still carrying on because of the war."

"And this would be in '18 or soon after. Frome, I see, had no children, so Mrs. Frome really got a gift?"

"I suppose so. From the way Tullis spoke, it wasn't much, considering what the fund has grown to. And Frome had been a trustee, which may have influenced them."

40

"Was James among the hard hit?" I asked.

"He was, by his own account," Puffin said. "Of course you don't know much about him."

"Only that he's something in the City, lost his wife a year ago, and can afford to send his boy to Cambridge."

"He's a stockbroker. What these City blokes call being hard up, you and I'd call rolling. Not that he'd much to say about his own affairs."

"He wouldn't have," I said, thinking of James Tullis's tight mouth and long Scots upper lip.

"No, he just groused about difficult times ever since the war. But one thing did come out. He didn't love Rowsell-Hogg."

"But he came to his dinner."

"Oh, well, his boy was there. And I don't suppose he'd quarrelled with Hogg, or anything of that sort. Especially as he tried to see him later on."

Maurice hadn't heard of this, and with his mania for unconsidered trifles wanted to know about it. Puffin told him how James had gone round to the 'Eagle' during the ball, but he didn't know why he wanted to see Sir Vyvyan at that hour.

"Matter of business, Tullis said. And Hogg was going early next morning. . . . Talking of Hogg, by the way, his people were the only ones who went on booming through it all, especially after the old man died and this chap ran the business. They'd always been the richest of the lot—stockbroking too, you know. It was a steady old firm, but young Hogg did a gamble on his own in marks, after the Armistice, and made a packet. Then he had the sense to get out in time and stick to legitimate stockbroking for the rest of his life."

"And Lanham?" Maurice asked.

"Just coming to him. He was hit worst of all. He was in some oil and colourman's firm—big wholesalers, and a family business, like Hogg's— and when his father died and he got made a partner it was going from bad to worse. The slump a few years back finished it altogether. Lanham got a job with some firm of the same kind, but only as a glorified clerk—two or three hundred a year—and the worry seems to have killed his wife, and if his girl hadn't had brains and won scholarships, he'd never have got her to Newnham. He has to scrape to keep her there. . . ."

"Poor creatures!" I said. "And now you're hounding them."

"Well, I can't help it," Puffin protested. "I don't like it any more than you do. I'm jolly well hoping there's nothing in it. . . . But we must find the man. Because all this seems to have turned his brain. He was always a queer bloke, Tullis says, with big ideas of his own importance, and theatrical, and so on—witness his club—and this come-down was too much for him. At any rate, some time before his firm went bust he'd been pestering the others for help—the other three club members who were left—Rowsell-Hogg, Tullis, and Farieigh. But Tullis and Farieigh hadn't any too much themselves, and Hogg, who was bursting with cash, wouldn't do anything."

"I'm beginning to agree with James," I said. "I don't think I could have loved the late Sir Vyvyan. Maurice has his faults, but he isn't mean."

"If you've got a name like Hogg," Puffin said, "I suppose you've got to live up to it. And he was a domineering sort of cove, evidently. Rush of money to the head. . . . But mind you, Lanham had put all their backs up to begin with. He wasn't exactly meek himself. And then, when they wouldn't help him, he said he'd got a claim on this precious fund. It was his idea, and he'd contributed his share to it, and he was entitled to draw on it."

"And the others wouldn't agree to that either?" Maurice asked.

"Rather not."

"Legally, they were within their rights, I suppose?"

"That's Tullis's attitude. He's all for the letter of the bond, and so on. Talked as if it would give him a pain to alienate a trust fund. That's how he put it."

I laughed. I could hear James Tullis saying it.

"And Farieigh," Puffin went on, "was an invalid then, owing to his heart—pneumonia finished him off a few months later—so *he* wasn't going to have his daughter's nest-egg whittled away—if you *can* whittle eggs. Hogg backed him up, and as they were both trustees, that was that. Whatever the third—the bank manager—thought, he'd be out-voted."

"If this was not long before Farieigh died," Maurice said, "it would be in 1924 or '25."

"I suppose so."

"How did they reconcile this action with the grants they made to the two widows six or seven years earlier?"

"Oh, it *was* six or seven years earlier. They were still boys then, and not so damned grasping. Though Tullis didn't put it like that. He pointed out that Lanham wasn't a widow, and hadn't died for his country."

"He'd only been ruined for it," I said.

"But I gathered," Puffin went on, "that he'd have got something if he hadn't expected too much, and gone on about his rights. If he hadn't been Lanham, in fact. Instead of a few hundreds, he wanted his whole thousand back, plus the interest to date, which had about doubled it by then. And he hadn't any rights."

"That sounds like Tullis on Trust Funds," I added.

"Without prejudice to Mr. Tullis, whom I don't know," Maurice said, with a look at me, "his old friend Lanham seems to have had hard luck. As Puffin pointed out, he waited too long. All the generous spirits among the Nine Bright Shiners had died young."

"Give James his due," I said. "He couldn't do anything. He wasn't a trustee then."

"No, but he soon was," said Puffin, "and that was the last straw for Lanham. He'd changed his mind about not being a trustee himself when he found he couldn't get his money back, and after Farleigh died he said he ought to have been made one as a matter of course, especially as it only lay between him and one other."

"Hoping," Maurice said, "to get the third trustee on his side sooner or later, when they'd out-vote Hogg. Which was why Hogg didn't want him. Which suggests, not only that Hogg had his reasons, but that the third trustee, at any rate the one then in office, was in Hogg's pocket."

"Seems to me they all were," Puffin agreed. "I told you he was bossy, and he was a big pot in the City, which would weigh with 'em all. Even bank managers are human. . . .As for his reasons, Lanham, by all accounts, had made himself quite impossible. Apart from the money, a much milder cove than Hogg would have shied at having a chap like that as a fellow trustee."

"You say 'by all accounts.' Whose have you had besides Tullis's?"

"The boys know all about it. It's family history to them. They've all been on the mat. Miss Farleigh too, and the Lanham girl, of course. And Mercer knew a bit."

Maurice was scribbling busily.

"H'm," he said. "By the way, how was this squabble carried on? By letter? Or did the old friends meet and go at it?"

"I don't think Lanham's met either of the others for years," Puffin said. "But he was always writing to someone, even to the bank managers, about what he called his claims. Of course it was Hogg he really had his knife into——"

Puffin caught my eye, realised that this phrase was a little unfortunate, and grinned sheepishly.

"He had a metaphorical one into James, too, I suppose," I said.

"Meta——? That's the word! Wonderful thing, education. . . . Oh, yes, he hates 'em all, but Hogg's name was simply mud to him, and every time he thought of the man, or some bill came in, he lost his rag and fired off a letter. . . . It's no good fixing me with an eagle eye, Maurice, and licking your pencil. This has been going on for years—ever since Farleigh died, anyway—so

43

you'll have to do without dates. But the worst of it began about then, when Lanham talked of going to law over the trusteeship, as I told you. Anyway, Hogg soon stopped answering letters, and then Lanham went to his office and made a scene, and had to be chucked out. The next thing was, he started being libellous, and Hogg's lawyer had to threaten him with proceedings. He seems to have lain low for a bit after that, and then he tried another tack. This was only a few months ago. He had the nerve to write to Lady Hogg, pointing out that when he'd had money himself he'd been fool enough to cough up several hundreds for a diamond for her, and that she owed him and his daughter some return now. . . ."

Puffin stopped and shrugged and reached for the gin-and-lime-juice again.

"He must be mad," I said.

"That's the trouble," said Puffin, mixing himself another drink. "Help yourself, Myra."

But I was thinking of the girl, whose whole life too must have been embittered by the Nine Bright Shiners and their good intentions. That these were her father's own ideas, and youthful, generous ones too, was the tragical irony of it.

"What does Miss Lanham say?" I asked.

"Thinks Hogg's better dead."

"Have you seen her?"

"Not I. I may have to, and I'm not looking forward to it."

"One sees now," I said, "why she doesn't come to these dinners."

"She wasn't asked, or her father either. You can't wonder. Skeleton at the feast, and all that. Not that they'd come, anyway. There have only been three, all in Lanham's late worst period, so to speak. Hogg started 'em when his boy and one or two of the others came up."

"Interesting point, that about the pendant," Maurice remarked.

"Ah, you see it?" said Puffin.

I saw it, then. And I remembered, with some pride, that I'd seen it dimly before, earlier in the day, when I asked Puffin if the theft of the pendant alone wasn't suggestive, and he'd shown by his manner that it was. That letter to Lady Rowsell-Hogg explained why.

3

At this point Vera Nugent, just back, appeared from the drawing-room window to welcome Maurice.

For a few minutes we chatted about pleasanter if less exciting things than murder and robbery. Then Vera said she was going in again to rest. She was taking Averil to the Pembroke Ball that night. I'd cried off. I love dancing, but one can have too much of it in the middle of June, and I decided I preferred a quiet evening with the men. I should then be on the spot, too, if any fresh news turned up. My education, as Maurice said, was progressing. I used to be rather superior about his detective fever, and call him Gabriel Betteredge, but it had bitten me now.

"No, I won't stop," Vera said. "I know what you're discussing, and I've had quite enough of it for one afternoon. I've been having tea with tutors' wives, and we've talked of nothing else. Chester, I shall have to refuse all engagements while this wretched case is on. Because I'm your wife, people think crime's a pet hobby of mine, like gardening or collecting butterflies. I'm sure they say, 'That Mrs. Nugent's coming to tea. Have you read up the police news. . .?' And they *will* try to pump me. So for heaven's sake clear it up soon."

"What does Cambridge think?" Puffin asked.

"Oh, what you'd expect. Every one takes it for granted that this unhappy man Lanham is guilty. How *do* things get about so quickly?"

"I told you this would," Puffin reminded her. "Too many people know about it, and there must be plenty of old hands, like Mercer and some of your pals' husbands, who'd remember the whole story from the beginning, and put two and two together. What's twenty years or so in a place like Cambridge, where they're still talking scandal about Cardinal Wolsey?"

Maurice took up this point after Vera left us.

"You don't seem to have wasted your day, Puffin," he said, looking at his notes, which covered pages already.

"Oh, it's just routine work." Puffin talked as if he'd been a policeman all his life. But he looked pleased. "Iliff's an energetic bloke, and I haven't had much sleep. And it helped, though it was a damned nuisance in some ways, having everybody up and about all night, and most of 'em at this ball. We had Tullis and Mercer and the boys through it before the old lark was up."

"That's how it got about so quickly, of course. But who put you on to Lanham in the beginning? The helpful Mr. Tullis?"

"Oh, lord, no. We had to prise things out of him. It was young Rowsell-Hogg."

"How did he come to do it?"

"Ah," said Puffin. "Now we're coming to the confirmatory evidence, and it's what I don't like. The rest's nothing. Lanham's letters and talk might be just hot air. But you remember the mysterious gent at the 'Eagle'?"

"Of course?"

45

"He stammered."

"Well?"

"So does Lanham."

"Oh, does he?" Maurice said, while I opened my eyes at this piece of news.

"When he's nervous or excited," Puffin went on. "And though that fellow seemed as cool as ten cucumbers, I'll bet he was both just then. . . . Well, as soon as young Hogg heard the maid's story, of course he thought of Lanham, and told us about his stammer, and a lot more we couldn't make head or tail of—he was in a deuce of a state, poor chap—till we had it confirmed by Tullis and the others."

"H'm," said Maurice. "Anything else?"

"Oh, yes. Lanham always carried a thick malacca."

"A sword-stick?"

"They don't know about that. But it's just the sort of silly gadget a theatrical bloke like Lanham *would* carry."

"Don't let your imagination run away with you, Puffin," Maurice said. "The proportion of swords to malaccas must be very small. And you keep calling the man theatrical, apparently because he wore a blue dress coat when he was a boy."

"Damn it, Maurice," Puffin said, "the man's an *actor!*"

"You never said so. You said he was an oil and colour merchant."

"So he is—or was. But he used to be a keen amateur actor. Leading light of the A.D.C., and kept it up afterwards, till his troubles took up all his spare time."

"An actor with a stammer?" I said.

"Your James says it never bothered him on the stage, because he was never nervous when he was acting. It's his natural rôle, Tullis says—meaning he's always posing and dramatising himself. And then he used to take Shakespearian parts—blank verse, and all that. It's a sort of cure for stammering, like singing. Takes your mind off it, or something. . . ."

"Well, what next?" Maurice said.

"There's the pendant, of course. Why was that taken, and half a dozen valuable rings and things left?"

"Yes, it's a suggestive point."

"And then there's the drawing."

"Ah, the drawing," said Maurice. "I wondered when we were coming to that."

"Like to see it?"

"Of course. Have you got it?"

Puffin produced, this time from a suitable place, his breast-pocket, a stout envelope, and took from this a piece of crumpled paper about the size of a postcard.

"Iliff didn't like letting this out of his sight," he said. "But we can't do anything with it till to-morrow. There's one of those handwriting blokes here, a professor of something—every want supplied in a university town—but he's away to-day. So I brought it along."

We bent over the bit of paper. On it was drawn, in what looked like ordinary blue-black ink, a rather crude figure in armour, with bare knees, a round shield, and a sort of cuirassier's helmet. Above this was scrawled, in a running hand, the word "Hector."

"Can the versatile Lanham also draw?" Maurice asked.

"Tullis says he used to, after a fashion," Puffin said. "Designs for costumes and things, for plays, you know. Don't know much about it myself, but that looks pretty amateurish to me."

Maurice was still peering at the sketch through his eyeglass.

"It seems to me rather interesting," he said.

But he wouldn't explain what he meant, and went on to ask if the police had any of Lanham's handwriting.

Puffin said they had a letter—a line or two Lanham wrote to his daughter saying he was coming to Horningsea to stay with the Devines. The writing looked very like that of the "Hector" of the drawing, but they were waiting for the expert to give an authoritative pronouncement.

"So you see how it is," Puffin went on peevishly. "Curse it, I wish my imagination *was* running away with me. When it's a case of housebreaking, or arson, or handing out gold bricks, you know where you are. You're dealing with professionals. They're fair game. Even if a navvy hammers his wife, or some shopkeeper does *his* in, it's different from this. I'm not a snob, heaven knows"—(I'm sure he believed this)—"but with fellows of this sort it's a foul business. I'm still hoping this chap Lanham will clear himself, but I don't like the look of it. There's the stammer, and the stick, and that infernal pendant, and the drawing, and when you add to 'em Lanham's grudge against Hogg and the way he's been carrying on for years, what *are* you to think? And then on top of it all, he comes to Cambridge and vanishes...."

This naïve speech left him a little breathless. I caught Maurice's eye, but concealed a smile. Puffin's a dear, but his idea of what was, and what was not, fair game in crime was rather comical.

"You don't know that Lanham did come to Cambridge," I said.

"He said he was coming there, and I'll bet he did."

"What's your theory, then?" Maurice asked.

"Mine? Well, it's Iliff's, really, but it's common sense. At least it explains things. . . . Lanham knew he was coming to stay with the Devines. It was fixed up some time ago. Perhaps he meant to behave himself then, but he got brooding again over the old trouble, and thinking of Hogg there at the 'Eagle,' doing himself well and showing off before all those kids at the dinner, while he—Lanham himself, I mean—would be skulking out at Horningsea, keeping away from Cambridge because Hogg and Tullis were there, and having to slink in down back streets to see his own daughter so that he shouldn't meet 'em, as if they owned the place. And it was as much his university as theirs, and if it hadn't been for him there wouldn't have been a dinner or any thing else. ... So he began to see red. Perhaps he hadn't even made up his mind when he started, but the idea was there, and he came all ready, with his sword-stick, or whatever it is, and a false moustache and dark glasses——"

"From his property-box?" Maurice put in.

"Well, he must have had all that sort of thing at one time. Or he may have bought 'em for the occasion. We shall know about it before long. If we don't get news of him by to-morrow, I shall send a man up to town with a warrant to run over his flat."

"What's he like without these adornments?"

"Rather a striking - looking chap, Tullis says, though he hasn't seen him for years, of course. But he was grey then, and wore his hair long and straight, and he has queer light grey eyes. He kept his hat on at the 'Eagle,' so the maid never noticed his hair."

"Go on," Maurice said.

"Well, in the train or somewhere," Puffin went on, "Lanham made up his mind. Or he may have made it up before, and come down by another train, to dodge Devine, though it would be easy to do that at the station any evening in May Week. . . . Once in Cambridge he'd know where to look for Hogg. Hogg always stayed at the ' Eagle,' and there was the dinner there, and it was a certainty he'd go on to the ball afterwards. Anyway, whatever Lanham was doing in the early part of the evening, he must have been hanging about Trinity or the 'Eagle' at midnight. He saw Lady Hogg go in, and then followed Hogg and Mercer to Queens', and waited outside. I dare say it was while he was waiting that he thought of putting a finishing touch to a good night's work by pinching the pendant. He'd know by then that the first part of the programme was going to be easier than he could have hoped. Hogg was playing into his hands by walking up King's Lane alone at one in the morning. . . ."

Puffin leaned back and took a long drink, like a man who'd done well. So he had: it was a jolly good imaginative effort for him, or the Superintendent, or both, and I told him so.

Maurice, of course, was critical.

"It leaves a lot unexplained," he said.

Puffin looked a little pained. "Of course it does," he said. Then he remembered why he wanted Maurice's help, and cheered up. "Well, the more holes you can find in it the better I'll be pleased," he admitted. "And if you can prove that Hogg was murdered by a dago waiter because he passed him a dud sixpence, I'll join the Society of Antiquaries. So have another whisky and get down to it, there's a good chap."

But before my husband could get down to it we were disturbed by noises without. Loud hails from the river preceded the disembarkation of Averil, escorted home by the mothers' joy.

Of course Mr. Ince had to be introduced and given a drink. He was obviously much impressed at meeting England's premier amateur sleuth, who quite cast a chief constable in the shade. Then Mr. Ince propounded a scheme, all cut and dried, for the following night, which was that of the Jesus Ball. Vera and Averil were going anyway, and now the whole household was invited as the amiable Patrick's guests. Otherwise, he said pathetically, he'd be all alone, except for some girl, whom he didn't seem to want now. Here he grinned at Averil. To draw me, he'd already invited Ian and his father. I thanked him, especially for James. Maurice and I left our acceptance in the air, but with all this the dressing-gong went before we saw the last of Mr. Ince, and discussion of more serious topics had to be adjourned.

4

We had another visitor that evening. Vera and Averil had just gone off to Cambridge, and the two men and I had settled ourselves in the garden again, when Superintendent Iliff was announced.

"Oh, lord," said Puffin. "What's up now? Can't a fellow have any peace? All right, Hammond—send him out. And bring some drinks. We shall want 'em."

The Superintendent, no doubt, had expected to be invited to the study for a private conference. Though a well-disciplined man, he couldn't quite control his features when he saw Maurice and me—especially me.

"Come along, Mr. Iliff," Puffin said, judiciously blending formality and heartiness. "Pull up that chair. This is Major Hemyock. You've heard of him.

49

He's known to the police. Mrs. Hemyock—Superintendent Iliff, my right-hand man. You can talk before 'em, Iliff. They know all about the case, and Major Hemyock's experience in this sort of thing will be useful, eh?"

Mr. Iliff looked stiff and doubtful, as well he might, but he had to do what he was told. He was a brisk, bullet-headed man, with bristling cropped grey hair and moustaches and greeny-brown eyes. There was little or no back to his head, but I rather liked him.

"Well, what is it?" Puffin said, when the Superintendent had pulled up his chair, in which he sat very erect. "News of Lanham ?"

"No, sir. Or there was none when I left Cambridge. I've been to Horningsea, and being so near I thought I'd better see you and report."

If this zeal failed to appeal to Puffin, he didn't show it.

"Have a cigarette," he said. "Horningsea, eh? What were you doing there?"

"I wanted to ask a few questions of Mrs. Devine and her son, sir."

"You saw young Devine this morning."

"One or two points have occurred to me since, sir."

While he lighted his cigarette, Mr. Iliff's greeny-brown eyes flitted from Maurice to me. Puffin adjured him, a little impatiently, to go on.

He went on.

"I forgot to ask Mr. Devine if Lanham had been there before."

"And had he?"

"He stayed there in March for a few days, sir."

"Anything in that?"

"What I wanted to get at, sir, was how friendly they were, and if Lanham made a habit of coming down."

"Which he did, apparently. At least I gathered that Mrs. Devine has only had the cottage since February."

"That's so, sir. . . ."

Here Hammond reappeared with the drinks, and there was an interlude while Puffin dispensed them. When a stiff whisky and soda had been put before Mr. Iliff, Maurice leaned forward.

"If I may butt in," he said, "I think I see what's in Mr. Iliff's mind. It's a question I was going to ask. Or rather several questions."

"Fire 'em off," Puffin said.

Maurice addressed the Superintendent, who was taking a drink and keeping a rather wary eye on him over the glass.

"You don't mind, do you, Mr. Iliff. . .? Well, who are these Devines? How did they come to know Mr. Lanham? And the third question you put yourself—how friendly are they?"

Maurice has a way with him when he likes, and he looks disarmingly simple and modest. A nice mixture of affability and deference, and perhaps the whisky and soda, perceptibly thawed the Superintendent. As discipline had to be preserved, however, he looked at Puffin, who nodded, before he answered.

"Well, sir," he said, "we don't know much about them. Mrs. Devine took this cottage in February. She seems to have a little money. She keeps to herself, but she's very well liked in Horningsea. She's been a nurse, and she's always ready to help when there's illness."

"A widow, presumably?" Maurice said.

"We've never heard of a husband, sir. The son writes for the papers— what they call a free-lance. He comes down quite a lot on his motor-cycle. They've both lived in America. And that's about all we know. We can't keep tabs on all the folk who take cottages in the country nowadays. It's become a regular craze. And in nine cases out of ten we've no occasion to."

"Oh, quite," said Maurice. "But I think you see my point, Mr. Iliff, or you wouldn't be keeping tabs on these Deviries now. Anyway, how did they come to know the Lanhams?"

"Neighbours, sir, in Chelsea. Lanham has a flat there, and the Devines had one in the same block before Mrs. Devine leased this cottage. Her son took a room then near by."

"And our thirdly?"

"Sir?"

"How friendly are they? Just acquaintances, or a good deal more?"

Mr. Iliff turned to include his chief in the conversation.

"Yes, sir, that's what occurred to me. Mr. Devine made out this morning that they didn't really know the Lanhams very well. He said they were sorry for them—Lanham had talked very freely about his troubles—and when Mrs. Devine took this cottage, so near Cambridge, they invited Lanham down for a night or two so that he could see his daughter on the cheap, so to speak. Expense, Mr. Devine said, was a consideration. Then they asked him down again for May Week—or rather, Lanham asked himself."

"Oh, did he?" Puffin said.

"I got that out of Mrs. Devine this evening, sir."

"And what exactly is the point, Iliff?"

"Well, I asked myself, sir, whether the Devines don't know Lanham a good deal better than they pretend. After all, an old Cambridge man ought to be able to find a friend there to put him up. He needn't walk about where he'd meet people he wanted to dodge. It's a large town, and Sir Vyvyan and

Mr. Tullis, anyway, wouldn't go far from the men's colleges, and Newnham's right off their track. But Lanham sticks himself away at Horningsea with folks he just knew as neighbours in Chelsea. It struck me as a bit thin."

"Yes, there's something in that," Puffin said, looking at Maurice, and then I rushed in rather rashly.

"Oh, I don't know," I said. "I think it's very natural. I've heard the whole story, Mr. Iliff, from several points of view, and I can quite understand why Mr. Lanham preferred to keep well out of the way. Remember it's May Week. Any other time wouldn't be so bad, but just now he'd feel thoroughly at odds with everything."

I looked as nicely as I could at the Superintendent—Maurice said afterwards that I made eyes at him—and he took it very well, but there was a slight return of reserve in his manner when he answered :

"Possibly, ma'am." Then he turned to Puffin again. "Anyhow, sir, I thought we ought to know more about it. Because if the Devines *are* more friendly with Lanham than they make out, where's he most likely to have run to? Back to Horningsea."

"But we discussed that this morning," Puffin said. "You put a man on the cottage, didn't you?"

"Constable Larkin wasn't sent there till ten o'clock, sir, you'll remember. After I'd been to Newnham. And he can't see through lath-and-plaster."

"Meaning that Lanham may have bunked straight there? I doubt it. He'll be a fool if he goes there at all."

"Not if you look at it this way, sir," the Superintendent said. "If I hadn't happened to find young Mr. Devine with Miss Lanham, and she'd held her tongue, we shouldn't have known of any connexion between them. Or not so quickly. If Lanham *was* hiding there, they'd have had the rest of the day, likely enough, to get him away. But owing to my meeting Devine, Larkin was out there on his heels. No one, except Devine himself, has left the cottage since then. He took out his canoe this afternoon——"

"He came to the motor-boat club," I put in. "I had tea with him."

Mr. Iliff gave me a sharp look. "Is that so, ma'am?"

"Then you really went out to have a look for yourself?" Puffin said. "Did you manage it?"

"Yes, sir. After I'd put one or two questions to Mrs. Devine and her son, he tumbled to what I was after, and said I could search the cottage if I wanted to. Seemed to think it rather a joke. I took him at his word—I wasn't going to slip up anywhere. But there's nobody there. The spare room's all made up ready for a visitor."

Maurice chipped in again.

"Well, that seems to answer our thirdly. I had the same notion about these Devines as yourself, Mr. Iliff—that they might have hidden Lanham, or helped him to get away, out of pity. I take it that's all you suspected."

"Yes, sir. I've never suggested they knew anything beforehand. But lots of people wouldn't give a friend away—even in a case of murder. And Lanham could have pitched them any tale. Mr. Devine didn't know what had happened till I told him this morning—or so he said."

"So my wife is probably right about Lanham's feelings, and the explanation given for his preferring Horningsea to Cambridge is the correct one. If he ever meant to go there this time, of course. . . ."

"Ah!" said Mr. Iliff darkly.

"But he told his daughter he was going."

"Well, he would, sir, wouldn't he?—either way? If he never meant to go beyond Cambridge, it would be a blind."

"You're inclining more to the theory that the murder was planned well ahead?"

"I am, sir—now. Perhaps from the time he invited himself to Horningsea, which was two months ago."

"Why was it staged in Cambridge?"

"That's what I'm getting at, sir. I think the setting—if you understand me—suggested the murder. Cambridge, and May Week, and Sir Vyvyan's dinner, and all the rest of it. Then there's that drawing of Hector. It means something in the place where the club was started. It wouldn't mean much in Eaton Square."

Maurice looked at Mr. Iliff with approval.

"Which implies," he said, "that Lanham, if he *is* the murderer—which is pure assumption at present—is in fact a madman."

"In one sense, sir. He's got this kink."

"But is otherwise sane enough?"

"That's what I think now, sir. If he planned the murder beforehand, he planned his escape too. He wouldn't need the Devines to help him. And he was cool enough to see his chance with that pendant."

"I can't get that part of it straight yet," Maurice said. "It seems to have been a desperately risky shot."

"We don't know how much Lanham knew, sir. And he'd two good reasons for running the risk. Revenge—he'd already committed murder for that—and money."

"You think he can sell the diamonds?"

"Sooner or later, sir—if we don't catch him first. They're good stones, but nothing special, and they can't be identified out of their setting, after all these years. We've been on to the jewellers who made the thing."

"Had he enough cash, do you know, to keep him for a bit?"

"We ought to know to-morrow, sir. As you say, it's all assumption at present, and we've got to go careful. But if we get a warrant to search his flat, the officer who goes to London can look into his banking account too. I'll lay we'll find he drew out all he could."

Puffin was listening to this with a gratified air. Both his exhibits were doing well, and growing quite matey into the bargain. Maurice looked at him before he went on.

"I won't," he said, "ask if you've taken the usual steps about ports and stations and so on——"

"Oh, we've got the net out," Puffin said.

"But there's one point occurs to me. Have you tried the cloak-rooms here?"

Puffin nodded, and looked at the Superintendent.

"Meaning that Lanham must have changed somewhere, sir?" Mr. Iliff said. "Of course we've thought of that. He can't be going about in evening dress. But the cloak-rooms can't help us. There's a fair rush at this time, and people were getting things out this morning as soon as the places opened. Some of 'em just run down for a ball, you know, sir, and then go on up the river for breakfast, and run straight back to London to their offices and such, and change in the train."

"A rackety life," Maurice agreed. "It wouldn't suit you or me, eh, Mr. Iliff?"

Mr. Iliff permitted himself to smile. He was growing quite human and expansive, and now treated Maurice, if not me, as a man and a brother. And when Puffin had pushed the decanter and siphon towards him, and he'd refilled his glass and half emptied it again, he favoured even me with a mellow look. Puffin keeps very good whisky.

"One or two last points," Maurice said. "I'm so beastly inquisitive. . . . How's the sword-stick theory progressing?"

"Ah," said Mr. Iliff. "That's one of the things I put to Mr. Devine this evening. He said he didn't know if Lanham carried a sword-stick. But when I pressed him, he owned he'd handled the stick, and thought it rather heavy for a malacca. He said he'd supposed it was weighted."

"The doctor talked of a French bayonet, didn't he?"

"Same sort of weapon, sir."

"Yes, I know. But does the word bayonet strike any familiar chord in your mind?"

Mr. Iliff looked puzzled. "In what way, sir?"

"I don't know myself. Never mind. . . ." Maurice frowned a little, shook his head, and went on. "The other point was, what exactly happened, if I may ask, when you went to see Miss Lanham at Newnham?"

"Precious little, sir," Mr. Iliff said, "so far as she was concerned. Mr. Devine was with her. I asked her if she knew where her father was, and she wanted to know why, and I told her, wrapping it up, of course. It was the first she'd heard of the murder. Or so she said. . . ."

"Do you believe her?"

"I think I do, sir. No one else at Newnham seemed to know about it, and I'm taking Mr. Devine's word that *he* didn't. At present, anyway. It wasn't in the papers then. But Miss Lanham went on at once in such a way that I never got any more sense out of her. Of course, knowing what she did about her father and Sir Vyvyan, wrapping it up wasn't much good. She knew what I was after, and went on something wicked. All about herself, it was, and the harm it would do her at college. Then she had hysterics, but if you ask *me,* sir, it was half temper. A nasty one she's got. . . . But there was no doing anything with her *then,* and Mr. Devine gave me a wink and we slipped out. He knocked up another young lady to look after her, and then we had our little talk in the court. . . . Anyway, I think it was all news to Miss Lanham."

"Poor girl," I said.

Mr. Iliff smiled dryly. "It's the other one, ma'am, *I'm* sorry for," he said. "All Miss Lanham's worrying about is herself."

He looked at his watch, and soon after this he left us. I don't think he had anything more of interest to tell us, and all that day's talks and discussions, though Maurice says they really told us a lot, were soon put in the shade by new sensations.

OPUS TWO

CHAPTER IV

WEDNESDAY MORNING

1

I HAD breakfast with Puffin and Maurice next morning. This was 16th June. Vera and Averil, having returned from Pembroke in the small hours, were still asleep.

Puffin, who is a hearty feeder, was prowling along the sideboard wondering what he'd have a second helping of, when we heard the telephone ringing in the hall.

"Damn!" said Puffin, cocking an apprehensive ear.

Hammond came in.

"Superintendent Iliff wishes to speak to you, sir. I've put him through to the study."

Puffin tore himself away from the kedgeree. " This is a dog's life," he said as he fled.

We seemed to have been waiting quite a long time before he burst in again, his eyes popping.

"Good God," he said, "he's done it again!"

Even Maurice was startled, and dropped his eye-glass in his cup.

"What do you mean?" I asked.

"Young Rowsell-Hogg. Killed in his rooms, not half an hour ago. Come along, Maurice, there's a good chap."

"Here, hi!" I said.

But they bolted and left me there.

I spent the next hour quivering with impatience. There was no one to talk to. I hadn't the heart to rouse Vera or Averil from their ill-earned slumbers. There was the Jesus Ball that night, of course—in fact, more than one, for May Week was nearing its climax. I could have taken the other car (Hythe House, as Puffin so originally says, is Liberty Hall) and run into Cambridge, pretending I wanted to buy a stamp or something, but that seemed even more heartless, not to say ghoulish. I tried to write a letter, and gave it up. I read the discreet account of the murder of Sir Vyvyan in *The Times,* and wished it was the *Daily Mail*—a paper Puffin doesn't recognise. Then I roved restlessly about the garden and stared malevolently at the Cam, a sort of pocket Old Man River, rolling along with complete indifference to death and disaster.

It was only ten o'clock when Hammond, apparently as unaffected as the Cam, sought me out to say that James Tullis had called to see me.

This was better than nothing, and when she brought James out into the garden I welcomed him with a fervour that must have surprised him.

"Now tell me all about it," I said, pushing him into a deck-chair.

"I should think," he said, trying to adjust himself—deck-chairs don't suit James, they're too unstable and undignified—"I should think you know far more about it than I do, Myra. Living, so to speak, at the fountain-head——"

"I only know the poor boy's killed."

James suspended his careful wrigglings to frown reprovingly.

"I should scarcely have described Vyvyan Rowsell-Hogg as a poor boy."

It dawned on me then that we were talking at cross-purposes. James hadn't heard of the latest horror. When I told him he went quite yellow, his jaw dropped, and he goggled at me. There's no other word for it.

"But this is dreadful!" he said, in a sort of squeak. "Good heavens, no, I knew nothing about it. . . ! I came out for a run—I hired a car—refreshing my memory of old scenes and trying to take my mind off other things—and finding myself so near here I ventured to call, early though it is. I will make suitable apologies to Mrs. Nugent. Blood is thicker than water. . . . But I can hardly believe you, Myra. It's appalling! Appalling. . .!"

At any other time, little as I knew of James, I'd have told him he was blethering. There's no blood connexion whatever between us. But I really don't think he knew what he was saying. He's a tall, good-looking man, if you like the ginger-headed Scots type, going a little grizzled and bald, but still a sturdy forty-five or so. He dressed well, had a permanent frown between his thick pepper and salt eyebrows, and very dark blue eyes, and as he was irritable and opinionated some people no doubt found him rather terrifying, an impression I fancy he cultivated. At any rate, he looked as if it would take a lot to throw him off his balance. But the news of this second murder had evidently given him a fearful shock, and he wasn't trying to make any impression at all.

"Have a cigarette," I said, with a vague idea of being helpful.

"I only smoke a pipe," James muttered. Sitting there looking up at me and goggling, half in and half out of his chair, he was rather comical.

"Then smoke it," I said. "And have a whisky or something."

"Not at this hour."

"You look as if you need it. And I thought the Scots drank it at all hours."

James smiled feebly and began to feel for his pipe.

"I've had a very trying time," he said. "Very trying. Do you know, Myra—perhaps—well, if you think your hosts won't mind, I do feel that a drop of something . . . "

While I went to fetch the whisky I pondered on James. In spite of what I'd said about the Scots, I didn't think he often wanted a drop of anything at that hour. And then I began to wonder why he'd really come. I'd introduced him to Vera at the Trinity Ball, but I felt sure it wasn't like him to call at a strange house at ten in the morning, even to see an alleged cousin, on the strength of a casual introduction. James would be nothing if not correct—normally.

When I got back he looked a little less liverish, and tried to be pawky about my encouraging him in bad habits. But from the stiff drink he poured himself he didn't need much encouraging just then.

It brought some colour back to his long face. Then he said:

"Now tell me again, Myra. I can hardly believe you. Young Hereward too! Poor lad! Poor lad. . . !"

But I felt somehow that he wasn't really thinking much about poor Hereward Rowsell-Hogg. And he began at once to press me for details, though I'd made it plain I knew only the bare fact.

"I suppose they're sure it's Lanham?" he asked after a while.

"They want to find him, of course," I said cautiously.

"The man's crazy," James said viciously. "He's a menace. He ought to have been shut up long ago. . . . Good heavens, if I'd known! But perhaps they've caught him by now."

"Do you mean you know something about him? Where he is. . .?"

"No, no. I haven't seen the wretched fellow for years. I meant I didn't even know he was coming down here."

"How would the knowledge have affected you?" I asked curiously.

But James wouldn't explain that, and, of course, he didn't mean what I thought, and was shuffling, anyway. I hadn't plumbed James then, though I did think he must have deteriorated since the days of the Nine Bright Shiners. I didn't like his vindictive tone. After all, Lanham, if he had done these hideous things, was mad, and they had been friends. At the same time I couldn't quite reconcile James's attitude with what Puffin had said about him. It was obvious that very little prising would be needed now to get him to talk. But somehow I didn't want to hear him, on that subject, at any rate, and I was glad when he changed it, which he did after brooding for a moment.

"Er—by the way, Myra," he said, "I hope I didn't give Nugent the wrong impression yesterday."

"About what?" I asked.

"I may have said something about Hogg. But really we were very good friends."

"I rather gathered he hadn't any," I said.

"Nonsense, nonsense!" said James tartly. "Vyvyan was a little masterful, but a very sound fellow. I've done business with him, off and on, all my life. A little friction now and then——"

"Is relished by the best of men?" I suggested.

"I was going to say, it means nothing between old friends."

"I don't know what you're driving at."

"Oh, that's all right, then," James said. "I was afraid Nugent might have been misled by something I let drop. Er—has he said anything about Cyprian Eagles?"

"Not a word. What are they? Birds?"

"No, no. Of course not. H'mph. . .! Well, never mind." James gulped down the rest of his whisky and became interested in the garden. "Charming place this, Myra. One of these days I hope you and your husband will visit my little house in Surbiton."

"Nice of you," I said, feeling sure that wild horses, if available, wouldn't drag Maurice there.

"I'm very anxious to meet the Major."

"Well, he's likely to be an uncertain quantity at present. You know he takes an unhealthy interest in crime?"

"So I've heard," James said. "Ian's full of it. It would be a privilege to hear his views on this miserable affair."

I made vague noises, and James came to the point.

"What are they? What does he think?"

"For a simple-looking man," I said, "it's remarkable how successfully Maurice conceals his thoughts when he wants to."

"Not from you, surely, Myra?" said James, trying, heaven help him, to be arch.

"Even from me."

"But he must have talked about this."

"He uses speech to conceal his thoughts too."

James gave me a suspicious look, which I returned with one of limpid innocence. Maurice isn't the only one who can conceal his thoughts.

"Ha, ha!" said James, rather hollowly, as they say. "You won't be drawn, I see."

"No," I said, deciding it wasn't worth while concealing them any longer. My first flush of enthusiasm for James had evaporated, and I didn't mind if he knew it. I looked at my watch, and this made him look at his.

"Dear me!" he said. "It's half-past ten. I ought to be going. But I should like to pay my respects, and apologise, to Mrs. Nugent."

"I hardly think she'd wish to see you now. She's in bed. I'll do all the apologising."

He gave me another look. But he said nothing more about going, and didn't even pretend to move. I couldn't exactly turn him out, but I could remove the only apparent attraction, so I rose myself.

"I'm afraid I've got some letters to answer," I said, which was strictly true, though they didn't get answered that day.

James, at a considerable disadvantage, for he was not skilful at rising quickly from a deck-chair, managed to extricate himself, and at last took the hint. But he was still obviously reluctant to go, and seemed so ill at ease that I was puzzled. As we walked round the house to where his car was standing in the drive he kept looking furtively about him. Then he suddenly wrung my hand violently, jumped into the driving-seat, and started the engine. At the last moment he leaned out for a final word.

"I think I shall stay in the hotel to-day. I'm not feeling at all well. A chill, perhaps. These late hours. The nights are quite cool. . . . Look here, Myra, can you come to lunch? Bring the Major, and I'll get Ian."

"We might catch your chill," I said unkindly. "Anyway, thanks and all that, but I'm afraid we can't do it to-day."

"Later, perhaps? What about tea? I'll ring up."

And he shot off, with a fearful grinding of gears. I stared after him, still more puzzled. I didn't believe in his chill, and the nights were far from cool. I was beginning, in short, to be distinctly sceptical about James, because I was quite sure of one thing. Blood might be thicker than water, and James's skin thicker still, but curiosity is the thickest of the lot. All this talk of old memories, and being in the neighbourhood by chance, was so much bunkum. James had come fishing.

2

I was in demand that morning, anyway, for not long after this I had another visitor.

Vera Nugent and Averil, blissfully unaware of the new horror, and of the fact that their guest had been deserted, even by her husband, were still asleep. I was still drifting restlessly about the garden. James's visitation, for some reason, had brought home to me the tragedy of young Rowsell-Hogg's dreadful end, besides inducing a lot of other depressing thoughts. Perhaps it was the contrast between the two generations. The poor boy had been so typical of his age and type, so full of what someone has called the temperamental gaiety of the well-born, in every way so different from James, who had grown into a canny humbug, if nothing worse—so different, too, from his own father, who had evidently been purse-proud and unpopular. And then there was Wilfrid Lanham. . . . Yet all these three, in the days when they dined in blue dress coats at the 'Eagle,' and instead of asking what their posterity had done for them, made lavish schemes for its benefit, must have been very like Hereward Rowsell-Hogg, and Ian, and the other children I'd met. Maurice had said that the generous spirits among the original Nine Bright Shiners had died young. Was it that, or, if they had lived, would they have altered and soured as the survivors had? And was this younger generation destined to go the same way? Probably, I decided, for by this time I was in a thoroughly pessimistic mood; and the natural conclusion from this was that we were all better dead.

Altogether, I was reduced to the depths of gloom, and when I was hailed from the river was ready to welcome any interruption gratefully.

It was the exquisite Mr. Armfeldt, in a hired motor-launch. Wearing a silk shirt and white trousers of some even more expensive material and cut, he was more exquisite than ever.

"Well, this is a bit of luck!" he said, drawing in to the bank.

In my pleasure at seeing a human being again I nearly said the luck was mine, but wisely thought better of it. Something told me that if you gave Mr. Armfeldt an inch, he'd take several ells. So I only said:

"Doctor Livingstone, I presume? And where's Miss Farleigh?"

"Why," he asked, "if one happens to be engaged, do people always hanker to know where one's fiancée is ?"

"A natural association of ideas," I said.

"Mid-Victorian ideas, surely?" said Mr. Armfeldt. "May I disembark?"

Reflecting that if Vera didn't want her lawns invaded by all and sundry she should have got up earlier, I told him he might. He landed and tied up his boat.

"Claudia," he said, "if it's really of interest to you, is probably still at Girton, asleep."

"Everybody seems to be asleep," I said rather crossly.

"Not in Cambridge. MacLanham has murdered it there."

Somehow I was surprised. "Oh, you know, do you?" I said. "Isn't it ghastly!"

"It's very inartistic," said Mr. Armfeldt, taking a gold cigarette-case from his hip-pocket. "MacLanham has no sense of values. May Week should be like a *fête-champêtre* by Watteau. He is turning it into a battle-piece. And he repeats himself, which is bad enough in history, but unforgivable in a crafts-man. . . . Will you have one, Mrs. Hemyock?"

"What do you mean, repeats himself?" I asked, waving the case aside impatiently. Mr. Armfeldt's epigrams were not amusing just then. He took a cigarette—a Russian thing, half paper tube.

"Same weapon," he said. "Or so I heard. A believer in the *arme blanche,* our MacLanham."

"But how did he *do* it?"

Mr. Armfeldt gave one of his slightly exotic shrugs.

"My dear lady, I know very little about it—though I may actually have been in Trinity when the distressing incident occurred. I'd gone to breakfast with a man there. Before we could begin his gyp burst in, full of the subject, and my host, of whom I'd thought better things, dragged me off at once to the scene of the crime. Fortunately I managed to escape him in the crowd—half the college was there by then—and as I had missed my breakfast, I returned to my hotel."

"Where I suppose you ate a hearty one?" I said sarcastically.

"I did. Why not?"

"And that's all you know?"

"Everything. Except that before I escaped from Trinity several high police officials arrived. One was pointed out as Colonel Nugent, and another military-looking man as your husband. It's wonderful how news gets round in Cambridge. Were they dragged from *their* breakfasts?"

"They were."

"Murderers are so inconsiderate."

"Other people," I said tartly, "seem to be very unfeeling."

Mr. Armfeldt gave me one of his liquid looks in full measure.

"My dear Mrs. Hemyock," he said, "what ought I to say? That I am shocked and grieved? I am neither, in the sense I suppose you mean. I have never met this boy——"

"But I have," I said. "I danced with him only two nights ago."

"Exactly. And you are a woman, to whom the personal equation is every-thing. But why should I further harrow your feelings by dwelling on that side of it? Surely a light touch is better? As a matter of fact," said Mr. Armfeldt, gazing at me with the soulful air of one who is misunderstood, "it is a self-protective measure on my part. I am an artist. I shrink from crudities like murder. That is why, instead of hanging about the spot among a morbid mob, I try to escape from realities on the river."

I thought of another character in *The Moonstone*—I have already referred to Gabriel Betteredge. The artistic Mr. Fairlie, admirers of that classic will remember, had nerves which were exquisitely sensitive to crudities. I naturally suspected that Mr. Armfeldt was no less of a humbug. But there are so many odd people in the world that one learns not to dogmatise by appearances. My visitor happened to be a healthy young man of six feet or so, whose rather saturnine air might be no more than a matter of the pigmentary glands; but if he had looked fragile and neurotic I should probably have taken him at his word. And artists, in these days, are particularly misleading people. So many of them might be tea brokers or farmers.

So I only said, a little dryly: "I seem to have introduced the wrong atmosphere again."

"Impossible," said Mr. Armfeldt firmly. He waved his hand to indicate the landscape, but continued to gaze liquidly at me. "This is what I needed."

"So glad. . . ."

"I may say it is what I hoped to find. I was at the Pembroke Ball last night. I saw Mrs. Nugent and her daughter, but you were not there. Then I saw your husband at Trinity this morning. You can follow my reasoning. . .?"

I could, and I didn't know whether to be amused or annoyed by his impertinence. I decided to be amused, but to restore the conversation to general topics. I pointed to the deck-chairs.

"We may as well sit down," I said. "And if your nerves have recovered, perhaps you won't mind talking about the only subject that really interests me just now."

His eye fell on James's glass and the decanter and syphon.

"Dear, dear!" he said, with a smile. "Have you been driven to that already?"

"No. I've had another case of nerves here."

He looked curious, but I didn't enlighten him. When we had sat down, and he had lighted a cigarette for me and taken another of his own abominations, he said:

"Well, now, if you like, we'll be morbid, and tell sad stories of the death of Hoggs."

But it seemed that he really knew no more than he had said about the murder at Trinity. The man he had gone to breakfast with had rooms in the Great Court, and those of Hereward Rowsell-Hogg were opposite. It was about half-past nine when the servant burst in with the news, and as Armfeldt and his friend ran out a crowd was already gathering. It struck me here that my sensitive companion must have lingered a little longer than he pretended, if he was still among the morbid mob when Puffin and Maurice arrived, though no doubt they made very good time.

I expressed surprise that young Rowsell-Hogg should be still in college, but Mr. Armfeldt, with his real or affected indifference to normal behaviour, seemed to think it quite natural.

Then he began to talk about Lanham. He had heard by now anything he hadn't known before about the heritage of trouble left by the famous fund—I gathered chiefly at the tea-party at the motor-boat club, after I left, for Miss Farleigh, apparently, had never discussed it with him, both their minds, no doubt, being attuned, as a rule, to higher things. Or perhaps they hadn't been engaged very long. Anyway, the opportunity having arisen, Mr. Armfeldt hadn't missed much, for all his pretences. He had the whole story at his finger-ends now. I was amused, too, to find that as he talked he grew so interested that he forgot himself, dropped more of his mannerisms, and became quite human. Even the slight foreign accent in his dulcet tones seemed more noticeable. And in his suave way, so different from James's, he insinuated a lot of questions about the police and Puffin and Maurice. What did they think? Were they sure it was Lanham? Were they going to call in Scotland Yard? Had they really co-opted my husband. . .? The crudities of murder, in short, no longer made Mr. Armfeldt shrink.

Presently I glided away from these inquiries—as Maurice's wife, I'm a good glider—by speaking of the Devines.

"This will cause them more worry," I said.

"It has," said Mr. Armfeldt. "I had a few words with Devine just now. He was out in that big canoe of his, and I overtook him. We lay alongside, as they say in marine circles, while I broke the latest news to him."

"I thought," I couldn't help remarking, "you took to the river to escape from realities."

"Not from all," he said, with a return of his old manner, and giving me a pointed look.

I brought him back to the topic I had perhaps unwisely left.

"Well, what did Mr. Devine say?"

"A mouthful, to use the language he sometimes borrows from Chicago. To continue our own nautical similes, he seemed all took aback—but the news made him think, I fancy. Because he let out one thing. It has been a byword in the Devine home for some time that Lanham is little short of certifiable."

"Then why on earth did they have him to stay with them?"

"They didn't want him again. But he invited himself, and kind hearts being much the same thing as lunacy——"

"Yes, I remember," I said.

"Oh, you've heard that, have you? Well, Lanham's talked to them, you know, and apparently he has only one topic, which, besides being very boring, has a possible significance—now."

"One had gathered that. Rowsell-Hogg."

"And his son. Both generations of vipers."

"But, good heavens," I said, "if that's the case, the Devines ought to have warned the police!"

"Yes, I think Devine feels that now. But probably he didn't think of it seriously before. And then he'd taken up the attitude that Lanham was his friend, and he wasn't giving too much away. A primitive fellow, in some ways, I should say," Mr. Armfeldt added, "with quaint conventions and inhibitions of that sort. . . ."

Rather unfortunately, I thought, for I was getting used to him, we were interrupted at this point by Averil, just up, who burst out full of excitement, wanting to know why her father and Maurice had rushed away in the middle of breakfast. She opened her eyes when she saw my companion. Of course she had to be told everything. She was genuinely shocked this time. Sir Vyvyan was nothing to her; but the dead boy, though she had never spoken to him, was very much of her age. But she recovered quickly enough to wink at me behind Mr. Armfeldt's back.

The atmosphere he needed being presumably thus broken, he took his leave very soon after. As we watched his boat sliding away up the river, I said to Averil:

"Who and what is he?"

I felt sure she'd know a good deal about him by this time, and she did.

"His first name's Paul," she said, "and he's Russian. He calls himself a painter, but he's really a house decorator. The modern sort of thing, you know—all cubes and pyramids and uncomfortable angles. Patrick Ince says—he told me all this—that Mr. Armfeldt makes a jolly good thing out of it because he's got such a way with middle-aged women. He just moons at them with those brown eyes of his, and they have the whole house done up like something out of Euclid on the spot. When their husbands see the results there are frightful rows."

She looked at me and giggled. A rather shattering thought occurred to me. Was I, in her eyes, one of those middle-aged idiots? Then I chuckled myself.

"What's the joke?" Averil said.

"I was thinking," said I, "of Maurice's face if I got Mr. Armfeldt to decorate our house."

65

CHAPTER V

I

Just before lunch Maurice arrived back in a taxi. I met him in the hall.

"Well?" I said.

"Ghastly business," Maurice muttered.

"Where's Puffin?"

"Staying on duty."

It was a long time since I had seen my husband looking so upset. The first murder had left him cold, so to speak—as it seemed to have left everybody else, whether they had known Sir Vyvyan or not. But there was something particularly horrible about this ruthless and determined killing of a boy. It had shaken me, though I had only met him once. And Maurice had seen him, lying as he had been struck down in those old rooms in Trinity, face forwards among the breakfast things.

During lunch, to which Vera, shocked and white, descended, we didn't talk much, and barely mentioned the murder, for Maurice obviously didn't want to discuss it then, and even Averil refrained from asking questions. Afterwards we all went out into the sunny garden again. I shall always associate that garden with horrors.

Maurice, still looking rather forbidding, lay on the small of his back in a deck-chair and filled a pipe.

"Now," he said grumpily, "I suppose you want to hear all about it."

"We don't *want* to," Vera pointed out gently, "but it has happened, and we shall have to, sooner or later. Or I shall. Chester isn't like you, Maurice. He can't keep things to himself. And this must be worrying him dreadfully."

"Sorry," Maurice said. "As a matter of fact, it's worrying me a bit. Well, there isn't much to tell—which seems to be a distinguishing feature of these murders. Someone called to see the boy while he was having breakfast, drove a bayonet or sword through his back, and went away. Just like that."

Vera shuddered.

"It seems impossible," I said. "Someone must have seen the man."

"Forty or fifty people, I dare say. There were plenty about the court, even at that time—including squads of horn-rimmed Americans with guide-books.

That's the trouble. Who was to notice another stranger—if he *was* a stranger? The gyp was busy, getting other breakfasts. He saw several men up and down the stairs about the time when it must have been done. Some he knew, and we've seen them. Nothing doing there. One or two the gyp didn't know, but he thought nothing of that. There are seven hundred undergraduates in Trinity alone, and he can't know 'em all. And this is May Week. . . . And the boy's own friends were keeping away from him. He said he'd rather be by himself."

"But why was he there at all?" I asked. "I should have thought——"

"He was staying up for the inquest on his father tomorrow. His mother went back to London yesterday, and he naturally preferred his own rooms to an hotel."

"Would he have let a stranger in?"

"He'd sported his oak, of course, but there were people he had to see just now: police, undertakers, the family lawyer—he's in Cambridge——"

"Who *was* it, Maurice?" Vera asked.

Maurice shrugged.

"Lanham, you mean?"

"Well, he's getting more and more badly wanted. They're detaining men with stammers all over the country, including an archdeacon in Cambridge itself yesterday, but Lanham himself still contrives to remain invisible."

"That doesn't seem possible either."

"Well, it has happened. Lanham or not, whoever has done thesemurders is either having astounding luck, or there's a lot of method in his madness. And in the latter case he'll have made his arrangements beforehand for keeping hidden."

"Yet you think he *is* mad?" Vera went on.

"If he's Lanham, undoubtedly. And I suppose all murderers for revenge are mad."

"But would this poor boy have let Lanham in?"

"He'd never seen him, as it happens. Or not since he was a baby. Long before Lanham quarrelled with Hogg senior, they'd gone their own ways. They had nothing really in common. And if young Hogg knew what Lanham looked like, a very simple disguise would meet the case. Lanham, we assume, has seen to that already. Cut his hair, and dyed it, and so on. Having been an actor, he'd do it artistically. He'd only got to say he'd come on some business——"

"But it means he must be actually hiding in Cambridge," I said, "or very near."

"Why?" Maurice inquired. "He's had plenty of time to run up and down from London or anywhere else."

"But you're still no nearer proving it was him."

"No one else with a speck of motive has been discovered yet. Against Lanham are the facts you know of already. You can add to them now a knowledge of Cambridge—the university side of it. The murderer, I should say, must have that. The murderer, again, continues to leave his visiting-cards——"

Vera said: "What do you mean?" And I cried Out: " Another drawing ?"

Maurice nodded. "Left on the table. A small figure being chucked off a tower by a larger one, and the name Astyanax."

"Who on earth——?" I began.

"You had no classical education, Myra. Hector had an infant son, Astyanax, who was thrown from a tower by Ulysses after the fall of Troy—Hector himself, incidentally, having been already killed."

We all sat and stared at Maurice for a moment.

"How dreadful. . . !" Vera murmured.

It did, for some reason, seem to make it more dreadful.

"Lanham, I suppose," I said, "had a classical education?"

"He would know enough for that. Though anyone could look up Hector in a dictionary. It's a further point against him, of course, that both these drawings are on his notepaper—or the paper he used to write to his daughter. And the expert johnny thinks the Hector and Astyanax are in Lanham's hand, though like most of   'em he won't commit himself definitely. After all, he's only got two words to go on."

" Lanham seems to have *wanted* to draw attention to himself," I said. "I suppose his finger-prints are all over them too? "

"Oddly enough," said Maurice, "there are fingerprints, presumably Lanham's, on the letter, but none on the drawings."

"And what do you make of that?"

"I? Or the police?"

"Both."

"Iliff thinks that Lanham remembered fingerprints too late, and wore gloves when he drew the sketches, forgetting that his prints were bound to be found somewhere—in his flat, for instance, eventually."

"It doesn't seem to me to tally with the rest," I said. "Using his own notepaper, for one thing."

"The Superintendent's argument is that the man, being mad, is cunning in some things and careless in others. One minute he doesn't care a button whether he incriminates himself or not—in fact he wants, as you say, to show off and say, ' Alone I did it'—and then the next the instinct of self-preservation pops up, and he takes futile precautions."

"Is that rational?"

"The whole point is that he isn't."

"Well, what *do you* think?"

"Not being mad yet, as I hope and trust," said Maurice, " I can't judge. The obvious beauty of Iliff's argument is that it reconciles everything. There's no illogicality, past or to come, that you can't fit into it."

"You wouldn't commit yourself, would you?" I said irritably. Maurice is so maddeningly cautious.

He grinned. "Well, I'm piling up the points against Lanham for you, and there seems to be no other candidate, which is the most telling of all."

"By the way," I asked, "who found the boy?"

"The servant—or to go on using the local jargon, the gyp. He went in to clear away. He had the sense to lock the door before he beat it for a bobby, so everything was just so when Iliff arrived."

"When do they think it happened?"

"It must have been between eight-thirty, when the breakfast went in, and just before nine, when the gyp found the body. Iliff was there in five minutes. He rang up Puffin before he left the station, and we were on the spot, thanks to a complete disregard of the speed limit, by a quarter past."

"When you were seen."

"Probably. But by whom, particularly?"

"Mr. Paul Armfeldt."

I'd mentioned the house decorator's visit at lunch, and James's too, but without going into details, and Maurice hadn't seemed much interested then.

"The fiancé of the Farleigh girl?" he said now.

"That's him."

"What was he doing at Trinity?"

I explained.

"H'mph," said Maurice, when I'd finished. "And Cousin James came too? Popular, aren't you?"

"You can't talk," I said. "What were you doing all the morning?"

"Standing by and looking intelligent—first at Trinity, and then at the police station."

"Holding Chester's hand?" Vera put in with a little smile. "I know your being here is a great comfort to him, Maurice."

"Glad to hear it," Maurice grunted. "I like to feel I'm of some use."

"Well, what have Puffin and his police been doing?" I went on.

"Exhibiting their well-known activity. Interviewing people mostly—including half Trinity, several dozen assorted tourists, and all the passengers they can find who came down by train on Monday evening. Puffin has sent a sergeant up to London now to search Lanham's flat and try to blandish his bank manager."

Averil, who very properly had been seen but not heard, broke a silence that must have been rather painful to her.

"What about the stick?" she asked.

"Eh. . .?" said Maurice. "Oh, you mean was anyone seen flourishing a malacca? No. Americans never carry sticks, and no one else in Trinity was likely to—not even the unauthorised visitor. I fancy he must have adopted Myra's plan, and be using his trouser-leg now. All Cambridge is looking for malaccas."

Averil's intervention was ill-timed, for it reminded Vera that her offspring had already heard more than was good for her. As I remarked to Maurice afterwards, the young, especially the modern species, must be more of a problem than usual in a policeman's household.

"Come, Averil," Vera said, getting up and fixing her daughter with a stern eye. "I want to talk to you about this evening. The Jesus Ball, you know," she added to me. "I don't know what to do about it. I don't feel at all like it now. . . . What do you think?"

I looked at Maurice, though I knew he wouldn't go, anyway.

"I think I've a job for Myra this evening," he said, rather unexpectedly.

Averil, who had been grimacing rebelliously, said:

"Not till then, Major? Good. I want your Watson to come to Horningsea with me this afternoon if she's nothing better to do. Girl Guides," she added.

"The very thing for her," said Maurice promptly. "And I want a nap. Tiring business, watching your police at work."

"Do come," said Averil to me. "I'll punt you down. . . ."

Vera, murmuring something about telephoning, swept her away. I turned to Maurice.

"What do you want to do this evening?"

"Thought we might call on your cousin James."

"I feel less like his cousin than ever," I said. "But he wanted us to go to tea. He was going to ring up."

"Six o'clock, not a minute earlier, or after dinner," said Maurice firmly. When he's not digging, he hates doing anything in the afternoon. "If he doesn't ring up, invite us yourself."

"Why do you want to see him?"

"Natural curiosity."

"He seemed very anxious to see *you,* and to know what you thought, and so on. Oh, and by the by, what are Cyprian Eagles?"

"Highly speculative oil shares. They've recently dropped heavily, I believe. Has James been bitten?"

"He seemed to think Puffin might know something about them."

"How did this come up?"

"He'd been talking about Sir Vyvyan."

"Hogg let him down over them, perhaps."

" I wonder. . . . Oh, and I say, Maurice, James hadn't heard about this poor boy's death, and when I told him he simply dithered. I had to fetch him a drink."

"Ah," said Maurice. "I wondered how he'd take it."

"What do you mean?"

"Well, if Lanham's a homicidal maniac, with a particular grudge against his surviving fellow members of this precious club, who's the next likely victim?"

"Good gracious!" I said. "I never thought of that."

2

The Nugents kept a punt and a skiff. Guests who appreciated comfort were not asked to endanger themselves in the latter. Averil and I, collecting cushions and chocolates, got out the punt about half-past two, leaving Maurice, his eyes already firmly closed, under a pink umbrella on the lawn. Pink, as I told him, was not his colour, and he looked like a large prawn in tweeds. Vera had gone indoors to lie down there. Inquiries by telephone had decided her to take Averil to the Jesus Ball. None of their friends, apparently, felt any scruples about enjoying themselves, and, as Vera said, May Week came only once a year, and a mother had a duty to her daughter. Besides, it was better for Averil to dance and sleep than to sit at home in an atmosphere of criminal investigation.

I left instructions that if James Tullis telephoned, Maurice was on no account to be roused. James was to make what arrangements he liked for the evening.

Averil's strong young arms propelled us rapidly up the river to Horningsea. It was very hot, and all I wanted to do was to lie about under a parasol. This was the first time we'd been alone together for a day or two, and rather to my surprise she began to talk at once about Ian Tullis, and kept it up till we drew into the bank again just below the trees round Horningsea. I was surprised because I'd thought she was more interested in Patrick Ince.

We landed where a grass lane came down to the river. Horningsea, like Clayhythe, lies on the east bank, a couple of miles nearer Cambridge. The country behind is a sort of tongue of the real fenland. It stretches away from here, as flat as a floor, all watercourses and dykes, past Ely and Fordham and Soham into Norfolk and Suffolk. In this tongue there are practically no roads, and all you can see in the distance, except an immense expanse of sky, are a few little church towers and windmills standing up on knolls that used to be islands. It is quite different country from that round Cambridge itself, though it is so near, and it has curious names of its own, suggesting water and mud and general sogginess. On a fine summer day, with willows whitening and aspens quivering, and so on, and big white clouds sailing overhead, it is very lovely: but it must be deathly in the winter.

Averil, who was a lieutenant in the local company of Girl Guides, was to act as quartermaster of a camping party at the end of the month, and she wanted to see some Horningsea maidens who were coming on this outing. I strolled up and down the village street, getting hotter and hotter and wishing I'd never left the punt, while she popped in and out of cottages. She was wearing the minimum of clothing, and I wished I'd gone one better and put on a backless frock. But I hadn't felt too sure how it would go down in these simple villages. As a chief constable's guest one had to be so careful.

Averil popped out for the last time and rejoined me.

"That's that, thank goodness," she said. "Walk to the end of the village and I'll show you the Devines' cottage."

"Is it far?" I asked suspiciously.

She pointed. "Just there."

I was sufficiently curious to agree. Where the houses ended another track turned down to the river through water-meadows yellow with buttercups. As we turned into it we met a large man strolling back to the road. He was in his Sunday best blue serge, and if he hadn't touched his cap to Averil, one would have known what he was. Without looking back, I knew he stopped to stare after us.

"They're still watching the cottage," Averil whispered, rather thrilled by this encounter.

The track ran into a perfect jungle of trees and cow-parsley, and then suddenly emerged on the river bank, by a little white cottage of lath-and-plaster and thatch. It was completely hidden from the road and village, but

I remembered seeing it from the river the day before, when Ian took me from the motor-boat club to Fen Ditton.

The cottage garden ran down to the river, and over the low hedge we saw a woman in blue sitting in a deck-chair on the tiny lawn. She looked round, and Averil waved.

The woman got up and came to the gate. She was very tall and very fair, though her thick hair was grey—she wore it long, in a big knot—and she made me think of one of Wagner's heroines, whom I've always pictured as large, statuesque blondes with tragic faces bound for unhappy ends. As I hate Wagner, and loathe opera, I'm rather vague about this, and I may mean Boadicea or Niobe or someone like that. Mrs. Devine, anyway, was a magnificent creature, with a lazy graceful walk that reminded me of an animal's—a cat's, probably, though a tigress's would sound more complimentary. But one doesn't often meet tigresses. I noticed how she got up from her chair (I've touched before on deck-chairs as tests of style) in one easy, sinuous movement, without using her hands at all. I hoped, dubiously, that I should be able to do that at her age. She must have been forty-five, but she still had a perfect complexion, with hardly a line on it, and very striking blue eyes, the deep blue of her dress, but cold, like ice. If there was nothing particularly tragic about her, she gave one the impression of tremendous hidden forces.

"I thought you were that policeman again," she said to Averil. She had a deep voice, the voice of a singer, in keeping with her big frame. Like her son's, but in some different way, it sounded to English ears a little oddly accented.

Averil was nervous and apologetic. Her father being what he was, the presence of the policeman hampered her socially. And then our own appearance in the lane, which led nowhere else, looked so exactly what it was too. She hastily introduced me and explained what we were really doing in Horningsea, adding, unconvincingly, that she thought there was a way back along the river bank to where we'd left the punt.

Mrs. Devine's blue eyes rested on mine. It was impossible to say what she was thinking. But when her lips smiled, it was rather a dry smile.

"Oh, we're getting used to our watch-dog now," she said. "In a way, I suppose, he's a comfort. To Harry, anyhow. He says he wouldn't leave me so much alone if I wasn't well guarded. Though I think"—she gave a low laugh—"I'm quite capable of protecting myself against Wilfrid Lanham."

I believed her. She was still smiling, as if at some thought of her own. Then one came into *my* head, and I smiled too.

"What sort of a man is he?" I asked. "Big or small?"

Mrs. Devine's fair eyebrows went up slightly as she replied: "Tall, but rather a weakling."

I had to explain then.

"I'm sorry," I said. "But your remark reminded me of something. An opera singer I know told me once how ridiculous she felt when she was playing Desdemona with some third-rate touring company in her early days. You know the smothering scene? My friend's a very powerful woman, and the man who took Othello was a fearful little shrimp. She said she could have smothered two of him at once with the greatest ease."

It was not a very funny story, and for a moment I was afraid Mrs. Devine thought it rather too pointed a one. Then she said abruptly:

"Desdemona was a fool. She deserved what she got. I never had any patience with Shakespeare's self-sacrificing women. My favourite plays are *Macbeth* and *Lear*."

I felt now that they would be.

"All the same," I said, "Lady Macbeth and Goneril and Regan came to bad ends, too."

"At least they knew what they wanted, and got it," said Mrs. Devine. "And they knew it was no good trusting men. . . ." She made a little gesture with one of her large white hands, which had been resting on the wooden gate, slowly closing her fingers together. She was still looking at me, and in the same abrupt way she went on: "I've heard of you, Mrs. Hemyock."

"I met your son yesterday," I said.

"And your husband's a detective?"

I smiled. "He wouldn't like to hear you say so. He insists he's only a retired soldier turned archæologist."

"I didn't mean professionally. But he helps the police, doesn't he?"

"Sometimes," I said, "when they let him. But he isn't helping anyone just now. We left him asleep on the lawn."

Mrs. Devine had a massive way of ignoring irrelevancies, and she merely went on fixing me with her blue eyes, like the Ancient Mariner, as if determined to keep me to the point.

"But he's interested in this case?" she said. It was a statement rather than a question.

"Who isn't?" I said non-committally.

"You can tell him," she went on, "that the sooner they catch Wilfrid Lanham the better, for his own sake and every one else's. He's mad. He won't hang; they'll send him to your Broadmoor."

"They've got to find him first," I pointed out.

"The sooner the better," Mrs. Devine repeated. "Aren't you related to a man named Tullis?'

"Scarcely related——"

"Tell him, anyway, to look out. I've heard Wilfrid Lanham talk about him."

I couldn't help smiling again as I thought of James, though it was no laughing matter for him.

"He *is* looking out, I fancy," I said. "For a weakling," I added, "Mr. Lanham seems to be making quite a lot of people look out."

Mrs. Devine frowned slightly.

"I was speaking of him as he used to be," she explained. "He's not a weakling now. I've been a nurse. I know what mania can do to people. And it doesn't need much physical strength to push a bayonet into somebody's back."

It came, I supposed, from having been a nurse, but the way she put this was extraordinarily matter-of-fact.

"Well, I don't know him," I said, "but I'm sorry for him. He seems to have been very badly treated. And then there's his daughter——"

"I do know him," said Mrs. Devine, "and I'm still more sorry for him." Her blue eyes remained expressionless, fixed on mine, but her lips smiled again, the same dry smile at some thought of her own. It was not a humorous smile. Mrs. Devine, I felt sure, had no sense of humour. Large fair women of her type seldom have one. Though here again, of course, it was scarcely a humorous matter we were discussing. "As you say," she went on, "he has been very badly treated. But he is not the only one. . . ."

One hand was smoothing her sleeve, and it closed again over the material, gripping it into folds. She had broad, ugly, powerful fingers, well kept but roughened with work. The blue frock, too, though perfectly laundered, had been mended here and there with beautiful neat stitches, and washed again and again. She wore no ornaments of any sort except a thick wedding ring. Behind her I could see the little garden, exquisitely tidy, the beds full of lupins and aquilegias, with not a weed to be seen. I was sure the cottage was equally faultless, scrubbed and polished, every bit of furniture in its right place and always in the same one. For some reason I wanted to see inside. Probably it was only because I was hot and thirsty and dying to sit down and drink gallons of tea. But, of course, Mrs. Devine herself interested me, though no one could call her easy to get on with—she was too remote from the trivialities that make life enjoyable for most of us. However, it was quite plain that she had no intention of asking us in. She just

75

stood massively at her gate, almost with the air of barring the way. She was obviously none too well off, and probably proud; and it occurred to me that two unexpected guests, even to tea, might show up deficiencies she preferred to keep hidden.

I felt suddenly sorry for her, while the thought of tea reminded me of the time.

"We'd better be going," I said to Averil.

Since our arrival Mrs. Devine had ignored the child, as if she were another irrelevancy. Now she remembered her, and smiled a little.

"You can walk back along the dyke," she said, pointing.

There was a trace of a path through the long grass, disappearing round a bend of the river bank, which is dyked. Having exchanged polite good afternoons, Averil and I departed by this route, in single file, Averil ahead. Looking back, like Lot's wife, as we got to the bend, I saw Mrs. Devine at her cottage door. She was looking after us. Then she went in. She had to stoop at the door.

The jungle growing inside the dyke, which shut in the cottage on every side except that of the river, hid it from us as soon as we were round the bend. At the same time the punt came into view, apparently about a mile off. We couldn't talk comfortably in single file, and we were trudging in silence when there was a rustling in the bushes ahead of us.

It was very slight, and I thought it was some animal or bird. And then suddenly a man climbed out of the cow-parsley and nettles on to the dyke, and stood facing us.

He was quite young, or at least I thought so at first. He wore a cloth cap pulled down over his eyes, a wasp-waisted grey jacket, and very full grey trousers falling over patent-leather buttoned boots. His clothes didn't look English, and when he spoke he didn't sound English, either.

"Sisters," he said, "you look kind. Say, where's that dick?"

We stared at him. I could see now that he was older than I'd thought. In fact in some odd, unpleasant way his face was very old, as if he knew too much, or had never really been young at all. It was a long, yellow face, wary and cunning, like a rat's, with a long, pointed nose and little black beady eyes that might have been buttons from his boots. They seemed to stare back at us without winking, and they made me think of wax figures— the worst kind, from the chamber of horrors. He was chewing something, and his jaw moved all the time. His arms were very long, like a monkey's, and as he slouched as he stood his hands hung down almost to his knees. His voice and language we'd both heard before, from Hollywood. But they sounded queer and sinister in Cambridgeshire.

As we didn't answer him he went on, keeping his voice low, in a sort of long-suffering way, as if we were children.

"Dontcher get me? The cop, flatty, bluebottle. Where is he?"

Averil, who had shrunk back against me, said over her shoulder: "He means the policeman."

"Sure," said the stranger. "Got me in one, sweetie."

"If you'll come with us," I said dryly, "we'll take you to him."

He grinned. It was an unpleasant, gap-toothed grin. Then he spat into the nettles.

"Quit stalling, sister," he said to me. "*You* ain't dumb, if that cop is. And he looks it. But I don't think he'd kinder take to me. That's why I'm asking you."

He kept shooting little glances past us all the time he talked, and listening, standing on the balls of his feet ready to jump and run. One hand slid into a coat-pocket, and I felt Averil, who had seen too many gangster films, shrink closer to me. The man saw the movement too, and grinned again as he produced a stick of chewing-gum and began to unpeel it. But he looked more wary and dangerous than ever.

"I don't know where the constable is," I said. "But he's not far off."

"Now isn't that a shame," said the man. He bit off a bit of gum with what teeth he had and started to chew again. "And all I want is a word with that dame there. What does she call herself? Armfeldt or something. Just a word, while her white-headed boy's away. I seen her—I'd have done my song and dance then but that dick came gum-shoeing along. . . . Just a word," he said again, trying to look persuasive but only succeeding in leering. " On the level, sister. Couldn't you slip back and take a look?"

"The lady there is not Mrs. Armfeldt," I said.

The beady eyes narrowed. " Now you *are* stalling," the fellow said nastily.

"On the contrary," I said. "Anyone in the village will tell you that that is not her name. And now we'll do as you suggest, and slip back to find that police-man. And if I were you I'd beat it, as I believe you say in your country. Come on, Averil."

I slipped round her so as to get her behind me. I'll admit I felt rather uneasy for an instant—the result, no doubt, of seeing too many gangster films myself.

The man snarled. "What the hell," he said. "I ain't done no harm. But I warn you. He's a killer."

Then he took me at my word, and made one jump of it down the dyke into the bushes. He disappeared at once. There was a little rustling, and then that died away.

77

I pushed Averil back along the path towards the cottage. I wanted not only to find the policeman but to warn Mrs. Devine. I still felt a little goose-flesh down my spine till we were round the bend again and the cottage was in view.

The policeman was still out of sight, but Mrs. Devine was in her garden once more, standing near the gate. She came to it to meet us, and looked at us without speaking.

I explained, a little incoherently, for it all seemed rather improbable already, what had brought us back. She frowned slightly, more as if she were puzzled than alarmed, but I noticed one of the large white hands grip the gate.

"Dear me," she said placidly. "How very strange. Thank you, Mrs. Hemyock. Who are these people, do you know? I seem to have heard the name."

"The Armfeldts?" I said. "I know a Mr. Armfeldt, slightly. Your son has met him. He was at this tea-party yesterday. I don't know anything about his mother. He's in Cambridge now, but I didn't think he lived about here. Averil says he's a fashionable house decorator."

"He doesn't live here," Averil put in. "At least, I don't think so. He has a studio in London, anyway."

"Perhaps he and his mother—or could it be his wife——?"

"It couldn't be," I said, "Or it oughtn't to be."

Mrs. Devine's blue eyes stared at me, while her lips smiled.

"I was going to say," she went on, "that perhaps they have a cottage too. It's quite a popular craze. Anyhow, I think this Mr. Armfeldt should be warned. I know the type of man you describe—I have been in the States. Perhaps Mr. Armfeldt has been there too ? "

"Yes. In Chicago," I said.

Mrs. Devine didn't claim acquaintance with that city. Instead she remarked, smiling again:

"After all, perhaps it's as well we're under guard here. It's a lonely spot. I must tell our watch-dog."

"We're going to tell him if we meet him," I said.

"I shall be grateful to you."

Before I could offer any other suggestions—and it *was* a lonely spot—she moved away a little, indicating quite clearly that there was nothing more to be said about it. A remarkable woman, Mrs. Devine. Probably, I thought, she felt as capable of dealing with an American tough as with Wilfrid Lanham.

We said good-bye once more and walked up the track we had come by, through the trees. As soon as we were out of them we saw the large figure of the watch-dog strolling back towards us. I stopped him and told him about our adventure, saying I'd report it to Colonel Nugent if he wished. He scratched his head and thanked me, and said he'd keep a good lookout in future and warn his colleague who relieved him. I thought he seemed rather " dumb," as our sinister acquaintance had suggested. Puffin admitted this afterwards, explaining that his force was so hard worked at the moment that he hadn't enough good men to go round. And then watching the Devines' cottage was the sort of routine job from which little was expected now.

Averil and I saw the watch-dog disappear in the trees before we went on to the punt—the longest and safest way round.

CHAPTER VI

WEDNESDAY EVENING

I

VERA NUGENT was a bit perturbed on her daughter's account when she heard our story, though by this time Averil herself was treating the whole thing as a rather exciting joke. Vera said what a good thing it was I was there, but I felt slightly uncomfortable, and wished Mr. Armfeldt and all his family in Jericho, because Averil would talk as if the decorative decorator was *my* friend and responsibility. Maurice —whom we found awake, by the way, but only just— merely listened and grunted with the callousness of a husband.

Then, with the tea, Puffin came home, very hot and bothered, and grew more so when the story was told all over again for his benefit.

"A Yankee crook!" he said. "In Cambridgeshire! Good gad, what next?"

"We don't know he's a crook," I said. "All we're going on is that he was hiding in the bushes, like Moses or somebody, and talked pure Hollywood."

"And said someone was a killer. Your Mr. Whatsisname, I suppose?"

"He's not my Mr. Whatsisname. And anyone less like a killer I never saw. Unless the man meant a lady-killer."

"What do you know about 'em?" Puffin asked.

"Which?"

"Killers."

"More than you do, Puffin," I said.

Which, thanks to Maurice's quaint hobby, was strictly true.

"Anyway," Puffin said, "I'm glad you tipped Larkin the wink. I know Larkin's a fool, but he won't let much get past him, and I'll see he's relieved by a better man to-night. Can't have harmless widows scared by your friend's crook pals."

I didn't trouble to correct him again. The poor man was really rather rattled by this complication. I only said:

"It will take a lot to scare Mrs. Devine."

"And anyhow," Maurice pointed out, "as Myra cleared up the little mistake of identity, presumably the American gentleman has confirmed it by now, and is gunning for this Mrs. Armfeldt elsewhere."

"Very consoling," Puffin said. "One killer at a time's enough for me. Three are altogether too much."

80

Maurice explained that he meant the word in a Pickwickian sense, and asked me if the man had used any threats.

"No," I said. "But I can't say he sounded as if he just wanted to make a social call. And why was he hiding?"

"He told you, didn't he?" Maurice said. "Antipathy to the police. Lots of people have it. And your gum-chewing friend's in a strange country, where I dare say he has no business to be. It needn't be anything more than that. . . . I'm trying to comfort Puffin," he added.

Puffin was gulping a third cup of tea. He handed over his cup for a fourth.

"Where's this bloke Armfeldt staying?" he asked.

I shook my head and looked at Averil, who shook hers.

"Perhaps with his mother," I suggested. "Miss Farleigh will know."

"Sort of dago, isn't he?"

"Russian," Averil explained.

"Same thing," said her father. "Well, we'll soon find out something about him—and his mother, too, if she's living about here. And we'll have the net out for your Yankee thug. Loitering with intent will do. Then we'll see who he is, and if he's registered."

He drank his fourth cup, and having got as good a description of our gum-chewer as Averil and I could give him, went into the house to telephone to his underlings about the man himself and the Armfeldts. A chief constable seems to have rather vague and wide powers—or perhaps Puffin assumed them—but I wondered what he could do with the Armfeldts, anyway, if they told him to mind his own business.

He was away quite a long time.

"Your cousin James held me up," he said to me when he came back. "He was on the line when I wanted it, and devilish effusive, for him. Wants you and Maurice to have a sherry with him about six. Won't I come, too, and all that. I've too many other fish to fry, but I shall have to run in again myself, curse it, so I'll take you along."

Maurice said that if he'd known we were going to have all this running about he'd have brought our car—or not come at all. What he'd been looking forward to, he said, was a spell of lying on his back in the garden. This was nonsense—he was as keen as mustard, really, and had suggested seeing James himself. But he's always like that when he has slept too heavily in the afternoon.

Next we tackled Puffin about the murder of Hereward Rowsell-Hogg.

It seemed to have happened a long time ago, instead of only that morning. I expected to hear of all sorts of developments. But Puffin's news, when boiled down, wasn't news at all. He'd nothing to add to what Maurice had

81

told us after lunch. The murderer seemed to have come and gone like a ghost—though this really wasn't surprising at that time of day in May Week, and in a big college like Trinity, full of tourists, too. Anyway, no one had seen or heard anything of him. There were no clues or finger-prints or any other sort of facts to work on, except the original ones—the nature of the wound and the drawing of Astyanax.

And, of course, the obstinate absence of Wilfrid Lanham.

Reports of men who might be him, with or without stammers, were still coming in from all over the country. Some came from impossible places like Land's End or John o' Groats. Those that seemed worth following up came to nothing. The man had now been lost for forty-eight hours. Only one definite point seemed to be established. He *had* come to Cambridge on the Monday evening, and by an earlier train than the one Harry Devine went to meet—the 5.10, which Maurice came by next day. Two other passengers by it recognised his description as that of a fellow traveller from King's Cross. So if Lanham had cut his hair, or otherwise disguised himself, it had been done after he reached Cambridge. But where? Inquiries had been made, without result, at all the barbers in the town.

"Any news from his flat yet?" Maurice asked.

Puffin shook his head. No report had yet come in from the detective-sergeant he'd sent off with a warrant to search the flat. Lanham, of course, had not returned there. The place had been watched by the Metropolitan Police since the morning before.

"There's one other thing," Puffin said, "if it means anything. We've found a taxi-man who picked up a fare off that train. Fellow walked out of the station, anyway, carrying a small suitcase. From the taxi-man's account it may have been Lanham. Or it may not. Fellow took his hat off, to scratch his head or something, and had longish grey hair. Not much to go by in Cambridge. . . . Anyway, he was driven to Butts Green. Know it? It's part of the Common. Bloke got out there and walked away across the Common."

"Where would he get to?" I asked. I didn't know much about that part of Cambridge.

"The river," Puffin said. "Chesterton's on the other side. But if he wanted to go there, why didn't he take the taxi on, up Victoria Avenue and over the New Bridge?"

"Economy, perhaps," Maurice suggested. "What about the footbridge?"

"You think he walked over that? But then he'd have taken his taxi to Abbey Road, not to Butts Green."

"Isn't the footbridge new? Would Lanham know about it?"

Puffin stared. "By jove, I wonder! He might not. It wasn't there in his day. There were two ferries then, I believe—one of 'em near the New Bridge. He might have been making for that. If it *was* Lanham. . . . Anyway, we'll do a bit of intensive combing in Chesterton."

He ruminated a bit, and then went on about other troubles. He'd had a harassing day altogether. Lady Rowsell-Hogg, when she heard of her son's murder, left her sick-bed to come down to Cambridge again, and made a dreadful scene, which was natural, but painful for Puffin. He said she didn't seem half so cut up about her husband's death—which perhaps was natural too. Then he had had a spot of bother with the college authorities. Our older universities are laws unto themselves—in fact they make their own (and some of their town's too), and one is that the police mayn't enter a college unless they're called in, and by someone a good deal more important than a gyp. According to Puffin, who was enjoying his first real tilt with the Medes and Persians, as he called them, he and his men ought to have waited outside Trinity till they got a formal invitation.

"One old boy told me it wasn't a common lodging-house," he said. "Lodging-house, indeed! It might be a bally embassy."

2

Just before six we drove into Cambridge. Puffin himself didn't know when he'd be back, and as Vera and Averil were going to the ball, Maurice and I decided to have a meal in the town. It was Maurice's suggestion, and I rather thought he'd got some plan in his head.

James Tullis was staying at Parker's, in Sydney Street, one of those small, quiet, respectable places where elderly Scotsmen put up. Having left Puffin at the police station, Maurice and I walked on to the hotel. At the top of Petty Cury, where there was the usual evening jam of people waiting for buses and things, we bumped into Harry Devine.

He was in flannels and an old tweed coat, and like every male under thirty in Cambridge was bareheaded. After what had happened that afternoon I felt I ought to speak to him. I introduced him, more or less in pantomime, to Maurice, and we all retired into the big entry conveniently provided at the corner by a popular chemist's. A lot of other people had had the same idea, but at least one could breathe there, and talk without screaming.

I asked Harry Devine at once if he'd been home that afternoon. He frowned a little and looked blank.

"No," he said, with the air of being politely surprised at my interest in his movements. "I've been around here since lunch."

"Averil Nugent and I were in Horningsea," I explained. "And we saw your mother."

And I went on to tell him about the man who was hiding. I did not, however, refer to killers. That remark, I thought, was better kept to official circles.

He listened without interrupting, and with the same blank face. I couldn't have said he was startled, or worried, or annoyed, or felt anything at all. He just stared at me, his light blue eyes as expressionless as his mother's dark ones. Once he ran his fingers through his straw-coloured hair, which was as thick as hers. But except for this, and his general extreme fairness, and his poker face, and something in the way he'd frowned at first, and a sort of wary watchfulness that one felt rather than saw, he wasn't really like Mrs. Devine. His long head was narrower than hers, and he was slighter and shorter.

"Well, you surprise me," he said at the end. It might have been his mother speaking now, in that cool, detached voice, though the inflexions were different from hers.

"I shouldn't have thought it," said I.

He smiled with his lips, like Mrs. Devine, showing his strong teeth.

"I'm grateful to you for telling me, Mrs. Hemyock."

"I thought you ought to know."

"I'll get back right now. Though at that, the fellow's probably here in Cambridge by this time. Chasing Armfeldt. Do you know anything about the man? Armfeldt, I mean?"

"I never heard of him before yesterday," I said.

"Same here. I knew Miss Farleigh's name, and that she was engaged, but I'd never met her before, either. You say this man who stopped you was an American? And small?"

"Weedy, and rather dressy, and like a rat." And I described the man more fully.

"You use your eyes," said Harry Devine. Then he shook his head. "I thought I might have seen him around. But I know the type."

"What they call a gangster?" I asked hopefully.

He smiled again. "There are all sorts of gangsters. And some of them look like Wall Street business men."

" Which they are, eh? " Maurice put in. He'd been listening and watching in his quiet way.

"Sure," said Devine, turning to look at him.

"It's a regular racket. I'm glad to meet you, Major Hemyock. The boys were telling me about you at the boat-club yesterday, after your wife left. If I'm not butting in, what do you think about these murders?"

"What does everybody think?" Maurice said.

"Not to be drawn, eh?" The white teeth flashed again. "Well, I guess what everybody thinks is right this time. I've heard Lanham talk. I feel now I ought to have done something about it."

They had both lowered their voices, though it was hardly necessary.

"I dare say he has talked in the same way to other people too," Maurice said.

Devine nodded. "He'd loose off to anyone about his troubles. He was like that. No self-control. And I reckon it's been getting worse. But my mother and I were used to it. We didn't know him really well, and we didn't know the rest of the bunch at all, and we thought he was just shooting his mouth off. I've heard men talk worse who hadn't the nerve to kill a cockroach."

"Apparently," I said, "he shot his mouth off about my sixteenth cousin James Tullis. Mrs. Devine suggested that he'd better look out."

Harry Devine turned his pale blue eyes on me.

"Oh, did she?" he said. He smiled again. "Well, it's different now, isn't it? That's the point. It struck me, of course, when I heard what had happened this morning. It seems to have struck Mr. Tullis too."

"How do you know?"

"Just left him, Mrs. Hemyock. I thought I'd better do something this time, you see. I didn't know Mr. Tullis, so I went along to Clare to find his son. He wasn't there, but the porter knew where the old man was staying, so I rolled off to the hotel. I'd made up a yarn—wanted to see young Tullis about something—but they were both there, and there was no need to pull any stuff. Mr. Tullis was on to me at once. What did *I* think? So I told him what I thought— that he'd better watch his step till they find Lanham."

Maurice was putting in his eyeglass. "The point struck even me," he remarked. "A homicidal maniac is a man with a fixed idea. It gets more firmly fixed as he goes on. I think young Mr. Tullis had better watch his step too."

"Oh, that's horrible!" I said.

James's panic had seemed rather amusing, and I hadn't taken his danger very seriously. Partly it was James's own fault. It was difficult to take *him* seriously. But Ian was very different. He was a boy, like Hereward Rowsell-Hogg, and natural and jolly, and I liked him.

Harry Devine had nodded. "I agree with you, Major," he said. "I told him so."

"Why don't they *find* the wretched man?" I said. "Things can't go on like this."

Maurice warned me not to talk so loud.

It seemed queer, when one stopped to think, that we were talking in this way at all, discussing wholesale murder in a mob of people shopping or waiting for buses. A woman crashed into me, apologised, and went on to her friend in the same breath: "Well, I said to the girl, 'Look here, young woman, I can get 'em twopence cheaper in the Market. . . .'" And then I heard another voice: "Murdered in our beds next, that's what *I* say. . . ." It reminded me that half Cambridge was discussing murder too. But not in quite the same way.

"It's easy," Harry Devine was saying, "to hide yourself for a few days, if you've fixed things up beforehand. You're almost bound to be caught in the long run, of course—in this country. But I dare say that isn't worrying our friend."

I asked him what he meant.

"He's nuts, Mrs. Hemyock."

"Nuts?"

"American for what the Major put in refined English. Homicidal. Lanham's out to bump these people off, and he won't care what happens after. I dare say he's fixed that up too. He doesn't mean to be caught alive—or that's my bet."

In spite of what I'd just said myself, and felt, about Wilfrid Lanham, there was something in Harry Devine's tone that jarred.

"Haven't you changed your mind, Mr. Devine?" I asked. "Yesterday you were talking about rational explanations."

He shrugged. "Yesterday there were at least four people there I'd never met before."

"And now there are only two?"

He gave me a twitch of a smile.

"And I'm an unfeeling brute?" he said. "It's a day later, Mrs. Hemyock, as I said just now, and things have happened. And the most important is what hasn't happened. Lanham hasn't shown up. Yesterday there was a chance he would, and I wasn't sure. I am now. Who isn't. . .?" He shrugged again. "I don't like it. The man's a friend of mine, in a way. I think he's had a hard deal. But you can't square hard deals with a bayonet."

Maurice, who had dropped his eyeglass, began to screw it in again.

" Ah, that bayonet," he said.

Harry Devine looked at him.

"Does it interest you, Major?"

Maurice dropped his eyeglass again. "Only from a professional point of view," he said.

"It's the girl," I said, "who interests *me*. Miss Lanham. I'm dreadfully sorry for her. Have you seen her again, Mr. Devine?"

He nodded. "This afternoon."

"What is she doing? Has she any friends?"

"She's in a college full of women, Mrs. Hemyock. Some of them seem to be kind. But she doesn't want them, anyway. I went along this afternoon with a message from my mother. Mary Lanham doesn't want her help either. She could stay with us if she liked. She won't budge. She says her father may come to her, or write, or telephone. I hope for her sake he'll have the sense to keep well away from Newnham. There's a policeman in the grounds, and another clamped to the 'phone."

"She doesn't believe he did these murders, I suppose?"

"I don't know,' said Harry Devine. "She says not, of course."

"Poor girl!"

"Yes, she's in a bad jam." He looked at his wrist-watch, and I noticed his hand—large and muscular, like his mother's, but, unlike hers, long-fingered. "Well, I must be going," he said; "though I don't think my mother's worrying any."

"She didn't seem to be," I agreed. "How do you come and go from Horningsea? Not in your canoe?"

"Not often," he said. "I have a motor-cycle."

He smiled, nodded, and left us rather abruptly.

3

James Tullis and Ian were waiting for us. Like his father, Ian hadn't met Maurice before, and they both regarded my husband with flattering respect.

James was himself again. I hoped I did him an injustice, but I suspected Dutch courage. He certainly put away two large whiskies while we were dealing in moderation with the sherry. Shaking off his chill, he called it. It had been a touch of hay fever, he thought.

Ian looked a little uncomfortable at this. He was not merely sober, but sobered. He'd known Hereward Rowsell-Hogg fairly well.

After James had blethered a bit about the family, I called him to order.

"We've just met Mr. Devine," I said. "He told us he'd been here."

"Ha, hrmm, yes, yes," said James. "Mr. Devine called to give us a word of warning. Very good of him, and all that, but as I told him, I think I can take care of myself. And of Ian too. Eh, my boy?"

"It's a lot of rot," Ian muttered.

I felt sorry for him. There comes a time, I suppose, when no father is a hero to his son.

"And what is your opinion, Major?" James asked.

"Everybody asks me that," Maurice said plaintively. "My opinion is worth no more than anyone else's."

"Oh, come, come! We know better." James tried to look knowing. "What I say is this, and I'd like your views—*I* say the time has come when Nugent ought to call in Scotland Yard. I don't mind telling you that there's a strong feeling about it in Cambridge."

Ian grinned, with a flicker of his normal spirits.

"Not very complimentary to Major Hemyock, Dad, are you?"

"My dear boy," said James, "the Major understands me perfectly. This is not a case where there is a mystery to be solved. The mystery, if there ever was one, *is* solved. We know who murdered the Rowsell-Hoggs. All that is left is to catch the murderer. And what is wanted for that is method, organisation, co-ordination. The county police have neither the experience nor the men. A wide net must be flung, every means employed——"

"Every avenue explored and every stone turned," I murmured.

James glared.

"Sorry," I said. "It was protective mimicry."

"I gather," said Maurice, "that Scotland Yard is giving all the help that seems necessary. If it is merely a question of running a known man to earth in Cambridgeshire, the county police should be quite capable of that."

"We don't know he's in Cambridgeshire," James objected. "No, no. I can't agree with you, Major. Co-ordination is wanted. In Scotland we have an officer called the Procurator-fiscal——"

I threw him out of his stride again by groaning audibly.

"What's the matter?" he asked testily.

"Scotland."

"What do you mean, Myra?"

"They always do things so well there."

"Ha, ha," said James, not very mirthfully. "Other countries, other methods, eh? Well, the point is——"

He was interrupted once more, by Maurice.

"We haven't very much time, Mr. Tullis"—we had all the evening, as a matter of fact—"and I wanted *your* views on one or two points."

James tried to look intelligent. "Well, well," he said. "Any way I *can* help——"

"How do you suppose," Maurice asked, "that Lanham got to know the Hoggs' movements on Monday night?"

"He waited in Trinity Street and followed them. Isn't that the theory? "

"It doesn't altogether satisfy me. Who *did* know of their movements? That they were leaving the ball early, for instance?"

"I really couldn't say, Major."

"Didn't you know, Mr. Tullis?"

"Certainly not."

"It wasn't mentioned at this dinner beforehand?"

"Not in my hearing." James looked at Ian, who shook his head.

"But you went to the 'Eagle,' " Maurice went on, "to see Rowsell-Hogg soon after he left Trinity."

James frowned. "Certainly I did. I failed to get a talk with him at the ball, and afterwards I was told he'd gone."

"Who told you?"

"Oh, several people."

"So you went after him?"

"Exactly."

"And missed him again at the hotel?"

"Yes. He'd gone on with Mercer. But you must know all this——"

"I've only heard it second-hand," Maurice said. "And I like to get things tidy. Well, there's one person, anyway, who knew beforehand what Hogg was going to do that night."

"Mercer, you mean?"

"Yes. They'd arranged it earlier in the day, hadn't they? Who is Mercer, what is he, besides being an assistant tutor at Queens'? Do you know him?"

"I can't say I *know* him," James explained carefully. "He was at Trinity when I was at Clare. I've met him again from time to time, on occasions like this. But he was Rowsell-Hogg's friend, not mine."

"What sort of a man is he? A typical don—if there is such a person?"

James's smile was a little wintry.

"No, I shouldn't call him that," he said. "A typical don would never have been a friend of Vyvyan Rowsell-Hogg. Mercer's a big, flamboyant fellow."

"A good mixer?"

"If you like the term, Major." James plainly thoughtit slightly *infra dig.* in connexion with any sort of don.

"I ask," said Maurice, "because I'm thinking of trying to see him to-night."

"Then you'd better pin him down soon. He's a regular gadabout. And in May Week . . ."

"Thanks. I'll ring him up." Maurice ignored James's look of curiosity, and went on: "Well, to get back to Lanham. Passing the first murder, what about the second? How could Lanham know that young Rowsell-Hogg would be in his rooms this morning? Or in Cambridge at all?"

James looked at Ian.

"A lot of people knew it, sir," Ian said. "All of us, for instance. All the poor chap's friends. All Trinity, for that matter. And the whole town was yapping about the Hoggs and their affairs yesterday."

"Naturally," said Maurice. "But how would Lanham hear even common gossip? If he *was* in Cambridge yesterday, he couldn't go about asking people questions. Wherever he is, he probably isn't showing himself at all, except when he has to."

"He took a chance," said James.

"I don't think there's much chance about these murders."

James looked at Maurice for a moment. Then he said: "Of course he's disguised."

"Very few disguises will stand the test of close inspection in daylight."

James smiled more genially.

"You don't know Wilfrid Lanham, Major. And you were never up here. He used to be a genius in that way. I don't mean only on the stage. Do you remember the President of Bolivia hoax?"

"I think I heard something about it at the time."

"Lanham was the President's *aide-de-camp.* A perfect South American. Even I shouldn't have known him if I hadn't been in it too."

I goggled at James. It was incredible to think of him taking part in a hoax. *Could* twenty-five years make all this difference in a man?

"An artist, evidently," Maurice said. "So you were an actor too, Mr. Tullis?"

James disclaimed the impeachment rather hastily.

"No, no. A practical joke or two—just a matter of dressing up. That was all. Boys will be boys, you know."

Still trying to imagine him in the retinue of the President of Bolivia, I thought it a pity so few of them remained boys.

"One other question," said Maurice. "What sort of a man is Lanham? Physically, I mean. Powerful?"

"No," said James. " I certainly shouldn't say——" He stopped and coughed and corrected himself. "Not exactly powerful, perhaps, but much stronger than he looked. Wiry. Yes, wiry's the word. Tough, you know. Middle height. Of course I haven't seen the man for years. If he's mad now, he'll have the strength of madness. He'll be a dangerous fellow. As he's proved, eh. . .?"

We left soon after this. James and Ian were going to dinner somewhere, and then on to the Jesus ball. The whisky had quite cured James's hay fever, and there was no more talk of his staying indoors. In fact, instead of going back to London next day, with Ian, as he'd intended, he was stopping on in Cambridge till a little matter of business was finished. Something to do with the trusteeship, he said. The death of Sir Vyvyan had raised all sorts of problems. He must discuss them with his friend Blewitt. Wilfrid Lanham might be a dangerous madman, but it would be a queer thing, said James, looking fierce, if he couldn't look after himself, and Ian too, by Jove. And forewarned was forearmed. Ian seemed chiefly interested in the news that Averil would be at the ball.

"I must cut old Patrick out," he said.

When we were in the street again, I said to Maurice:

"Well, you didn't learn much there, did you?"

"Oh, I don't know," Maurice said. "Your James, by the way, if I may say so——"

"You may say what you like about him."

"Seems to be a type I've met more than once. These belligerent-looking coves are apt to crack suddenly when a strain comes. From your account, he began to crack this morning——"

"And he's been busy puttying up the cracks—with whisky—ever since."

"Possibly. I wonder. He's not a fool, you know."

"He's a windbag," I said. "But what are you getting at?"

"I don't know myself. Now I want to ring up this chap Mercer. Feel like paying a call on him later? "

"If women are allowed to call on dons after curfew. I'm a bit vague about the rules. This was what you had in mind, I suppose, when you suggested dining out?"

"It was," said Maurice, and deserted me for a telephone kiosk.

He came out to announce that Mr. Mercer would be charmed to see us between eight-thirty and nine.

4

We had a quiet dinner at the 'Blue Boar', and then strolled along Trinity Street and King's Parade. I can never look at King's Chapel without a catch of the breath, and in the lovely rosy evening light it was like some enormous soaring piece of magic. All the same, I would have preferred to see it from the Backs, which had no horrid associations; but Maurice said he wanted to refresh his memory of the *locus criminis,* and we were following the route Sir Vyvyan Rowsell-Hogg had taken on Monday night. At the bend in King's Lane, where they found the drops of blood, two people were staring ghoulishly at the spot. I walked in the roadway, and quickened my steps.

The rooms of Mr. St. Clair Mercer of Queens' were in the beautiful Cloister Court, near the President's. I agreed with James when we saw the assistant tutor. He *was* big and flamboyant, and not at all my idea of a typical don. He was more like an actor of the old school (not public), with a mane of thick grey hair combed artistically back, a large florid face, and a blue jaw. His impressive manners were rather those of the actor of the old school too. But he had a magnificent forehead and a really superb voice, which he knew how to use. He was in evening dress, with a carnation in his buttonhole.

"Come in! Come in!" he said. "I have heard of you, Major Hemyock. Mrs. Hemyock, this is an honour indeed! You brighten my poor quarters!"

He really talked as if I did, and in exclamation marks too, and he looked at me in a way no woman could fail to appreciate. I was quite glad I'd put on a smart frock. I had feared it would be wasted on a don, as it had obviously been wasted on James. But Mr. Mercer had an eye.

His mellifluous voice flowed on.

"Try this chair. I had it made to my own design. A bachelor needs these small alleviations of his unhappy lot. If we must be lonely, let us at least be comfortable. . . . There! This cushion, now . . . so! How is that . . .? A cigarette? Turkish? I have these imported from Adrianople. And what about a glass of port? I can recommend that too. It comes from the cellars of the late Dom Miguel. Or sherry. . .?"

I said I would have port, without waiting to hear where the sherry came from. In the meantime I was looking round Mr. Mercer's "poor quarters" with interest. The beautiful old room was crowded with old furniture and knick-knacks, chiefly photographs, clocks, and watches. The assistant tutor evidently collected timepieces. There were clocks in china cottages, clocks in the middle of pictures, clocks that didn't look like clocks at all. One was a sort of brass plate, with a turtle swimming in it. The watches told the phases of the moon, the days of the week, the movements of the planets, and goodness knows what else. It was just half-past eight as I settled myself in the chair made to Mr. Mercer's specifications—and a very comfortable chair it was—and suddenly the room was filled with soft chimings and tinklings and little tunes as about forty clocks and watches went off like fairy musical-boxes.

"Pretty things!" said Mr. Mercer, busy in a corner with the port. "My singing birds, Mrs. Hemyock. And so much more satisfactory than nature."

His photographs were all inscribed, and the bigger they were the more sumptuous were the frames and the bigger and more legible the inscriptions, which was just as it should be, for at a glance I was able to read affectionate regards and remembrances from the Prince von This, the Count von That, the Grand Duke of Something and the Baron de Something Else. I thought of O.B., of whom my father used to talk.

Mr. Mercer approached me reverently—the reverence was delicately distributed between myself and the product of the late Dom Miguel's cellars—carrying, as if it were a chalice, a lovely cut glass. While he was supplying Maurice and getting his own glass he talked fluently about port.

There was a ritual silence while we sipped. The clocks and watches had ceased to chime, and only a tiny multiplied ticking was heard, a sort of refrain to the rite. When we had murmured appreciations —and like all that was his, Mr. Mercer's port, as even I could tell, was something very special—the tutor offered me a light for my cigarette.

I remembered just in time certain parental admonitions.

"Not till I've finished this, thank you," I said.

If I hadn't already won Mr. Mercer's heart, I won it then.

"Mrs. Hemyock," he cried, his fine voice trembling with feeling, "you are a woman in a thousand! You are the first in my experience to understand how port should be drunk. I shudder when I think of the glasses of this admirable wine that have been tossed off in this room—literally tossed off, as if it were Australian burgundy!—to the vitiating accompaniment of tobacco."

"Then this was a little test?" I said, holding up my cigarette.

"No, no! I had given up hope. But you have restored my faith in human nature." And he raised his glass to me. Then, turning to Maurice, who had paused in his study of the photographs to give me a wink, he suddenly became businesslike. "And now, Major, what can I do for you?"

"I explained over the 'phone," Maurice said, "why I wished to trouble you, Mr. Mercer."

"Yes, yes. About these shocking murders."

Maurice sipped his port again. "I've no standing in this, you know," he went on, "and you can tell me to go to blazes if you like, but I'm anxious to get an outsider's view of things. The relations between your unfortunate friend Rowsell-Hogg and this man Lanham, for instance. And this queer business of the Bright Shiners. I've heard Mr. Tullis's opinion, at second hand, but he's one of them, and possibly biased. You were their contemporary here, I'm told."

"I was," said the tutor.

"And probably knew most of them?"

93

"All of them. In those distant days, when together, *haud passibus aequis,* we trod the paths of knowledge, two of them were my particular friends."

"The late Sir Vyvyan being one?"

Mr. Mercer bowed his leonine head. "The other was a man named Jevons, of John's."

"Jevons. . .?" said Maurice. "Wasn't he drowned?"

"He was, poor fellow. He was only twenty-one. His father had some timber business, with connexions in the Baltic—was it Russia?—and after my friend Owen went down he was sent over there to serve his apprenticeship. When the war broke out he sailed for home to join up, but the ship struck a mine almost within sight of England. . . . There is his photograph," the tutor added, pointing to a small one, modestly framed, hanging on the crowded wall. "And *that*"—he pointed again— "is a self-portrait. He was clever with his pencil, poor Owen."

Maurice seemed to be interested in the photograph, and still more so in the sketch, which actually was drawn in pen and ink. He put in his eyeglass to peer at it.

"Very clever, I should say," he remarked.

Mr. Mercer drew his attention to a second drawing, rather more handsomely framed and mounted.

"You recognise this, perhaps?"

"Yourself?"

"Myself, when young. . . . Also by Owen Jevons, of course."

Not to be out of things, I got up to have a look. The self-portrait of Owen Jevons showed a long, intelligent head, deep-set eyes, and a cleft chin. It did not much resemble the photograph, but as Maurice said, it was a clever piece of work, with nothing amateurish about it. The drawing of Mr. Mercer, when young, was still more clever, with a touch of caricature, I fancied. Even then, no doubt, the subject lent himself to it. After twenty-five years, there was no mistaking the man.

Maurice wandered back to the sketch of the artist.

"This is like him?" he asked.

"For a self-portrait, yes," the tutor said. "It differs from the photograph, of course, but then the human eye and the lens of a camera view things differently."

"Have you any more of his work?"

"Somewhere I have a whole series of portraits and caricatures. Owen was always sketching people. I think his heart was more in it than in the timber trade. If you would like to see the drawings . . ."

Maurice, however, told him not to trouble.

"Another time, perhaps," he said. "We mustn't keep you too long now, Mr. Mercer, as evidently you are going out."

"My dear Holmes...!" Mr. Mercer chuckled. "Well, yes, one has one's social duties. Even the murder of an old acquaintance and his son——"

"Ah, yes," said Maurice. "That brings us back to the point. If it isn't an impertinent question, how friendly *were* you with Sir Vyvyan? You use the word acquaintance now. . . ."

"You are sharp, Major. As a matter of fact, that was all we had become."

"Yet, he came to see you here."

"Oh, we were perfectly friendly, in the technical sense," the tutor explained. "But in twenty-five years our paths had diverged widely. And financial success had rather gone to Vyvyan's head. However, when he was in Cambridge he usually looked me up. I am the only one of his old friends still here."

"So perhaps you don't know much about his quarrel with Lanham?"

"I know quite enough. Lanham was a common friend in the old days. At least, I knew him. We were in the A.D.C. together. And Vyvyan was always ready to talk about him to anyone who *did* belong to that era. I think—at any rate, I hope— that he felt himself to blame."

"In this matter of the club, and the fund?"

"Yes."

"You say you *hope*. He did not admit he was in the wrong?"

"Oh, dear me, no. Vyvyan would never do that."

"But he protested too much?"

"Exactly."

"Evidently, Mr. Mercer, you feel yourself that Lanham was hardly treated."

"Very hardly," said the tutor. He had dropped his affectations and spoke with obvious sincerity, and I liked him all the better. "Wilfrid Lanham," he added, "was always wrong-headed and egotistical, but he was impulsive and generous—the last man himself, at any rate in his early days, to hold an old friend to the letter of a bond."

"But after all, it *was* a trust, and there were other trustees besides Sir Vyvyan."

"They were his mouthpieces, Major—Farleigh, Tullis, Blewitt the bank manager and his predecessors, all of them. Vyvyan was like that. He always led. And then the trust, though cast in a legal form, was originally a friendly agreement. Moreover, it was Lanham's own creation."

"Oh, quite. What you say agrees with all I've heard."

"Mind you"—Mr. Mercer put up a large, plump hand and became slightly stagey again—"mind you, Wilfrid Lanham has behaved like an insensate child.

I say nothing about these appalling crimes. I am speaking of his conduct during the past decade or more. I hold no brief for him there. I have heard only Vyvyan's side of it, but that is enough. Only on Monday, not half an hour before he walked from these rooms to his death, he was telling me of Lanham's letter to his wife. You have heard of that?"

"About the pendant. Yes."

"It ought to have warned us," the tutor said. "It ought to have warned us. It contained threats. . . ."

"I didn't know that," Maurice said. "Threats against Sir Vyvyan?"

"Generalities, so far as I remember Vyvyan's account. I did not see the letter, of course. 'Don't drive me to desperation, or you and your husband will regret it. . . .' Something like that."

"Sir Vyvyan didn't take it seriously, I suppose?'

"Oh, no. He was merely angry and contemptuous. If only we had known! If only I had walked up with him to the ' Eagle'! I can see him now, turning to wave to me. . . ."

Mr. Mercer shook his handsome head and sighed.

"You saw no one else in Queens' Lane?" Maurice asked.

"No one. But Lanham could have been standing, as he probably was, a hundred yards away in the shadows. The Lane is badly lighted. . . ."

"By the way," said Maurice, "when exactly was this visit of Sir Vyvyan's here arranged between you?"

"Oh, in the afternoon. I met him in Petty Cury. He mentioned that his wife would be leaving the ball early, and as he was going back to London the next morning we agreed to come away at the same time and have an hour together."

"Did you mention this to anyone, Mr. Mercer?"

"Nugent asked me that. Yes, to one or two people—but only, as I remember clearly, at the ball itself. Which," said Mr. Mercer, with a smile, "would seem to dispose of what is in your mind, Major. Lanham can have obtained no knowledge of Rowsell-Hogg's movements through me."

"But Rowsell-Hogg himself may have spoken of them to someone earlier in the day?"

"Oh, of course. You may add poor Hereward, who was with him when we met that afternoon."

"The subject may have come up at this dinner at the 'Eagle,' for example?"

"Very likely it did. But who, among those present, could possibly refer to it in Lanham's hearing? Wherever he was, he wouldn't be in their company at any time." Mr. Mercer paused and looked curiously at Maurice. Getting no reply, he went on: "In any case, *how* Lanham obtained his knowledge—and my own view is that he simply followed us from Trinity—is surely immaterial?"

"Loose ends annoy me," Maurice murmured. "I suppose in your view whether or not Lanham knew that young Rowsell-Hogg would be in his rooms this morning is also immaterial?"

"I don't see that it matters," said the tutor. "Personally, I imagine that both these crimes were premeditated up to a point, and that Lanham then seized his opportunities."

"It seems to me a very risky method."

"All murders are risky. And a homicidal maniac will run more risk than most of us."

"You may be right." Maurice finished his port and dismissed the point. "When did you last see Lanham, Mr. Mercer?" he asked.

"I have not seen him since he went down—that is to say, since 1912."

"How would you describe him? Was he healthy, robust, athletic?"

"No," said Mr. Mercer thoughtfully. "No, I should say he was rather frail. He lived too much on his emotions. He should have been an actor, not a man of business. He certainly never went in much for athletics—though I believe he did some mountaineering in a small way. Of course, he may have altered very greatly in twenty-five years—physically, I mean. Some of these weedy-looking boys develop surprisingly. But I should be surprised myself if Wilfrid Lanham were one of them."

Maurice's empty glass caught his eye and reminded him of mine, which I was just emptying, and he became the host once more, busying himself with the decanter. Both men had been standing all this time, and Maurice turned again to peer through his monocle at the sketch of Owen Jevons.

When the tutor handed me my glass I remarked on its beauty.

"Lovely things, are they not?" he said. "I still have a score. They belonged to Louis-Philippe. . . ."

But I thought he spoke with less than his usual relish of his possessions. He had lost much of his theatrical manner, and looked rather tired and old.

"Why not sit down, Major?" he went on, sinking heavily himself into a chair beside mine. Maurice found another. Mr. Mercer was running his fingers through his thick grey hair. "This is a dreadful business!" he said. "A dreadful business. All this talk brings it home to one. . . . Vyvyan, at any rate, had lived the best part of his life—for a man of our age he was wearing none too well,

I thought—but that poor boy. . .!" There were certainly no histrionics about the tremble in the fine voice. "I did not see much of Hereward, but he was a good lad. A good lad. He had harmed no one. . . . It is a sad reflexion, Major, that things would never have come to this fearful pass if Vyvyan and his fellow trustees had performed one small, graceful act in the beginning. For which, by the way, there were precedents. . . ."

Maurice nodded. "So I hear. You mean the cases of the two widows?"

"Yes. Mrs. Frome and Mrs. Henderson. There was also, of course, a precedent on the other side."

"That I didn't know," Maurice said, looking interested.

"It is a painful story," said Mr. Mercer. "I hardly know whether I should repeat it now. Or, at any rate, in this company."

His eye rested on me before travelling to the self-portrait of Owen Jevons.

"A story concerning *him*?" Maurice inquired.

"As you say. No, no, I hardly think . . . Besides, it has no bearing on these murders."

"All the same, I should like to hear it, if I may."

Mr. Mercer still hesitated. He looked at me again, and coughed.

"I don't know what the story is about," I said, "but I'm quite grown up. And if my husband really wants to hear it, you'd better tell it now, or you'll get no peace. He's very persistent."

"It is not strictly confidential," Mr. Mercer said. "At any rate, Tullis knows all about it—more than I do, in fact. Well—hem !—in short, these are the facts. I give them to help you to understand Vyvyan's curiously narrow outlook. In justice to him, in a sense—for though in this case, too, I consider he behaved wrongly, he quite sincerely never thought so himself. He came of a rigid Puritan stock, you know. . . ."

"That breaks the ice," I said. "I'm prepared for anything now."

Mr. Mercer gave me a little smile.

"And in theory, if not in fact," he went on, "the blame again should be apportioned between Vyvyan himself and the other trustees. . . . At any rate, this, briefly, is the story. Owen Jevons, as I told you, left England in 1913. Wherever he went—I am vague about the timber trade, but probably it was to one of what were then the Russian provinces on the Baltic—he met a girl there. Not to put too fine a point upon it, she became his mistress. Within a year Jevons was drowned. Five or six years later, after the war, the girl came to England, bringing with her a child—a son—whom she said was Owen's. She was in very poor circumstances; she knew that Owen had been well-to-do, and she thought his family should help her. His family thought differently, though I believe they did a little. However, they told her about the Nine Bright Shiners and the fund, and she next applied to the trustees. . . ."

Mr. Mercer paused to sip his port.

"One foresees the result," said Maurice. "By the way, was this before or after assistance from the fund was given to Mrs. Frome and Mrs. Henderson?"

"After," the tutor said. "It was these grants, I believe, which suggested the idea to Owen's parents. But of course the cases were not similar, and the trustees were adamant."

"Or Sir Vyvyan was?"

"Shall we say he persuaded them? Poor Owen's *liaison* was a type of lapse with which he had no sympathy. I spoke of his Puritan stock. He had all their hair-splitting ethical notions. An irregular union was moral turpitude, but, on the other hand, anything was fair in business. For example, only on Monday he was telling me of another piece of persuasion, in his eyes equally justified. He had obtained inside information about some shares in his possession. They were going to slump, as I believe the phrase goes. So he induced his old friend Tullis, who was not so well informed, to buy them at a good price. When they slumped, Tullis was naturally indignant. But Vyvyan couldn't see that he had done anything even censurable. Tullis, he said, should have kept his ears open."

"Cyprian Eagles," said Maurice, looking at me.

"Yes," Mr. Mercer said. "That was the name. Tullis has been talking, I suppose. . . ?"

He was plainly unaware that James and I were in any way connected, so I made no comment. But the more I heard of Sir Vyvyan, the less I regretted his decease.

"To go back to this girl," I said. "It was dreadfully hard luck on her."

"Particularly so," said the tutor, "if her own story was to be believed. *She* said that Owen had promised to marry her as soon as he came of age. Until then he was financially dependent on his father, who had other views for him, I understand. At any rate, he was keeping this affair quiet for the time being."

Maurice had pulled out his notebook. Mr. Mercer, with a slight smile, watched the amateur sleuth at work over his glass of port.

"If this was just after the war," Maurice said presently, "the other trustees would be Farleigh and the first or second bank manager?"

"Farleigh was one, certainly," Mr. Mercer agreed. "It was some years before he died."

"Do you know what became of the girl?"

"I have no idea. All I know about the affair I heard from Vyvyan, and that was a long time ago."

"But you say Mr. Tullis knows more than you do?"

"Only because Vyvyan told me that after the girl had been turned down by the trustees she applied to both Tullis and Lanham for help. They, too, had been Owen's friends, and by that time they were the only other surviving members of the club."

"Lanham, eh. . .?" said Maurice. "Did either of them help her?"

"I don't know about Tullis. Lanham assisted her, or said he did. He was always citing her case in his letters to Vyvyan about his own grievances."

"At any rate, they would both know her?"

The tutor shrugged. "There again I can't say. I have an impression that one of them knew her, but I may be wrong. She may merely have written to them."

"A Russian, or Lithuanian, or whatever she was?"

"More often than not, Major, educated Russians are good linguists. And if Owen Jevons really intended to marry this girl, no doubt she was a lady."

"Do you know her name?" I asked.

"I remember her family name," Mr. Mercer said. "It was Daal. D, double-a, l."

Once more all the numerous clocks and watches began to chime. It was nine o'clock. I caught Maurice's eye.

He seemed quite ready to go, and we left a few minutes later. Mr. Mercer was apologetic, but he *had* an engagement. With a return of his old manner, he implored us—with a speaking eye on me—to visit him again soon and try his sherry. It came, if I remember correctly, from the cellars of the late King of Bavaria.

As soon as we were in the court again, Maurice said:

"Are we both invited to this ball?"

I stared at him. "Do you mean you want to go, after all? Vera has tickets for us, of course. Mr. Ince sent them."

"Who'll be there among the dramatis personæ? Besides young Ince and the Tullises?"

"I don't know about the Henderson boy," I said. "I should think he's doubtful. But Mr. Armfeldt said something about hoping to meet us there before he left this morning. That will mean Miss Farleigh too, I suppose."

"And his mother?"

"Goodness knows."

"Well, do you feel equal to it?"

"Oh, perfectly. But you realise it's after nine now, and we've got to get back to Hythe House and change."

"We'll ring up Vera. If she doesn't want to wait for us she can leave the tickets."

Vera, however, said that she and Averil were still dressing, and didn't propose to start much before ten. They would wait for us. We got a taxi, and were back at Hythe House before half-past nine.

IMPROMPTU—*and* OPUS THREE

CHAPTER VII

THURSDAY MORNING

1

STRICTLY speaking, half this chapter belongs to the last one. But as the sensation which was to make the Jesus ball one of the most notorious entertainments ever known in Cambridge happened, so far as I was concerned, after midnight, I'm lumping everything connected with it under "Thursday Morning." To quote Maurice again, it's so much tidier. One can't cut a dance in half.

I'm not fond of dragging on my clothes at short notice, but I managed it in half an hour. Maurice, of course, was down first, and had ten minutes' talk with Puffin, who'd got home to dinner. Puffin was distinctly fretful, but I only had time to gather from his grumbles that there was still no fresh news of importance.

When the four of us set off in the Nugents' big car I sat by Maurice, who drove.

I asked him what *had* happened.

"What hasn't happened," he said, "would be the better way to put it."

"Lanham's still the Invisible Man?"

"He is. And though they've turned his flat upside down they've found nothing incriminating except his notepaper."

"It's the same as that used for the drawings?"

"Yes. But we knew that before. It's quite a common brand, by the way. And the fact that the finger-prints on the note to his daughter are really his only confirms another natural assumption."

"Well, they wouldn't be anyone else's."

"It was as well to be sure."

"Who looks after him? Is it a service flat?"

"Nothing so modern. He has a woman in daily. She hasn't noticed anything unusual in his behaviour lately. She says he's always irritable and queer. He told her he'd be away for a week, and the people he works for confirm this. He was taking half his summer holiday."

"Half?" I said. A fortnight in the year must have seemed a pittance to a man who had been a partner in a big firm. "What about his bank?"

"The manager, under pressure, gave a few details. But only, as he said, because they could do his customer no harm. Iliff guessed wrongly there. Lanham only drew out a fiver for his holiday. But then there was precious little to draw."

"He was counting on the jewels, perhaps?"

"Unless," said Maurice, "he knows some shady diamond dealer, I don't see how he's going to raise anything on them for some time to come—in this country, anyway. Every man in the trade will be dashed careful with embarrassed strangers who try to sell them unset stones, to say nothing of pendants."

"There's Mr. Devine's suggestion, of course—that Lanham isn't worrying about the future."

"Then why did he bag the pendant at all?"

"Just to get his own back on Lady Rowsell-Hogg, I suppose."

Maurice shrugged.

"Any sidelights on sword-sticks?" I asked.

"No one knows of one—not even the charlady."

"Have they asked Miss Lanham?"

"Oh, yes—in vain. But she wouldn't know about it either, now, would she? The malacca, on the other hand, like Gilbert's cotton broker, is a familiar object from Fulham to the City."

We were held up for a moment by the traffic at the Fen Ditton cross-roads. When we were over the railway, making for the Newmarket road, I asked if there was any news of my American gum-chewer or the Armfeldts.

"Not to date," Maurice said. "Except that Armfeldt's mamma *is* in Cambridge. Staying at the ' Granta' with him. But they've both been in London all day with Miss Farleigh. However, they're due at this ball."

"All three?"

"Apparently."

We got to Jesus at a quarter-past ten. For the ball they lay down a floor in Cloister Court and rig an awning over it. There was a fearful jam, and at first I didn't see anyone I knew. Averil was whirled away at once by some youth of her acquaintance who seemed to have been waiting for her. Maurice led Vera into the crush. He's quite a good dancer when he chooses to exert himself. I was left *plantée là* under an arch of the cloisters, which were hung with coloured lights in a way that would have surprised the nuns of St. Radegund. But then the whole thing would have surprised them.

Suddenly a liquid voice addressed me.

"My dear Mrs. Hemyock!" said Mr. Armfeldt. "How delightful! And how charming you look! That frock . . . You have the art few English-women possess—you know how to dress. Do you know, I have been looking all over the college for you."

I refrained from asking him why, or inquiring after Miss Farleigh. I merely remarked that I hadn't said definitely I was coming, or something equally non-committal.

"Shall we try this one?" he said persuasively.

We tried it. He was a really beautiful dancer, as I'd felt sure he would be, and his own clothes were too perfect for words. After a few inanities he explained that he and his Claudia had been in London all day.

"And Mrs. Armfeldt?" I said.

He didn't seem surprised that I knew of his mother's existence, or of her presence in Cambridge. After all, most of us had mothers, and quite a lot of them were there.

"Yes," he said, "she went with us. The International Surrealist show opened to-day. I am exhibiting."

"Cheers!" said I. "At last I've met a Surrealist. And you can tell me what Surrealism surreally is."

"The exploitation, Mrs. Hemyock, of the fortuitous encounter of distant realities on an unconventional plane."

"Can't you make it simpler?"

"That is as clear a definition as any I know."

"Well, I can believe you. I'll try to think it out. What *are you* exhibiting?"

"Two symbolic paintings and an abstract composition of three pieces of coal, a toothpick, and an elastic-sided boot arranged on a plate round a bottle of ketchup."

"And what on earth does that symbolise?"

"I call it 'Portrait of a Bishop.' "

"But you might call it anything you like, I suppose ?"

Then he smiled. "Perhaps I might," he said. "One has to do it, you know."

I very naturally asked why. But at this moment the music stopped and I never got an answer.

"I should like you to meet my mother," Mr. Armfeldt said, leading me tenderly into the cloisters. "She's here, you know. She pretends she's chaperoning Claudia, but she isn't really as Victorian as that. The truth is she enjoys these affairs as much as anyone."

This gave me my opening, and I said casually:

"Averil Nugent and I were in Horningsea this afternoon, and we met a man who wanted to see Mrs. Armfeldt. An American . . ."

I felt my companion's arm stiffen against mine, and he gave me a quick glance which was a good deal less liquid than usual.

"Oh. . .?" he said slowly. "So it was you, was it?"

His tone, like his look, had changed. I remembered suddenly and uncomfortably the gum-chewer's last words. "I warn you. He's a killer." And though the idea seemed even more mad than Surrealism, with so much sudden death about I felt quite glad for an instant that several hundred other people were about too just then.

Before I'd time to feel ashamed of myself, Paul Armfeldt was his own airy, affected self again.

"Ought I to apologise?" he asked lightly, fingering his silky black moustache. "Because we don't know anything about it. When we got back from town there was a policeman at the hotel with a story of two ladies who'd been pestered by a sinister American asking for my mother. But it's a complete mystery to us both. I give you my word on that, Mrs. Hemyock. Besides, why should anyone look for us at Horningsea? We have never even been in the place."

"Apparently he muddled you up with the Devines."

"So that was it. . . ." He stroked his little moustache again and looked thoughtful, and when he did that a sort of mask fell over his dark face. "Can you describe the man, Mrs. Hemyock, and tell me exactly what he said?"

I was able to oblige, but once more I felt it would be tactful to omit any reference to killers. Paul Armfeldt listened with the same expressionless face. At the end he shook his head.

"He's no friend of mine. Even I draw the line somewhere. But you'll find him by the thousand in Chicago or New York."

"Yes, Mrs. Devine seemed to know the type."

"Oh, she was over there too, was she. . .? Well, it's a puzzle, I can assure you."

But he was still a little pensive, for when he pulled out another gold cigarette-case—a dress one, this time—from a waistcoat with onyx buttons, he forgot at first to offer it to me. He had just rectified the lapse, with abject apologies, when a striking figure came majestically through the crowd in the cloisters towards us.

"Here's my mother," he said.

Mrs. Armfeldt must have been nearly six feet tall. Though she was in the late forties, her glossy hair was still black. It was piled high on her head and surmounted by an enormous tortoise-shell comb which towered another foot above everybody. She wore a perfectly lovely gown of stiff wine-coloured shot brocade with an immense puffed skirt and train, which she carried over her arm. There must have been yards and yards of that skirt. With her free hand she held up a jewelled, gold lorgnette. Jewels sparkled on her dead-white fingers and two great purple stones dangled and shimmered from her ears. She was handsome in a big, baffling, nondescript way, chiefly because of a pair of very lively dark eyes. Every one stared at this exotic and impressive figure, rustling and flashing at every step, which might have walked straight out of a canvas by Velasquez. Mrs. Armfeldt, in fact, made all the bright young things present, to say nothing of their mothers, look insignificant and provincial. I even had momentary doubts about my own frock.

"Zere you are, Paul," she said.

"This is Mrs. Hemyock, Mother."

"Ah, I have heard of you, Mrs. Hemyock." Mrs. Armfeldt showed beautiful small white teeth as she surveyed me through the lorgnette. There was nothing impertinent about this scrutiny—she used the thing with an air, a natural manner, very different from that of English dowagers. She spoke excellent English, except for a small difficulty with her " th's." "My son," said Mrs. Armfeldt graciously, "has talked much about you. I am pleased to meet you."

Her manner was rather regal. I murmured something appropriate.

"Mrs. Hemyock," Paul Armfeldt said, in his ordinary easy style, "was one of the heroines of the adventure of the sinister American at Horningsea this afternoon."

The lorgnette fixed me again, "*In-deed*?" said Mrs. Armfeldt. "It was you? Quite a coincidence. Zat is a funny business, eh?"

"He was rather a funny figure for this part of the world," I agreed.

"And he wished to see *me?*"

"So he said."

"I've told you of Devine, Mother," her son put in. "The newspaper man who has a cottage at Horningsea. This fellow seems to have mixed us up."

"But why?"

"Heaven knows."

"He did not explain, Mrs. Hemyock?"

"I'm afraid we didn't give him time. He only referred to Mr. Armfeldt"—I chuckled as I looked at that sleek, dark, exquisite young man—"as your white-headed boy."

The white-headed boy fingered his moustache and smiled a little absently. Mrs. Armfeldt, after looking at me for a moment through the lorgnette, lowered

106

it and smiled too, showing her small, perfect teeth again. She shrugged, and all her jewels spun and glittered.

"Pfui!" she said—or something that sounded like that. "I do not understand it. Some low friend of Paul's, perhaps—but he says no. And I ask you, Mrs. Hemyock, do I look as if I live in a cottage?"

"Scarcely," I said, smiling.

"It is true that we have visited ze United States. . . . Have you ever been zere?"

"Never."

"Everyzing is upside down. You stay with some millionaire, in a house as big as Blenheim, and ze gardener has been at school wiz your host, and calls him Jake. So you see. . .?"

"You may meet anyone?"

"Zat is it. Tell me, what are zese Devines?"

"I really know nothing about them. I met Mrs. Devine for the first time yesterday afternoon."

"She is like me?"

"Not in the least, Mrs. Armfeldt."

"Zen I do not understand it at all. Let us forget about it, eh? Zere are no Yankee crooks here. Paul, Mrs. Hemyock would like an ice. I would like one too. Where are zey?"

But the music had begun again, and as I saw a group consisting of Vera and Maurice, James Tullis, Ian, Averil, and Patrick Ince standing together across the court looking about them (I correctly assumed for me), I made my excuses and went to join them.

2

I had a two-step with Maurice, while James steered Vera round in his stiff way, as if she was a ship. Then I had to suffer James himself, and heard a lot more about his Great-aunt Julia, whom he seemed to think was a suitable topic for a ballroom. Afterwards Vera and Maurice sat out, raking up old scandals from Simla or somewhere, and I rang the changes on Ian and Patrick Ince, dancing with whichever of them wasn't partnering Averil. They had both attached themselves firmly to her, and carried on a public competition for her favours. During one dance with me Ian said rather seriously: "Old Patrick's a bit of a thruster, don't you think? He only met the girl yesterday." Ian himself had only met her the day before that, but as a sort of connexion he had my backing, and I more than guessed now that he had Averil's too. The pushing Mr. Ince, however, had a slight local advantage, for it was *his* college ball, and we were all having supper with him. As for the youth who'd claimed Averil when we arrived, I saw him hovering wistfully in the offing once or twice, but I don't think he got another dance with her.

Paul Armfeldt danced busily, chiefly with Claudia Farleigh, who had turned up in white satin, and not much of that. She gave me a cool nod. Mr. Armfeldt looked at me tenderly every time we passed in our respective orbits. Once he went round with his mother, who stepped out with a stateliness that dignified even the modern shuffle, the brocade train over her arm, the immense tortoise-shell comb sailing high above the crowd of heads. I took an opportunity to point out the pair to Maurice.

Of the other dramatis personæ, young Roy Henderson was not there, and though Patrick Ince had invited Harry Devine, and kept looking for him, I never expected to see him—in which I was wrong.

When I rejoined Vera and Maurice at the interval before the supper dance, Maurice suggested a stroll round. Vera said she would stay where she was.

"We might run across your pals the Armfeldts," Maurice said to me.

From the determined way he led me through the passage by the kitchen into Pump Court it was obvious that this was a figure of speech. He'd just seen them go that way.

We overtook them almost at once in the gardens, which were hung with coloured lights. Claudia Farleigh and another man were with them, but as a dutiful wife, and an inquisitive one, I went more than half-way to meet Mr. Armfeldt's encouraging smile. We bandied introductions, though I never caught the strange man's name.

Mrs. Armfeldt studied Maurice through the lorgnette.

"Ah, ze detective," she said. "And what do you zink of our little mystery, Major Hemyock? Your wife has told you, eh? Ze American crrrook."

She mimicked excellently the rolling "r's" of melodrama.

"I have not thought about it, Mrs. Armfeldt," Maurice said rather stiffly. He hates being ridiculed about his detective hobby.

She showed her small teeth in a smile.

" It is too petty a zing for you, eh? And wiz all zese real tragedies."

"They seem rather more important."

"I am crushed," said Mrs. Armfeldt, with her mocking air. Then, with a sudden change of tone, she went on: "Yes, they are terrible. Terrible. I tell you what I zink. You will never catch zis man Lanham alive. No, never."

"That," Maurice said, "seems to be quite a common view."

"You zink so yourself?"

"I don't say that."

"No. You will say nozzing. You are discreet. You have a poker face—like so many Englishmen. So often zere is nozzing behind it, eh? But not so wiz you, Major."

"I hope you are right," said Maurice.

Paul Armfeldt, stroking his minute moustache, was listening with a somewhat set smile. His dark eyes seemed to be trying to read the poker face. But Maurice was looking particularly blank.

"Well, I want to dance," Claudia Farleigh drawled.

The band had struck up again, and we all drifted back to Cloister Court. Maurice and I fell behind the others. The strange man—I heard afterwards that he was a fellow of the college, a friend of the late Mr. Farleigh, and Claudia's godfather—led her on to the floor. Paul Armfeldt was just giving me a speculative look over his shoulder when I was startled by a voice behind me.

"Hullo, Mrs. Hemyock. Have you seen Ince anywhere?"

"I didn't expect to see *you*, Mr. Devine," I said.

"Deserting my post, eh?" Harry Devine smiled at Maurice. "Evening, Major. Oh, yes, I was going to mount guard, but my mother wouldn't hear of it. We've got a new night patrol parked plumb in the garden—a whale of a fellow—and, anyway, we've heard nothing more of the mysterious gent from the States. As I said, he's probably in the town now, chasing Mr. Armfeldt there." He gave a cool nod to Paul Armfeldt, who was staring at him with a little frown. "If the police haven't rounded him up yet," Harry Devine added, his light blue eyes still on the other's dark ones. "Any news of that, Major?"

"None that I know of," said Maurice.

Paul Armfeldt murmured to his mother, who put up her lorgnette to examine Mr. Devine. Then she sailed towards us, her son following.

"Introduce me, Paul," she commanded.

He waved a graceful hand, but his eyes were still wary.

"Mr. Devine—my mother."

"I have seen you, Mr. Devine, in ze street, eh?" Mrs. Armfeldt said. "But we have not been introduced."

Harry Devine, no less watchful, it seemed to me, smiled with his lips.

"Pleased to meet you, Mrs. Armfeldt."

The lorgnette looked him up and down. "How familiar zat sounds," said Mrs. Armfeldt, with her faint air of mockery. "And ze voice. . . . One can tell you have been in ze States, Mr. Devine. A long time, eh?"

"A good many years."

"In Chicago, my son says."

109

"That is so."

"We must talk about it one day. It is a link, eh? Like zis sinister perrrson"—
she rolled the "r's" again, her lively dark eyes still mocking him—"who has come
all ze way from zat country to find us— perhaps—and finds you and your muzzer
instead."

"That little mistake seems to have been put right," Harry Devine said.
"I was just saying to Mrs. Hemyock and the Major that we've heard no more
of him. And you. . .?"

Mrs. Armfeldt laughed lightly and waved the lorgnette.

"No. He has not called. We have not been zhreatened. Or blackmailed. It
is disappointing, eh?"

Harry Devine's eyes met the exquisite Paul's squarely again. He looked
well himself in evening dress, which showed off his broad shoulders and
narrow hips. He was the shorter of the two, but probably, I thought, much the
more wiry and powerful.

Paul Armfeldt, without relaxing his watchful stare, was tapping a cigarette on his gold case. There was a definite tension in the atmosphere.
The pair made me think of a couple of dogs—hostile, suspicious, ready
to fly at one another, but not sure if it was worth it, or even what there was
to fly about. Mrs. Armfeldt, however, seemed to find it amusing. At least
she smiled in her slightly sardonic way, her bright eyes flitting between
the two.

"It is no good glaring at Paul," she observed. "If zis man is some low friend
of his, he will not say so—even to me."

Harry Devine laughed. He had a pleasant laugh. He seemed to shake off
his humours.

"Well, it's no business of mine, anyway," he said. "I dare say Mr. Armfeldt
can deal with it, if it's any of his."

"Which it isn't," Paul Armfeldt said shortly. It was the first time he had
spoken directly to the other.

"Oh, sure!" said Harry Devine lightly.

"Bah!" Mrs. Armfeldt exclaimed. "It bores me. Let us go and have supper."
She picked up her train, adding to the company in general, with a wave of
her lorgnette: "But it is a pity, eh? All zis crook stuff for nozzing."

She sailed away, her son turning rather abruptly to follow.

Harry Devine looked after them. "I wonder," he said. He shrugged. "Well,
I'll have to go and chase Ince. He'll be feeling sore. There's some girl I'm to
take care of for him, so he can give his whole mind to Miss Nugent. I hope
she's a good-looker."

"I haven't noticed him bothering about any other girl," I said. "Anyhow, I suppose we shall all be at the same table for supper."

"Oh, that's fine."

He gave us a friendly wave—he seemed in unusually good spirits now—and went off.

"Well, well," Maurice said, putting in his eyeglass to stare after him. "And what do you make of *that* little scene?"

"I don't make anything of it."

"Nobody seems anxious to claim your American friend."

"I don't wonder."

"But there's an interesting unanimity of opinion about Lanham's intentions."

"Well, that's natural enough too."

"Oh, quite. . . ."

"What's biting you?"

"I wish I could tell you. . . . There, the band's stopping. I'm hungry. Let's follow Mr. Devine's excellent example, and find our host."

Supper was a very cheery affair. They'd cleared the long tables out of the Hall, and dotted it with small ones. At ours were Vera and Averil, James Tullis and Ian, Harry Devine, Maurice and myself, and, of course, our host. Despairing of Harry Devine's appearance, the resourceful mothers' joy had contrived to wish on to some other party the girl his friend was to have taken off his hands. Averil was in clover with two strings to her bow, chaffing each other across her. Ian referred to Mr. Ince as Pushful Patrick, and Mr. Ince retaliated by quoting a song he'd adapted with his usual ingenuity—"It's little for blushing they care at Clare." Ian, of course, would be leaving in a couple of days with his father, who was only hanging on for his little matter of business with the bank manager ; but the pushful one was staying on in his rooms (he lived out of college) for a week or two of the Long to catch up arrears of work. Term, with Mr. Ince, was not the season for this—there were too many games—and his tutor had told him that if he wanted to pass his Tripos he'd have to buckle to. And there was £5000 in the offing, as he remarked. He added that he'd no home to go to, anyway, and went on to try to make a few dates with Averil. It was during this talk, I think, that I learnt that young Roy Henderson was staying up too—partly for the same reason—work—and partly because his mother, who was still alive, was abroad.

Of the rest, Harry Devine had shed altogether a certain reserve he'd shown at our other meetings, and told amusing transatlantic stories. He seemed, as I'd noted before, in almost unnaturally good spirits. And even James Tullis, under the influence of more drink and excellent food, became pawky and paid heavy compliments all round.

The Armfeldts, with Miss Farleigh and her godfather, were at a table near by. Paul Armfeldt, too, seemed to have recovered his poise, or pose, and favoured me with the famous liquid look from time to time, when his Claudia wasn't watching. But it was his mother who dominated the table.

This party went down before ours. It was some time after midnight when we left the Hall. Dancing had begun again. Vera met some friends, and stayed talking to them. Ian whisked Averil on to the floor, where Claudia was dancing with her godfather. James wanted to finish a cigar, and wandered off somewhere. The Armfeldts were not to be seen, and Harry Devine had drifted away too.

After looking on for a few minutes, Maurice and I strolled out into Front Court. It was not lit up, and other people there were just blurred shirt-fronts and frocks in the starlight. Like the courts of so many Cambridge colleges, Front Court and Pump Court at Jesus are three-sided. The west side of both is formed by one long stretch of railing. They make a sort of letter E, with Pump Court, which is much the bigger, on the north. The middle arm of the E, separating them, is a block of buildings which replaced the thatched barns and byres of the nuns of St. Radegund. You get from one court to the other round either end of this block. At the east end a dark tunnel runs obliquely past the kitchens, and close to where it opens into Pump Court a second tunnel opens too—the one from the cloisters through which Maurice and I had followed the Armfeldts before supper. These two passages, in other words, converge from the smaller courts into Pump Court. This, as I've said before, is laid out as a huge garden, with lawns and flower-beds and a few shrubberies. Another garden stretches beyond the railings and all this was thrown open that night.

Maurice and I had ambled round Front Court, avoiding the cobbles, and were standing by the entry of the slanting tunnel when a man came out of it and walked quickly past us. I didn't even notice what he looked like. It was too dark, anyway.

A moment after another figure came out of the entry, saw us and stopped. I made out that it was Harry Devine.

"Hullo," I said.

"Oh, it's you, Mrs. Hemyock." He was breathing rather fast, and peering past us. "Did you see a man come out just now?"

"Yes."

"Where did he go?"

"Towards the Gatehouse, I think."

This, of course, is the main entrance of the college. You reach it from Jesus Lane by a walled alley known as the Chimney.

Harry Devine was still staring. He took another step, and hesitated.

"I could have sworn——" he said.

"What's the matter?" Maurice asked.

"You know, for a moment I could have sworn it was Lanham, I know his walk. Did you see his face?"

But neither of us had. All we knew was that the man was in evening dress, like everybody else.

And before we could do anything more about it a third figure came flying out of the dark entry and bumped into us. It was James Tullis, and he grabbed Maurice's arm as if he was sinking. He began to stutter.

"I—I—I——"

"All right, James, the ayes have it," I said.

He goggled at us. I could see his eyeballs shining in the starlight, and suddenly it didn't seem funny.

"Is that y-you, Myra?" He was still spluttering, and he jerked round to look back into the black mouth of the passage. "G-good God!" he said. "D'you know what's happened? I've been shot at!"

3

There was a moment's astonished silence, and then Harry Devine cried out:

"Then it *was* him!"

And he flew off towards the Gatehouse.

"Who?" spluttered James. " What does he mean? N-not—not Lanham?"

I said: "Well, he thought he saw him. A man passed us——"

"Then it must have been! Good God . . ."

"Look here, Tullis," Maurice said firmly. "What *has* happened? And when? And where? We haven't heard any shot."

James was now shooting nervous glances all round the court.

"Hadn't we better get into a doorway, or something?" he said. "He may be dodging about anywhere in this mirk. Best get Myra out of it, what. . .?"

He was looking behind him again, and edging backward. He was obviously badly shaken. Within two yards of us, beside the tunnel mouth, was the entry to a set of rooms. We took James's disinterested advice and crowded into the lobby, where it was almost pitch dark.

"Well, what about that shot?" Maurice asked.

He sounded sceptical, but he kept in front of me. I was too interested to be frightened. I was straining my eyes to see if anything was happening at the Gatehouse. People seemed to be walking about the court just as before.

"You wouldn't hear it from here," James said. He muttered rather, but he was pulling himself together. "That devil's using a silencer. I've heard one before—a man I know brought it home from the States. You don't often see them in England. That's how I knew. Otherwise I'd have thought someone was chucking a stone——"

"Oh, go on!" I said. I didn't want a lecture on silencers. There was still no sign of any excitement in the court.

"Well, it was like this. I was just the other side there, in Pump Court, walking back to find some of you. There are a lot of people about in the gardens, but there was no one near me at the moment that I could see. There are one or two largish shrubs in a bed, and I was just passing them when I heard this noise. Like a bark, or cough—muffled, you know. Something went *phut* past my nose and smashed a window. I didn't stop to think. Subconsciously I must have guessed what it was. I just bolted for cover. . . ."

James was still talking rather jerkily, and much less pompously than usual.

"How long ago was this?" Maurice asked.

"Just now. A couple of minutes ago, perhaps."

"Where did you bolt to?"

"Into a doorway. Backing on to this, you know, but a bit farther along. I was close to it."

"And then?"

"Well, nothing happened. People were walking about all over the place, but no one seemed to have noticed anything, though some of them must have heard the shot. But then they wouldn't know it was a shot. Those footling fairy lamps didn't give enough light for me to recognise anyone. If I'd been armed myself, if I'd had a stick"—invisible, and well in the rear, James began to talk with a touch of trucu- lence—"I'd have had a hunt for the fellow. I could see those shrubs. But as it was——"

"'You are brave, Mr. Hodgitts,'" I murmured— a little unkindly, perhaps, but I was excited. "'Do not be rash.'"

"Eh. . .?" said James.

"Nothing. Go on."

"Anyway, if he *was* in the shrubs, he must have cleared off when I turned my back. I couldn't see a movement. Then after a while a couple came by—

a man and a girl—and I slipped out behind them, and dodged through that tunnel, and ran into you."

"You say a window was broken?" Maurice asked.

"I heard the glass go."

"No one else heard it?"

"There was no one else near enough. But it will be there for you to see for yourself——"

"Oh, quite," Maurice said. "I wonder what Devine's up to?"

We got an answer to this at once. Perfect peace still reigned in Front Court. We could hear the saunterers talking and laughing, and the music of the band filtering through from the cloisters. From somewhere near came Harry Devine's low voice:

"Major Hemyock?"

Maurice stepped out. "Here I am."

"He hasn't gone that way," I heard Harry Devine say. "The porter says no one has passed out for half an hour or so. How's Mr. Tullis? Hurt?"

"No. What other bolt-holes are there?"

"I don't know this place well. There's that passage into the cloisters, and a lot of doorways, of course, in that block of rooms there by the gate. There's another garden behind them. He could have nipped into that round the end of the block, or doubled back round the end of this one into Pump Court——"

"Too many possibilities altogether," Maurice said.

I stepped out and joined them.

"I've had enough of the Black Hole," I said. "What are we going to do next?"

"You'd better go back to the ballroom, Mrs. Hemyock."

"Nonsense, Mr. Devine. I'm not going to be done out of the fun."

"It isn't fun," he said seriously.

He was looking about him all the time. We kept our voices low because of the other people in the court, and Maurice expressed what was in our minds when he said:

"It won't do to raise a scare."

James, after hovering uncertainly in the doorway behind us, came out and completed the party. Harry Devine dropped his voice lower still.

"What *did* happen, Mr. Tullis?"

James told his story again, in fewer words. It sounded less heroic than ever, but Maurice, though for a minute or two he'd had his own doubts about the whole thing, told me off afterwards when I said so. *He'd* have thought a good many times, he said, before he went hunting in the dark, with only his bare hands, for a man with a pistol. Of course he was quite right, and I was unfair to James.

"Well, suppose we go and look?" Harry Devine said at the end. "If Lanham was crouching in a flower-bed, there may be footprints. They'll settle if it *was* him, anyway."

"Who else could it be?" James muttered.

They made another attempt to get me away, but I threatened to scream, and they had to let me go with them. I don't want to be unfair to James again, but I fancy he'd have preferred to escort me to safe quarters.

Harry Devine leading, we went through the dark tunnel into Pump Court. There were a number of people strolling about among the coloured lights, as James had said. Obviously rather ill at ease, he took us along the path which ran beside the back of the block facing Front Court. It was in a doorway in the front of this, of course, that we'd taken shelter.

Half-way along was another of these entries.

"Here we are," said James, peering nervously about him. "And there are the shrubs."

They stood up about ten yards away, across a strip of turf.

"Let's look for your window," Maurice said.

We soon found it, and James was justified. Dark though it was, we could see quite a big star in one of the panes. It was a few inches above the level of a tall man's head. James is fairly tall. Anyone firing from a crouching position behind the shrubs could have put his bullet just about there.

So that was that. Maurice went back to the doorway, struck a match, and poked about.

"Myra," he said, "you stop here with Mr. Tullis. Don't argue. Mr. Devine and I will have a look at that shrubbery."

James and I obeyed. I was quite willing this time. I didn't imagine that Lanham, or whoever the man was, was still hiding in those shrubs, but that star in the window had brought things home to me. Up till then, I suppose, James's story had hardly registered properly. I didn't want Maurice to go routing about there in the dark, but I knew I couldn't stop him.

I remember I held my breath as we watched the two figures cross the turf. Then they were lost in the shadows of the shrubs. Then a match scraped and flamed, and another, and a third. We could hear the murmur of talk and laughter all over the gardens, and I jumped when a man and a girl came by along the path, saw us standing in our doorway, and passed on with a little giggle from the girl. At another time this would have amused me. It didn't then. Just after this came one of those odd lulls when every one must have stopped talking at once, and I heard Harry Devine's voice quite clearly.

"There they go," he said. "After you, Major."

There was a lot of soft rustling from the shrubbery, and matches shone in it like fireflies. Then I heard a sudden exclamation. More matches crackled and flared. Another couple sauntered by our doorway, looking over their shoulders.

"Lost something, I suppose," said a man's voice.

I think I had a premonition that they'd found something. A moment after a figure loomed up on the turf. It was Maurice. He called to me in a low voice, and I joined him.

"Look here, old girl," he said, taking my arm—and he doesn't often talk like that, "can you stand a nasty shock? You'll have to go through it later, anyway. I don't think there's anything to be afraid of. There's no one in those bushes—alive."

"What do you mean?" I said.

"Come and see. It may help us to know if we're right. But it isn't nice, you know."

He led me across to the shrubbery. Harry Devine, somewhere in the thickest part, lit two or three matches to guide us. I thought of my frock, but it was no good worrying about that.

We stooped and pushed our way through the bushes, making a sort of little circuit—to avoid messing up marks in the soil, I realised later. I could see Harry Devine's shirt-front in the light of the matches he kept striking. He seemed to be on his knees.

"Woa!" said Maurice. "Now take a breath and look. For God's sake don't yelp, or make any noise. We don't want a panic."

"What is it?"

He was still between me and something over which Harry Devine was kneeling. He said over his shoulder:

"It's a dead man. Can you stick it? One look will be enough."

He pulled me, bent double, beside him. Harry Devine lit another match and held it low.

There was no wind, and the little flame burned almost straight. It spirited out of the blackness just one thing—a face, staring upwards from the soil among the shrubs. The eyes were closed, but the mouth was open, showing gaps in the discoloured teeth. A trickle of blood ran down the unshaven chin from the corner of the snarling lips.

I clapped my hand over my own mouth, or I *should* have yelped. Maurice's hand tightened on my arm.

117

"Do you know him?"

"It's the gum-chewer," I said in a whisper. "The man who stopped Averil and me on the river bank by Horningsea."

The match went out and the face vanished.

"That's my last," said Harry Devine.

4

Maurice Says I behaved very well. At any rate I didn't go into the vapours, or do anything silly. I remember saying:

"Is he dead?"

"Yes," said Maurice. "Stay where you are, Devine. "I'll be as quick as I can."

He began to lead me out of the shrubbery again.

As soon as we were on the turf we saw a white shirt-front. It was James, who'd followed us to see what was up, or because he didn't like being alone. Maurice gave him no time to ask questions.

"Tullis," he said, "get hold of the Master, or someone in authority here. Just say there's a spot of bother—a police matter. I'm going to the porter's lodge to ring up——"

"What is it?"

"Never mind now. Do what I ask you, there's a good chap. Don't say a word to anyone else. Tell whoever you find to come to *me,* at the lodge—not here. Devine's standing by, and we want to keep it quiet, if we can manage it. That'll appeal to the authorities. And bring Myra a stiff drink."

"But what——?" began James again.

Maurice gave him a push. "Off you go," he said.

James went. People were walking about all round us, just as usual, but the little lamps were rather confusing, and no one seemed to have noticed us creeping out of the shrubbery. We followed James, but turned off through the covered passage into Front Court, where there were more people, and where we could hear the band again. It was playing an old foxtrot, "Anything Goes," which was somehow horridly appropriate.

We walked across to the porter's lodge in the Gatehouse. Luckily there was nobody else there at the moment. I was beginning to realise what had happened. My knees were feeling a bit wobbly, and my shoes were full of grit, and I was glad to sit down while Maurice rang up the police station, with the porter gaping at him. Maurice was very guarded, but I could hear that he'd got the Superintendent, who like the rest of us, but for different reasons, was keeping late hours just then. Not so poor Puffin, who was in bed when Maurice telephoned to *him.* There was really nothing Puffin could do, but he had to be kept informed of things like murders—especially at this time.

When Maurice had finished, he came over to me and said:

"How are you feeling?"

"Oh, all right."

"I'm sorry, Myra. But we had to know who the man was as soon as possible. Though I guessed, of course, from your description. And it was either you or Averil."

"Look at my frock," I said.

"Well, we couldn't move him. Anyway, you're going back to bed in a few minutes."

At this moment James appeared, like a Scottish Bacchus, hugging lovingly a bottle of whisky, a siphon, and two tumblers. With him was a stout, oldish man who was one of the tutors of the college. He kept saying peevishly:

"What's wrong, heh? What's wrong?"

I was feeling a little hysterical, and I giggled at James.

"Where are your vine leaves?" I said.

Maurice kept them both waiting while he mixed me a drink. Then he took them into a corner and told them what had happened. I could hear the tutor clucking away like an old hen. He was annoyed because Maurice had taken things into his own hands and telephoned to the police. Who was Maurice, he wanted to know. Then he veered round and was all for sending the porter out to fetch in a constable from Jesus Lane, but Maurice said no, let them wait till the Superintendent came. He'd asked Mr. Iliff to bring plain-clothes men, if he could find any at that time of night—I had a picture of a crowd of detectives in pyjamas—and they might manage to camouflage the business till the ball was over.

In the middle of this Mr. Iliff came in. He was not in uniform, and he looked very tired. He'd left his posse, or as much of it as he could collect at such short notice, outside the gate, in the Chimney. He and Maurice and the tutor went off at once, and I was left with James and the porter. I didn't feel like talking now, and I let them get on with the whisky. I kept seeing that face staring up in the blackness, with little lights and shadows wavering over it as Harry Devine moved the match, and the trickle of blood running down the chin. It was like a horrid, confused dream, and I don't remember much more of what happened that night.

Maurice, however, must have been back in less than ten minutes. I remember having an argument with him. I said I was going to stop, and he wouldn't hear of it. With my face, he said, to say nothing of my frock—I'd put my foot through it, crawling under those bushes—I'd give the show away at once. They were still hoping to keep it quiet for a bit. Vera could be told later, and Averil, with luck, needn't know anything about it that night. In the end he bundled me off to the car, just as I was, without my cloak. We must have passed Puffin somewhere on the road.

Maurice left me in bed with another whisky and three aspirins, and then went back to Jesus.

CHAPTER VIII

1

WHEN Maurice got back about four in the morning I was sound asleep. I just muttered at him and went to sleep again. It was midday when the maid brought us tea and I woke up. Then I had to wake Maurice, and it was only after he'd had three cups that he was fit to talk. By this time I'd got all my senses back, and remembered everything, and I was wild to know the rest.

Maurice said if he wasn't allowed to sleep he'd get up, and did I call this a holiday, anyway?

"No one else will be up," I said.

"Puffin will, poor devil."

"When did he come back?"

"Lord knows. After we did."

"Did you bring Vera and Averil?"

"Yes."

"Did they know what had happened?"

"Vera did, of course. We told Averil you felt queer, and had gone home."

"Then it didn't get out?"

"Not far, anyway."

"Have they caught the murderer?"

"No."

"Any news of Lanham?"

"No."

"Give me a cigarette," I said, "and stop this staccato dialogue, and tell the story properly. We're not characters in an American novel. Who was that man, and how was he killed, and who killed him, and why, and how did you stop it getting out, and all the rest of it."

Maurice yawned. "You don't want much, do you? We don't know who the man was—yet. There was nothing in his pockets but some money, chewing-gum, a time-table, and a fully loaded automatic. He'd been shot twice—through the heart and lungs."

"There, in the court?"

"Presumably. Whoever shot him must have dragged him into those shrubs, and with all those people about he can't have been dragged far. He'd only been dead an hour or so."

"And no one heard the shots?"

"If they did, they can't have known they *were* shots. Remember the case of Cousin James."

"Gosh! I'd forgotten James. *Was* he shot at, too?"

"There was a bullet through that window. They found it in the wall of the room."

"Was it Lanham? It must have been, I suppose?"

"We don't know who it was."

"But why should he kill that other man?"

"We don't know that he did. It's only safe to assume that the same person fired all three shots. It would be too much to suppose that there were two assassins, each armed with a silencer, prowling about Jesus last night. Anyway, they'll know about that by now."

"How?"

"They'll have got the bullets out of your Yankee friend, and compared them with the one fired through the window."

"Well, tell me something you *do* know. Start at the beginning. When you and that tutor and Mr. Iliff went to see the body, leaving me stuck in the lodge with James. You never even told me that part."

"You'd had enough horrors then," Maurice said. "As a matter of fact, we had all our work cut out persuading Iliff to leave things alone for a bit—till the ball was over, anyway. He wanted to get all his men in—flashlight photographers and the rest of 'em—but I pointed out that with five or six hundred people there he'd have chaos in a quarter of an hour. And it would soon be daylight. One or two people we wanted to see we *could* see, on the quiet—and did. I don't suppose another twenty knew that anything was wrong, and they thought it was an accident or something——"

"Who did you want to see?"

"If I'm to start at the beginning, I'll start at the beginning. It was only possible to hush the business up because Jesus is such a whacking big place, with four courts and all those gardens and the cricket ground beyond. The darkness helped, and so did the authorities. On with the dance was their motto, and very naturally. Nearly everybody will be going down to-day, and the place will be empty. . . . So while I was running you back here Iliff and Devine and one or two others carried the body across to the cricket pavilion, well out of the way. They only met a few people, and Iliff spread the tale about an accident. It's bad form to be inquisitive, thank heaven. . . . In the meantime, the local constabulary had been filtering in unobtrusively, through the Master's garden, and so on, so as not to attract notice. A man was planted in the shrubbery, and others round about at strategic spots. Then Puffin turned up, tails and all, with his tie under his ear——"

"He *dressed?* Whatever for?"

"Because his wits worked quicker than Iliff's, though I did get him out of bed. I'd told him I'd try to keep things quiet, and why, and evening kit was the best disguise. He'd have to mix with the mob. Besides, people know him. . . ."

"Go on."

"That's about all."

"Nonsense. You were there for hours. Who did you put through it?"

"Oh, your friends the Armfeldts, among others."

"Heavens!" I said. "I'd forgotten them too."

"The deceased," said Maurice, "having inquired so tenderly after them, they were naturally in request."

"What did they say?"

"What you'd expect. Knew nothing about it."

"Did they actually *see* him?"

"Oh, yes. Puffin and I hunted 'em up. Separately. We found Armfeldt first and took him over to the pavilion. We didn't want to tell him we were confronting him with a corpse—that was the little surprise—and it was a bit difficult, talking airy nothings and parrying his questions. Of course he knew something was up, and by the time we got him there he was well on his guard. Puzzled but polite, and with a mask on."

"Yes, I know," I said. "He put it on when I told him about the man. Well?"

Maurice frowned. "I don't know. . . . He didn't turn a hair. Just looked blank and said he'd never seen the man before. But if he had, he'd had plenty of time to put two and two together. If he'd been more natural, or even a bit startled, I'd be more ready to believe him. He's hiding something."

"That's what I thought. And Mrs. Armfeldt?"

"Mrs. Armfeldt," Maurice said, with a smile, "was Mrs. Armfeldt. Herself, in fact. I went across to fetch her while they kept her bright boy in play."

"I wonder she came at all."

"You don't do justice to my charm of manner. As a matter of fact, I told her her son was with the police, and had asked me to bring her along to clear up a little misunderstanding. That fetched her all right."

"It would fetch any mother," I said. "You've got some nerve. And to look at you—especially now, with your hair on end—anyone would think you without guile, and rather soft."

Maurice tried to smooth his hair down and went on:

"She gave me a look when I mentioned the police, as if she'd heard the name somewhere. But all she said was, 'Has zat bad boy been drinking too much?' Which was nonsense, because he was dead sober, and she must have seen him not long before. Anyway, she came like a lamb—or rather, like a duchess, sailing along and prattling about the pretty lights. But her brain was working hard all the time, because she never even asked me what *had* happened. She's as clever as that son of hers, or cleverer, and she knew I wouldn't tell her. But again it wasn't natural."

"And did you make *her* look at the body?"

"I handed her over to Puffin, and watched through the door."

"Poor Puffin!"

"Yes, he was a bit taken aback. He hadn't met her before. But he needn't have worried. She just put up that lorgnette of hers, and said, 'Who is zis?' as if it was something the cat had brought in. Then she tumbled to it—I told you she's quick—and asked coolly if it *was your* friend."

"I like that—from her!"

"Oh, she said it quite nicely. Then she wanted to know where her son was. He was in the next room, among the lockers and cricket gear, and Iliff fetched him in. She fixed him with a stern eye and said, 'Paul, do you know zis man?' And Paul said meekly, 'No, mother.' It was as good as a play."

"If confronting people with corpses at one in the morning is your idea of a play——"

"It's the right word," Maurice said. "Whether either of them recognised the man I still don't know. Even Iliff, with thirty years' experience of this sort of thing, can't make up his mind. But both of them were afraid of something, and it wasn't the first time they'd been in a fix. They were altogether too calm about it. And Mrs. Armfeldt, at any rate, is a first-class actress. I don't even know whether that accent's genuine."

"Oh, I think it is," I said. "They're not English. You've only got to look at them."

"You may be right. Anyway, they've got us puzzled."

"What did you do with them in the end?"

"Oh, let them go. . . ."

"And they didn't complain? You seem to have been carrying things with a rather high hand."

"It was a case of striking while the iron was hot. . . . No, they had no complaints."

"Wasn't that odd? I don't somehow see Mrs. Armfeldt taking your irregular methods lying down."

"Unless she had cause to. Yes, the point was noted too. She did remark, by the way, that they weren't the only people at the ball who knew Chicago."

"Meaning Mr. Devine, of course. Where was he while all this was going on?"

"Mostly with Cousin James, I believe. I'd suggested before I left with you that he might be detailed to see that Tullis didn't talk—and *vice versa.*"

"How cunning of you," I said. "But what's going to be done about the Armfeldts?"

"Oh, they won't be allowed to run away. Scotland Yard's looking up their careers in this country, and by now the Chicago police will have had a cable asking for news of them on that side. Also about the unknown deceased, and on general principles about the Devines too. With an addendum suggested by myself."

"What was that?"

Maurice began to get out of bed. He sat on the edge and lit a cigarette.

"It's the Lanham case. This bayonet business started a notion in my mind at the beginning, but I couldn't track it down. Then we met Devine yesterday, and he talked about squaring accounts with bayonets, and I remembered. Association of ideas. He's been in the States, and not long ago a bayonet was used in some gang murder, or murders, there. It was reported in the papers here, and it stuck in my memory."

"It would. But was Lanham ever in the States? And how could he be mixed up with a gang, anyway?"

"Ask me another—to both questions. But with all this transatlantic atmosphere, on top of bayonet work, I suggested inquiries."

"If they come to anything," I said, "I suppose it will be a sort of silver lining to your morbid passion for police news, home and foreign. . . . But seriously, Maurice, where *does* this last horrible affair come in? It can't really have any connexion with the other murders, can it?"

"The only tangible one is the shot at Cousin James."

"Oh, that must have been a mistake. Or anyone might take a pot at James. Lanham, anyway, doesn't use a pistol."

"There's no rule against his using one. If he was in evening dress he'd find a bayonet a deuced awkward thing to wear. He wouldn't dare to bring his sword-stick—if he has one. A silencer, of course, makes any pistol bulky, but

125

it could have been smuggled in, say in an overcoat pocket, done up in brown paper, to be fetched from the cloak-room when wanted. Iliff's looking into that."

"But how would Lanham get *in*? He couldn't have a ticket for the ball. And all Cambridge is looking for him."

"If his disguise is good enough he could have walked in earlier in the day and hidden himself somewhere. But Iliff's got a better idea than that."

"What is it?"

Maurice was getting into his dressing-gown.

"Aren't you going to get up?" he said. "Or don't you want any lunch. . .? Iliff's notion is that Lanham's been hiding in Jesus all the time. It's an enormous place, and half-empty now. Term's over, and only the fellows staying on for the ball, or doing extra work, or both, like young Ince, are still up. Lanham, at any rate, must know the college fairly well. Apparently his best friend in the old days was Ince's father, his fellow Shiner, who was also at Jesus."

"Yes," I said, "that *is* an idea. It would account for a lot. Or he may be in some other college. They must be all full of odd rooms and attics. What about King's? He'd know that inside out."

"It doesn't lend itself so well as some of the others. But Iliff's thinking now of combing the lot, starting with Jesus."

"He's got his work cut out. But how would Lanham get in at night? After he'd killed Sir Vyvyan, for instance? Wouldn't the gates be shut then, even in May Week?"

"He may have waited till they were opened. But there are other ways and means. Witness the Alpine Club."

"What's that?"

"A set of young lunatics who climb about over college roofs, and so on, and specialise in getting out of bounds by unorthodox routes. Lanham may have used some of 'em in his time. Remember he mountaineered a bit. Unlike his dinner club, this one's a hardy annual."

"He's middle-aged now," I objected.

"So are lots of genuine Alpine fanatics."

Maurice had collected his sponge and towel and wandered to the door.

"Talking of that," I said, "how did that American get in last night? They'd never have let *him* through the gate."

"Alpine methods, too, probably. He found out where the real Armfeldts were staying, and where they were going in the evening. They'd been away all day, and it was his first chance. A good one, too—much better than holding them up in the street, with the police, for all he knew, looking out for him——"

"Were they?"

"Not very earnestly. They've got their hands full with other things. . . . Well, he could get into Jesus over the railings along the Common. He could choose his time, after dark, and we can assume he'd done a bit of climbing too. He'd have had a job at most of the colleges, but Jesus is admirably situated for that sort of game. Once inside, he could go anywhere. Everything was thrown open, and the place was full of caterers' men and what not. . . . Now I'm going to have my bath."

He went off to have it. Twenty minutes later, when I'd had mine—I rushed it, against the habits of a lifetime—the discussion was resumed. I wanted to hear the official theory of the last murder.

Maurice was putting on his collar. "There are three," he said. "You pays your money and takes your choice. One: Lanham was hanging about, waiting for a chance to take a pot at Tullis. He fired from the shrubbery, and then found the American tough hiding there too, so he removed an awkward witness by putting two more bullets into him. Objections to this: *(a)* the doctor says the man had been dead at least an hour when we found him about twelve-thirty, and *(b)* the man's own automatic, unused, was in his hip pocket. It wouldn't have stayed there long after Lanham crawled in beside him and blazed away."

"No, I don't call that a good theory," I said. "If there were three shots, someone must have heard *something*. And James only heard one."

"Oh, he was running away. And three shots *were* fired. But not necessarily together, or recognisable as shots. However, I agree with you. It didn't happen like that."

"What's the next theory?"

"The man was shot by Armfeldt, not knowing who Armfeldt was. Hence the automatic still in his pocket. They bumped into one another, or he asked Armfeldt the way or something, and the immaculate Paul recognised him from your description, or guessed who he was. His language would give him away at once. There couldn't be two of his type in Jesus last night."

"That isn't very convincing either," I said. "He *must* have known the Armfeldts. He'd come four thousand miles to find them."

"It was dark. And when I said Paul, I meant either. Did he know *Mrs.* Armfeldt? From your account he mistook Mrs. Devine for her."

I stared at Maurice. "You mean *she* may have shot him?"

"It's an alternative. I should say she has more nerve and quicker wits than her son."

127

"Good heavens. . . ! Of course, she could stuff half a dozen silencers under that skirt. But on this theory, what about the shot at James?"

"Oh, that would still be Lanham."

"He was there too?"

"Devine thought he saw him, remember—and just after."

"Yes, I'd forgotten that. So much happened. . . . How frightfully complicated! And to make things worse, my boy friend, or his mother, or both, dragged the body into the very bushes where Lanham happened to hide later. I say, Maurice, isn't that too much of a coincidence?"

Maurice had begun to fuss with his tie.

"Oh, quite," he said. " I'm only telling you. I'm pretty sure it didn't happen like that either."

"Well, give me a chance with the mirror, if you want me to get any lunch, and tell me theory number three."

He removed himself reluctantly—he's very faddy about the set of his ties— and tried to see what he was doing over my shoulder.

" Number three would be the most rational of the lot," he said, "if it wasn't for the doctor's evidence. And it explains the silencer business. I can't and won't believe there were *two*. As your James says, they're not much used in this country, and not easy to get. . . . Anyway, the idea is that *three* shots were fired at the man in or near the shrubbery, one missing him and nearly hitting Tullis. If it was the first, Tullis, thinking of his skin and busy ducking into doorways, mightn't hear the other two. You remember he said there was no one near him just then? He meant on the paths, of course. He wouldn't see a couple on the turf, behind the bushes."

"But someone else might have seen them. It sounds fearfully risky."

"However the man was shot, it was risky. Appallingly risky. Whoever shot him must have had very urgent reasons. It couldn't wait."

"Well, it sounds a much simpler theory than the others," I agreed. "What about the doctor?"

"He was a cocksure young man. One of the guests. I haven't heard what the police-surgeon says."

"The idea, of course, is that Armfeldt did the shooting? Or Mrs. Armfeldt. Though that seems too fantastic——"

"The female of the species . . . But we'll say one of them. Forgetting the doctor, and putting all three shots at twelve-thirty, where were they then?"

"I don't know. They went down from supper some time before we did."

"Having been under our eye in the Hall for at least three-quarters of an hour—say from eleven-thirty to twelve-fifteen."

"And before that. You hauled me out after them during the interval before the supper dance. We found them *with* Miss Farleigh and the other man, and we all went in together, and met Mr. Devine."

Maurice frowned. "Yes, and they hadn't been out long. Five minutes, perhaps. I saw them go. Was that time enough? Hardly. And they were cool enough when we found them in the court. *And* that other pair were with them. . . . Damn! It would fit in with the doctor and everything if they could have done it then, about eleven-fifteen."

"By the way," I said, "they weren't searched, I suppose?"

He grinned. "Lord, no! Puffin couldn't take a high hand, if he'd wanted to. There wasn't enough against them. And can't you see him asking Madame Armfeldt if she'd mind being searched. Iliff might have had the nerve, but he knew there'd be no weapon on either of them then. As soon as there was a spot of light he started a hunt for it by having the flower-beds dug over, and as I came away the welkin was ringing with roars of anguish from the head gardener. . . ."

Just then something else rang—the luncheon-gong. I made a hasty finish and we went down.

2

Vera and Puffin were alone. Averil, at the end of a hectic week—socially, I mean, and she was going to a private dance that night—was putting in more and more time in bed. She hadn't any idea yet how hectic last night had been.

Vera looked white and strained, and Puffin declared he was a wreck. He hadn't got to his own bed till nearly five, and he said he wasn't going to leave home again till he'd sandwiched in another nap before tea. So far there was no more important news. The police-surgeon agreed with the other doctor that the man in the shrubbery had been killed about eleven o'clock, or soon after. There'd been no reply yet from Chicago, or even from Scotland Yard. The Armfeldts were in their hotel. The pistol was still missing, and so was Lanham. Old and New Chesterton had been combed for him in vain. Puffin was now becoming resigned again to his guilt—of all three murders—and was talking seriously of calling in the Yard to take over everything. This multiplication of violent crime was getting him down, besides raising a fearful hullabaloo in Cambridge, where he was between Scylla and the other thing—the Town complaining that the tourist season would be ruined (I should have thought myself that a few murders were a draw), and wanting to know why something wasn't done about it, while the attitude of

129

the university authorities to the police (so Puffin said) was still that summed up in a song lately popular—"Anywhere else you can do that there, but you can't do that there 'ere." Someone, too, had coined a *bon mot,* "A murder a day keeps the doctor away," which was enjoying considerable success. In other circumstances Puffin would have thought it intensely funny, but it didn't appeal to his sense of humour just then.

Lunch was nearly over, and food and drink had restored us all a little, when the telephone went in the hall. Puffin swore. But the call was for Maurice.

When he came back he said:

"That was Miss Mary Lanham."

"Wanting *you?*" Puffin asked.

"Yes. She wants me to go and see her this afternoon. Any objections?"

"None at all, my dear fellow. You have my blessing. Perhaps you can get something out of the girl, and save me seeing her at all. I'm still putting it off. Iliff's seen her again, and by his account she's a snorter. . . . Well, well! So your reputation *does* exist, Maurice. What's the betting she hopes you'll do us in the eye, and rehab—ab—whatever it is, her papa? Good luck to you. I can't say fairer than that."

Maurice looked at me.

"Care to come along, Myra? When pain and anguish wring the brow you may be a help. And you know your own sex better than I do, even now. You're quicker at telling when they're lying."

I told them they were both treating a tragic case with objectionable levity. But I admit I was quite willing to go. I was curious to see Miss Lanham, as well as sorry for her, though I pointed out that it was doubtful if she was equally curious to see me. Maurice said if I liked I could pass as the indispensable mug who trots round with every amateur detective.

We took the Nugents' second-best car. Near Fen Ditton we met a motor-cyclist whom I recognised as he flashed past as Harry Devine. I think he saw us at the same moment, for when I looked over my shoulder he was looking back too. I wondered what time *he* had got to bed.

It was nearly three when we reached Newnham. Many of the students had gone down, and the buildings had a deserted, holiday air. A very obvious policeman in plain clothes, planted in the porter's box, looked at us curiously when Maurice asked for Miss Lanham and gave his name. The man would know this, of course, but though policemen's faces seem to be constructed so as to give as little as possible away, I thought there was more than mere interest in that look. And the porter, who was in his undress uniform, a baize apron, to show that vacation was icumin' in, appeared rather agog. I wondered if something fresh had happened.

A maid led us out of the Pfeiffer Building along a corridor to Sidgwick Hall, where Mary Lanham roomed. To one not educationally minded, there is something rather awful about the very names of these seminaries. How different, one feels, from us, Miss Sidgwick and Mrs. Pfeiffer. We were taken upstairs to a door on the first floor. The maid knocked, and a sharp voice said, "Come in."

I'd made up my mind what Wilfrid Lanham's daughter ought to look like, and I was entirely wrong. Instead of a tragic, distraught creature, we saw a self-possessed girl of the school-marm type. She was small and plain—an insignificant little thing, as Claudia Farleigh had said. Her complexion was muddy, her dark, frizzy hair unbecomingly dressed, and she had round, staring, pale grey eyes, magnified by enormous spectacles. Her clothes were good, but she had no sense of dress whatever. "Prig" was written all over her.

Her stare was on me as she shook hands with Maurice, who explained untruthfully that I always came to hold his hand on these occasions.

"We must have our Watsons and Van Dines," he said.

This humour passed completely over Miss Lanham. I was sure she had never read a detective story in her life—or anything but instructive literature. She gave me the stare and a limp hand—I loathe limp hands—and said casually:

"Well, I don't mind. Do sit down."

Her voice was commonplace—thin and rather acid, like her peaky features. We found chairs. I was then ignored (the fate of all Watsons, Van Dines and similar mugs), and the stare was fastened on Maurice again. The girl began on him at once, as if she was reading him a lecture.

"I want you to help me, Major Hemyock. I never read the police news as a rule, of course, but I have to see what the papers are saying about all this, and they've mentioned your name, and had a lot about your other cases. And Mr. Devine has spoken about you too."

Maurice murmured something about his blushes, and added: "How can I help you, Miss Lanham?"

"By showing the police, of course, what an idiotic mistake they're making. While they're wasting time looking for my father, the murderer is doing just what he likes."

"I have every sympathy with you," Maurice said, "but I can't teach the police their duty. I'm only an outsider who happens to be staying with the

Chief Constable. You're not a fool, Miss Lanham. You must see that the best thing for your father to do, if he is innocent, is to show himself."

"Of course he's innocent," the girl said sharply. "And he *has* shown himself," she added, with a little air of triumph.

"Oh?" said Maurice. "I hadn't heard of it."

"He telephoned to me, not half an hour ago."

This *was* news. It accounted for the subdued excitement in the porter's box, where the policeman was planted to tap any telephone message to Mary Lanham.

Maurice took out his eyeglass and screwed it in again.

"Indeed?" he said thoughtfully. "Where did he telephone from, and what did he say?"

"I don't know where he was. He just said he was all right, and that I wasn't to worry, and rang off."

"You're sure it was your father?"

"Of course it was."

"You recognised his voice?"

"Of course I did." (The words "of course" were in permanent type on Miss Lanham's lips.)

"And that was all he said?"

I found myself murmuring, "Of course it was," but this time she changed the refrain.

"Just what I told you," she said.

"Not a word of explanation?"

"No. I was asking him where he was and what had happened to him when he rang off."

"Anyone," Maurice said, "might pretend he was your father. As a practical joke, for instance. There are plenty of people, I'm sorry to say, who will do that sort of thing. That's why I want you to be quite sure about the voice—*and* the words. What exactly *did* he say?'"

"He said," Miss Lanham replied patiently, as if she was addressing a backward school-child, " 'Is that you, Popsy? Father speaking.' And I said, 'Good gracious, father, where *have* you been?' or something like that. Then he said, 'I'm all right. Don't worry,' and rang off."

"H'm," said Maurice, while I was trying to visualise our hostess as Popsy. "You couldn't tell, I suppose, whether he was speaking from near at hand or some distance away? Trunk calls are sometimes difficult to catch."

"His voice was rather faint."

"Not many people, I dare say, know he calls you by that name?"

"Of course not."

"You think it excludes the idea of a practical joke?"

"Of course it does. I *know* it was father. Who else could it have been?"

"Echo answers 'who'. . . ? It's a pity Mr. Lanham wasn't slightly more communicative."

"He'd guess there'd be a policeman sitting at the telephone. He only wanted to ease my mind."

"He'd have eased it more satisfactorily by turning up in person," Maurice said. "Have you any idea, Miss Lanham, why he should be hiding himself in this way?"

Mary Lanham leaned forward. "*I* think," she said, "he's trying to track down the murderer."

I revised my ideas about her literary pabulum. This sounded exactly like something out of a book, and not a very instructive one. Maurice didn't seem to think highly of the notion, either.

"What you mean," he said, "is that you *don't* know of any real reason for his disappearing just now?"

"Or at any time. Only what I said," Miss Lanham hastened to explain away, at her father's expense, her lapse into sensationalism. "Father's incurably old-fashioned. He's a romantic—the last of them, I should hope. He was always doing silly, theatrical things when he was younger."

"But lately, I understand, he's had rather too many worries to leave him much inclination for drama."

"He's been abominably treated, if that's what *you* mean," the girl said viciously. Her large round glasses gleamed. "Both of us have. I've no pity whatever for that odious Sir Vyvyan. *Sir* Vyvyan, indeed! He ought to have been in jail, instead of in Debrett! Stealing our money. . . ."

" If you're referring to the trust fund, Miss Lanham, he hasn't had the use of it," Maurice objected. "Nor, I gather, the need."

"How do you know? It all comes to the same thing, anyway."

"But you will get your share when you graduate."

"I ought to have had it long ago. If I hadn't slaved and slaved I shouldn't be here. And now all this has come to upset me when I want to be working. As if my whole life hadn't been cramped and spoiled already, just because a pack of thieves wouldn't let us have back the money father put in in the beginning—his *own* money—*our* money——"

Her sharp little voice was rising. Her eyes glittered behind the glasses, and her cheeks were flushed. When she began I felt sorry for her again, but as the shrill voice went on, dwelling only on her own grievances, though she put my very thoughts into words, sympathy dwindled. I remembered Superintendent Iliff's account of his first meeting with Miss Lanham. He was right. She had a nasty temper, and what mattered most to her, now or at any time, was Mary Lanham.

Maurice broke in, rather curtly:

"Well, we're getting off the point. You still want me to help you?"

"Of course I do." She was a little breathless, and white now with anger, except for the red spots on her cheeks.

"The only way I can do it, remember, is by trying to find out the truth."

"Well?"

"Can I ask you some questions?"

"Of course. Go on."

Maurice took out his eyeglass and began to polish it.

"Was your father ever in the United States?" he asked.

She looked surprised. " No, never," she said.

"When did you see him last?"

"At Easter. I was home for the vacation."

"Did he talk then of coming here for May Week?"

"He never talked of coming *here*." Miss Lanham was at pains to be precise. "He talked of coming to stay with our friends the Devines at Horningsea. He never wanted to see more of Cambridge than he could help, and you can't wonder——"

"This second visit to the Devines was his suggestion?"

"I don't know what you mean. They invited him, I suppose, like they did before."

"When did he come the first time?"

"In March. But he only had a week-end then, of course."

"Had he any reason for choosing May Week for this visit?"

The girl gave a bitter little laugh. "Choice didn't come into it. You forget that my father is now an employee. He has to take his holidays when he is graciously permitted, not when he *wants* to. Of course, he wouldn't have *chosen* May Week, with all this foolery going on, and all the people we detest here too—the Hoggs, and that toady Tullis——"

"What I'm getting at," said Maurice, avoiding my eye, "is that this visit was fixed some time ago. Your father couldn't change his mind, and come earlier or later."

"That's what I'm telling you. It was arranged early in the spring. As a *great* favour, so that we could go away together later, he was allowed to take his fortnight in two parts—a week now and a week in September. So kind of them. And a whole fortnight, too! Aren't some firms generous? Of course, to a man who's had a big business of his own, and has been accustomed to going away for *months* to the Riviera or Scotland or anywhere, without thinking of expense, it seems just a *little* niggardly——"

Maurice said, patiently but firmly, "With term over, Miss Lanham, and your father having a natural prejudice against Cambridge at this festive time, I rather wonder you didn't go away somewhere together now."

"Beggars can't be choosers," the girl snapped. "I can't go away at present. I'm working—or I'm supposed to be. I'm staying up for a few weeks to get in some vacation courses and lectures. At least I *was*. I don't know if they'll let me now. And my father wanted to see *something* of me. When I'm at home *he's* working all day, and anyway, in that pokey little flat . . ."

She was well away again with her grievances. Being a mere spectator, I was putting in the time looking round her room. It was a pleasant, light room, with a big window facing an inner garden across which was another red-brick Hall named after some depressing feminine educationalist. In one corner a screen concealed a bed. There were a lot of books, and everything was dreadfully tidy, but at the same time it was fussy. There were far too many knick-knacks, and the walls were hung all over with prints and photographs and little sketches of landscape, cottages, and so on in water-colour and pen-and-ink.

Maurice, I noticed, cast more than one speculative glance at these—to my untutored eye they looked very amateurish—and when he stemmed the flood again it was by switching on a new topic connected with a more macabre style of art.

"To return to our muttons, Miss Lanham, you've heard about these drawings found on Sir Vyvyan and his son?"

Her mind still on her own ill treatment, she said automatically, "Of course I have."

"You know they are drawn on notepaper similar to that used by your father?"

"Harry—Mr. Devine—told me so. I wondered why that fool of a Superintendent went off with a note father wrote me. For that matter, I use that paper myself when I'm at home. It's common and cheap, like everything else we have to use now. . . ."

I thought this new grouse was rather hastily whipped up, and for the first time she began to fidget, twisting her fingers together.

"All the same," Maurice said, "it's a curious coincidence it should be used for these drawings."

"Of, of course, if that's what you think——"

He checked her again. "Do be patient. I was merely making a statement of fact. It *is* a curious coincidence. Too curious to be true."

"I don't know what you mean."

"I'll put it another way. Quite a lot of people must know that your father uses this paper. His friends, and yours, for instance."

"I suppose so, if they notice that sort of thing."

"Has he used it for long?"

"Oh, yes, for years and years."

"Is your address on it?"

"We haven't got a die. We don't go in for luxuries. We use one of those little stamping machines at home."

But she was looking less belligerent now, and watching him closely.

"Anyone," he went on, "could buy a pad of the paper?"

"Of course. We always get ours at the same shop, but most big stationers sell it."

"Among the people connected with this case, who would know that you use it?"

She stopped to think. "What do you mean by 'connected'?" she said. "That brute Hogg knew, of course. Father wrote to him a lot at one time. His wife would know, and his son, I dare say. He may have shown the letters to people. His dear friend Tullis saw some of them, I expect, and laughed over them with him. And the other humbug, the third trustee—the bank manager here, Blewitt. And that man Mercer may have seen them. He knew father and the rest in the old days, and Hogg seems to have been thick with him, and I'm sure he'd enjoy the joke too——"

"Your friends the Devines have seen the paper, of course?"

She stopped, stared, and repeated, "Of course," twisting her fingers and frowning.

"There was a man named Farleigh," Maurice said. "A trustee at one time. Do you know his daughter?"

"I don't *know* her. I've seen her once. A stuck-up cat. She called in my first term and tried to be patronizing——"

"You have never written to her?"

"Of course not."

"Or Mr. Lanham?"

"I'm sure he never did. Why should he? He may have written to her father, but that would be a long time ago. . . . Oh!"

"Well?"

136

"I've just remembered something. I don't see that it helps, but you asked about anyone *connected.* . . . That girl's engaged to a man called Armfeldt."

"My wife and I have met him," Maurice said.

She remembered my existence and gave me glimpse of the stare.

"Mr. Devine has met him too," she said to Maurice. "Anyway, about a month ago he called to see father."

"Oh, did he?"

"Yes. It was one evening. Father was out, and I was here, of course. Our woman was in the flat, getting father's dinner, and Mr. Armfeldt asked if he could come in and write a note. She let him, and, of course, he must have used our notepaper. You were asking about people who knew——"

"What had Mr. Armfeldt come about?"

Miss Lanham sniffed. "More condescension!" she said scornfully. "Father told me about it in his next letter. He's with Drew's, the oil and colour firm, you know. Lanham's, our old business, was the same, of course, but much bigger. Before the Japanese and the Germans got into the market, it was———"

Maurice said patiently: "We're talking about Mr. Armfeldt."

"Oh, yes. . . . Well, he's a house decorator or something, and he said in his note that he'd heard of us from his precious Claudia Farleigh, and thought perhaps he could put something in father's way. The impertinence of it! As if father was a commercial traveller, touting for business. He may be only a subordinate now, but he has a *little* pride left——"

"What did he do, Miss Lanham?"

"Told Mr. Armfeldt off, he said."

"By letter?"

"Of course."

"He didn't see him?"

"Certainly not."

"He hasn't heard from him again?"

"Not that I know of."

"Are you on the 'phone at your flat?"

She looked surprised. "No," she said.

Maurice began to polish his eyeglass again. When he'd got it to his liking, he took another look at the sketches on the walls. Mary Lanham watched him impatiently.

He turned to her again. "Have you heard what happened at the Jesus ball last night?"

"No," she said. "I'm not interested in balls."

"It wasn't in the morning papers, but news of it must have got here by now."

"Well, I haven't heard anything. I don't see any more people than I can help. What *did* happen?"

"There was another murder."

This shook her. Her hands began to work together again.

"Not—not another of the——"

"No. An American."

"An *American*? So that's why you asked. . . ."

"And someone apparently took a shot at Mr. Tullis."

Her eyes were enormous behind the spectacles. Then she asked: "Was he hurt?"

"No."

Miss Lanham laughed. "What a pity. . . ." Then she frowned. "I don't believe it," she said.

"I'm not romancing, Miss Lanham."

"Oh, I don't mean about this American, whoever he was. That can't be anything to do with *us*— father and me—thank goodness. But James Tullis. . .! Did anyone see him shot at?"

"No."

" I thought not. You said 'apparently.' I guessed there was something fishy about it." Her spectacles flashed as she leaned forward, her face flushed and vicious. "Do you know what *I* think, Major Hemyock?"

"I shall be interested to hear."

"If that hypocritical Scotsman *was* shot at, he fired the shot himself, to draw you all off the trail. Pretended it was father, I suppose! The brute! I've wondered about him all along, and I'm sure now. Where was he when Sir Vyvyan was murdered? Not at Trinity. He'd just walked to the hotel and back, hadn't he? But he took a long time about it. Have the police asked him where he was the *next* morning, when the boy was killed? If not, they'd better!"

She spat all this out with extraordinary venom. Maurice took a look at me, but I lay low. I was quite interested in the theory too, and, having seen James after the incident, could be amused by it. If Miss Lanham had heard that he was a connexion of mine—and it might have got round to her through Harry Devine—she'd forgotten about it. Not that a consideration of that sort would have stopped her, of course.

"Well, well," Maurice said mildly. "Putting other things aside, Miss Lanham, why should Mr. Tullis commit these crimes?"

"That's for the police to find out," she snapped. "Have they asked about his dealings with Rowsell- Hogg & Co. ? Or why he was so anxious to see Sir Vyvyan that night? He's a stockbroker, too, isn't he? And they were hand in glove at one time. Thick as thieves would be a better way to put it. And I know they've quarrelled before now—father heard that somewhere—and probably his fellow thief let him down, and serve him right too. It will serve them both right when he's hanged for murdering the other——"

At this new flare up Maurice said, not so mildly: "You're not helping by throwing wild accusations about. If you've any facts to offer—about *anybody*—let me have them. They won't go further unless I see cause. But this sort of thing is wasting time."

She stared at him sulkily. "You're all the same," she said. "Facts! Well, here's one. There's another thousand pounds or more coming to James Tullis now. The Hogg boy's share of the fund will be divided up among us."

"You mean it will come to young Tullis. Which," Maurice added dryly, "is equally incriminating for all of you. Besides, where does the murder of Sir Vyvyan come in?"

"Oh, that was a quarrel, as I said, over business. Perhaps it suggested the other."

Maurice shook his head. "You're ingenious, Miss Lanham, but you must do better than that."

She was still sullen. "It's for *you* to do something, if you really want to help. I've told you what I think, and I've thought of nothing else for the last three days——"

"Yes, I know. You've had a rotten time. That's why I'm here. But we must do our thinking tidily. Your idea about the fund *is* a fact, at any rate, and though I don't see yet that it leads anywhere, we'll file it. Have you any more?"

"Not what you'd call *facts.*"Her tone was scornful, but she was calming down. She paused, her forehead puckered over the round glasses. "Though there's this, too. . . . Have you or the police thought about that man Mercer?"

"I haven't—seriously."

"No, he's a don. Almost as respectable as a stockbroker. But he was the last person to see Sir Vyvyan alive, except the murderer. And he knew beforehand about that visit to Queens'."

"And the motive?" Maurice asked.

"How do I know? Perhaps he's been swindled, too. He's another old friend. He and Tullis may have been in it together."

"Well, we're accumulating suspects," Maurice said lightly. He caught my eye, and got up from his chair. "And you've given me something to think about, Miss Lanham, if that's any consolation to you."

He strolled away to look at some of the sketches hanging on the wall. The girl stared at his back. I rose too, and then she got up herself.

Maurice said, over his shoulder: "Are any of these your work?"

"Some of them," she said indifferently.

"This one?"

"No; father did that."

"Ah, yes." Maurice gave his eyeglass a screw and peered through it at a pen-and-ink sketch of some cottages. "I remember—he used to draw. And this? I like this."

He'd turned to another pen drawing. I looked at it too, but I couldn't see anything particularly striking about it. It was a drawing of some lock gates, with an old man standing on them. Mary Lanham was plainly rather irritated by this sudden interest in trifles.

"No," she said shortly. "That's one of Mr. Devine's."

"Oh, he draws too?"

"A little." She was fidgeting impatiently with her hands.

"And this thing in pencil?"

"That's mine."

"Do you ever use a pen?"

"I've tried. I like water-colours best."

Maurice went on calmly examining the picture gallery, while we stood by. Then he turned to the girl again.

"I'd like to borrow three or four of these sketches, if I may," he said.

"*Borrow* them?"

"Yes. You shall have them back in a day or two. I'd like this one of your father's, and this—it's his too, isn't it?—and this of Mr. Devine's. And can you put your hand on a pen-and-ink drawing of your own anywhere? This pencil one would do, perhaps, but I'd prefer pen work."

"Whatever do you want them for?"

"A little experiment." He was coolly taking the sketches off their nails. "Do try to find me one of your own, Miss Lanham."

She looked puzzled and exasperated. It wasn't often anyone dared to be so free with her possessions, and if Maurice had been younger, or a woman, he wouldn't have got away with it as easily as he did. But he was a new type to her, and for all her precocious airs she was only nineteen. After staring at him for a moment, she shrugged and went to a drawer of her desk, where she rummaged impatiently, finally fishing out a small drawing on a piece of cardboard.

"There's this. . . ."

At any rate I was able to recognise the subject at a glance—which is more than can be said for Surrealism, for instance. It was the Devines' cottage at Horningsea. Maurice appeared to compare it with his other loot, which he'd laid out on the table.

"That'll do nicely," he said. He stacked the four sketches together, put them under his arm, and collected his hat and gloves. "Come on, Myra. Time we were moving. . . ."

He bustled me off, giving Mary Lanham no chance to ask any more questions. She was staring at him with the same puzzled look through her round spectacles as she saw us out. She ignored me to the end. She'd classified me at once, Maurice said, as a social butterfly. I hadn't uttered a word except "How do you do" and "Good-bye"—a common experience for Watsons and Van Dines, but a most unusual one for me.

I made up for it as soon as we got into Sidgwick Avenue. (The higher education of women has blighted even the streets round Newnham.)

"Why on earth," I asked, "are you going off with those things?"

"For an experiment, as I told her." Maurice began to put his precious drawings on the back seat of the car. Withdrawing his head, he added: "And we're going to try to borrow one or two more presently."

"Who from this time? A secondary school drawing-class?"

"No. Mr. St. Clair Mercer. Hop in. I want to go to the police station first."

"What I need," I said, "is tea. That girl leaves one with a dry feeling in the mouth." Here, not being used to the eccentricities of the car, Maurice started off with a jolt. When I'd recovered myself and put my hat straight, I went on: "Look here, Maurice, I don't like her, but why did you let her go on, raising false hopes by listening to all that rubbish about James Tullis and the rest of it?"

"I hadn't much option, had I? And it did her good to get it out. By the way, how do you feel about your James?"

"How do I feel about him?"

"Have you got a weak spot for him?"

"Good heavens, no. I only stick him because of Ian. Why?"

"Oh, ' because,' as we used to say. Anyhow, we got some suggestive information, one way and another."

"Do you mean about *James?* Can you *see* him. . . ? Now that story about Paul Armfeldt *was* rather odd. He's never mentioned knowing anything about the Lanhams. And then her father's telephone message. Popsy, indeed! I don't want to be catty, but parental affection's a queer thing."

"Puffin's merry men will know all about that by now," Maurice said. "I hope it helps them. Mr. Lanham, incidentally, seems to have been thoroughly in character in his dealings with your friend Paul. By the by, Myra, did you notice her hands?"

"Miss Lanham's? They were nothing to write home about. Thick fingers——"

" She wasn't wearing any rings."

"Why should she?"

But Maurice enjoys being cryptic, even with me, at times, and he pretended to be busy with the traffic in Silver Street.

Not being drunk and disorderly, I knew I should be parked with the car outside the police station, so I got him to drop me at the 'University Arms' for tea while he got his business over. I made him promise to make it snappy. It was early-closing day, and I didn't want to be marooned in the lounge for hours with nothing to do. When he left me it was about four o'clock.

CHAPTER IX

1

THE first people I saw in the lounge were the Armfeldts and Claudia Farleigh, with a party of bright young things. Mrs. Armfeldt was superb in magenta, with a little black straw *tricorne,* worn well over one eye, perched on the piles of her dark hair. I could see the lorgnette flourishing. They didn't see me, and being doubtful of the etiquette with suspected persons, I slipped by into the corner farthest from them.

As suspects, Paul and his mother seemed in first-rate form. I could hear her laughing and talking, obviously holding the stage as usual, and making the girls at her table—even the supercilious Claudia—look like something out of a cheap store. Her son was flashing his smile and the liquid glance about, apparently equally at ease. I looked in vain for anyone who might be a detective watching them. Most of the other men present were definitely parents, the Church predominating.

The liquid glance didn't miss much, in the feminine way at any rate, and presently it found me out in my corner. Paul Armfeldt got up and bowed, and Mrs. Armfeldt turned to stare through the lorgnette and then waved it, and every one else in the lounge stared too. It was like being recognised by the viceregal party at Simla.

Mr. Armfeldt came over in his graceful way. He was very beautiful in double-breasted grey suiting.

"*Alone,* Mrs. Hemyock?" he said, with just the right shade of incredulity.

I explained that I was waiting for Maurice.

"Shame on him!" said Mr. Armfeldt. "He doesn't deserve you. Won't you join us? My mother would be so pleased."

I was firm about this. He stroked his little dark moustache and looked liquidly at me.

"I wish I could join *you,*" he said. "But it's our party, and I have to make myself polite to those children."

"Does that term include Miss Farleigh?"

"Oh, she's growing up. Too fast, perhaps. But she'll get over that." His look conveyed that he and I understood these little facetiae at Miss Farleigh's expense. Then he said lightly: "My mother and I are celebrating, you know."

143

"A birthday, or something?" I asked politely.

"You might call it that. The birth of freedom. You know what happened at Jesus last night?" (I tried not to give away, even by a look, how much I knew about it.) "Well, that's all cleared up. So far as we're concerned, I mean. We're discharged without a stain on our characters. My mother is rather disappointed, really. She'd like to make a dramatic entry at the Old Bailey, if they'd let her spend a few weeks with her dressmaker first. However, as I tell her, cells are so uncomfortable, so it's all for the best."

"I'm glad to hear it," I said. " I didn't know. . . ."

I left it at that. The liquid glance was still on me, a little acutely, I thought.

"A queer business," Paul Armfeldt said thoughtfully. "You've heard who the man was?"

"Our mutual friend."

"Not *ours*. We've never seen him before."

"And that's all that matters, I suppose, from your point of view?"

"Well, I should say he was no loss to anyone. But my mother and I are naturally curious. The police won't say what they think, but they'll be making inquiries, and we should be interested to know what they find out about him."

"By way of my husband and me?"

"I wasn't going to put it quite so crudely, Mrs. Hemyock."

"No, you're never crude, are you, Mr. Armfeldt? Well, I'll put it to my husband. But I can't answer for him, of course."

"Naturally. Thank you so much. You are always kind. *And* you have a flair for dress, which is so much more important. Another charming frock. . . ."

After a few more compliments he went back to his party. A little later Maurice came in.

He spotted the Armfeldts, of course, and they saw him too, and more bows and waves of the lorgnette were exchanged.

"Our stock's going up," I said, as he joined me. "Try not to look self-conscious. Behave as if you're used to nods and becks from the *gratin*. By the way, they want to pump us."

"I thought they might."

"But they say they're cleared."

"It begins to look like it," Maurice said. "They've been busy. They've produced about twenty people to say they were never out of their sight for two hours before supper. On the doctors' evidence that seems to let them out. It's an unsatisfactory sort of alibi, of course—people don't really keep tabs on one another at a ball, and they aren't always looking at their watches—

but that cuts both ways, and at present Puffin's all for letting sleeping dogs lie."

"Has he fallen for Mrs. Armfeldt?"

"She's a bit overpowering to a modest chap like Puffin. And then one of the witnesses for the alibi is Miss Farleigh's godfather. He carries a lot of weight in Cambridge, and he's taken a high tone about it. Then again they haven't found the weapon, and the cloak-room idea's petered out—too many people went to them for things—so Puffin and Iliff are inclining now to theory number three, or some variation of it. Lanham ran into the man in the bushes or somewhere and polished him off, they don't quite know why, before he could get his own gun out. Then, an hour later, Lanham took a pot at James. It's too involved for me. However . . ." Maurice shrugged. "Soil's too dry for footprints, and there are only the marks where the fellow was dragged into the shrubs, that Devine and I spotted right away."

"Well, you said yourself it was difficult to believe in *two* murderers."

"I said two *silencers.*"

"But that man *asked* about the Armfeldts."

"Oh, obviously there's a lot we don't know yet. . . ."

The waiter came, and when I'd ordered more tea, and he'd gone again, I said:

"You've seen Puffin?"

"He's just come, rubbing his eyes."

"And what's the news?"

"That's what I was coming to. They've had a cable from Chicago, via the Yard. The Armfeldts left for England two years ago. Mrs. A. ran a dressmaking shop, a fashionable affair, which closed down in rather mysterious circumstances, apparently. The Chicago police say they've nothing against her, but sound as if they wish they had. They evidently suspect some underhand game. But it may only have been liquor. They can't say much in a cable. Details are following."

"And my beautiful Paul?"

"Helped his mother design frocks."

"He talks as if he knew a good deal about them. At any rate, he says nicer things about mine than you ever do. Where did they come from originally?"

"Russia. Refugees—or that's their story."

"What about Mr. Armfeldt senior? Or was he a prince or something?"

"Nothing known about him. Believed to be dead, in Russia."

"Such a convenient country," I said. "And what's their record over here?"

"Blameless, so far as the Metropolitan Police know. They seem to have brought some money away with them, because they took a biggish house with a studio on Campden Hill. Mrs. Armfeldt retired into private life, while your Paul launched out as a painter and decorator to the nobility and gentry with advanced ideas, and has done very well. The coteries think highly of him too, so he's made the best of both worlds."

"Yes, I forgot to tell you he's a Surrealist," I said.

Maurice's tea arriving, I looked across at the Armfeldts, and found them anticipating the compliment. Mrs. Armfeldt smiled graciously, and the Surrealist stroked his moustache.

"I bet they'd like to know what you're telling me," I said. "Go on. Any news of our mutual friend from the shrubbery?"

Maurice nodded. "Yes. We guessed correctly. He's from Chicago too. He's got some good identification marks on him—a scar down his back, a malformed toe, and one or two more—and the police there knew him as Bud M'Ginnis, among other things. He was a member of the Tonello gang."

"What were they?"

"Racketeers, apparently."

"What *are* racketeers? I never know."

"I understand they succeeded the bootleggers."

"Thanks so much. This is rather thrilling. We seem to have walked into an American novel."

"I should have thought," Maurice said, "we were providing enough home-grown produce for you. Be patriotic, and buy Empire thrills."

"You're very chirpy," I remarked.

"Give me some more tea. One of my long shots has found the mark. I told you I suggested a rider to Chicago about bayonet murders."

"Yes."

"The late Mr. M'Ginnis had a brother, also a member of the Tonello gang. Last autumn the Tonellos had a war on with another gang. One evening in October M'Ginnis's brother was found in his garage, pinned to the wall with a French bayonet. That's what I saw reported over here. I thought there was some rather *outré* feature about it, but I'd forgotten the details."

"*Outré* is the word," I said. "I congratulate you, anyway, on the silver lining. Go on."

"Our acquaintance, Bud, went about looking for his brother's murderer, and then disappeared. This was last month."

"He came over here then?"

"Presumably. The Yard know nothing about him, but they're looking into it."

"Do the Chicago police know who killed his brother?"

"Probably not, as they don't say so. But *he* may have known. It looks as if he knew something."

"But where does it fit in?" I asked. "The bayonet business, I mean. Has this M'Ginnis been going about killing people with one? And if so, why? Or did Lanham get the idea from the papers, like you? Or is it just a coincidence? And what about the Armfeldts? If they've been here for two years they can't be in it. And yet that man was trying to find them."

"You ought to give notice of these compound questions," Maurice said. "Anyway, I haven't finished yet. The cable had news about the Devines, too. Or rather no news, which was odder."

"It must have been a very long cable."

"It was. You can have a lot of fun at the taxpayers' expense. I told you Puffin asked about the Devines, just to cover the ground thoroughly, and because they'd been in Chicago too. But they're not known there—at any rate under that name."

"It's an enormous town."

"True. But Devine is supposed to have been a journalist, isn't he? None of the local papers have ever heard of him."

"The police can't have had enough time to make thorough inquiries. Or he may have used a pen-name or something."

"Oh, quite. The Yard has looked him up in some book of reference, and he does write—over here, anyway. Articles on life in Canada and the States, chiefly. Camping in the great open spaces, hunting 'possums, how to build birch-bark canoes, or light fires with two twigs and a grasshopper—that sort of thing. Boys' papers and the popular weeklies. . . ."

"Well, that's no more discreditable than Surrealism," I said.

"Lord, no. I'm only telling you. Now I'll tell you something else. The City thinks there was some very dirty work behind the slump in Cyprian Eagles. A reputable stockbroker would have fought shy of them, anyway—unless he was sure he could get rid of them at once, before the buyer smelt a rat."

"That doesn't sound very reputable. You mean that Sir Vyvyan *knew*, and deliberately bought some to get rid of to chumps like James?"

"That's the idea. Tullis oughtn't to have been caught, of course. But Hogg was his friend, and he forgot that all's fair in business, as Mercer said."

I looked at Maurice. "Why are you worrying about James?" I asked.

"I'm not worrying about him particularly. I'm assimilating information about everybody concerned. And a nice muddle it makes." He passed his cup again and looked at his watch. "There are two other scraps of news," he said. "The inquests on Rowsell-Hogg and the boy were opened together this morning and adjourned at once. A pure formality——"

"I'd forgotten about the inquests," I said. "Things seem to move so fast just now. . . . Horrors! Of course there'll be one on this man M'Ginnis. Shall I have to identify him or anything?"

"I think we can get you out of that. After you met him he took your advice and made inquiries in Horningsea. A woman there confirmed what you told him—that the occupants of the cottage were not the Armfeldts. She's quite willing—anxious, in fact—to do any identifying that's wanted."

"Thank heaven."

"Finally," said Maurice, "the telephone message to Miss Lanham this afternoon came from a call-box at the station here."

"That's not much help, I suppose?"

"None whatever. Except as some sort of proof that Lanham is still about. And Puffin doesn't think that a help either. He wishes the fellow was anywhere else. He cheered up a bit when I reminded him that it may not have been Lanham at all."

"But remember 'Popsy,'" I said. I added the stock question: "No real news of Lanham, I suppose ?"

"None. Iliff's had Jesus thoroughly combed, without finding any sign of unlawful occupation. They're still hunting the gardens for last night's weapon." Maurice finished his tea and beckoned to the waiter. "We've got one or two calls to make," he said, "if you care to come."

"Where to?"

"I've made an appointment for five o'clock with Blewitt, the bank manager—the third trustee. Then I want to see Mercer again, if he's about, to borrow another drawing or two. You can try his sherry. And while we're at Queens' I'd like to meet that Henderson boy. You can introduce me."

I couldn't go into all this because the waiter was there with the bill. Then Maurice hustled me out. He didn't want to be cornered by the Armfeldts, he said, and they were showing signs of moving too. So with bows and smiles to them we beat it rather hastily, followed, I felt sure, by inquisitive stares from Paul and the lorgnette.

2

The National Southern Bank was quite near, in Sydney Street, and we walked there, Maurice having parked the car in the Market Place. The staff was still at work on ledgers and things when we were let in. Maurice had used Puffin's name and authority in making the appointment, and if Mr. Blewitt was surprised to see me he concealed it politely. He was a tall man like a crane—I mean the bird—all neck and legs, with an embarrassing Adam's apple which moved up and down in a startling manner. It fascinated me, and I had a job to keep my eyes off it.

"I shan't keep you long, Mr. Blewitt," Maurice said. "All I want is a little information about this trust fund of the Nine Bright Shiners."

"What sort of information?" Mr. Blewitt asked cautiously.

"What exactly it amounts to, the conditions of its disposal, and so on."

"And so on? Let us be precise, Major Hemyock."

This was pot calling the kettle black, and I grinned at Maurice.

"I mean," he said, "that further questions will arise as we go on. I don't know myself where this is leading, if anywhere. I'm digging up anything that has the slightest connexion with these murders. Detection is an empirical science, like archæology. You never know what you may turn up."

"Why not apply to my fellow trustee, Mr. Tullis?"

"I shall do so, if it seems advisable. At the moment, Mr. Blewitt, I want to hear you on the subject. I have, as I told you, full authority from Colonel Nugent to carry out these inquiries in my own way. You can confirm that, if you like."

"I have done so," the bank manager said. "Hum. Well. Reserving the right to decline to answer any questions I may think improper, I see no objection to giving you the financial details you ask for. They are not confidential." He put on his glasses and turned over some papers on his table. "As it happens, recent deplorable events have caused me to go into the matter. You ask for the exact amount of the fund. I have a note somewhere. . . . Hum. Yes. Here it is. On June third next—that is, in little less than a year from now—the fund, if untouched, would reach the total of thirty thousand, four hundred and seventy-seven pounds, three shillings, and tenpence halfpenny."

Maurice had got out his note-book. "But it has, in fact, been drawn on," he said.

"That is so. In 1919, sums aggregating eight hundred pounds were granted by the trustees, using their discretion, to the widows of two members of the club who lost their lives in the war. And at the end of last summer term the first of the beneficiaries under the deed of trust, Miss Farleigh, graduated and drew her share—a matter of some four thousand pounds."

"Leaving, roughly, twenty-five thousand pounds to be divided among the four other beneficiaries now surviving?"

"As you say—*now* surviving." The Adam's apple was moving in sympathy with these enviable figures. "When Miss Farleigh graduated there were six others. Shortly before Christmas young Mr. Rex Henderson was killed in a motor accident. And yesterday poor Hereward Rowsell-Hogg was brutally eliminated from the list. A most promising lad. A chip of the old block," said Mr. Blewitt, almost lyrically. Suitable words failing him, perhaps, he added: "As the poet says—

> " 'Prophetic Granta, with a mother's joy,
> Saw greatness omen'd in the manly boy. . . .' "

Maurice is never lyrical. He only said dryly: "However, these eliminations leave more for the others."

"Hum. Yes," said Mr. Blewitt, crashing to earth again after his unexpected flight.

Maurice went on: "Do the terms of the trust provide for such a case as this? The possibility of one or more of the intended beneficiaries dying, before they could qualify, must have been foreseen. Yet Miss Farleigh, as things are, gets less than she would have got had she graduated this summer, *after* young Henderson's death, instead of a year ago; and less again than if she had waited a little longer, till after yesterday's murder. She suffers through being the eldest."

"If you can call it suffering," I put in, "to get a buckshee four thousand pounds."

Mr. Blewitt, the apple working hard, looked at me with a mixture of rebuke and approval.

"The trust," he said, "was established on this basis. An arbitrary period was taken—twenty-five years. The total which the fund would attain by the end of that period could be calculated to a halfpenny. It seems to have been assumed that by that date—which is June third next year—the list—hum—of candidates would be closed, in the natural course of things, and that all of them would either be undergraduates, would have very recently graduated, or would be within a matter of a few years, or terms, of coming up. It was left to the trustees to adjust, as they saw fit, any discrepancies in the shares arising out of such circumstances as you mention. Miss Farleigh's share, for instance, was calculated on the basis of the ultimate total—*not* on the aggregate of the fund last summer. True"— Mr. Blewitt put up a finger—"the fund was thus diminished by a sum slightly in excess of that warranted by a strict apportionment at the time; *but,* on the other hand, with the probable beneficiaries thus reduced to six, the balance would right itself, or approximately so. To my fellow trustees and myself it seemed an equitable decision. It was a question of striking a happy mean. Hum. Yes. I am endeavouring," said Mr. Blewitt kindly, "to put it in simple language. The administration of such a fund, however, is decidedly complex. . . ."

He talked just like that. I tried to follow his simple language, but all I really grasped was that his last remark was an understatement.

Maurice has a better head for this sort of thing. "It comes to this," he said. "Unless all the beneficiaries graduated together, or *after* June third next, their shares couldn't be exactly equal."

Mr. Blewitt nodded. "As you say. The inequalities, however, will be small, and we do not anticipate complaints. The sums, in any case, are handsome."

"Oh, quite. And buckshee, as my wife puts it. They are surely much more handsome, by the way, than the original Bright Shiners expected. The nine of them must have counted on more than seven children between 'em."

"No doubt," Mr. Blewitt said. "No doubt. But to go back a moment first. You spoke, Major, of their foreseeing the possible demise, prematurely, of one or more of these candidates under the deed of trust. The deed itself is silent on this point. Understandably, I think. Actuarially, with persons of the youthful age envisaged, a death-rate of, say, one per cent, would probably be accepted as a basis of computation. So that even had there been twice as many of the younger generation, the contingency you indicate would seem a remote one. You can calculate the odds for yourself. Hum. Yes. Now to come to your last point," said Mr. Blewitt pitilessly, his Adam's apple running up and down the scale till it made me giddy, "still less could the authors of the trust anticipate the war, in the course of which three of them were to die childless, while two more were cut off—hum—in the flower of their manhood. . . ."

He had to get some breath here, and Maurice seized his chance.

"In both cases," he said, "there was a miscalculation. I grant you, though, that no actuary could be expected to foresee what has just happened—the death of two out of seven young people within six months or so."

"Indeed, no." Mr. Blewitt looked a little pained. Evidently he had *not* finished his speech.

"Boiled down," Maurice said, "this is the situation. Instead of ten or a dozen youngsters drawing perhaps a couple of thousand apiece, you're left with five, each of whom will net round about five thousand."

Having his oratory boiled down did nothing to remove Mr. Blewitt's look of disfavour. But he agreed.

"That is so."

"Now suppose," Maurice went on, "for the sake of argument, that four more were to die before graduating. The survivor would scoop the whole remaining twenty-five thousand."

The manager's apple wobbled wildly. "It is an unthinkable assumption, Major."

"But the conclusion from it is correct?"

"If you choose to put it that way."

"Assume the survivor to be Miss Farleigh, who has graduated and drawn her share. Would it apply to her?"

"We—the trustees—have never even adumbrated such a possibility."

"Of course not. But would she get the balance—on top of her four thousand?"

"There would be no other person entitled to the money," Mr. Blewitt agreed reluctantly. "But these hypotheses, Major—if one may call them even that——"

Maurice went on firmly. "Well, we'll leave them. There's another point. I'm told there are no more candidates to come up."

"That is so."

"And there aren't likely to be any?"

"You must see that for yourself." Rallying from the shock of the hypotheses, Mr. Blewitt smiled bleakly. "Unless, of course, Mr. Tul—that is to say, unless one or both of the two surviving founders of the trust, who are widowers, should marry again, and have children. And then . . ."

"And then there'd be no money left by that time, or very little?"

"It would seem so."

"The possibility of second marriages, or at any rate late ones, was not taken into account in the deed of trust?"

I foresaw another speech coming. It came.

"To be frank, Major, many contingencies were not taken into account. The trust was constituted long before my day, of course, but one is forced to conclude, from its conditions, that its authors did not look very far ahead." The Adam's apple did a record lap, and up went Mr. Blewitt's finger. "I may go so far as to say that in my considered opinion the whole scheme was entered upon with undue haste. From the fact that the fund was to accumulate for twenty-five years, without any provision for later eventualities, it seems clear that second marriages were among the possibilities overlooked. Very early ones, of course, would have presented no difficulties. But if it had not been for the war, instead of two survivors of the original Nine Bright Shiners— to give them their somewhat fantastical appellation—there might to-day be seven or eight: instead of two widowers, three or four men still in the forties, who might marry again; or who, if their wives were alive, might yet have more children. . . . Hum. This is only one instance of a lack of foresight shown by these youthful enthusiasts——"

"They must have taken advice at the time," Maurice put in.

"Ha. Hum," said Mr. Blewitt. "As to that, I cannot say. The question involves the judgment of one of my predecessors here, and I have scrupled to raise it. Had I myself been in his position . . . Hum. However. No doubt these young men were in a hurry——"

"If youth but knew," I said brightly.

Warmed by his eloquence, the manager beamed on me.

"How true, Mrs. Hemyock. How true!"

"One more question," Maurice said, the tide being now stemmed.

Mr. Blewitt inclined his head. "And that is?"

"Sir Vyvyan Rowsell-Hogg being dead, who is now the third trustee?"

I thought Mr. Blewitt was going to swallow his apple. He recovered it with a gulp, and managed another smile—one of his bleaker ones. He said, rather wryly:

"You have a positive gift, Major Hemyock, for putting your finger on—hum—delicate localities. By the conditions of the trust, which stipulate that two of the trustees must be founders, the vacancy is automatically filled by Mr. Wilfrid Lanham."

"Yes, one supposed so. That puts you in a difficulty?"

"It creates a most perplexing situation."

"Are you doing anything about it?"

"Mr. Tullis and I have discussed it briefly."

"Have you agreed upon any course of action?"

Mr. Blewitt hesitated. "Hum," he said. "No. We do not see precisely eye to eye. . . . I have suggested that three heads are better than two, and Sir Vyvyan's solicitor, Mr. Rooke, who of course is well acquainted with the business, is coming down to Cambridge again to-night to go into it with us. Mr. Tullis and he are dining with me. Mr. Tullis was returning to London to-day, and wanted the meeting to be there, but we are very busy here at the end of the summer term. So many accounts to be closed or transferred. I shall be working till the last moment. . . ."

He looked significantly at the books and papers on his table.

"Well, we'll leave you to it," Maurice said. "To return, for one moment, to Mr. Lanham, I'm told he felt aggrieved because he wasn't made a trustee when the last vacancy occurred, in 1925."

153

"So I hear," said the manager. "I was not a trustee myself then. I only came to Cambridge in 1929."

"Have you ever met him?"

"Mr. Lanham? No."

Maurice got up. "By the way," he asked, "if Mr. Tullis were to die now, what would happen with regard to the trusteeship?"

Mr. Blewitt gulped again. The finger had been planted on another delicate locality. This unpleasant possibility, which had struck James himself, had obviously struck the manager too. He said, with a slight shudder:

"You delight in suggesting fresh dilemmas, as if we were not already faced with enough. It was never foreseen, of course, that the founders would be so reduced in numbers. In the lamentable eventuality you envisage—I do not pretend to misunderstand you—it would become necessary to apply to the court for authority to co-opt."

"To fill the one vacancy? I take it that Mr. Lanham, unless also incapacitated in some way, is now irremovably your colleague?"

Obviously, again, the horrid thought had occurred to Mr. Blewitt. He winced, and replied cautiously:

"In the peculiar circumstances, Major, that might also become a question for judicial decision. But I trust the necessity will not arise. One has hopes— hum—in short . . ."

Maurice smiled. "I won't pretend to misunderstand *you,*" he said. "Well, I really think that's all. I'm exceedingly obliged to you, Mr. Blewitt."

The manager said, "Not at all. Not at all," but he was clearly relieved. He'd been wondering what new dilemmas Maurice was going to envisage. He got up with alacrity to show us out.

As soon as we were in the street, I said, "I love him. He's a lamb. I never knew anyone could talk like that."

"It won't do you any harm," Maurice said, "to hear a few drops from a well of undefiled English."

"Drops? There were buckets. But what were you getting at, Maurice, with all that talk about second marriages? Not my *James?* The complete widower. . . ."

"I wasn't getting at anything, except information."

"And all that gup about the fund, and the share out?"

"Ditto. Filling in the background. We don't know what may be important. I'm beginning to think—— But we can't talk here."

We were obstructing about a third of Cambridge in one of its narrowest and busiest streets—which is saying a good deal. Though May Week was officially over, and the town, socially and educationally speaking, already half empty, while it was early-closing day as well, I didn't notice much difference, except that perhaps there were a few thousand less bicycles than usual. You could actually *see* Holy Trinity, which as a rule is hidden behind a pile of machines, like What's his-name under the Trojan corpses. Maurice dragged me across into Petty Cury, where there are no bus stops. By contrast it was a desert. Then he went on:

"I'm beginning to think, a little late in the day, that we've been harping too much on the revenge motive, and neglecting another side of the case. There's a sum of at least twenty-five thousand pounds in the background. Take Lanham's own position with regard to this, for instance. It's quite altered by Rowsell-Hogg's death. Lanham has got what he's wanted for ten years or more—a hand in the disposal of the money."

"But it's a *trust,*" I said. "And they wouldn't let him——"

"He may not see it that way. And they can't stop him trying, if he turns up with a good alibi, which might happen yet."

"Then who——"

"Of course that isn't all. As his daughter pointed out, everyone concerned is the gainer by the murder of that boy yesterday. She and the other youngsters will get an extra thousand or so. That brings in their parents, fiancés, and what not. Lanham himself, Armfeldt, your James——"

"James again? Why, he's scared stiff for his own skin."

"I'm only stating a case. And Tullis isn't too scared to stay on in Cambridge, which is an unhealthy locality."

"But the case doesn't account for the murder of Sir Vyvyan, to begin with."

"Cyprian Eagles," Maurice said darkly. "Or the pendant may come in there, after all."

I didn't take him seriously, of course. I said, "And the American gangster?"

"He's another puzzle, I admit. The fact is, we don't know half enough yet. There may be a dark horse we haven't thought of at all. It might be young Devine, or his mother, or both, or even the mellifluous Mercer. . . ."

"Where on earth," I said, "can *they* come in? You're thinking of Popsy and her ravings again. You'd better go back and harp on the revenge motive. I can grasp that. It's simple. Besides, all these horrors for a thousand pounds and a few diamonds. . . . It isn't *likely.*"

"Murders have been committed for much less. And in this case one more will make it two or three thousand, two more will double the whole——"

"Maurice! You don't *really* think that?"

But we'd got to the car, and he only shrugged.

We drove to Queens'. Mr. Mercer was out, but his man said he'd be back by six-thirty, as he was going out again to dine. At Roy Henderson's rooms we found the oak sported, and though Maurice, who seemed anxious to see the boy, hammered on the door, there was no reply.

It was now about a quarter to six. Maurice had become uncommunicative, and said he wanted a walk to think things out. He thinks better walking, or says he does, and the result is that he tramps faster and faster, wrapped in happy meditation, while anyone with him toils panting behind. Having left the car in Queens' Lane, we went through King's to Clare and over Clare Bridge. Among the tennis courts Maurice began to put on pace. As he was generally ahead of me, and we hardly spoke, except when I pulled him up, we must have looked like a study for "A Rift in the Lute," or something of that sort. Once he stopped to ask me where Patrick Ince had his rooms, but I didn't know.

It was a lovely evening, but very hot, and I was soon boiling. We turned back again over Trinity Bridge, and I made Maurice halt there. It cooled me a little just to look at the water. While we were on the bridge a canoe came dashing up stream round the bend from St. John's. It was really coming very fast. There was one man in it, in flannels and a tweed coat. It was Harry Devine.

He looked up and saw us, checked for a moment, waved a hand, and shot under the bridge. I walked across to watch him streaking along, with quick, regular strokes of his paddle, under the willows which overhang the straight reach past Trinity Hall.

Maurice crossed to join me.

"He's a powerful chap," he said. "That's a big canoe—one of those Canadian birch-barks. Come from Horningsea, I suppose. It must be four or five miles by water."

"We passed him going out there as we drove in," I said. "He was on a motor-bike then. He seems to be as ubiquitous as Mr. Armfeldt."

The canoe shot under the next bridge out of sight. We walked on through Trinity to Trinity Lane and King's Parade. Maurice wanted to turn down King's Lane, but I said I'd had enough of it, and preferred Silver Street, where there hadn't been a murder. We had plenty of time. It was only just after six.

You can see a long way down King's Parade. Just as we moved on, Maurice looked back. Then he said quickly:

"Here's the other ubiquity—Armfeldt. I want something from him. It's a good chance. Nip across, Myra, and stop him, and make an excuse to get him to draw something——"

"Draw something. . .?"

"Yes. Don't waste time. There's that antique shop over there. Pretend you want a sketch of that dresser, or a chair—anything you like. Got a pen?"

"Of course not. . . ."

"Here's mine. And a blank sheet. . . . He'd better not see me. He might smell a rat. Join me at Mercer's."

And he bolted down King's Lane, leaving me clutching his fountain-pen and a sheet of paper torn off a letter.

Luckily Paul Armfeldt was some way off. He was on the other side of the road, coming from Trinity Street, and walking quickly. I hurried across, trying to collect my wits and think of some plausible story. One came—Maurice says all women are born liars—as soon as I'd planted myself in front of the antique shop. There were a couple of beautiful old brocade chairs in the window. I rested the sheet of paper on my bag—it was one of those flat, stiffened *pochette* things—and poised the pen, and waited.

Out of the corner of my eye I could see Paul Armfeldt coming up under full steam. He must have been doing a bit of thinking, too, because he never saw me till I turned with a happy cry.

"Mr. Armfeldt! The very man I want!"

He gave quite a start. "Mrs. Hemyock. . .?"

"In person," I said. "Are you in a frightful hurry? Can you spare a moment to do something for me?"

"My dear lady! *Can* you ask?" he said.

But I thought that for once he wasn't really very pleased to see me—or perhaps anyone he knew. Only it was a habit with him to gush over any woman who wasn't absolutely hideous, and he'd reacted automatically.

"I *can't* draw," I said plaintively (and this, at any rate, was the truth). "You see those chairs? A friend asked me to match some for her—it's a wedding present—and I believe they're the very things. But the wretched shop's shut, so I can't get a description, and I was going to try to sketch one of them. I want to write to Lucy to-night. But probably my drawing wouldn't even *look* like a chair. . . . You're an artist. Be an angel, and draw the thing for me. It won't take *you* a minute."

I pushed the pen and bag into his hands. He was really in a hurry, or wanted to be alone, because he didn't waste time over any more gushery, but started to draw the chair at once. To anyone who can't draw, to watch an artist at work is like watching a miracle. A few strokes, and the chair was there. And though he was in a hurry, Paul Armfeldt couldn't help being thorough over his own job. He even sketched in the pattern of the brocade, and added some notes. Evidently he knew something about furniture. Considering that his tools were a fountain-pen, a *pochette,* and a bit of notepaper, and that he had to do it all standing in the street, it was very clever—and quick. It *didn't* take him much more than a minute.

"Will that do?" he said, turning on the liquid look. "If you're really thinking of buying them, Mrs. Hemyock, don't give more than twenty pounds for the pair. The left-hand one's faked a bit. Look at that leg. The carving's not quite the same, eh . . .? Genuine, I should say, but off another set. . . ."

I thanked him fervently. He seemed inclined to linger now, but I felt a fearful humbug, and wanted to get away. I was afraid, too, that he might try to pump me again.

"I must run," I said. "I've got to find my husband. He's gone to ask about some man he used to know at Caius."

The truth wouldn't save me now, and I had an idea that the less said about Queens' the better. Besides, Paul Armfeldt was heading that way, and Caius would take me in the opposite direction.

We parted tenderly, and being thorough in my own way I went to Caius. Not wanting him to meet me again, *sans* Maurice, I took a roundabout way back, thinking what a tangled web we weave when first we practise to deceive, and wondering when I was going to get cool. I went through the Market Place and Benet Street, buying an evening paper on the way. I've said nothing about the Press, but all this time, of course, Cambridge was full of yelling newsboys and huge headlines, and reporters from London were nosing about everywhere. At Hythe House, mercifully, we were free from this nuisance (though one man did try to interview Maurice), and getting so much inside information myself the most lurid headlines left me cold.

In the Market Place I thought I caught a glimpse of James Tullis, cutting down towards King's Parade by St. Edward's Church. All that matters of Cambridge is a small area, but it was surprising how many of the dramatis personae seemed to be about just then, and all apparently heading the same way, even by river. I didn't feel equal to James, if it *was* him, so I slowed up. When I got to King's Parade again myself, there was no sign of him.

With all this furtive dodging, it was after half-past six when I staggered into Queens' for the second time that evening. Maurice was nowhere to be seen, so I went up to Mr. Mercer's rooms.

The tutor opened the door to me, and welcomed me in his richest voice.

"I am honoured again. Come in, Mrs. Hemyock. Come in. Your husband is here."

Maurice was standing, with a small parcel under his arm.

"Oh, here you are, Myra," he said. "Well, we mustn't keep Mr. Mercer any longer. He's going out."

This was pretty thick. There he was (Maurice, I mean), full of sherry—the decanter and glasses were on the table—and after I'd toiled half round Cambridge for him, and told lies wholesale, he wanted to whisk me off at once. What I wanted, even before a drink, was to sit down and get my shoes off. I couldn't say so, or even tell Maurice what I thought of him. But fortunately Mr. Mercer had better instincts, and was very properly horrified.

"Nonsense," he said. "Mrs. Hemyock, you are tired. Here is your chair. I shall always think of it as yours. Another cushion. . .? There now. And a glass of sherry? You like it dry? I have an Amontillado, a slightly fuller wine, but in summer I recommend this. It comes from the cellars of . . ."

As I was busy making faces at Maurice I shall never be quite sure whose cellars the sherry came from. The tutor handed me a glass, and then gave me a cigarette from Adrianople. One may smoke with sherry, I was glad to find, for I wanted that cigarette too. The wine was very good, and the chair more comfortable than ever, and I was soothed by the soft ticking of all the clocks and watches, which mingled with Mr. Mercer's fine rolling voice. I dare say I did look tired—I felt like a rag—for he left me to recover, and talked to Maurice. I paid very little attention to what he was saying. It was something about a Prince, I think. Maurice wasn't paying much attention either. He stood there with the parcel under his arm, looking fidgety and saying "yes" and "no" at what I hoped were appropriate intervals, and he kept catching my eye and casting meaning glances at the nearest half-dozen timepieces. There wasn't much chance of forgetting the time in that room, anyway, but I wouldn't understand him till I'd had another glass. Then a perfectly ferocious frown made me suspect he was thinking of something besides the tutor's engagement. I gulped down the sherry and dragged myself to my feet. Before I was on them Maurice had reached for his hat and gloves.

The clocks and watches were chiming seven as Mr. Mercer pressed my hand sympathetically and bowed us out, overwhelmingly polite to the last. This was more than I felt, and as soon as we were down in Cloister Court I said to Maurice:

"Never again. If you want me to be a stalking horse, or a red herring, or whatever it is, you might at least let me enjoy the perquisites in peace. I've walked *miles*. . . . *Now* what's the hurry?"

For he was pounding along the cloisters as if we had to catch a train.

"I don't know," he said. "I don't know. I'm worried. . . . Did you get that drawing?"

"Yes. And told enough lies——"

"Good work. Where was he going?"

"Mr. Armfeldt? I didn't ask him. What have you got there?"

He didn't bother to answer. We were rushing through the archway into the front court. Maurice made straight for the entry, up near the big Tudor gate, where Roy Henderson had his rooms.

These were on the ground floor. When I overtook Maurice, I found the outer door open. He was knocking on the inner one.

There was no reply. Maurice was just about to hammer again when a young man came in behind us. He was in evening dress.

"Hullo!" he said. Looking for Henderson, sir?"

"Yes," said Maurice.

"He ought to be in," the young man said. "He's coming out to dinner with me. Excuse me, sir. . . ."

Stepping past Maurice he threw the door open, calling out:

"Roy——" His voice jerked up to a shriek. "Oh, my God, look at him! *Roy* . . ."

He ran in. I heard Maurice swear as he plunged after him.

I was standing in the doorway. I could see about half the room. I can see it now—the end of a table, with books scattered on it, an arm-chair, a gown flung over the back, a pair of slippers. . . .

In the foreground, Roy Henderson was lying on his face on the floor. The opening door had missed his head by inches. He was in his dress-shirt and trousers, and in one hand, crumpled by his grip, was a collar. Glass from his broken spectacles glittered on the carpet. I caught a dreadful glimpse of a great crimson stain on the white linen of the shirt, between his shoulder-blades.

I turned away, sick and dizzy, clutching at the door-post. The door had swung wide, and as the two men bent over the sprawling form a draught from the open window blew a small sheet of paper off the edge of the table to my feet. Hardly knowing what I did, I stooped and picked it up.

It was another crude drawing of a man's figure. He wore a crown. Above it was written the word "Solomon," and at the foot of the sheet were the initials "W. L."

FINALE: UNREHEARSED

CHAPTER X

1

MAURICE pulled the young man out of the room and closed the door gently. I'd never seen him look so stern and angry. He turned to me.

"Are you all right, Myra?"

"I can manage," I said. "Give me something to do."

Roy Henderson's friend, with a face like paper, was leaning against the door-post, staring over his shoulder at the closed door. A shudder shook him. Maurice said to him:

"Pull yourself together. What's your name?"

The boy looked round. "Dutton," he muttered.

"Do you know if there's anyone else on this stair now?"

"I don't think so. I think they've all gone down, except . . ." His eyes slid back to the door. " Oh, God. . . .!"he said.

Maurice said again, more sharply: "Pull yourself together, Dutton. Run to the lodge and telephone to the police. Stay there."

Young Dutton lurched out. I heard him begin to run.

"Fetch Mercer," Maurice said to me. "Stay in his rooms, if you'd rather. I'll stop here. What's that paper?"

I gave him the drawing I'd picked up. He stared at it for a moment. "H'mph," he said. "Well, off you go."

I ran out. I almost bumped into an elderly couple, a man and a woman, who were strolling round the court. The man was reading aloud from a guide-book: "This court was built immediately after the foundation of the college in 1447. Note the seam in the brickwork where the first work ends. . . ."

I rushed by them, leaving them staring after me.

Mr. Mercer's man opened to me, and said his master was dressing. I could hear the bath running. I told him I must see the tutor at once, and he showed me into the rooms with the clocks and left me there. My voice was shaking, and he looked at me oddly, but he was too well trained to say anything.

The sherry decanter and glasses were still on the sideboard. I went straight to them and helped myself. Then Mr. Mercer came in, wearing a blue silk dressing-gown with scarlet cuffs. His fine hair was on end. Before he could speak I said:

"Young Henderson has been murdered in his rooms. My husband wants you to come at once."

He kept his wits. It was startling news to have hurled at him in this way, but all he said was: *"Henderson?* Henderson *too* . . .? Where is it going to end . . .? Poor lad! Poor lad . . .! But you, Mrs. Hemyock—you must have had a great shock. Sit down, sit down, and let me give you something."

"I've helped myself," I said. "Please hurry."

He went out of the room. I took his advice then, and helped myself again, liberally. Then I lit a Turkish cigarette, and began to feel better. Maurice says that when you're frightened or shocked you can drink intoxicants as if they were water without their going to your head.

Mr. Mercer was back well inside a minute. He'd only exchanged his dressing-gown for a jacket. He was without a collar, and hadn't touched his hair. He began to say that I was to stay there as long as I liked, but I told him I was coming with him. I couldn't sit alone twiddling my thumbs and thinking.

We hurried off. In the front court the elderly couple were still pottering round. Maurice was waiting in the doorway where I'd left him. The college porter was with him. I saw the white face and shirt-front of young Mr. Dutton in the door of the porter's lodge under the big gate. There seemed to be no one else about the place. Almost everybody had gone down.

Maurice took the tutor into that dreadful room, while I stayed outside with the porter. The man wanted to talk, but I was in no mood for that. The elderly couple went by us again, gave me a curious look, and passed under the archway into Cloister Court.

In a few seconds Maurice and Mr. Mercer joined us again. Maurice was saying:

"He's still warm. It happened while I was with you. I'd called here twice before—at a quarter to six, and a few minutes after, on my way to your rooms the second time. His oak was sported both times. He may have been in, of course, but I don't think so. I knocked, and the second time I tried to look in at the window, and tapped the glass. I think he came in soon after that. Then he started to dress. He wouldn't sport his oak again. He wasn't working. He was going out. When the murderer came, he probably walked straight in, as we did just now. Henderson may have told him this young Dutton was coming, because the man seems to have been in a hurry to get away. He didn't even think of shutting the outer door, which would have kept the thing quiet a little longer."

162

"Why should Henderson talk about his engagements to a stranger?" the tutor asked. "Lanham was a stranger to him—or this ghastly affair would never have happened."

"Perhaps to get rid of him," Maurice said.

Mr. Mercer looked terribly shocked now, and old. That room had upset him, and I didn't wonder. He ran a hand through his thick untidy hair.

"You must have been very anxious to see that poor boy, Major," he went on.

"I'd begun to be afraid," Maurice said.

The tutor stared for a moment, and then looked round the empty court, so mellow and peaceful in the evening light.

"Oughtn't we to *do* something?" he muttered. "The President is away already, you know. There's no one else. . . ." He turned to the porter. "Who has come in lately, Strudwick?"

The porter answered rather defensively. "No one, Mr. Mercer, since half-past five or thereabouts, that I know of, except this lady and gentleman, and them two who've just gone through, and Mr. Dutton, of course—I know *him,* sir, he's at Pembroke, and often in to see Mr. Henderson——"

"You didn't see Mr. Henderson himself?"

"Not when he came back, sir. I saw him go out about five. But I'm not looking out all the time, as you know, sir, and he may have come in again by the bridge."

"I've gone into that," Maurice said. "Almost certainly the murderer used the bridge. And there's nothing we can do *here*—now. He was out again, the same way, probably some time before my wife and I left your rooms five minutes ago. Perhaps half an hour before."

Instinctively I looked at my watch. It was only nine minutes past seven now. I remembered Mr. Mercer's clocks and watches chiming the hour as we left. It seemed incredible.

Then another thought struck me. "I might have met him," I said.

"You didn't see anyone?" Maurice asked.

"No. Both the courts were empty then."

But I shivered a little. In my mind's eye I saw a figure hurrying ahead of me, through the little tunnel before us into Cloister Court, cutting across it to the other archway and the humped wooden bridge spanning the river. . . . Then I shivered again. Suppose he hadn't been ahead of me? Suppose he'd been in Roy Henderson's room *then,* when I went by. . .?

A similar train of thought was disturbing Mr. Mercer.

"He must have come and gone by my rooms while we were sitting talking," he said.

"There's a chance," said Maurice, "that someone noticed him in the new buildings." (Queens' has built a big new block across the river, joined to the old part of the college by the bridge.) "But I don't see," he added, "that it's going to help us. . . . Hullo, here they are."

We heard the grinding of brakes as a car drew up at the gate. A little crowd of men poured through. There was Puffin and Mr. Iliff, a tall man carrying a black bag who was obviously a doctor, and two or three more, as obviously policemen in plain clothes, also with bags and things. I saw a constable in uniform taking up his stand in the gateway. The boy Dutton, looking white and forlorn in his evening dress, trailed after the party as it hurried to join us.

Puffin and the Superintendent stared when they saw Maurice and me.

"*You* here?" Puffin said.

Maurice said bitterly: "On the spot, all the time. I've been called a Jonah before this. It'll stick now. And I came to warn the boy."

"To *warn* him?" Puffin said. "Damn it, what *has* happened? The same again?"

He and all his policemen looked worked up and grim. Mr. Iliff's little grey moustache really bristled, and his greeny-brown eyes were like flints. I shall always remember that angry group of men, feeling this new crime as if it were a slap in the face, and chafing like dogs to get their own back.

Maurice had merely nodded. "Come and see for yourself," he said. "Then I'll leave you to it."

They trooped in, Mr. Mercer with them. I was left outside again—and gladly—with Mr. Dutton and the porter.

I don't know what we talked about, if we talked at all. The boy brought out a cigarette-case, and offered it to me, and I took a cigarette thankfully. His hand was still shaking as he lighted it for me. But it wasn't many minutes before Maurice and Puffin came out. Puffin's jaws were clamped together, and he was quite pink with rage. Maurice had gone rather white, as he does when *he's* angry.

"It's my job now," he was saying, "and I'm going to get on with it. I'll tell you the whole thing, as I see it, later on. We've both got a lot to do first."

Puffin looked at me and gave me a rather wintry smile.

"Poor old Myra," he said. "And we asked her down to give her a good time. . . . What are you going to do, Myra?"

"Going on with the war," I said. "Sticking to Maurice."

Maurice looked dubious. "How are you feeling?" he asked.

"Fine. Only keep me on the move. I must be *doing* something. I can't sit about by myself and think. Where are you off to now? What's this job?"

He shrugged. "Come along, then. We're only going to pay some calls."

We left Puffin talking to young Dutton and the porter, and walked out of the college to our car. One or two idlers had stopped at the gateway to stare at the constable there.

All this time Maurice had been carrying the parcel he'd brought from Mr. Mercer's under his arm. He put it with the other sketches on the back seat. As we got in he asked:

"A drink do you any good?"

"I've had several," I said. "Mr. Mercer's sherry."

"I thought you seemed to be bearing up well. I'm sorry to have let you in for this, Myra. And for the second time in twenty-four hours."

"You couldn't foresee it."

"I did foresee it. At least I was afraid of it. It might have been one of the others, but being here I ought to have sat outside that boy's rooms till he came in."

I remembered what he'd said after we left the bank. I glanced at his face.

"You look like doom," I said.

"I feel like it."

He let in the clutch savagely, backed into the gateway, and we jerked round and shot into Silver Street. When I'd got my breath back I asked where we were going.

"To run your young cousin to earth, if we can find him. Then we'll chase Ince. His rooms are in Maid's Causeway. And I want to see Miss Farleigh. . . ."

We swung into Trumpington Street. Where it becomes King's Parade the antique shop caught Maurice's eye.

"You've got that sketch of Armfeldt's?" he asked.

I patted my bag. "Here."

"Did you see which way he was going?"

I nodded backward. "He was still heading that way when I left him. I didn't look round."

Maurice pulled up by the Senate House, and we left the car there and walked down the passage by Gonville and Caius to Clare. But Ian wasn't in his rooms.

Maurice looked at his watch. "Twenty-five to eight," he said. "If Blewitt's so busy, he won't dine before eight. Depends on where he lives, of course, but Tullis might still be at Parker's."

"He was out an hour ago," I said. "Or I thought I saw him, anyway, on my way back to Queens'."

"Where was *he* going?"

"Cutting down towards King's from the Market Place."

"This was about half-past six?"

"Yes." Mention of Mr. Blewitt's dinner-hour reminded me that at Hythe House, at any rate, they did dine at eight. "Do you realise," I said, "that Vera will be expecting us back?"

Maurice was hurrying me up Senate House Passage again.

"We'll phone her," he said, "and pick up a bite somewhere. Then you can taxi back—unless you like to try your hand with the car. I shall probably be here till late."

I said I preferred a taxi, and that I hoped he was going to charge up all this transport to somebody.

We drove to Parker's, and Maurice went in. He was there some minutes, and came out looking bothered. James had gone—he hadn't been back since I thought I saw him an hour before—and no one in the hotel knew anything about Ian. Maurice had rung up the bank manager's house, which was in the Trumpington Road, but James wasn't there yet, and wasn't due till eight.

"You're fussing a lot about James," I said.

"It's the boy I'm fussing about," Maurice said.

"Maurice, you *don't* think——"

"I'm not taking any more chances. We'll try young Ince now."

We shot off again towards Jesus Lane.

As soon as we'd turned into it, Maurice said: "Take your mind back to that tea-party at the motor-boat club on Tuesday."

"It seems a long time ago now," I said.

"Didn't you say that young Tullis told every one there about his father going to the 'Eagle' the night before to see Rowsell-Hogg?"

"Yes, he did."

"Every one. . . ? They weren't all there at the beginning, were they? You said something about Devine and someone else turning up later. Who was actually there when Tullis told the story?"

It was just like Maurice to fling that sort of question at me. He's got an uncanny memory himself. I tried to remember what *had* happened on Tuesday afternoon, but it wasn't easy. It seemed weeks ago, instead of only two days.

"I know," I said at last. "Ian was telling the story just before Patrick Ince turned up. So there were only the Farleigh girl and Paul Armfeldt and young Henderson there. And Averil and me."

"I forgot Averil," Maurice said. "One sees so little of her these days. Of course she stayed on. . . ."

166

I asked him what he was talking about, but by this time we'd reached our destination.

2

Maid's Causeway is a continuation of Jesus Lane. Patrick Ince's rooms were on the ground floor of a house looking across a part of the Common— the Butt's Green which has figured already in the story —to the river and the boat-houses on the other bank.

Mr. Ince was in. I didn't see why I shouldn't pay a few calls too, and I went in with Maurice. We were shown into the sitting-room. There, with the mothers' joy, was Harry Devine.

"Well met, gossips!" said Mr. Ince. "Or in words more suited to my elders and betters, how do you do? Devine, clear that chair. It's my second best, Major. Can you bear it? Or, what's more to the point, can it bear you? Mrs. Hemyock, try this one. It doesn't fire on all its springs, and the less said about its legs the better, but when you get used to the knobs you'll appreciate it. There's a subtlety, *a je ne sais quoi,* about it. And it's an historical piece. Forty generations of undergraduates have sat, sprawled, lounged, or slept in it. It was an antique when Bishop Alcock suppressed the nuns for brewing bad beer. There were only two of them. The stuff had killed off all the rest. . . . And talking of beer," said Mr. Ince, going off at a natural tangent, "fish it out, Devine, will you, and the sherry, if any, and anything else you can find in liquid form. And why weren't we drinking, anyway? The way the best years of one's life are frittered away, reading and all that, when there's good liquor eating its head off in the cellarette—my landlady's English—is a sin and a shame. And as Devine's been making my flesh creep, he might have thought of it before. . . ."

Maurice had said that we weren't going to stay. But overwhelmed by this barrage I was insinuated into the historical piece before I knew what I was doing. After Mr. Mercer's super-stuffed balloon furniture it certainly felt a little knobby. Harry Devine, after giving us both a quick glance, had swept a lot of books off the second-best chair. But Maurice was firmer than me, and declined it.

"We're not stopping," he said. "I only want a word with you, Ince. How has Mr. Devine been making your flesh creep, by the way?"

Harry Devine was stooping over the cellarets, otherwise a converted coal-box with a leather seat for a top. Patrick Ince said:

"*Imprimis,* with the true story of the American yegg." He looked at Maurice reproachfully. "And oh, Major, why, oh why, didn't you let me in on it? In my own college, and you my guest? Was it kind? Was it the behaviour of an officer and a gentleman? Dash it, you might have tipped me the wink."

"It was the behaviour of a very busy man," Maurice said. "Well, what next?"

"Eh. . .? Oh, Devine, you mean? Poetry, and thrown off just like that. Oh, the lad's been trying to put the wind up me thoroughly. Lanham, you know. Fly for your life, and so on."

Harry Devine straightened himself and turned towards us, beer in one hand, sherry in the other. He looked at Maurice.

"I was putting it to Ince," he said, "that he might come away with me for a week or two, that's all."

"You think he's better away?" Maurice asked.

"I think this may be an unhealthy place for him just now."

"You've been putting two and two together, Mr. Devine?"

The latter nodded without speaking. The room was rather dark, thanks to some appalling lace curtains, but his light blue eyes seemed to shine in it. I could see a little colour in his fair cheeks. Under the reserve he was wearing again I thought he was really worked up about something.

The mothers' joy had gone to the sideboard for glasses.

"A life for a life," he said over his shoulder. "I saved *his* once—or I might have done if he wasn't the best swimmer in Michitoba. Or is it Manichigan? Anyway, I owe him a canoe, and he will have those whopping Canadian things. It'll be cheaper to go to Scotland."

"Scotland, eh?" Maurice said. "I thought you were working."

"Capital place, Scotland, for work." Mr. Ince was setting the glasses on the table. "No distractions there in the summer. No cricket—though I believe they do think they play it, but they mix it up with curling and golf, and score by holes and haggises. When they score at all. . . . Now, Mrs. Hemyock, a spot of sherry? Or do you feel beer is best, like our brewers?"

>" ' Beer, happy produce of our isle,
>   Can sinewy strength impart. . . .' "

I thought it unwise to mix my drinks, and said I'd have sherry.

Mr. Ince was much too voluble to be observant, but I met the luminous eyes of Harry Devine, standing in his quiet way in the background, studying my face. They moved to Maurice's.

"Anything fresh, Major?" Mr. Devine asked suddenly.

Maurice was having beer. I'm sure he needed it. He emptied his glass and put it down carefully. Then he screwed in his eyeglass and said:

"Yes, I'm sorry to say. You seem to have put two and two together correctly." Patrick Ince, filling his own glass, looked up. Maurice turned to him. "Your friend Henderson has been murdered"

"Oh, good lord. . .!" Patrick said. He went on pouring beer, his startled eyes on Maurice, till it overflowed on to the table.

Harry Devine drew in his breath with a hissing sound, but he didn't speak till Maurice turned to him again and asked:

"Is this what you were afraid of, Mr. Devine?"

Devine made a little gesture. "No, no. . . . I just had a hunch. That was all. I've been thinking. . . . But *this*—so soon—of course I didn't expect it."

"You expected something of the sort sometime?"

Harry Devine made the same helpless motion with his hands.

"I tell you it was just a hunch," he said. "I hadn't worked it out to decimals."

"You had a hunch about young Tullis."

"Meaning I ought to have warned Henderson too ?"

"Well, I take it," Maurice said mildly, "you've been warning Ince here."

"I hadn't got as far as sending out a general alarm. At that, you your-self, Major, or the police, have as much to go on as I had. . . . No, it was this way. It was thinking of Tullis and his old man that put me on to it." Harry Devine ran a hand through his thick hair. He took a step forward. "Any hick could see where *they* stood," he said. "Tullis senior was the last of the old crowd. Lanham had it in for him too. And the boy's *his* son. . . . Well, you know all about that. I ran round to warn them both, and found old Tullis had beaten me to it by a mile. . . ."

Patrick Ince was staring, with the same blank, startled look, from one to the other of them. He lifted his dripping glass and drained it and set it down, apparently without knowing what he was doing.

Maurice prompted Harry Devine. "And then?" he said.

Devine shrugged. "Well, I was milling it over, and it came to me. Suppose it didn't stop there? When a guy starts killing, he keeps on. It gets him, like drugs. He needn't be a homicidal maniac right off, but after the second or third time you'd need a microscope to see the difference. And Lanham started at scratch. He *is* mad. He's killing for revenge. I'm telling you how I put it to myself. I thought, what about Ince here? Lanham probably hates him like hell. He's never seen him, but he's the son of his father, same as young Tullis, and that Rowsell-Hogg boy. . . . Well, Ince is my friend. I came round right away to throw a scare into him."

"You were coming here," Maurice asked, "when we saw you on the river?"

Harry Devine took up his own glass of beer. "Sure," he said. "And at a good lick too. I'd thrown a scare into myself, just by thinking of it. My machine's giving trouble, or I'd have been here sooner."

Maurice said: "It's a pity, you know, you didn't think of Henderson, too, while you were passing Queens'."

The glass went down on the table with a bang, slopping the beer over to mingle with what Patrick Ince had spilled.

"D'you think I don't know it?" Devine cried. "D'you think I couldn't kick myself? But I haven't met the kid more than twice. He didn't mix, like the rest of them. His twin was smashed up—you know that? He took it hard. . . . Anyway, I just never thought of him. I guess I hadn't worked it out that far."

"Oh, I'm not blaming you," Maurice said. "If anyone's to blame, *I* am. I had the same hunch, Mr. Devine, though I arrived at it by a different way. I'd tried to warn the boy. I was still in Queens' when it happened. I shan't soon forget that."

Harry Devine stared. He gave a curt laugh. "The hell you were?" he said. "Well, if that wasn't a bad break. . . ."

Patrick Ince spoke for the first time since he heard the news.

"He was killed there?"

"In his rooms," Maurice said. "About an hour ago."

"Who found him?"

"My wife and I, and a young man named Dutton."

"Dutton of Pemmer? Oh, I know *him*. Great pal of Roy's. But my hat, isn't it a ghastly thing! There wasn't a more harmless chap. A dream walking, we used to call him. Remember the song. . .?" Patrick Ince stopped, biting his lip and frowning. "How was it done?" he asked abruptly.

"The same way."

The young man shuddered. He had enough imagination to picture that scene. Then he laughed harshly.

"A murder a day keeps the doctor away! Oh, damn and blast the brute! Why the *hell* don't they catch him?"

"They will," Maurice said. "And I think before any more harm's done."

"Got a line on him?" Harry Devine asked.

Maurice merely nodded. I wondered if he really meant anything. Then he said to Devine: "By the way, your hunch didn't include Miss Farleigh either, I suppose?"

"Lord, no." The blond young man had picked up his tumbler again. His eyes narrowed over the rim. "I never gave her a thought," he said. His lips curled. "I seem to be a way behind, don't I? And I fooled myself I'd done some swell thinking. . . . But I only met the girl the other day. And she's gone down. Quit these halls of light and learning. That's why she didn't seem to fit, I suppose. Is she still in the town?"

"She's staying another night at Girton, I believe."

"What are you going to do about it, Major?"

"Warn her," Maurice said.

"And you came here to warn Ince?"

"Chiefly. And found you ahead of me again."

Harry Devine smiled ruefully. "I didn't see so far ahead, by a long chalk," he said.

Patrick Ince, looking from one to the other, still with a slightly dazed air, shook himself like a great dog. Then he suddenly remembered my presence. He became apologetic.

"I say, Mrs. Hemyock, I'm awfully sorry. Language, and all that. And talking all that rot before. You must have been through it. . . . But I didn't know."

"Of course you didn't," I said.

He turned to Maurice. "Can't I take a hand, Major? I'd give my share of this ruddy fund to see Lanham well and truly scragged."

"Keep it," Maurice said. He walked to the window and parted the curtains and looked out for a moment. "My advice to you, Ince," he said, when he turned again, "is to stay here till it's all over. You'll be watched and followed from now on. Only don't go out after dark. And don't make a fuss about it. Get on with your work, and let the police get on with theirs. They'll be keeping an eye on young Tullis, too, and Miss Farleigh, as long as they're here. The Tullises go to-morrow, anyway, I believe, and Miss Farleigh may decide to go tonight, when she hears. . . ."

"If you think *they're* safer out of Cambridge——" Harry Devine began.

"I don't say that. They, as well as Ince, will be under supervision wherever they are, till this business is cleared up. But the police here have got the thing in hand at last. They know what they've got to look out for."

"Do they know where Lanham's hiding? That's the point."

"I can go so far as to say they think they do."

We all stared at Maurice. Harry Devine frowned. He went on abruptly:

"They're not trying to use Ince as a decoy?"

"Certainly not," Maurice said. "But I'm sure Colonel Nugent won't want him to go as far afield as Scotland just now. That is, if you were thinking of pushing off in the next day or two."

"I wasn't going to waste time, once we'd fixed it up."

"Well, put it off. You know, Mr. Devine, you can be useful here yourself, perhaps. You know Lanham, as he is now, better than anyone in Cambridge except his daughter."

"All right, Devine," Patrick Ince put in. "I'm not going now, anyway."

Devine shrugged and nodded. "It's for you to say. It was only a notion. If you're being trailed, you ought to be O.K."

Maurice looked at me, and I got up. He said to Patrick:

"There's another thing I came to see you about. Take your mind back to that dinner before the Trinity Ball on Monday. Did you hear Sir Vyvyan say anything about leaving the ball early, and going to Queens'?"

The boy shook his head. "No. The police asked me that at the time. He may have done, of course. I was at the other end of the table." He looked at his friend. "*You* had some story, Devine. . . ."

Harry Devine smiled at Maurice. "Still on that tack, Major? Well, as I told Ince, two people, outside his crush, knew beforehand where Rowsell-Hogg was going that night."

Maurice put in his eyeglass. "Indeed?" he said. "You might have passed this on, you know. Who were they?"

"I was one," Devine said. He smiled again. "And I reckoned *that* wasn't worth passing on."

"And the other?"

"Mrs. Armfeldt. But I didn't know who she was then. It was this way. On Monday afternoon I ran into her and Sir Vyvyan in King's Parade. I'd met *him*—his boy introduced me at the races. He said, 'Har are yah? Har are yah?' in his toplofty way" —Harry Devine showed his white teeth as he mimicked the stockbroker—"and I was pushing on, when I remembered I wanted to ask the boy about some man he knew in London. They were going back next day, you know. So I asked if he was around. The old boy mumbled something about waiting for him, or I thought he did, and I stood by. I heard him say to this duchess—I took her for that, at least—that he was sorry, but he had his evening all fixed up. His wife wasn't feeling too good, and he was leaving the hop early with her, and then going with some old friend to Queens'. He dressed it up with a lot of 'har-hars'—you wouldn't know his style, of course—and madame waved that gold eyeglass on a stick, and they looked pally enough, but I could see he wished her at Halifax. Then she took the hint and sailed off. It turned out I'd got him wrong—what he'd said to me was, he was tired of waiting for the boy— and as he showed pretty plainly that that was where I got off too, I faded away. . . . That's the story. Hardly worth passing on, Major, was it? And anyhow, it was only at Jesus last night that I found out who the duchess was."

"You can never say what will be worth passing on," Maurice said. "It's news to me, for instance, that Sir Vyvyan knew the Armfeldts."

"We all met them during the bumps," Patrick Ince said.

"I take it they weren't at the Trinity Ball, though?"

"You can," I put in. "I shouldn't have missed *her.*"

Patrick had raised a grin. "There was a spot of bother over that," he said. "It was poor old Hoggins's party, and Claudia was going, of course, but the old man didn't cotton to the Armfeldts, and wouldn't let Hoggins ask them. What he said, went, you know. Claudia was rather huffy about it, and though she came to the dinner, she cut the ball, and went off to some do the Armfeldts themselves had got up at the last moment, to show her independence. High-brows and what not," said Mr. Ince, with some contempt. But he added candidly: "Not that I blame her. *De mortuis,* and all that, but the late Sir Vyvyan did think he owned the earth."

"Mrs. Armfeldt's a good trier," Harry Devine said. "When I met them she must have been having a shot at roping him in for this party of hers. I guess she hadn't exactly grasped his meaning before."

"What time was it when you met them?" Maurice asked him.

"Round half-past four."

"Do you happen to have told this story to anyone else?"

"Only to Ince. I didn't think it was a very good one."

"And you, Ince?"

"Lord, no, Major. I forgot all about it till just now."

Maurice moved to the door. As the boy went to open it, he took his arm and led him into the hall, giving me a look over his shoulder which I interpreted correctly. Harry Devine was waiting for me to follow. When he did so I'd dropped my gloves behind the historical chair. Mr. Devine obligingly went to look for them, and by the time he'd found them and we'd left the room the other two were standing on the steps in the street.

"There's your guardian," Maurice was saying, nodding to a man walking slowly towards us. "He'll introduce himself, and expect you to tell him your movements. Otherwise he won't worry you."

"Well, I don't want him," Patrick said, eyeing the man with a frown. "Makes a fellow feel so damned silly. But I suppose I can't help it. I only wish," he added grimly, " that Lanham *would* have a try at me. I'm itching to get my hands on him now. . . ."

The plain-clothes detective, ignoring us all, had turned about. Harry Devine stared at his broad back. As we crossed the pavement to the car he said :

"By the way, Major, what's the news about *our* corpse?"

Maurice was opening the door of the car. He answered over his shoulder: "There's none that I know of."

We got in and drove off, leaving them standing together. When we'd turned and passed them again they were going in. They stopped to wave. The plain-clothes man was walking back towards the house.

I said to Maurice: "I'm glad you don't leave all the lying to me."

"I'm selecting what I broadcast," he said.

"It was another judicious selection, I suppose, when you said the police had got a line on Lanham?"

"Well, Iliff thinks he has. At least he's made up his mind now that Lanham's hiding in one of the colleges."

"Do you think so yourself?"

We were in Jesus Lane. Instead of answering, Maurice nodded towards the college and said: "The gun's still missing."

"Well, it would be if it's Lanham's," I said. *"He'd* have no reason for burying it in flower-beds."

Then I asked how the plain-clothes man had got to Maid's Causeway so quickly. Maurice explained that when we left Queens' the Superintendent was just going to arrange all that by telephone.

"By all that," I said, "you mean looking after Ian and Miss Farleigh as well? And James too?"

"The infants, anyway. It's a bit of a strain on Iliff's resources just now, but I don't think he'll have to keep it up long."

At the head of Jesus Lane we turned left into Sydney Street.

"Where are we going now?" I asked.

"The police station. They may have found out where young Tullis is."

The police station is in St. Andrew's Street, a straight run. We were there in a couple of minutes. Maurice ran in. When he came out again he was looking less bothered.

"He's just where we want him," he said. "Having dinner at the 'Corner House' with some of the lads of the village who're doing overtime. I've phoned Vera, and we'll run along there now and have a bite ourselves." He looked at me as he got in. "You're a bit white," he said. "Effects of restoratives wearing off?"

"I could do with some food," I said, suddenly realising the fact. Thinking of it made me hollower than ever, and when we got out of the car at the 'Corner House' a few minutes later I felt as weak as a rat. Though why a rat?

Several thousand hearty feeders having just departed for the Long, or to begin real and earnest lives, the 'Corner House' was not too crowded. As we made our way through the inner room we saw Ian with three other youths. They were laughing away, and Ian didn't see us, but when we'd found a table, and Maurice had ordered a couple more restoratives, he left me with the menu and went to speak to the boy.

When he joined me again he said: "I've asked him to come over in a few minutes, when you've had time to get some food down. He knows he's being trailed—did you spot the fellow outside?—and seemed to think it rather a joke. They hadn't told him about Henderson, so I did."

"You might have let him finish his dinner," I said.

"I didn't want to tell him here. Haven't you had enough of breaking bad news? But he's got to know, for his own sake."

The waitress came with the soup. We'd nearly finished the fish, and I was beginning to feel a little better, when Ian arrived.

He was very subdued. I said all the usual silly perfunctory things about poor Roy Henderson. It was a consolation, though a poor one, that Ian had never seen much of the dead boy. When the other twin was alive, the two Hendersons had kept to themselves. But apart from the shock, this news had made Ian realise that being watched over by the police was by no means a joke.

The waitress having brought the entree and gone again, Maurice said to the boy:

"You remember your party at the boat club on Tuesday?"

Ian nodded vaguely, his mind on other things than parties.

"You were telling them about your father going from Trinity to the 'Eagle' the night before, to see Sir Vyvyan about something."

"Yes, I think I did."

"Myra thinks there were only Miss Farleigh, Mr. Armfeldt, and Henderson there at the time. Is that right?"

After the shock he'd had, Ian naturally found it as difficult as I had done to remember the precise order of events on Tuesday afternoon. But when he'd thought a bit he agreed.

"That's right."He began to look interested. "Why, sir?"

(To make up for calling me Myra before all and sundry, Ian was always very punctilious with Maurice.)

"Yours not to reason why," Maurice said. "Now just think, Tullis. Did you repeat the story that afternoon?"

175

Ian thought again. "No," he said. "No, I'm sure I didn't. Why should I?"

"You might have told it to Ince. He came after, my wife says."

"Oh, Patrick *knew*. I'd told him before."

Maurice nodded. "He said you'd told him, but he wasn't sure when, except that it was at the club that day."

"It was before I came to fetch Myra," Ian said.

He was obviously getting curious, but Maurice changed the subject by talking about the murder at Jesus, a sort of homoeopathic treatment that at any rate served its purpose by taking the boy's mind off his friend's death. Ian had heard from Averil at the ball all about our famous encounter on the river bank, and there had been some joke at the Armfeldts' expense during supper, and now he wanted to know where *they* came in. Maurice was careful to explain that they didn't come in at all, and knew nothing about the man, and, of course, he didn't mention the scene in the cricket pavilion.

Ian seemed slightly disappointed. "Can't say I care much for Armfeldt myself," he said. "And it wouldn't hurt Claudia to be taken down a peg. Of course I don't mean in any beastly way, like murder," he added hastily, and then looked rather dashed again as another thought struck him. "I suppose, then—I suppose it was Lanham again. . . ?"

Maurice said something non-committal and steered the talk away from that topic. Presently he asked:

"By the by, talking of America and the Americans, have you ever been over there, Tullis?"

"I? No, sir."

"Or your father?"

"He went to the States once when I was a kid."

"I'd an idea he'd been lately. I must have been mixing him up with some friend he was talking about."

"It was fifteen years ago," Ian said.

Soon after this he went back to his own table. Maurice gave him the same advice he'd given to Patrick Ince—to stay in after dark, and not to worry. It was easy to say this, and the poor boy was looking very shaken. He had more imagination than the mothers' joy, and I knew he was thinking again of Roy Henderson. However, he was going back to London with his father next day, and then they were off to Cornwall or somewhere remote. When Maurice heard this he didn't seem to mind, in spite of his objections to Scotland.

When we were alone again I said, "Now what have you been getting at?"

"I'm only trying to clear the ground. You can think it out for yourself, Myra."

Half a bottle of white wine, as I told him, on top of all the other drinks I'd had on an empty stomach, was now beginning to go to my head a little, and I didn't feel like hard thinking. So I left James's visit to America for later consideration. It was fifteen years ago, anyway.

"I suppose," I said, "you got that bit about the party out of Patrick Ince when I dropped my gloves?"

"Is that what you did? Yes, I got it out of him then."

"I don't see where it leads. Anyway, what do we do now?"

"Aren't you tired of this careering about?"

"I want to be tired," I said. "I want to sleep to-night. Are you going to Girton?"

"No. Miss Farleigh can wait. In fact, I don't want to see her now."

"Women and children last? But I suppose the police are mounting guard over her too by this time."

"I'm not worrying about her any longer," Maurice said. "But I want to see the other blue stocking again."

"Mary Lanham? Why?"

"To ask her a question. Are you coming? I shan't be more than a minute, and you needn't see her if you don't want to."

"I feel sorrier for her when I don't," I said. "I'll wait outside."

It was after nine o'clock when we left the 'Corner House.' Ian was still with his friends, drowning trouble with an extra drink or two, and on our way out Maurice left me for a moment to speak to him again. Ian gave me rather a wan smile, and the others stared at Maurice with interest.

At Newnham I sat in the car while Maurice went up to see Mary Lanham. As he'd promised, he wasn't long.

He said with a smile when he came back: "I think I prefer Miss Farleigh."

"What did you want to ask the girl?" I said.

"Why her father put off coming down here till the Monday. You'd think he'd have made the most of his holiday by coming on Saturday."

"Perhaps he wasn't thinking much about holidays. Well, what's the answer?"

"He *was* coming on Saturday. But a few days before he heard of another job, and he had to see some man about it on Sunday."

"I shouldn't have thought he'd be bothering about other jobs, either, just now."

"That's the story he told the girl," Maurice said. "Or so she says. . . . And that's all for to-night, so far as you're concerned. We'll find a taxi, and you'll go back and keep Vera company and go to bed early."

"And you?"

"I've got a lot of work to do here."

I was suddenly feeling too tired and sleepy to want to career about any more, or even to be curious. We met an empty taxi at the Queens' Road crossing, and I was transferred. As I drove out of Cambridge some enterprising local paper was already splashing the murder at Queens'. *Opus IV,* it called it, with an appropriate scholarly touch. But as Maurice said later, strictly speaking it was *Opus III.* There had been one impromptu.

CHAPTER XI

FRIDAY MORNING

1

I FELT a complete flop by the time I got back to Hythe House, and after very little talk Vera put me to bed. She knew what had happened, though Maurice had said nothing about it, for Puffin had telephoned later. He was still in Cambridge, of course, and Averil had just been fetched to her last dance. Vera said now she wished it wasn't the last. She realised that these entertainments were a blessing in disguise. After a week of them, her daughter was too tired when she was at home to bother about anything but the next one, and anyhow she'd already talked her head off about the latest excitement. A dance a day, said Vera, adapting the current witticism, kept horrors away. The last trump, she added, would have a job to wake Averil just now.

It would have had a job to wake me that night, rather to my surprise. Though I felt so whacked, I expected to be wakeful, in the horrid nagging way one is when one's nerves are edgy, from the moment I got into bed, but I went off like a log. I half woke when Maurice came in, looked owlishly at the bedside clock, saw it was 1.30 a.m., and drifted away again. The next thing that roused me was his getting up, and even then I couldn't keep awake. When I finally shook myself out of this stupor I was furious to find it was nine o'clock and that he'd actually left the house again, and Puffin with him.

Vera had very little to tell. Puffin had come home with Maurice, but he was too tired then, and too sleepy and rushed when he got up, to go into things. He didn't seem to know when either of them would be back. All this, as Vera said, made housekeeping very difficult. She took it with her usual calm, but she was feeling the strain too. She said she wished Puffin would shuffle his troubles off on to Scotland Yard. But she seemed to put a lot of faith in Maurice. He'd got something up his sleeve, she told me. Puffin had let out that much. Even Vera was bound to be a little curious to know what it was, but I couldn't tell her.

I was much less patient. I haven't got her placid temperament. Ten hours' sleep had put me thoroughly on my feet again, and after all that had happened yesterday it was dreadfully boring to be stuck away at Hythe House wondering what was happening now. I couldn't exactly say this to Vera, but she understood. After breakfast, which they brought me in bed, I wandered about and got in the way and made myself a general nuisance. Averil, who'd come home with the milk, was still asleep, and I had to talk to someone. Though Vera was very sweet about it, I know I made housekeeping more difficult still. And I needn't have worried, after all. I ought to have remembered that Friday's a lucky day for me. A good deal depends, of course, on what you call luck. Some people might not agree with me, and I wasn't too sure about it myself at one time. And it was to prove a very unlucky day for some others of my acquaintance.

All the week it had been getting hotter and hotter, and the morning was sulphurous. There had been summer lightning during the night, Vera said, and she pointed vaguely about and prophesied thunder. About eleven o'clock I said I must do something, and I was better out of her way, anyway, and I'd take the skiff out. It would be cooler on the water, and the exercise would work off some of my restlessness. Vera talked about thunder again, but I said I didn't mean to be long. Maurice, of course, would have looked at the glass, and read the weather report, and weighed all the pros and cons. These preliminaries to any expedition are half the fun to him, but I don't know an isotherm from a depression.

I sculled away upstream, towards Horningsea, because I thought it would make the return journey easier. But there isn't much current on the Cam, and feeling so restless and vigorous I went a good deal farther than I meant to. I was enjoying it, and I'd plenty to think of, and altogether before I knew where I was I was passing the Devines' cottage. There was no one to be seen in the garden, but Harry Devine's big canoe was tied up to the bank. And I noticed now that the sun had suddenly gone in, and that a wind was getting up, rustling the willows. But I'd forgotten about Vera's prophecies, and owing to the trees I couldn't see any real clouds.

A little way beyond the cottage was Baitsbite Lock, on the other side of which the bottom eight starts in the Bumping Races. I decided to row to the lock. By the time I'd got there the sky overhead was a copperish green, and the wind had dropped again, and an inky black cloud, which the trees had hidden, had soared up over them like magic, and was shooting out sinister fingers into the copper colour above. Not for the first time, I felt I'd been a fool. I didn't particularly mind getting soaked, as all I had on was a backless linen garment and a pair of sandals, but one *looks* so silly, dripping all over the carpet and with one's hair in rats' tails. And I'm not frightfully fond of thunderstorms in the open. One didn't need to know anything about isotherms to guess that a pretty nasty storm was on its way. It gave a preliminary bang and rumble as I was turning.

Of course I thought at once of the Devines' cottage. It was the only refuge between the lock and Hythe House. I could have sheltered at the lock itself, but I didn't see why I should. Mrs. Devine knew me, and was mixed up, in a way, with all the trouble at Cambridge, and I'd seen quite a lot of her son. I only thought twice about it because of a sort of defensiveness in her manner when we'd met, and because she hadn't asked us in then. But she couldn't object to my sheltering from a thunderstorm. Anyway, I'd turned the skiff, and I could see the cottage, and I put my back into it and shot down stream.

The black cloud was overhead already. There was another fearful bang, and the first drops fell, tepid and heavy and the size of half-crowns, just as I shipped my sculls and ran alongside the canoe. I tied up the skiff and landed on the lawn.

I was half-way across when I stopped and stared.

An extraordinary procession was hurrying out of the trees down the track by which Averil and I had reached the cottage two days before. Puffin was leading. Behind him—I could hardly believe my eyes—was Mrs. Armfeldt, in her magenta and black *tricorne.* Behind her was her son. Maurice, James Tullis, and Superintendent Iliff brought up the rear. They were all doing a jog-trot to get out of the rain—all, that is, except Mrs. Armfeldt. She managed even to hurry majestically.

Puffin was opening the gate for her when he saw me. He was looking pretty harassed anyway, and at this shock he let out a sort of yelp.

"Good gad! Myra!"

"More orphans of the storm?" I said. "What *is* this—a pilgrimage, or a Rotary convention?"

Then I caught Maurice's astonished eye. At this moment Mrs. Devine, in her blue cotton frock, appeared at the door of the cottage.

She looked from me to the procession, and back to me again. It struck me then that of course she didn't know any of them, except the Superintendent.

I was still standing in the middle of the lawn, and she called to me:

"Mrs. Hemyock, what is all this?"

"I'm wondering," I said. "I've only just come ashore myself, to beg for shelter."

And as the huge raindrops were falling more heavily, I made for the door again, arriving there with Puffin, who'd bustled past Mrs. Armfeldt. He gave me a queer look.

"Mrs. Devine?" he said. "My name's Nugent. I'm the Chief Constable. Hope you'll forgive this invasion. We've been having a council of war—these murders, you know—and we thought you and your son ought to be in it.

Representing Miss Lanham, eh. . .? As we were at my place, just down the river, it seemed the simplest thing to run along here. Saves time, and so on. Bit of an infliction, though, I'm afraid—I hadn't counted on this weather, — thought we might sit in your garden, what?—but as it is . . ."

Under Mrs. Devine's cold, blue stare he trailed off rather feebly. Mrs. Armfeldt, who had followed him, filled in the gap.

"As it is, may we come in?" With a gesture and a roll of her dark eyes she indicated the black sky, the rain, her magenta silk, and the consequences of staying outside a minute longer. She found time to incorporate a bow to me.

Mrs. Devine had not spoken again. She stared from Mrs. Armfeldt to Puffin and then past him to the other men coming up from the gate. She stepped back quickly, bending her head to clear the low door. Her hand went out to the door-knob, and for an instant I thought she was going to shut us out in the downpour.

Mrs. Armfeldt said crossly: "See, my hat will be ruined. And my dress. May we come in at once, please?"

The other was still blocking the doorway. The two women, face to face, one so fair and statuesque in her faded cotton frock, one dark and vivacious and expensively dressed, were almost of a height, thanks to Mrs. Armfeldt's heels. They must have been almost of an age, too.

Then Mrs. Devine, with a little shrug, turned abruptly and went in. Mrs. Armfeldt, ducking the *tricorne,* followed at once. Maurice and Paul Armfeldt had just joined us. James and the Superintendent were at their heels. Puffin was standing aside to make way for me.

An enormous drop of rain rolled down my bare back, and there was a terrific peal of thunder overhead. As I looked instinctively upward I saw Harry Devine's face at a dormer window over the door. It vanished as the rain began to pelt down in earnest.

Maurice grabbed my arm. "What on earth are *you* doing here?" he said. He sounded quite angry about it.

I made a face at him, shook myself free, and dived into the cottage.

2

The front door opened into a living-room. It was low and square, its walls distempered primrose.There were two small windows, one near the door, looking over the sloping lawn to the river, the other opposite, showing the gloomy trees and undergrowth beyond a tiny kitchen garden. Both were open. In the room there were a gate-legged table, two armchairs in cretonne covers, a big divan against the end wall, and a writing bureau under the back window. A few pen-and-pencil and water-colour sketches hung on die walls. A bowl of roses stood on the table. The floor was tiled, and there was one cheap rug in front of the little grate. I could see no reading matter except a book on a chair and a pile of newspapers on a low stool by the hearth. One got the idea that everything not in use was put away in drawers and places. The effect was bare and rather poverty-stricken, but everything, as I'd expected, was scrupulously neat and clean.

There were two more doors in the party-wall. Through the nearest I saw a kitchen. The other, across the room, showed the end of a flight of stairs. Feet were pounding down these, and as I took in the scene—what with the small windows, the trees at the back, and the thundercloud overhead, it was very dark—Harry Devine, stooping, swung himself through the door, stood erect, and stared round, frowning.

"What's all this?" he said, just as his mother had done.

Mrs. Armfeldt was already settling her full skirt in one of the armchairs. She inspected him through her lorgnette. Mrs. Devine, her back to me, was standing facing him. Her thick grey hair was within an inch of the ceiling. She went up to him and whispered. Mrs. Armfeldt was trying to hear what was said, but there was a lot of noise now at the door, where all the men were crowding in out of the rain. Harry Devine frowned and whispered back, his pale blue eyes luminous in the dark room, his head thrust forward as he watched the newcomers. I thought he was urging his mother to do something, but she shook her head.

Puffin and Maurice had come in first, then Paul Armfeldt and James and Mr. Iliff. James was rubbing his head, having cracked it on the door. They made the room seem lower and smaller and (as they were blocking the doorway and the only window that gave any light) darker than ever.

Outside the rain pounded and the thunder rolled. Before anyone could speak again, there was a vivid flash of lightning. Mrs. Devine, who still had her back to us all, went quickly to the bureau and closed the window. Over her shoulder she said:

"Please close the door and that window too. I don't like lightning."

James obliged, just as the next crack of thunder banged like a salvo, and the room became darker still. Mrs. Devine turned round. She was putting on, of all things, a pair of tinted glasses.

"My eyes," she explained. "The lightning hurts them."

Harry Devine came forward. "Well?" he said.

Puffin began to explain all over again. He was too hot and bothered to remember to introduce the Armfeldts or Maurice or James to Mrs. Devine, but I suppose she guessed at once who they were. Or her son may have told her when they whispered together. Puffin's tale didn't sound very convincing to me. It would have been much simpler for every one to meet somewhere in Cambridge, and I wondered how he'd induced the Armfeldts to come out to Hythe House in the first place. All I could see dimly, in every sense, was Maurice's hand behind this move. Puffin would never have thought of it himself.

Maurice, who still looked cross, drew me back against the wall, between James and Paul Armfeldt. The latter, or what I could see of him in the gloom, wasn't at all his debonair self. He never even looked at me. James was scowling, perhaps because his head hurt him. Only Mr. Iliff, his broad back to the window and his bristles brushing the ceiling, was aloof and composed. His greeny-brown eyes were taking stock of everything and everybody. Presently he stepped a little aside, which let in a shade more light.

Mrs. Armfeldt, of course, kept her poise and stared round too through the lorgnette. Mrs. Devine, standing in the shadows by the bureau, half hidden by her son, was just a tall blur of blue cotton, with a whitish face and two dark discs above it. There was an uncomfortable air of tension in the crowded room.

Harry Devine was saying to Puffin, rather curtly: "I still don't see where we or Miss Lanham come in."

Another dazzling flash made faces leap out of the gloom and fade again. Mrs. Devine put a hand to her eyes. She moved past her son, pushed the newspapers off the stool by the fireplace, and sat down, turning her back to the front window and all of us who stood there. It seemed odd to see this big, masterful woman almost crouching on that absurd little seat. But the most unlikely people are upset by thunderstorms.

Harry Devine, after one glance at his mother, was looking at Puffin again. Puffin was looking at Maurice, as if this was *his* cue.

"Perhaps I may explain," Maurice said. "The idea was mine." He stopped while the next peal deafened us, and then went on: "You and I, Mr. Devine, arrived at the same conclusion yesterday. We agreed that this series of murders is intended to continue."

The other nodded. "Yes, that's my idea."

"Until the murderer is caught, then, three people may be in continual danger."

Harry Devine moved restlessly. "We went into all this," he said. "Though I make it four."

"You're including Mr. Tullis?"

184

"Sure. Lanham's had one try at him, hasn't he? Or have you got some new theory about that gunplay at Jesus? I saw him, remember."

"You said you thought you did."

"It's good enough for me, after what happened."

"We may come back to that," Maurice said. " *Your* theory is that we're dealing with a madman, killing for revenge?"

Harry Devine said in a surprised tone: "Of course."

"That's where I don't agree with you."

"How, Major?"

"I don't think now that revenge is the motive for these crimes—or at any rate, the only motive."

"I don't get you. There's only that jewellery——"

"There's also twenty-five thousand pounds."

Maurice paused to put in his eyeglass. What he really wanted in that room was a pair of night binoculars. It was growing darker and darker. The thunder was rumbling now all the time, and the rain was sousing down. I could just see Harry Devine frowning thoughtfully. Mrs. Devine still had her back to us, and Mrs. Armfeldt, forgetting her lorgnette, was watching Maurice.

Another flash lit up the room, bringing out faces like ghastly violet masks.

Maurice went on, turning a little to include us all: "You'll see that if I'm right—if we're right, for Colonel Nugent is inclined to agree with me now, but he's letting me do the talking because he's good enough to say I've got the gift of the gab—if we're right, then, this alters the whole position. Instead of looking for *one* man, the only man we know of who has the motive of revenge, we have a much wider field. We're bound to consider *anyone* who will benefit by these deaths. . . ."

Someone stirred near me. Maurice looked round.

"This is a purely academic discussion," he said. "Let me go on. . . . To run over the situation, as it was and as it is now, what do we find? A few days ago, five young people stood to gain by the trust fund established by their parents and others to the tune of some five thousand pounds apiece. *To-day,* three of them stand to get over eight thousand pounds. *To-morrow.* . . . But you can calculate for yourselves how the sum will work out if there are any more eliminations."

The storm was passing over the river towards Cambridge. The lightning flash that came then was fainter. But it was no brighter in the room. The rain still thudded on the cottage roof like something solid.

I could see Harry Devine's pale eyes fixed on Maurice.

"I seem to be a few laps behind again," he said. " I hadn't thought of it this way, Major. I—*we,* my mother and I—*know* Wilfrid Lanham, you see. We've heard him talk. He's mad. He's vamoosed. . . . Anyway, it just didn't occur to us, I suppose, to look at it from the money angle." I could just see his lips smiling. "We weren't raised," he said, "among people who toss thousands of pounds around like so many cents. This trust business sounds like a fairy-tale to us."

"The theory," Maurice said, "doesn't exclude Lanham, by any means. His daughter benefits by the fairy-tale. . . . By the way, Mr. Devine, if it isn't an impertinent question, where *were* you raised ?"

Harry Devine stared a little, but he answered carelessly:

"I was born over here, in London."

"A Cockney, like myself. . . ."

"Meaning I don't talk like one? No, I've been too long knocking round the States. . . . Well, go on, Major. What are you leading up to?"

Mrs. Armfeldt interrupted. "Zis money angle, as Mr. Devine calls it," she said, putting up the lorgnette, "did not occur to me eizer." She shrugged, with a little laugh. "It is interesting, but it is no concern of ours—my son and me. Why——"

Maurice said quickly: "On the contrary, you and your son are among the runners, Mrs. Armfeldt."

She sat up with a start and a rustle of silk. "Eh? Ze runners? What do you mean?"

"Mr. Armfeldt is engaged to Miss Farleigh."

"Well?"

"Even as things are, the trustees may decide to make up to Miss Farleigh what she has lost through graduating before these recent deaths. And if the three other surviving beneficiaries were to die, before *they* graduate, she will get everything—twenty-five thousand pounds plus what she has already drawn."

"But zis is monstrous!" Mrs. Armfeldt cried. "Paul, do you hear? Colonel Nugent, how dare you allow zis man——"

Puffin looked uneasily at Maurice, who went on dryly:

"I'm only clearing the air. I'm not making accusations. What I'm pointing out, Mrs. Armfeldt, is that not only you and your son, but Mrs. Devine and hers, and Mr. Tullis and his, must all be more or less under suspicion now. It's better to be frank. . . ."

It might be, but I thought that if this was Maurice's idea of clearing the air he'd borrowed it from the thunderstorm. Quite a good little tempest in miniature blew up at once. James spluttered, "Damn it, Hemyock. . .!" Mrs. Armfeldt half rose from her seat. Her son brushed roughly past me as he walked to her and faced us, his eyes black and glittering. Even Mrs. Devine's tinted glasses turned sharply. And Harry Devine took a quick step towards Maurice.

He said, in a nasty, quiet voice: "How in hell can you fix anything on *us*?"

A pallid flash lit up angry faces and cast weird flying shadows on the walls. They fled, and we were in twilight again. Maurice was looking round placidly through his eyeglass, like a showman rather pleased with his exhibits. He smiled at Harry Devine, but left his question unanswered.

"Perhaps now," he said, "you're all beginning to understand what Colonel Nugent meant by a council of war. Suspicion apart, you're all involved in another way, through your interests, affections, however you like to put it. . . . You *must* put your heads together, and help *us*. Let's be academic again, and tidy. And please don't keep interrupting. You can have my blood later. Well, these are the alternatives. . . ."

He dropped his eyeglass and began to polish it with maddening delibera-tion. Every one was watching him except Mrs. Devine, who'd turned away again, and Mr. Iliff, who was watching the watchers.

"*One,*" Maurice said briskly, like an auctioneer." If the murderer is Lanham, then Ian Tullis, young Ince, and possibly Miss Farleigh and Mr. Tullis, are in danger. I include Miss Farleigh because we're assuming that Lanham is out for revenge as well as gain, and he may have felt a particular grudge against her father. *Two.* If the murderer is Mr. Armfeldt——"

Paul Armfeldt muttered something, and his mother bounced in her chair again. Maurice turned on them.

"Please be quiet! I'm treating you as arguments, not as human beings. And if you feel that's scarcely complimentary, Mrs. Armfeldt, I apologise. . . . Now if your son is the murderer, obviously the potential victims are the younger Tullis, Ince, and Miss Lanham. Coming next to *Three,* Mr. Tullis"—James began to gobble, but subsided when I pinched him hard—"in this case we have to look after Ince and Miss Lanham again. And on the fourth supposi-tion, that the dark horse is Mr. Devine, the two boys are *his* quarry. . . ."

Maurice peered through his eyeglass, seemed satisfied with it, and screwed it in again. This time no one spoke. It was odd how they seemed tamed by being treated as arguments. Or perhaps they were getting interested, in spite of themselves. Even Harry Devine showed no resentment at Maurice's fourthly—in fact, I saw his lips twitch a little. Once he had looked round at his mother, or rather at her stiff blue back, for she hadn't stirred again. I won-dered if the thunder made her so ill that she couldn't even feel interest. But the peals were banging and rumbling farther away now, and the room seemed to be growing lighter. Only the rain beat down as heavily as ever.

Maurice went on:

"I suppose we're agreed that the murderer is a man. I think we can wash out the idea of an outsider—someone unknown to us. He's one of the four I've mentioned. He may, of course, have an accomplice, who in at least two of our imaginary cases is presumably a woman. . . ."

At these unpleasant reminders there was a little stir. Somebody drew in a breath with a tiny hissing noise, and Mrs. Armfeldt's silk skirt rustled as she jerked in her chair again. Maurice went on again quickly:

"There's still one more possibility. The murderer may have an accomplice outside his own household. That's to say, two of our alternatives may be working together. Lanham, for choice, with one of the other three——"

Harry Devine said: "So that's what you meant?"

"Well," Maurice said amiably, "if Lanham *has* a confederate, you're cut out for the part."

Harry Devine, I thought, didn't know whether to take him seriously or not. He said, with a touch of mockery:

"Granted. But is that all you've got against me? "

Maurice took him up promptly. " As the principal, you mean?"

"If you're going back to that, Major." His tone was still mocking.

"Why not? Let's consider you as the principal. We'll see afterwards how Lanham fits in as second murderer."

"Go right ahead," Harry Devine said. "This is interesting."

Maurice smiled. " I'm glad you take it so reasonably. . . . Well, to begin with, Mr. Devine, you've known for some time the whole story of the Nine Bright Shiners and the fund and Lanham's grievances. You're his neighbour in Chelsea, and his friend—his only friend, apparently, among the present company, by the way. You're well aware, of course, of his peculiarities—his stammer, for instance, and his theatrical bent. You could get his notepaper and imitate his handwriting. Whether or no the famous malacca is a sword-stick, it's a familiar object to you, and might suggest the weapon used in these crimes. You can draw"—Maurice glanced at the sketches on the walls—"and could turn out the figures of Hector and so on found on the bodies. . . ."

It *was* lighter in the room. I could see Harry Devine's frown of concentration. His eyes, narrowed, never left Maurice's face. His mother had turned again to stare at Maurice too, her dark glasses gleaming blankly, but it was the only movement she made.

Harry Devine was saying: "Go on."

"There are other items," Maurice said, "but we can fit them in later. Well, with these advantages, you worked out a scheme something like this. You and your mother took this cottage. You invited Lanham down for a week-end. You already knew Miss Lanham, of course, and you next got in touch with the other beneficiaries under the trust by the ingenious process of allowing Mr. Ince to upset you into the river."

Harry Devine gave a short laugh. "Did I?" he said. "Well, I call that pretty smart."

"Yes, it was quite neat. Mr. Ince is a hearty, friendly soul, and he made amends for what he thought was his error by introducing you to his set and the amenities of Cambridge generally. You could now mingle with your victims in the most natural manner."

I could feel James fidgeting beside me. Puffin, just in front of us, was rubbing his fingers up and down the seams of his trousers, a trick he has when he's on edge. Mrs. Armfeldt stared from Maurice to Harry Devine's broad back, her lorgnette still lying forgotten on her magenta lap. It was impossible to tell whom Mrs. Devine was staring at through those spectacles. I wished I could read her face. If I had been her, I thought, I couldn't just *sit* there, like an image.

"Go on," Harry Devine said again.

Maurice took out his eyeglass and screwed it in more firmly.

"To come to the murders," he said, as if he was talking about a picnic, "what you meant to do, still speaking academically, you know, was this. You intended to kill, first Sir Vyvyan, and then four out of the five beneficiaries under the trust still up at Cambridge, during the last five days of May Week, beginning last Saturday. You chose this time——"

"Heh?" Harry Devine interrupted. He was frowning again, his lips twisted in a sardonic smile. "Saturday? Why then? And why didn't I kick off till Monday?"

"We'll come to that. . . . You chose this time," Maurice went on, "because it was the only period at which Lanham and the rest of them could be got together conveniently in the same place. Lanham's holidays are strictly limited, and arranged for him beforehand. You persuaded him to ask for a part of them in May Week, so that he could be here with his daughter, giving out that he'd invited himself. Four of your other victims were here already, and Sir Vyvyan, you knew, would be coming down for part of the time. . . ."

Paul Armfeldt, who'd been fiddling about with his ring while he stood watching, pulled it off his finger and dropped it. It clattered on the tiles and for an instant broke the tension in the room. When he'd retrieved it, Maurice began again.

"A murder a day for five days," he said, "meant fast work, but these shock tactics would so hustle the police that before they'd got a clear idea of what they were up against, everything would be over. And this would include a sixth murder, carried out immediately after the others. Lanham's body would be found, with appropriate indications of suicide—an outcome at which you, who knew him so well, had already hinted. The police wouldn't look any farther. The case would be regarded as closed. And the surviving benefi-ciary, Miss Lanham, would get twenty-five thousand pounds."

Harry Devine had listened with the same sardonic smile on his lips. Otherwise his face was blank again. He inquired with an air of mild interest:

"But would she, Major? If her father was suspected of making a pile for her in this way——"

"Come, come!" Maurice said. "You wouldn't—in our supposititious case—have overlooked that point, Mr. Devine. You'd have made quite sure before-hand that as the money is a trust fund, by which Lanham couldn't benefit directly, and which wouldn't even come to his daughter through *him,* nothing could prevent her getting it—provided, of course, she had no hand in the crimes herself. No amount of suspicion of her father could affect her posi-tion. And anyway, there'd be no other candidate for the money left alive, except possibly Miss Farleigh. She might put in a claim for a further share. But perhaps, to be on the safe side, her elimination was intended too. . . ."

"Sure. It would be," Harry Devine said easily. "And the Vice-Chancellor's and the Archbishop of Canterbury's as well. What's another killing or two when you've got your hand in. . .? But haven't you forgotten something, Major?"

"Very likely. What is it?"

"Why am *I* doing all the donkey work? What do I get out of this? If you think there's a rake-off coming to me when things have simmered down, you don't know Mary Lanham. Unless it's your notion that she's in cahoots with me. And even then, I don't see her parting with enough to make it worth my while."

"I can imagine circumstances," Maurice said, "in which you could see to it you got a good rake-off."

"I'd like to know them."

"I should say your intention was to marry Miss Lanham. If you haven't married her already——"

Harry Devine's pale face flushed. He took a step towards Maurice. For the first time his temper had cracked.

"You," he said, "might leave that sort of talk out of it!"

"As you like," Maurice said. "You asked me. Anyway, as no doubt you know, proof of motive isn't necessary for conviction in a case of murder."

"You're changing your ground, aren't you? You were making a song about the motive just now. . . . Oh, hell!" Harry Devine got himself under control again. The colour ebbed from his face, leaving it a pale mask again, in which only the blue eyes shone. He shrugged. "What are you really getting at, Major?"

"I'm trying to get at the truth."

"You're going a swell way round. And you've still missed it. . . . Are you through now?"

"Not quite," Maurice said. "I like to finish things tidily. Let's run over the rest of the story."

"The rest. . .? Oh, how I did it, eh?"

"Yes, how you did it."

"Well, I ought to be interested in that, too, come to think of it," Harry Devine said.

He was smiling again, or his lips were. He really seemed interested, in a detached way.

For some time I hadn't had eyes for anyone else. I saw vaguely the other faces watching in the shadows—Mrs. Armfeldt's, from her chair, and the immaculate Paul's, up near the ceiling, and the black discs of Mrs. Devine's glasses midway down by the fireplace. Now, at last, she was roused enough to keep her head over her shoulder. The lenses were never off Maurice and her son. But she still sat there on her stool, unnaturally quiet, never moving or protesting or showing any sign of feeling.

Not that any of us stirred much. We were all absorbed, like people at a play. With James on my right, near the door, and Mr. Iliff on my left, and Puffin just in front of us, our little group was separated from the other by Maurice and Harry Devine, in the centre of the stage. It was growing lighter in the room, but so imperceptibly that it might only have been one's eyes that were getting accustomed to the gloom. With the door and both windows shut, it was also growing very close, and I was thankful I had so little on. Puffin, in tweeds and a stiff collar, was dabbing his neck with his handkerchief. Outside, the rain made less noise, but it was still coming down in sheets, and the thunder rumbled in the distance. As a matter of fact, only five or ten minutes, though they seemed like hours, had passed since we all crowded into the cottage.

Maurice, for a moment, had been ruminating on his shoes. He looked up and said, in a conversational way:

"I suggested just now, Mr. Devine, that these murders were meant to begin on Saturday."

"So you did, Major," said Harry Devine, quite as airily. "And I asked you why I didn't kick off till Monday. What's the answer?"

"Obviously, because Lanham wasn't here. Your time-table was thrown back by an accident. You'd arranged with him that he was to come down as soon as he got off work on Saturday. That would have given you five clear days, for all the other persons concerned, except Sir Vyvyan, were staying up till Wednesday at least, for the Jesus Ball. But at the last moment Lanham heard of some new job, hung about in London over Sunday to see a man about it, and finally didn't come down till Monday afternoon. . . ."

Harry Devine corrected him. "Monday evening."

"I think not. But we'll come to that. . . . This delay must have rattled you a bit. Your time-table had been carefully calculated. Now the whole scheme would have to be put off two days, at the last moment. Ince and Henderson were staying up, and could wait, but you were left with very little margin for the first three murders. They'd have to be managed strictly to schedule, at the rate of one a day. And Sir Vyvyan *had* to be disposed of on Monday night, as he was leaving Cambridge next morning. . . . However, here you had a bit of luck."

"I must have needed a break," Harry Devine said.

"You ran into Sir Vyvyan and Mrs. Armfeldt, and heard he was leaving Trinity early and going to Queens'."

"Well, I didn't make any secret of that. I told Ince, and he passed it on to you."

"Oh, quite," Maurice said. "We might have learnt the fact from Mrs. Armfeldt, so you very wisely got in first. It looked better, coming out that way."

Harry Devine smiled. "I'm not so dumb as I thought," he said.

Maurice went on: "Now we'll go back to Lanham's movements on Monday. *He'd* suggested, probably, coming down by that train in the evening that you went to meet. During the morning you sent him a telegram, telling him to catch the four o'clock, which reaches Cambridge at five-ten. You made up some story. He was to take a taxi to the Common and meet you on the river bank, where you'd have your canoe, and you'd bring him here by water. Perhaps you added that you'd tell his daughter, if he wanted her to know. That would prevent him ringing her up to say he was coming earlier than he'd told her. But there was no particular reason why he should want to. She wasn't expecting to see him at all that evening. The objects of these manoeuvres, of course, were *(a)* that you shouldn't be seen with Lanham at the station, and *(b)* that you wanted him down as soon as possible. You had a lot to do that night."

"I must have had," Harry Devine said. His lips still smiled, but his pale eyes were not amused. "Go on, Major. What did I do next in this dime novel?"

Maurice said placidly, "You brought Lanham here, doped him, and put him away in storage till he was wanted again. Your mother is a nurse—she would know what to give him, if you didn't——"

At this first direct reference, since the very beginning, to Mrs. Devine, the still figure by the fireplace stirred. The dark glasses gleamed. I thought she was going to get up, but as her son broke in angrily she checked herself.

"My God, Major!" Harry Devine cried. "I've had enough of this!"

"As you like," Maurice said. "I thought you were interested."

"I'm not keen enough to have my mother dragged in——"

"But my dear Mr. Devine, your mother has been in all along. We agreed on that to start with. Just as Mrs. Armfeldt is in, with *her* son. And Mr. Tullis. And, of course, first and foremost, Lanham——"

"I reckoned you'd forgotten him," Harry Devine rapped out.

"Not at all. As you say, this is only a dime novel. And it's only in dime novels that one can bet on the improbable. In real life it's the obvious that turns out to be the truth, nine times out of ten. Ask the Superintendent."

Harry Devine flashed a look at that officer, who was effacing himself so thoroughly that one forgot he was there.

"I thought," he said to Maurice, "you were aiming to prove this was the tenth time."

"Purely academically—at present. And though I happened to begin with you, your fellow suspects here will have their turn. I can assure you it's possible to work up almost equally good cases against them."

Harry Devine's face was still dark. His right hand was gripping the lapel of his coat, the other was thrust into his pocket. His feet were a little apart. His narrowed, luminous eyes glanced sideways at his mother, sitting erect now, her own blank stare on Maurice, and then shifted round to Mrs. Armfeldt, who had jerked up in her chair. He relaxed slightly, and his lips twitched.

"I don't see," he said to Maurice, "how this academic stuff's going to help you. But please yourself. Only step on it."

Maurice stepped on it. He went on quickly:

"I said, Mr. Devine, that you had a lot to do on Monday night. Having brought Lanham here, you left him unconscious in charge of your mother and went back to Cambridge. On your motor-cycle, was it, this time. . .? You wanted to find someone who knew you, so that you could spread your tale of being there to meet the later train, and of Lanham's non-arrival. Your luck was in, because you ran into Ian Tullis, who would be certain to broadcast this little fiction later on, when it became important. . . . Then, I think, you came back here, to see how things were going on and to make one or two small preparations. Two or three hours later you set off once more, no doubt by road again. And at midnight you were waiting for Sir Vyvyan and Mr. Mercer to leave Trinity for Queens'. . . ."

Harry Devine opened his lips, but Maurice checked him.

"Ask your questions at the end," he said. "Well, to go on, you killed Sir Vyvyan in King's Lane on his way back to the 'Eagle.' Perhaps you stopped him, perhaps you came up behind, and he never knew who struck him. You dragged his body into a doorway, walked on into the hotel, went through that little scene with the maid, and lifted the pendant. Of course you'd reconnoitred the place beforehand, and had decided where to hide and how to get away. Possibly you walked quietly out again, minus moustache and glasses, in the confusion caused by the body being brought in. You went to wherever you'd parked your cycle, and rushed back here. You had still several hours of darkness. You put Lanham in your big canoe and took him to some hiding-place down the river. You've had six months in which to look for such a place, and the fenland in that direction is not a populous part of the world. It wouldn't be difficult to find a corner where an unconscious man could be left safely for four or five days—provided, of course, he was kept unconscious, and you would see to that. At nights, or perhaps even in the daytime, you'd paddle down and dose him again as required. No doubt you tied him up too. The weather has been fine, and he wouldn't come to any harm——"

Harry Devine spoke before he could be stopped. "Have you ever tried lifting an unconscious man in and out of a canoe, Major?"

"It wouldn't be easy," Maurice agreed. "But you're a powerful man, Mr. Devine, and Lanham is a light-weight, as every one who knows him has admitted—before they thought of correcting themselves. And your canoe isn't one of the flimsy things ordinarily used on the Cam. Of course this business of carting Lanham about, and keeping him doped and hidden for five days, is one of the most difficult, and one of the biggest risks, you've had to take. You might have handled it differently, by killing him outright. But you would have to dispose of the body, and it would be both more artistic and more convincing if he could be kept alive till you could produce him, dead, and apparently by his own hand, at the end of the series. There'd be no need to forge a confession. Facts would seem to speak for themselves. . . ."

The rain was beginning to pound down again, but it was the last of the storm. Gleams of sunlight shone through the dripping trees beyond the back window, and I remember thinking that there must be a rainbow there. The room was much lighter now. Mrs. Devine had turned her face away once more. Her son, with a fixed little smile on his lips, said to Maurice:

"You have an explanation for everything."

Maurice said: "One tries to be tidy. . . . Now let's get on to the next two murders. I needn't go into details. I'll only point out, with regard to Hereward Rowsell-Hogg, that you could learn, from your common friends, that he was staying in college over Wednesday, while we know you were in Cambridge early that morning because Mr. Armfeldt told my wife that he *overtook* you on the river on his way to Hythe House. . . . As to last night, you could find out Henderson's movements in the same way—perhaps from himself—and *I* saw you, again on the river, heading towards Queens', not half an hour before he must have been murdered. Having tied up your canoe at the Mill Pit, you would walk over the wooden bridge into the college, kill the boy, and be out again and paddling home in three or four minutes. There was no one about. The college was almost empty. You ran a slight risk of the porter seeing you, if he happened to put his head out of the lodge while you were coming or going, but he didn't. . . ."

The room was getting stifling, and even Maurice felt warm. He stopped to mop his face before he went on again.

"So far," he said, "everything had gone according to plan. You had kept to your time-table. You and your mother had fostered the idea that Lanham had been mad for some time, though you made out you didn't realise how mad he was till after the second murder. You both harped on the suicide ending. You both went so far as to draw attention to the danger in which the two Tullises stood. You, yourself, even warned them—quite a clever move. The police might begin to suspect at any moment that other murders were due to follow. This you couldn't help, so you turned it to your own advantage. To this fabric of suggestion you then added one or two touches which I think were afterthoughts, and perhaps not quite so clever. On the drawing of Solomon which you left in Henderson's rooms you put the initials 'W.L.' And during yesterday afternoon you telephoned to Miss Lanham, pretending you were her father. It was not the sort of message one would expect him to send in the circumstances. You hadn't thought it out beforehand, and you were hurried, because you knew the police were tapping all calls. Perhaps, too, you weren't sure of keeping the imitation up for more than a few words. . . . Anyway, it wasn't one of your most successful efforts."

"It happens," Harry Devine said, "to be the first I've heard of any message. This is a darn good story, Major, but don't twist facts too far. How do you know I was in Cambridge yesterday afternoon?"

Maurice said sharply: "How do *you* know the message was telephoned from Cambridge?"

For an instant I thought Harry Devine was taken aback. But it *was* only for an instant that he hesitated, if he hesitated at all. Then he smiled.

"Ask the Superintendent," he said. "It's all over the town where *he* thinks Lanham's hiding. And I'd say he's right. We ought to have thought of the colleges before."

"However," Maurice said, dropping the point rather meekly, I thought, "you were there yourself at the time, because my wife and I passed you coming out on our way in."

He looked at his watch and then glanced round the company.

"I'm sorry to be so prolix," he said, "but I've nearly done. With Mr. Devine, that is. . . ." He turned to Harry Devine again. "We've got to the position yesterday evening," he went on. "There were still two murders to come, not counting Lanham's suicide. In your original order Ian Tullis must have been marked down for early disposal, because he was leaving Cambridge with his father yesterday. But on Wednesday afternoon, when you thoughtfully went to warn the Tullises, you found they were staying another day. Ian was reprieved for a few hours. Perhaps you couldn't see a way of getting him alone just then. Anyway, his case was put back while you dealt with young Henderson. . . . But in the meantime, during yesterday, you changed your plans much more radically. Did you hear, or think, that inquiries were taking an awkward direction. . .? Whatever the reason, there was some hitch. You decided to carry your scheme one stage farther, and then to pull up for the time being. This must have involved other rearrangements. You couldn't, for instance, keep Lanham drugged and a prisoner indefinitely. It would be interesting to know what you proposed to do with him, now that the rest of your programme was postponed. For postponed it was. You went straight from killing Henderson to young Ince's rooms, with a proposal that for his own safety he should go to Scotland with you. His own safety. . .!" Maurice paused. "Would he have come back, Mr. Devine?" he asked. "Or would there have been a convenient accident? And would you have rested content with that, and with half the twenty-five thousand pounds, or with Lanham at the bottom of the Cam would you still have used his ghost to eliminate Ian Tullis later on. . . ?"

There was a queer silence. Maurice had rather worked himself up, as he very seldom does. Harry Devine faced him with the same blank, watchful face, but towards the end a flush spread over it. A hand gripped the lapel of his coat again, and I could see the other clench in his pocket. Again his mother had turned round, but the room wasn't light enough yet for me to read her face. Those baffling glasses were like a mask.

Every one else shifted a little. I could hear the rustle of Mrs. Armfeldt's silks, and Puffin's shoes scraping on the tiles of the floor. I could see his fingers twitching. Paul Armfeldt, fiddling with his ring, had it half off. Mr. Iliff took a short step forward. Something, I felt, *must* happen now. If it didn't, if this silence went on, I should laugh hysterically. . . .

But nothing happened. Or rather, it was Harry Devine who laughed, and somebody (James, I think) breathed noisily, as if the breath had been held back.

"Well, well!" Harry Devine said, his pale eyes watching Maurice like a cat's, while his lips still smiled. "I call that a swell novel for a dime, Major. Isn't it my turn now? I've got a few questions to put to you."

I could only see Maurice's back, but I knew he was watching the other just as closely. He seemed to be thinking. Then he shrugged.

"If you like," he said. "Fire away."

It was an anticlimax, somehow. I didn't know whether to be relieved or disappointed. I thought even Harry Devine himself was a little puzzled. But he went off the mark promptly.

"Go back to the beginning, Major," he said. "Granting everything, for the sake of argument, why in Hades should I kill old Rowsell-Hogg? I've nothing coming from *him.*"

"Obviously," Maurice said, "his murder was a blind, to fix suspicion on Lanham from the start. The theft of the pendant was part of it."

"You're making me out a fine picture of a whole-hogger. Hell, I didn't mean a joke. . . ."

The white teeth flashed, but it was a forced smile. Harry Devine was feeling the heat, for he ran his hand over his forehead, where the sweat glistened. The lightning was a long way off now, and I wondered no one thought of opening the door or a window. We were all too absorbed, perhaps—all too keenly watching and waiting for something.

And then I wondered if it was coming now, after all. There was another little pause, while Harry Devine's smile died and he stood there frowning. I realised that under his cold self-possession he was very tired. He was suddenly feeling the strain after an ordeal that must have taxed his will and nerves to the utmost. The reaction had set in, and he was struggling to clear his thoughts, as his next words showed.

"Hell," he said again, "you've talked so much I can't think. What does it matter, anyway? It's all boloney, and you know it, Major. Leave me alone, and get down to cases."

Maurice said, with an air of surprise: "I thought it was your turn now. But if you like, Mr. Devine, I'll give you another opening. What can you tell me about that business at Jesus the other night? That's the one thing I haven't got quite clear."

"You don't tell me!" Harry Devine said, with a sneer. "And I thought you'd an answer to everything. . . . But I'm through, anyway. I've had enough of this third degree, in my own house. I'll only say this. I'm not the only one in this room who's been in the States." He turned abruptly on the Armfeldts. "Try *them,* for a change," he said.

Maurice focused his eyeglass on the pair.

"Why not?" he asked.

3

It was like a sudden transformation scene. One moment Harry Devine was the centre of interest, the cynosure and all that. The next he was forgotten as Mrs. Armfeldt, who had sat silent and almost unnoticed for so long, bounced in her chair.

"How dare you!" she cried. "Colonel Nugent——"

Paul Armfeldt put in, "Yes, we've had enough of this——"

"Enough?" Harry Devine said jeeringly. "You haven't begun yet."

Maurice said sharply, "Mr. Devine has stood it, Mr. Armfeldt, and very patiently, I think. Why shouldn't you? If you've nothing on your conscience you've no reason to object. . . . I'll run over a few of the points against you. Your motive, unlike Mr. Devine's, is in evidence. On Monday night, you and your mother gave an impromptu party at your hotel. The 'Granta' is within two minutes' walk of King's Lane, and you could easily have slipped out for a quarter of an hour. You knew, from your mother, that Sir Vyvyan was going to Queens' that night. . . . To come to Wednesday morning, you were in Trinity when his son was murdered——"

"I wasn't!" Paul Armfeldt cried. "I didn't get there till nine or after."

"Can you prove it? Again, yesterday evening you were walking towards Queens' just before the third murder there——"

I received a look that was anything but liquid as Paul Armfeldt said quickly, "I was going to see a man at Peterhouse."

"Did you see him?"

"No, he was out. But the porter will tell you——"

"It wouldn't take you long to get back to Queens'. To dodge the porter there you'd go down Silver Street and over the wooden bridge. . . ."

The sweat was standing out on Paul Armfeldt's forehead now. Harry Devine was watching him maliciously. He began to protest again, but his mother, who had risen, silenced him with some dignity.

"Be quiet, Paul! I zhought we were going. I certainly do not wish to hear more of zis. But *you* will hear more of it, Colonel Nugent! Come, Paul——"

But here James, to my surprise, put in his oar.

"No, you don't!" he said truculently, getting in front of the door. "You'll hear it out."

Face to face, he and Mrs. Armfeldt glared at one another, while Maurice went on calmly:

"Yes, I haven't done, by any means. I was going to point out, Mr. Armfeldt, that of course you and your mother have learnt from Miss Farleigh all about Lanham and the club and the fund. You could do those drawings in your sleep—you're an artist. You had, or made, an opportunity to get Lanham's notepaper——"

Paul Armfeldt exclaimed shrilly, "How? What do you mean?"

"You called at his flat, when he was out, and wrote a note to him. From his reply you could imitate his handwriting."

"Good God, Major, this is lunacy! I did go there, but I'd quite forgotten it. It was Claudia's idea—she thought I could do him a good turn with his firm by putting some work in their way. Instead of being grateful, he wrote and abused us both. And you twist round a thing like that——"

Mrs. Armfeldt, her magenta breast heaving, her dark eyes flashing, had turned away from the immovable James.

"Colonel Nugent, I insist on being allowed to go! Zis *is* lunacy! And worse, as you'll find——"

Puffin looked very uneasy. Even Mr. Iliff, standing in his corner like a piece of furniture, glanced doubtfully from his superior to Maurice. But Maurice went on, like the brook.

"As Mr. Devine points out, Mr. Armfeldt, you have also been in the States, which suggests a link with that affair at Jesus on Wednesday night. What's more, last autumn you were back in America for some months. Does that recall anything. . .? To go on, you have made one or two obvious attempts to pump Mrs. Hemyock about my views on these crimes, and those of the police. You were in Cambridge at the time of the telephone call yesterday afternoon——"

Paul Armfeldt said hastily, "I wasn't trying to pump Mrs. Hemyock. At least, not for that reason——"

"You admit you did try?"

"Well . . . I was interested, of course. And then——"

"Paul!" Mrs. Armfeldt said sharply.

They exchanged a glance. Paul took out a yellow silk handkerchief and passed it over his forehead. There was a little pause while Maurice dropped his eyeglass and stared thoughtfully at his shoes. He seemed suddenly to have forgotten all about Mr. Armfeldt.

The rain was now easing up again. The thunder rumbled over Cambridge. By comparison with the late Stygian darkness the low room seemed quite full of light. In the breathing-space I found myself taking stock of the company again. Most of us were now gathered near the door and the front window— James Tullis in front of the door, myself next to him, Mr. Iliff against the wall on the other side of the window, with Puffin, Maurice, and Mrs. Armfeldt a little in front of us. Facing us stood Paul Armfeldt, with Harry Devine now behind him. Mrs. Devine sat where she had sat all this time, upright on the low stool by the fireplace, her back to us. I felt again how extraordinary her attitude was, how unnatural and how *unlike* her, as I'd imagined her to be. Though she might, of course, be feeling really ill—I've heard of thunder having the queerest effects—yet nothing, I should have said, would have stopped this big, masterful woman from having her say about Maurice's nerve, and in her own house too. But while he'd piled up his points against her son, in a way that sounded very nasty, whether he was in earnest or not, all she did was to look round once or twice through those baffling tinted glasses. After complaining about the lightning, she hadn't uttered a word. I didn't see Goneril or Lady Macbeth, unless struck dead by a flash, taking it so quietly for one second. It was uncanny. . . .

I was jerked back from these thoughts, and my eyes from Mrs. Devine's long, motionless blue back, by Mrs. Armfeldt saying suddenly, in a conversational tone:

"Well? Well? Is ze play over?"

She had got back her normal poise, though with an obvious effort, for she was still breathing fast, and her dark eyes sparkled.

Maurice looked up. "Oh, do go if you want to," he said. "You won't mind waiting in the car?"

He nodded to James, who flung open the door. Quite a flood of light streamed into the room.

Mrs. Armfeldt, not unnaturally, looked rather taken aback. Her son, having adjusted *his* wits to Maurice's *volte-face,* joined her with a briskness that was quite comical. He refrained carefully from looking at me.

"Yes, let's go," he said eagerly.

She looked out at the rain. "*I* certainly do not wish to stay," she remarked, as if someone had asked her to. "We will wait in ze car, since I suppose we may not drive it away. Will somebody lend me an umbrella?"

It was an absurd little interlude. Harry Devine, who all the time Paul Armfeldt went through it at Maurice's hands had been keeping his own blank face at its blankest, seemed to wake up to his duties as a host, if an unwilling one. He glanced round at his mother, and took a step towards the kitchen door. But Maurice forestalled him.

"In there?" he said. And then to James: "Find it, will you, Tullis?"

For one moment the mask lifted again from Harry Devine. He looked wicked. I knew then that he was far more angry than he'd ever shown, and that this new trifling interference galled him almost to the limit of his self-control. But he still had himself in hand. He shrugged. His face became blank again.

James dived into the kitchen, and we heard him routing about. But he reappeared almost at once with a lady's umbrella, large size, suited to Mrs. Devine. Paul Armfeldt took it from him. Mrs. Armfeldt, without a look behind her, dipped her *tricorne* at the door and sailed out. As her son stooped to follow her, opening the umbrella, he turned his head to say waspishly:

"I suppose it's Mr. Tullis's turn now."

James gave a snort.

I saw the two figures hurrying past the window on their way to the cars, Paul holding the umbrella over his mother.

As if some tension had been eased, or some new act was beginning, every one left in the room made a slight movement. James drew closer to me. Puffin shifted his feet and coughed. Superintendent Iliff, in an absent sort of way, took a step or two forward. (It struck me then, for the first time, how extraordinarily out of the picture the forces of law and order had been so far.) Harry Devine put a hand to his coat lapel and moved a little to one side, towards his mother. And even her straight back, though I could not say it stirred, seemed more rigid.

Maurice was putting in his eyeglass again. He glanced casually round at James.

"Ah, yes, Mr. Tullis . . ." he said.

Mrs. Devine, of all of them, came suddenly to life. She rose abruptly from her stool, still without turning to face us. It was quite startling to see that blue statue move so quickly and supply.

She said in a low voice: "I'm going upstairs, Harry."

Like a slow-motion film that jerks suddenly out of control, everything seemed to happen violently at once. Maurice snapped over his shoulder to James: "Get Myra out of it!" James grabbed my arm and pulled me through the door into the garden. I caught a glimpse of Harry Devine stepping between his mother and Maurice, of Puffin and the Superintendent starting forward. And I heard Maurice say sharply:

"*Not* upstairs, Mrs. Devine—*or should I say Daal* ?"

Then I was struggling with James on the sodden lawn, with the rain beating on us. I was struggling because I was afraid for Maurice. A fearful shindy was going on in the cottage. A shot cracked. A police whistle blew. James kept saying, *"All right, Myra! All right!"* I said much more unkind things to James and I've apologised for them since. But though he played his part nobly, I shall always believe he thought it the better part. He wasn't really anxious to be back inside that room.

A man came running round the side of the cottage and plunged in through the door. A herd of elephants still seemed to be trampling about there. I was exhausted, for James was really strong. Suddenly, up above, at the dormer window, Maurice's face appeared. He was a little pinker than usual, and obviously rather blown.

"Oh, there you are," I said stupidly.

"Well?" James cried. "Is he there?"

Maurice wiped what appeared to be a cobweb out of his hair. Inside the cottage the tumult and the shouting had suddenly died.

"Yes, he's here," Maurice said. "In the loft."

"Do let go, James," I said. "I *will* be good—now. Who are you talking about?"

"Lanham," Maurice said.

CHAPTER XII

"It put years on my age," Puffin said. "Rotate the port, Myra."

We were in the garden at Hythe House once more. That's to say, Puffin, Maurice, and I were. I'd been hearing for the first time what happened in the cottage at Horningsea after James manhandled me out of it. Because immediately after that Maurice made me go off with the Armfeldts in the car that had brought them out. Somehow I didn't need any persuading. I might have joined in the dog-fight, to help Maurice, but that was over, and I wasn't at all keen on hanging about to see the Devines come out with gyves on their wrists, like Prince Eugene or whoever it was. It would have seemed indecent. There are one or two jobs for which women definitely are not suited. Soldiering is one. A policeman's is another.

That short drive with the Armfeldts was an unsociable one. Paul drove, and his mother sat beside him, and neither said a word to me till they dropped me at Hythe House. They had to go out of their way to do that, of course, and they didn't do it just from kindness. What Maurice called his charm of manner persuaded them. In other words, they were still anxious to keep in with him and the police. But that didn't make them go out of their way to be sweet to me. They didn't even ask what had happened. All they wanted, I fancy, was to get well away as quickly as possible. Not that I wanted to chatter just then, anyway. I was feeling rather shaken myself.

When I got out, Mrs. Armfeldt said distantly, "*Good* morning, Mrs. Hemyock," and her son gave me the liquid smile a good deal under proof, so to speak. They drove on at once, and out of this story.

I had lunch with Vera and Averil. Then Vera, saying that her daughter was *not* to talk any more about it, whisked the child off to say good-bye to the Tullises. Immediately after, Puffin and Maurice came back from Cambridge, where the Devines—I couldn't think of them as anything else yet—had been taken in the second car and locked up, charged with aiding and abetting, or obstructing the police, or something equally trivial. But of course this was only till the real charge could be worked up. You have to go about things in this way in England.

The two men had had a sandwich or something, but not nearly enough to drink, Puffin said. He wanted port, and lots of it. He always drinks port when he can spare time to go to sleep after it. It runs in the family. His great-grandfather commanded his brigade at Waterloo from a barouche, because he couldn't put his gouty foot to the ground.

The thunder had rolled away out of sight and hearing over the home counties. The sun blazed down again. It was queer to be sitting there once more, feeling that everything else was over, too—bar the explanations. The detective, in life as well as in fiction, usually has the last word, and as Maurice's wife I was getting used to these anticlimaxes where the hero tells you how he did it. One always wants to know, so one can't grumble.

It was Puffin, as a matter of fact, who began, with the story of the dog-fight.

Mrs. Devine, he said, was the worse of the pair. When she did come to life, she was like a tigress, and nearly as powerful. Luckily, she hadn't a weapon. It was her son who pulled a pistol from a holster under his armpit, where his hand had hovered so often at the lapel, but Maurice, who'd had his eye on that hand, tackled him low before he could aim, and as they came down in a heap the automatic followed its bullet into a corner. Then the four men—Puffin, Maurice, Mr. Iliff, and the constable watching the cottage, who ran in when the whistle blew—managed after a while to master the other two. In the process Mr. Iliff had his face clawed, and the constable's thumb was bitten. It sounded a horrible business altogether, and I was thankful I hadn't been able to break away from James.

It was after this that Puffin said, referring to what had happened before: "It put years on my age."

Maurice nodded. "I'm afraid I did spin it out," he said. "Finding Myra there made things doubly awkward. I knew we could get rid of Mrs. Armfeldt when we wanted to, but Myra never knows when she's in the way. . . . I was thinking hard all the time. And to the very end I was bluffing. I hadn't convinced you and Iliff. I'd hardly convinced myself. If you could have got a search warrant——"

Puffin said: "My dear chap, I told you no magistrate would grant one on that evidence. You've just said you weren't even sure yourself. As it was, Iliff and I risked our heads by being there at all. It was the most irregular business I ever heard of. I'm damned grateful now, and all that. . . ."

"So am I," said Maurice. "For your moral support. It kept 'em all fairly quiet. They wouldn't have listened for thirty seconds to me alone, but they didn't know what to do with you standing there. You lent dignity to impudence, and kept them guessing to the end."

"Like you, apparently," I said.

He nodded again. "There were times, as I said, when I wasn't any too sure. After all, what *had* I to go on? And Daal's as good a bluffer as I am, or better. He ought to be. He must have had more practice."

"Why did you go about it that way?" I asked. "Couldn't you have waited? You said yourself that Harry Devine—Daal—whatever his name is—had changed his plan. There were to be no more murders for the present. Or were you guessing then, too. . .? Anyway, those boys were being guarded, and Ian's off to-day. Why did you rush in with your performing troupe?"

"Because of Lanham. They couldn't keep him alive while they waited to resume operations. Still less if they weren't going to resume them."

"*Was* he in with them, or not? I haven't got *that* clear yet."

"Lord, no. He's been lying doped since Monday night. We got the district nurse in, you know, and then had him taken to Addenbrooke's. They say he's full of the stuff, and a mere bag of bones."

"So you were right about him, too?"

"Yes, but I was only guessing again. I didn't know. Or he might have been in with them. It was a distinct possibility. But if he was, he was none the less in danger. From all accounts of him, he'd be the weak link. They'd have to get rid of him. They were flitting, you know. They'd got the wind up. They knew that affair at Jesus must start inquiries that might be very awkward. And then I was nosing round where I wasn't wanted. I think they'd decided— or Daal had—to drop the Cambridge end for good, get Ince away to Scotland, where there'd be one more death—an accident—and be content with half the profits."

"Leaving Ian alone, you mean?"

"Yes. He'd get twelve thousand, five hundred pounds, or thereabouts, and the Lanham girl the same. Then I made a mistake—or I think I did. When we all left Ince's rooms last night those sketches I'd borrowed from Miss Lanham were lying on the back seat of the car. They weren't tied up, like Mercer's. I wasn't expecting to meet Daal. He may have seen them, and if he did he's quite sharp enough to put two and two together. I didn't think of it till this morning, but when I did I began to worry about Lanham. If I'd been sure he was in that cottage I shouldn't have had much hope for him. But I thought they probably had him tucked away somewhere else, and neither of them left the place last night. So there seemed to be a chance. . . . The performing troupe, as you call it, was roped in to provide an explosive atmosphere. I hoped if we got 'em all together something would go off."

"It took a long time," I said.

"So long that in the end I chucked a match in myself. But I was pretty sure by then."

"About Lanham being in the cottage?"

"That was one thing."

"But Mr. Iliff went all over it on Tuesday."

"Yes, when Lanham *was* lying under a hedge or somewhere, trussed up and doped. *After* the cottage had been searched, what place could be better?"

"They were running an awful risk, though."

"Not so big a risk, when you come to think it out, as if they'd left him somewhere out of reach, where they might be prevented from getting to him to give him his daily dose. And it was only for five days, according to their original time-table. And they're used to running risks, anyway. They're born gamblers."

"I suppose," I said, "they got him back somehow on Tuesday night, in spite of the cottage being watched then?"

"Probably," said Maurice. "You saw yourself how it *was* watched. Until you came in with your story of the gangster, Constable Larkin and his relief were quite happy patrolling the track from the road. From there the cottage, *and* the river, are masked by the trees. When Daal brought Lanham back in his canoe from wherever he'd parked him on Monday night, he'd only to wait till his mother signalled that the coast, literally, was clear. One of the lessons of this case is the use of water transport in crime. We're not river-minded in this country. Even here, on the edge of the fens, people have got out of the habit of using their waterways, except for pleasure. But it was our talking about the Cam that gave me a hint to begin with. You remember Puffin's story of the taxi? When he mentioned Butt's Green, and you asked where the passenger would get to from there, he said, 'the river.' It stuck in my mind, and when I was wondering where Lanham was, and how he—or the murderer—got away every time, I began to think amphibiously. And that suggested Daal's big canoe. . . ."

"Now tell me about *them*" I said. "The Daals. I shall learn to think of them by that name in time."

Maurice finished his port. "You ought to be telling this, Puffin," he said.

"None of your mock modesty," Puffin said. "I haven't grasped the whole rigmarole myself yet. And I don't care if I never do. Confessions of a chief constable. Carry on."

He reached for the decanter again and settled himself in his chair with the air of one who after stormy seas has reached port (in two senses) at last. Maurice carried on.

"Some of the facts," he said, "we only got an hour or two ago. And some we don't know yet. But it's all pretty clear now. . . . You know the beginning, anyway, Myra. The Nine Bright Shiners and the trust fund and the rest of it. The real story dates from 1913, when Owen Jevons went to Norway to learn the timber business at that end. . . ."

"I thought he went to Russia," I said.

"That was only Mercer's guess, and he guessed wrong. The firm's still flourishing, though there's no Jevons in it now, and we rang up this morning to find out where Owen Jevons did go to in 1913. He went to Norway. There he fell in love with a girl named Karen Daal. You know the rest of that story too—up to the time when she came to England, and Jevons' people and the trustees of the Shiners' fund refused to help her. Soon after this—we don't yet know exactly when—she took the boy, Jevons's boy, to America. She settled in Chicago and took up nursing. The boy may or may not have taken up journalism, but later on he certainly took up bootlegging, or something of the kind, and became a member of the Tonello gang."

"Then it was he——?"

"It was he who killed a man named M'Ginnis by pinning him to the wall of a garage with a bayonet. Puffin had another cable from Chicago two hours ago. The police there have found out somehow that the murderer's name was Daal. If we'd known that before we set off this morning it would have saved us a lot of trouble."

Maurice took the decanter. When I'd declined it, he filled his glass again and went on.

"After this murder Daal found Chicago too hot for him. M'Ginnis's brother and his friends were after him, and one presumes the police as well. So he and his mother skipped back to England, where they took a cheap flat in Chelsea, in the block where Wilfrid Lanham lived."

"Did they know that?" I asked.

"I refuse to believe it was a coincidence. I think Mrs. Daal, to give her the title she naturally used, though she now called herself Devine, always bore a grudge against the members of the club and their children. Especially against the children, who were getting all that her son, in her opinion, ought to have had. I think she always had the idea of revenge at the back of her mind. She'd been brooding over it in the States, and back in England she'd begin to wonder what she could do about it. The boy would be brought up with the same idea, though I dare say he thought chiefly about the money. His mother wanted another sort of revenge as well. Anyway, they couldn't get one without the other. . . . What I think happened was that they hunted up Lanham among the rest of the surviving Shiners, found out where he lived and that he had a daughter, and saw how they could make use of both to square a hard deal with a bayonet, as Daal himself put it. They came over here some time before Christmas, and quite possibly Rex Henderson's death in a motor smash was the germ of their scheme. It must have suggested possibilities. There were only four lives left between them and twenty-five thousand pounds. Sir Vyvyan, no doubt, was included in the list of victims for the reasons I suggested this morning—partly to incriminate Lanham, but quite as much to please Mrs. Daal, who hated him worst of the lot. . . ."

"Do you think Lanham knew who they were?" I asked.

"We shall know when he's fit to talk," Maurice said. "But personally I feel sure he didn't. He'd never seen the woman before—we do know that, from Tullis. Lanham had helped her, in the old days, as he said, but he was away at the time, and it was done by letter. On the other hand, your James *had* met her."

"Oh. . .!" I said.

"Yes, she called to see him at the same time, when she was begging for help. We'll come back to that. . . . Well, at Chelsea it was easy for the Daals to get in with Lanham. He'd talk to anyone about his grievances. The next step in the plan was for Daal to get round the girl. I dare say that wasn't very difficult either. You've seen both of them, and you know more about that sort of thing than I do. Anyhow, it came off. They were married at a registry office last May."

"Good heavens!" I said. "Then you weren't bluffing when you said that at the cottage this morning?"

"Yes, I was. At my suggestion, last night, Puffin had inquiries made through Scotland Yard. We didn't know definitely when we should hear, one way or the other. If they were married—and logically they *must* be, if I was right— they might have been married anywhere. As it happens, they were married in Chelsea, the obvious place to try first. But this news, like that from Chicago, didn't come through till after we'd started."

"Does her father know, do you think?"

"I doubt it. Daal wouldn't want anyone to know. It mustn't leak out too soon. And Lanham seems incapable of keeping his mouth shut. It would have to be kept from the Newnham authorities, anyway, and Daal could use that, among other arguments, to prevent the girl telling her father."

"Poor creature!" I said, and once more sincerely.

"Yes, she's well out of it."

Maurice sipped his port and lit a cigarette, in defiance of the purists.

"Go on," I said.

"The rest you know—or most of it. The Daals had already rented this cottage, and I think we shall find they carried out the rest of the scheme, including the first three murders, very much as I sketched it for their benefit this morning."

"What really happened at Jesus on Wednesday night?"

Maurice smiled. "Oh, that was a tragi-comedy of errors, so far as one can piece it together. The murdered M'Ginnis's brother must have tracked the Daals to England. Obviously he'd never seen either of them. Somehow— Daal no doubt made some shady acquaintances in London, where he'd naturally gravitate to what the press calls the underworld, and the news perhaps got to your friend Bud that way—somehow, anyway, the unfortunate Bud learned that his quarry had come to Cambridge. So he came to Cambridge after him. Inquiries there—he'd have to be careful, and couldn't ask too many questions—informed him that a gentleman, recently of Chicago, was living in a cottage at Horningsea and mixing with a particular set of undergraduates. Unluckily there were two such persons, and Bud M'Ginnis very naturally confused them. That both their mothers happened to be here at the time helped on the error. He thought Armfeldt was his man. What he was trying to do when you met him one can only guess. Probably he was going to pitch some tale of old Chicago days to Mrs. Daal, or Mrs. Armfeldt, as he thought she called herself, hoping to be in the house when his brother's murderer came back. He must have heard in the village that Daal was out just then, without hearing his name."

"He little knew either of the mothers," I said. "And then?"

"Then he took your hint, found out that the people at the cottage were called Devine, and still working on his original error went off to Cambridge to find Armfeldt. Armfeldt and his mother were in London for the day. When they came back M'Ginnis followed them to Jesus and got inside. But by this time he must have been trailed himself—by Daal. *You* told Daal about him—and he took it pretty coolly, I admit. Though he half gave himself away when he asked you what M'Ginnis looked like. He said he thought he might have seen him about. That struck me as a bit odd at the time. You don't see many American gangsters in Cambridge. Anyway, Daal daren't let M'Ginnis live—daren't let him speak to the Armfeldts, if he could help it. He didn't want any hint of his murky past coming out just then. So somewhere in those gardens, before he could get near the Armfeldts, the unhappy Bud was accosted by a friendly gent who wanted a match or something. And that was the end *of him*. . . ."

I shivered. "And he came to us straight from that murder?"

"Yes. He was rather late, you remember. And in particularly good spirits. He's a killer, as Bud remarked, and coves like that get a kick out of their murders. That's one reason why they go on. . . ."

"I think that's horrible!" I said. "And I saw him again just after he'd killed that poor boy Henderson. . . . But he didn't seem so cheerful then."

"No, he was beginning to get worried by that time, though he hadn't given up. He was still hoping to do something with Ince."

"What about that shot at James?"

"One of Mr. Daal's afterthoughts, I fancy. There he was with a weapon, and there was your James, strolling about with his cigar. It was an opportunity to carry on the Lanham theme. Of course something of the sort may have been intended from the first. But it was a tactical mistake to use an automatic with a silencer. It was out of character. I'd begun to wonder, and it made me wonder again."

"And when he said he saw Lanham. . .?"

"Another piece of opportunism. He saw us first, from the archway."

"And the Armfeldts?" I said. "Where *do* they come in? And what were they scared about? They *were* scared—apart from the fright you gave my poor Paul."

"Oh, something in *their* past in the States, no doubt," Maurice said. " I told you the police there seemed interested in them. And Paul, by the way, *was* in Chicago again nine months ago, round about the time of the M'Ginnis murder. If I had a guess, I'd say he's still doing some little side-line to the decorating business. Smuggling antiques, perhaps. Your poor Paul is a wrong 'un, all right, in his small way."

"That's just prejudice," I said, "because he isn't the army style, and is much better-looking than you are."

Maurice grinned. "The point is, they've got a position here now. The intrusion of a gangster, asking all over the place for them, must have been a little unnerving. It was by moral suasion on these lines that Puffin and I induced them to join the troupe this morning. They don't like the police, for old acquaintance sake, but they're precious anxious to keep on the right side of them. The precise why and wherefore are no business of ours now, so I didn't press the point."

"Did you ever really suspect them?"

"For a few minutes, perhaps, at Jesus."

"Why did Paul Armfeldt call at Lanham's flat?"

"I can't answer everything. But the reason he gave may have been the true one. Under her top-lofty exterior, which probably is only youth and Girton,

Miss Farleigh may conceal a kind heart. The Lanhams have no telephone, so Armfeldt would have to call."

"Who else did you suspect?"

"Your James, for one."

"Yes, I did wonder," I said. "But I couldn't believe it, like the man who saw the giraffe."

"Well, he had plenty of motive. He's in a hole, thanks to his old friend Sir Vyvyan. Paying for those Cyprian Eagles has crippled him, and he hasn't settled in full yet. Rowsell-Hogg was pressing him. The trust fund, as a source of supply, is as obvious in his case as in the others. Then, though he pretended to be so dour and discreet with Puffin, he managed to give away a whole lot that was very damaging to Lanham. He wanted to see me, so far as I could make out, chiefly to carry on the good work. He gave you the same impression. . . . The truth is, I should say, that he's really no hero, and he saw where he stood, or might stand. Apart from other things—his funk after the second murder seemed genuine enough—I couldn't reconcile him as the murderer with his obvious keenness to have a bigger say in the trusteeship. Why should he worry about that, if he was aiming at getting the money another way?"

"Do you know why he followed Sir Vyvyan on Monday?"

"Yes, to eat humble pie. He wanted to put settlement off. Afterwards, with the wicked baronet out of the way, he thought he might do something with Blewitt—get his boy's five thousand pounds advanced, perhaps. You can't blame him. His position, substantially, is the same as Lanham's, though he couldn't very well stress the point. The boy's share, or part of it, was *his* money, originally. But Blewitt wasn't having any—wouldn't even see Tullis on trust business till he had the support of Hogg's lawyer. Hence the dinner last night."

"Poor James!" I said. "He must be in a hole, or he would never have stopped on for it. Because he *was* frightened. . . ."

"You can't blame him for that either," Maurice said. "I told you he's the kind that cracks under a strain, and anyway, no one really likes to feel that another chap's after him with a bayonet. And Tullis did nobly this morning. I told him roughly the part I wanted him to play—to let me roast him too, if necessary, and to keep the Armfeldts from bolting till I gave the word, and to be on hand generally. The most I could ask of Puffin and Iliff was to stand by. I wanted someone unofficial who could do or act a little rough stuff——"

"Rough stuff is the word," I said. "He made me black and blue. But I'm grateful now. I hope he gets some cash for it."

Maurice smiled. "I should like to be at the next full meeting of the trustees," he said. "With Lanham present. I bet Blewitt's rather sorry things have turned out as they have. He was hoping to get this lawyer in. He'll probably side with Tullis now, to keep Lanham in order. It's an ill wind. . . ."

Puffin sat up and blinked. I believe he'd nearly been asleep.

"You haven't told Myra about the picture gallery," he said.

"Picture gallery?" I repeated. "Oh, I know. . .! Those sketches. Yes, Maurice, what in the world did you want *them* for?"

"Deuced clever of him," Puffin said. "A bit beyond me, of course, but then I'm a mutt about art. And if we'd had to bring 'em in as evidence, can't you hear counsel for the defence on the subject?"

Maurice said, "Well, we've agreed about that all along. That's why we staged that highly irregular third degree scene this morning."

"Go and fetch 'em," said Puffin. "See if Myra can spot what you mean."

Maurice went into the house. He came back with a brown-paper parcel. When he'd untied this, he laid the picture gallery out on the grass. There were the three sinister crumpled drawings of Hector, Astyanax, and Solomon, the sketch of the chair Paul Armfeldt did for me in King's Parade, the three little pictures borrowed from Mary Lanham (to call her by the name she has taken again now), and two more from Mr. Mercer's collection. We all knelt on the grass to study this array.

Maurice said, "You see that drawing of Hector? Call it Exhibit A. When I first saw it one thing struck me. It's obviously the work of an amateur, but of an amateur who knows something about penwork. The way that hair's done, for instance. . . . Well, that fitted in all right. Lanham could draw a bit. Now look at Exhibits B and C, of the same series. There are the same tricks of style."

I saw what he meant. But it was only what was to be expected, and I said so.

"Oh, quite," Maurice said. "Now by way of contrast, consider Exhibit D. Chair, by Mr. Armfeldt. Equally obviously, it's drawn by a trained artist. Every line tells. There's no waste. And there are no tricks in it, I may as well say at once, that you'll find in any of the other exhibits. So we'll put it aside. We don't want it. But now look at these—Exhibits E and F."

He pointed to the two sketches he'd borrowed from Mr. Mercer. One was the self portrait of Owen Jevons, the other a little picture of a man standing by a boat. Both were drawn with a fine pen in black waterproof ink, unlike the crude things left on Harry Daal's victims, which were done in broader lines with what appeared to be writing-ink of the usual blue-black variety.

"Look at that hair again," Maurice said, "and compare it with Hector and Co. And the way that fellow's coat is drawn with the robes, or whatever they are, of Hector and Solomon. Do you see any similarity?"

I thought I did, vaguely. "But what about it?" I said. "Hair's hair, and one coat, in a drawing, is very like another. And these sketches of Mr. Mercer's were drawn twenty years ago."

"That," said Maurice, "is the extremely interesting point. Because the tricks of style *are* the same. Hair is by no means always hair—at any rate, at the hands of the amateur. He'll nearly always make a thing like a sparrow's nest. The hair in all those sketches is *drawn*—roughly, but definitely. Same with the clothes. And the identical tricks are there, as I said—in the drawings of Owen Jevons, twenty years old, and in those caricatures scrawled in the last few days."

"Do you see it?" Puffin said to me. He was as keen as a boy over this game.

"I suppose so," I said, peering at the drawings and shutting one eye, as one always does, why, I don't know. "But it doesn't make sense. The same man can't have done both lots. Jevons is dead."

Puffin chuckled.

Maurice said: "True. But before he died he passed on his tricks of style to his son."

I sat back on my heels. "Is that possible?"

"Possible? It's the commonest thing. It will go on for generations, like handwriting. I've known children who can't draw a line, in the artistic sense, or their fathers either, but whose grandfathers have been draughtsmen, and those grandfathers' tricks of style crop up in the kids' scribbles in their old copy-books. And it's always in things like hair and clothes that the inherited method comes out. Now look at these. . . ."

He pulled forward the three sketches from Mary Lanham's room.

"Exhibit G," he said, "is Lanham's. H is his daughter's. *He's* got some idea of the thing—she has none. But there are the similarities again."

It was becoming plainer to me now, as he put his finger on arrangements of lines and bits of cross-hatching. And when he placed the two sketches beside what he called the Hector series, Exhibits A, B, and C, it was equally plain, after a little examination, that these three had never been drawn by Wilfrid Lanham.

"And here," said Maurice, hooking his third sample from Miss Lanham's collection towards us, "is the *pièce de résistance*. Exhibit I. A work by Mr. Daal. Compare it with Hector and Co."

It was the pen-and-ink drawing of the old man standing on the lock gates. It was Baitsbite Lock, and the lock-keeper there, as I discovered later.

"Note the trousers and the hair," Maurice intoned, with the enthusiasm of the expert. "Those lines *there,* and these on Solomon's vague but voluminous garments. See what I mean. . .? And now study Owen Jevons, the father, again. Here are the same old tricks. In other words, *in three sets of drawings,* two done twenty years ago, one admittedly by Daal-Devine, and one by the murderer. . . ."

I sat back again and clapped my hands.

"I agree with Puffin," I said. "I call that jolly clever of you, Maurice. And praise from a wife of ten years" standing is praise indeed. Was it those things of Mr. Mercer's that made you suspect Harry Devine—or Daal, as the case may be?"

He nodded, and began to collect his trophies.

"Yes," he said. "There's even a look of Daal in that self portrait of Jevons. . . . In some ways, you know, Lanham didn't seem to fit in from the very beginning. Even if mad, he wasn't the man, from all accounts, to go in for mass murder in such a methodical way. Stealing the pendant, too, required a cold nerve you wouldn't expect in an excitable, impulsive type. Then how did he know of Hogg's movements, and why didn't he draw more money? You'd think he'd want every penny he'd got. And then, of course, other little pointers, indicating Daal, began to come along. There were small contradictions about Lanham's visit. His daughter knew nothing about his having invited himself. Whenever we talked about Daal she looked self-conscious. Once she called him 'Harry.' She kept fidgeting with the third finger of her left hand——"

"Curse you, Maurice," I said. "I'm a woman, and I never spotted that."

"Well, I happened to spot it, and it suggested that she sometimes wore a ring on that finger, and that Daal's name reminded her of it. Then, again, she let out that she knew all about your James's wanderings on Monday night. This was yesterday. How would she hear that bit of news? It wasn't in the papers. The only person she'd seen in the interval who'd be likely to tell her anything confidential about the case was Daal, who'd called at Newnham on Wednesday. But how would *he* hear the story? He joined your party at the boat-club on Tuesday *after* Ian Tullis told it, and it wasn't repeated again there. I had that from Ian himself, Ince, and Averil. So far as I could discover, Daal could have got the tale only through some means of information of his own. . . ."

"You mean he *saw* James that night?" I said.

"I think so, while he was waiting himself in King's Lane."

We had all risen, and Maurice was tying up his parcel again, less the Hector series, which he handed over to Puffin.

"Well, what else?" I said.

"Did you notice Daal's hands?" Maurice asked. "Long, artistic fingers, very unlike his mother's short thick ones. Jevons had hands like that, Mercer tells me. And then last night, in Ince's rooms, didn't you think Daal's behaviour rather queer? His excuse for overlooking Henderson's danger was plausible, but if he was so bent on warning *any* of these children he could scarcely forget Miss Farleigh. Lanham had no grudge against the elder Henderson, and Ince's father was his chief friend when he was at Cambridge, but he must have hated Farleigh, who as a trustee had sided with Rowsell-Hogg on a certain famous occasion. Yet Daal had never thought about the girl. He'd never thought about the money, either, which, as he's no fool, seemed to me unlikely. The whole case reeked of that trust fund. I didn't pay enough attention to it myself, I know, till after that talk with Blewitt, nor did anyone else, but it was always in the background. And Daal, mixing with these boys, and hearing about their shares, and what they were going to do when they went down, couldn't overlook it as a motive-—except on purpose. And finally, he never asked how Henderson had been killed. He showed no curiosity whatever. . . ."

Maurice had finished tying up his parcel. He yawned.

"These were all little things," he said. "But they struck me as odd. The oddest thing of all never struck me till it was too late. It will be a long time before I forgive myself for that. Do you remember standing on Clare bridge and watching Daal go under in his canoe?"

"I'm not likely to forget it," I said.

"He was wearing a tweed jacket."

"Why shouldn't he?"

"After paddling four or five miles, and paddling fast, on a hot summer evening? He isn't the man to coddle himself, at any time, and a jacket was absurd then. I ought to have tumbled to it. He had to wear it, you see. We found an ingenious gadget in the cottage—an adaptation of the pistol holster under the armpit, which he also wore on occasion, as you know. It's an American dodge, by the way. This thing's a scabbard for his bayonet. Much easier to get at there, and much less troublesome, than if he'd worn it down his leg. The bayonet—it's the standard French type—has been filed down to the length of a little more than a foot. Goes comfortably under a jacket. But a jacket must be worn. The only sort of costume it wouldn't go well with is evening dress, but the only time he wore that, except at Jesus, when he was otherwise armed, was for the first murder, when a malacca was part of the correct *ensemble*. We found that too, by the way. His bayonet fits into it. And Lanham's own stick is there—a perfectly normal one. *And* the pendant. . . ."

Maurice yawned again. Puffin caught the infection. I was clamping my teeth together when I remembered something.

"What's this about James knowing Mrs. De-Daal?'

"He met her that once," Maurice said. "Fifteen years ago. I hoped he'd know her again. That would have settled everything. But she's a clever woman, and a cool one. She saw him coming through the gate, and knew *him* all right. Of course she was on her guard, knowing he was in Cambridge. . . . Anyway, she ducked into the house. When I came in she was whispering to Daal, with her back to us, probably telling him——"

"I think he was urging her to do something," I said.

"Wanted her to go upstairs, I expect. But she could bluff too, and take chances. They're both born gamblers, as I said before. And fatalists too. I think she knew then—perhaps they both knew—it was all up. But they went on bluffing to the end. And then perhaps she wouldn't leave him to face the music alone. You never know with women. . . . However, she took advantage of the thunderstorm, put on a pair of dark glasses, talked a lot of nonsense about the lightning, and sat through it with her back to us. And Tullis never recognised her after all We fetched him to see her, without her glasses, at the station. He says he wouldn't have known her again. . . ."

"I wonder," I said, "why she wanted to run upstairs at the end. Because it was getting lighter?"

"Ah, I wonder," said Maurice. "She might have had time to give Lanham something stronger than dope. It would have shut *his* mouth. And I wonder, if things had gone differently, what would have happened to his daughter?"

Puffin said, with another yawn: "They ought to be damned grateful to you, old chap."

"They won't be," said Maurice.

He was quite right.

Lightning Source UK Ltd.
Milton Keynes UK
UKOW020111110212

187093UK00001B/35/A